ONLY YOU

AN ADAIR FAMILY NOVEL

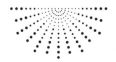

SAMANTHA YOUNG

Only You

An Adair Family Novel

By Samantha Young
Copyright © 2023 Samantha Young

ALSO BY SAMANTHA YOUNG

One King's Way (a novella)
On Hart's Boardwalk (a novella)

Hart's Boardwalk Series:

The One Real Thing
Every Little Thing
Things We Never Said
The Truest Thing

The Adair Family Series:

Here With Me
There With You
Always You
Be With Me
Only You

ABOUT THE AUTHOR

Samantha Young is a *New York Times*, *USA Today* and *Wall Street Journal* bestselling author from Stirlingshire, Scotland. She's been nominated for the Goodreads Choice Award for Best Author and Best Romance for her international bestseller *On Dublin Street*. *On Dublin Street* is Samantha's first adult contemporary romance series and has sold in 31 countries.

ACKNOWLEDGMENTS

For the most part, writing is a solitary endeavor, but publishing most certainly is not. A massive thank you to my lovely friend Catherine Cowles for reading the first version of *Only You* and for providing insight and support that means the world to me. Love you loads!

Of course I have to thank my amazing editor Jennifer Sommersby Young for always, *always* being there to help make me a better writer and storyteller. On top of that, Jenn, you are just the best cheerleader and most supportive human. Thank you for being you. I love ya!

Thank you to Julie Deaton for proofreading *Only You* and catching all the things. You have an amazing eye for detail and I'm always reassured my stories are going out into the world in the best possible shape.

And thank you to my bestie and PA extraordinaire Ashleen Walker for handling all the little things and supporting me through everything. I appreciate you so much. And miss and love you loads.

The life of a writer doesn't stop with the book. Our job expands beyond the written word to marketing, advertising, graphic design, social media management, and more. Help from those in the know goes a long way. A huge thank-you to Nina Grinstead at Valentine PR for your encouragement, support, insight and advice. You're invaluable to me and I hope you know how much I cherish you. Thank you to all the team at Valentine who work so hard to make sure my books find readers. You all are amazing!

Thank you to every single blogger, Instagrammer, and book lover who has helped spread the word about my books. You all are appreciated so much! On that note, a massive thank-you to the fantastic readers in my private Facebook group, Samantha Young's Clan McBookish. You're truly special and the loveliest readers a girl could ask for. Your continued and ceaseless support is awe-inspiring and I'm so grateful for you all.

A massive thank-you to Hang Le for once again creating a stunning cover that establishes the perfect visual atmosphere for this story and this series. You are a tremendous talent! And thank you to Regina Wamba for the beautiful couple photography that brings Brodan and Monroe to life.

As always, thank you to my agent Lauren Abramo for making it possible for readers all over the world to find my words. You're phenomenal, and I'm so lucky to have you.

A huge thank-you to my family and friends for always supporting and encouraging me, and for listening to me talk, sometimes in circles, about the worlds I live in.

Finally, to you, thank you for reading. It means everything to me.

AUTHOR NOTE

Dear Reader,

Many years ago, I was inspired to write this series set in my picturesque, fictional village in the Scottish Highlands. Because of obligations to other books, I put this series on hold. For that I am thankful, because over the years it evolved into something so three-dimensional in my mind, sometimes it seems impossible that Ardnoch and its characters are not a living, breathing reality. The love and support readers have given me and this series has blown me away and made writing it even more special. Thank you so much. You'll never know how much I appreciate you.

When I realized I'd so quickly come to the last chapter in this family saga, it filled me with a sense of restlessness. Usually when I finish a series, it feels right. Complete. However, as much as I believe Brodan and Monroe's epic love story signals the end of the trials and tribulations of the Adair Family (can you hear them breathe a sigh of relief?), I am not yet ready to leave Ardnoch behind.

Beyond the Thistles is the first book in *The Highlands Series* and set in this world I have grown to love so much. Once you finish Brodan and Monroe's story, I hope you'll be excited about what and who is coming next. You'll find all you need to know once you scroll to the last page... but don't rush there in a hurry. Take your time. Find a place to curl up for a while and let the pages guide you into the rugged beauty of the Scottish Highlands and a love story I felt deep in my soul with every word I typed.

With love and gratitude,

Sam x

PROLOGUE

MONROE

YEARS AGO ...

The cinema was a quiet place on a Monday morning, even if it was summer and the school holidays. Only a handful of people waited in the large foyer. Nothing to distract me from the vertical ceiling banner with Brodan Adair's gorgeous face plastered over it. I couldn't believe it the first time I saw his brother Lachlan on a chat show promoting his debut Hollywood film.

From there, Brodan started appearing in secondary roles. Nothing that tempted me to watch his movies and TV shows. However, it had been hard to miss his escalating success. Now, there he was on a giant poster advertising his first big lead role in a blockbuster movie.

An ache I'd carried around in my chest for years splintered painfully.

Turn around and get the hell out of here, I urged myself. *Stop being such a masochist.*

But I couldn't.

The desire to see what had become of him was too great. I thought years apart would numb it, might even erase it … but ironically, the distance had only made my heart stubborn.

Fuck.

Throwing my shoulders back, I marched across the foyer to the ticket counter and bought a ticket to the next showing of Brodan's movie.

There he was. That horrible ache bloomed hotter as I stared up at a larger-than-life Brodan, playing the role with a flawless American accent. It almost made him seem like a different person. Except for those eyes. Everything was always in Brodan's eyes. It was a wee bit disconcerting to see he was such an excellent actor because, for a while, I could almost forget this leading man was once my best friend.

Until he kissed the leading woman with genuine passion.

Rumor had it they were dating in real life.

Watching them, I couldn't believe it wasn't true—their chemistry was fire.

Ridiculous hurt and jealousy filled me. Possessiveness.

He was mine first, I thought childishly.

Brodan had never really been mine in the way I wanted, but when we were children, he was my everything. Memories I tried so hard to forget consumed me, whirling before me, blurring the sight of Brodan Adair, Hollywood actor …

I knew by my mum's cut lip as I walked into the kitchen that it was one of those days. I opened my mouth to talk, and she shook her head frantically.

2

Shit.

We lived in a small row cottage on the edge of Ardnoch. Our village was tiny, but not so tiny that we didn't have streets that were known for housing folks who had less than other folks. We lived on one of those streets.

"That Monroe?" *Dad yelled from the living room across the hall.*

Mum mouthed, "Leave."

My heart lurched in my chest, and I turned to go just as Dad appeared in the kitchen doorway.

His face was red, his eyes bright with whisky, fists clenched at his sides.

As a kid, I didn't know Dad was an alcoholic. Or at least I didn't understand it. I was twelve now, in my first year at Ardnoch Academy. So I knew. I knew things now that I didn't know then. I knew it was the drink that turned my dad into a monster.

My hands became clammy.

"Hi, Dad."

"Where you been?" *He stepped toward me belligerently.*

"School."

"You should be out working, helping," *he snarled.*

"I'm t-twelve," *I quietly reminded him.*

"I was working at twelve, you lazy wee bitch."

"I have to go to school, Dad. It's illegal not to."

His nostrils flared. "You think I don't know that? You trying to be smart with me?"

"No. It's just ... few places here will hire you for a part-time job until you're fifteen." *Plus, I wanted to go to school. I wanted to do something with my life.*

"Try harder. We've got bills to pay."

I don't know what came over me, if I was sick of walking on eggshells with the man, but I muttered, "Maybe if you didn't spend all your money on drink."

As soon as the words were out of my mouth, I froze, nauseated with fear.

His expression darkened. "What the fuck you say?"

"Dad—"

"Callum, don't," Mum pleaded.

"Cheeky bitch. Come 'ere!"

Everything from that point was a blur of black and red and pain. I could hear Mum screaming, "Stop!" She must have finally gotten him off me, but my face hurt everywhere, and I couldn't open one of my eyes.

"Why?" Mum hissed. "Why did you provoke him?"

I tried to speak through the agony, but the only thing I could think of was my best friend's face.

Brodan.

I wanted to be with Brodan.

He made me feel safe.

My right side screamed with pain as Mum pulled me up onto unsteady feet.

"Look what you made him do," Mum cried softly. "This is your fault."

My fault?

Was it?

Maybe it was.

Brodan's dad would never dare hurt his children. I knew Brodan wished he was around more. Looking after the Adair brothers and their sister, Arrochar, had mostly fallen to the eldest, Lachlan, but still, Mr. Adair was a gentle man. He'd never beat his daughter to a pulp.

"Now we'll have to keep you off school for Christ knows how long," Mum huffed, and I could see through my one eye that she was tearing up. "Let me get some antiseptic for your lip, and then we'll get some ice on your face."

On which part? *I thought numbly.*

As she walked dejectedly out of the kitchen, I got up. Dad was still here. He could come back and do more damage. Maybe even kill me this time.

So I stumbled toward the kitchen door, the floor bobbing up and down like waves in the sea. I pushed past the strange feeling and threw myself out of the house.

Terror made me pick up my heavy legs, and I ran. I took the back streets toward the road that led to Ardnoch Estate. Brodan and his siblings rode their bikes to the castle they called their home. In a few years, Lachlan would be old enough to drive them to school.

Sharp pain cut through my ribs, and I had to slow to a walk. It would be ages before I got to the drafty old castle, and I hurt so much, I didn't know if I could make it.

"Roe!" a familiar voice called.

I lifted my head, trying to see through my one good eye. Blurry figures appeared on the road ahead.

On bikes.

Brodan?

Brodan! I tried to open my mouth, but suddenly the world tilted and my legs disappeared.

Pain shot through my knees.

"Monroe!"

Brodan.

It seemed like only seconds later that hands were on me, and I looked up into Brodan's frantic face. Tears glimmered in his eyes. "Arran, get Dad."

"What ... what's going on?" I heard his brother Arran whisper.

"Arran, get Dad!" Brodan yelled. I could hear the panic in my friend's voice.

Then his arm was around me, and he held me to him. "You'll be okay, Sunset, you'll be okay. I won't let anything happen to you ever again. You're safe. I've got you, Roe."

. . .

I blinked, coming out of one of the most vivid memories of my childhood. Tears wet my cheeks, and I glanced around to make sure no one paid attention.

There were only two other people at the screening, and their attention was glued to the film.

To Brodan.

From the moment my father had begun beating me, Brodan, my best friend since our first day at primary school, had become my protector. Even at twelve, he'd been determined to take care of me. Because of him and his father, my life changed after that day.

And I'd stupidly thought Brodan's passionate commitment to my well-being meant something.

I would be fourteen years old when I finally admitted to myself that I loved Brodan more than just a friend.

Hope had bound me to him until he shattered it.

In my hurt, I'd acted impulsively.

We ruined everything, he and I.

So why couldn't I be free of him?

My emotion spilled over as I looked at his face on the screen.

So familiar.

Yet so much a stranger.

I didn't know who that man was. That knowledge was so fucking painful I couldn't stand it.

Wiping angrily at my tears, I pushed up out of the seat and turned my back on the screen.

On him.

Enough. It was enough now.

I had to forget him. To move on.

I had to.

1

MONROE

PRESENT DAY

ARDNOCH, SCOTLAND

I tried desperately not to think of the pile of jotters that needed marking piled on the back seat of my car as I miraculously found a parking spot on Castle Street. Renovations were ongoing at the local hotel and restaurant, the Gloaming, so the car park was filled with work vans, vehicles, and the camper vans of the very last tourists of the season.

Mum's food shopping was in the car's boot, but I'd promised her I'd pick her up a to-go coffee from Flora's, and I had a package to collect from the post office before it closed. Then I had to drop off the food, make Mum's dinner, get back to the caravan, make my dinner, and spend the rest of the evening marking my primary five class's math and their online work while bingeing episodes of *Gilmore Girls* on my laptop.

What a glamorous life I led.

The sooner I got to Mum's, however, the sooner I could return to the caravan Gordon had rented to me for peanuts at his beachside caravan park.

It turned out returning to my hometown of Ardnoch wasn't as simple as I'd thought it would be. When my mum's neighbor called to tell me that Mum had broken her hip and wasn't coping on her own and that there was an opening for a teacher at the village primary school, I really had no good excuse to not run to Mum's rescue. But after accepting the job, I tried to find somewhere to rent and realized my hometown had risen from my financial reach. I made a fairly good salary and there was only me. However, the rent was high in the village. That, plus the average council tax, made living in Ardnoch almost impossible. I just couldn't afford anything that was available, not with rent and all the other bills. Not on my own. So now I was stuck in Gordon's caravan park and trying not to panic about it.

I could always move in with Mum, but after a few weeks of living with her when I first returned, I vowed to never do so again, else I resign myself to a life of misery.

No, my only real sensible option was to tough it out in the caravan for the year.

Worries up to my eyeballs, I strode down Castle Street toward Flora's to grab myself and Mum a coffee. I nodded hello to a few locals as I made my way to the counter. Flora looked up from cleaning and gave me a wide smile.

"Monroe. How are you today, sweetheart?"

Flora was always lovely to me. Her mum, Mrs. Belle Rannoch, was Mum's neighbor, and while Flora was older than me and we didn't exactly grow up together, she'd known, as her mother did, what my family situation was like. I didn't confuse their kindness for pity, and I was grateful to them both. Coming home had not been easy, so having a couple of friendly faces among those who gossiped about my return meant a lot.

"Rushed off my feet, as usual." I smiled at her. "How has your day been?"

"Quieter. There are only a few tourists left now. Usual?" she asked.

"Please." I popped in nearly every morning and afternoon for my coffee.

Flora got the fancy artisan coffee machine going and then turned to me. "So, reconnected with any old friends yet?"

I tried not to wince at the pointed question. Flora had encouraged me to make more of an effort to rekindle my old friendships. Unfortunately, all three of my old friends belonged to the same family—the Adairs. The Adairs were part of what was once known as landed gentry, their castle and large estate passed down through the generations. When we were kids, they were also what was known as land rich but cash poor. Until the eldest of the five siblings, Lachlan Adair, made money as an actor and businessman, and retired from acting to transform their home into a members-only club for those in the film and TV industry. Thane, the second eldest, was a respected architect; Brodan obviously was an even bigger Hollywood star than Lachlan; Arran had returned from his travels to buy the Gloaming with Lachlan, renovate it, and run it; and the youngest, Arrochar, was a forestry engineer. As close as I used to be to Brodan, I'd also been good friends with Arran and Arro … once upon a time.

While Arran had already made it quite clear that he wanted to be friends again, there was just too much water under the bridge. I'd avoided Arro, and she'd made no attempt to reach out, so I think avoidance was the right way to go.

As for number three, he was probably off in some exotic country filming his latest movie.

It didn't matter, anyway. I'd already started reaching out to schools along the Central Belt in the Lowlands, enquiring about open teaching positions for next year.

At the abrupt shake of my head, Flora frowned but turned back to finish the coffees. With two to-go cups in hand, she rounded the counter to hand them to me. "On the house."

"Flora, you have to stop giving me free coffee."

"I have to do nothing of the kind." She pushed them toward me.

With a grateful smile, I took them. "Thank you."

She refused to let go of them, however, as she bent her head to give me a very serious look. "There's something you should know about Brodan—"

"If it's about his collapse at the wedding, Flora, I already know." I cut her off, my heart racing at the mere mention of his name. I'd escaped seeing Brodan Adair when he was in town a few weeks ago, but not only had the villagers told me about him collapsing at his brother's and sister's double wedding, the tabloids discovered it from someone at the hospital where he was treated.

"No. It's about—" She cut off as the bell above her door rang, and she turned to see who'd stepped in. Flora released the coffee and tensed before shooting me a worried look.

Pulse racing at her strange reaction, I looked toward the door, and it felt as if the floor gave way beneath my feet.

Brodan Adair.

In the flesh.

More handsome now than he even was as a young man. Brodan was classically good-looking with a strong, straight nose, beautiful pale-blue eyes, and a mouth with a lower lip much fuller than the upper. He had lines around his eyes that didn't use to be there, but they only made him more attractive. As did the five o'clock shadow.

He was thirty-seven now. We both were.

It's so unfair that men age into their looks, I thought.

I hadn't seen Brodan in real life in almost eighteen years.

And he was staring at me as if he'd seen a ghost.

Strain tightened his features as our gazes connected across the room. Those pale-blue eyes used to give away everything Brodan felt. Now there was nothing in them other than polite coolness.

Even anger would have been better than that.

A man shifted at Brodan's back, and, for the first time, I realized he wasn't alone. How I had missed his companion was evidence of Brodan's ability to make me forget everything else around me. His friend was at least six foot four, six five, and ruggedly handsome. He had a trimmed beard and dark hair that was shaved at the sides and longer on top. His chest was as broad as Brodan's, and the two of them seemed to fill the entire café.

Feeling attention on us as patrons watched the reunion of Brodan and Monroe, my cheeks grew hot, and I felt more than a bit sick to my stomach.

The nausea only increased when Brodan strolled toward the counter, his gaze moving to Flora. "Flo, how are you?" he asked, moving behind me and not acknowledging my presence. "Can we have two Americanos, please?" I tried not to shiver at the rumble of his familiar voice.

Flora gave me a pained look I couldn't stand.

"I'll see you later," I whispered.

"Okay, sweetheart."

I walked away without a backward glance, but Brodan's companion blocked the door.

His face was expressionless as he moved to the side and pulled the door open for me.

"Thanks," I murmured and hurried out before I allowed myself to really feel my first encounter with my ex-best friend.

He'd ignored me.

After all these years, he just ignored me.

Like I'd meant nothing to him.

Then again, it shouldn't come as a surprise, since he'd thrown me away and never looked back.

A chasm so painful, it made me breathless, opened in my chest. That man had occupied my mind more times than I liked to admit, which was shitty considering he obviously never thought of me.

Blindly, I made my way to the post office just before it closed to grab my parcel. I couldn't tell you what words I exchanged with the postmistress, my mind still reeling from the café encounter. The parcel, however, pulled me out of my stupor. It was a large, awkward box containing craft supplies for a project I had in mind at school. Unfortunately, like most schools I'd worked at, the budget wasn't there for these kinds of things, so like many of my colleagues, I bought it out of pocket.

In the end, I precariously balanced the two coffees on top of the box and ambled down the street. While I'd never been so grateful to see my old Yaris, the situation was a distraction from the arsehole who'd returned from my past. Until I reached my car.

He'd ignored me!

Lowering the box to the ground, I opened the boot and realized I needed to make space, so I pulled out shopping bags filled with my mum's groceries.

As I lifted one out, the bottom of the bag gave way, and Mum's milk, bread, fruit, canned soups, and all went flying every bloody where.

Tears of frustration burned in my nose, and then I made the mistake of looking straight ahead.

My heart skittered as Brodan stood outside Flora's with

his silent friend and stared impassively at the sight of me surrounded by fallen groceries.

Then he abruptly looked away, and those tears tried their damnedest to spill, but I forced them back, pinching my lips together as I bowed my head to collect the groceries.

Once upon a time, Brodan would have been the first person rushing across the street to help me.

I was vaguely aware of footsteps as I crouched and stretched under my car for the milk. When I finally got it and pulled it out, I turned to see Brodan's friend gathering the other groceries.

Straightening, I looked back at Flora's. No Brodan. I searched Castle Street. No sign of him at all.

His quiet friend came to me with an armful of food. "Where do you want them?" he asked. He was Scottish too.

"Uh, in the boot, thanks." I gestured.

He drew up to me, and I could smell his attractive aftershave as he leaned in and dumped the items in for me.

"Thanks," I repeated.

He met my gaze as he stepped back. "No problem."

"I'm Monroe."

"I know who you are," he said mysteriously.

"Do you have a name so I can thank you properly?"

"Walker."

"Thank you, Walker."

He gave me a stoic nod before he turned and strode away.

If I lived in a world that gave a shit about me and what I needed, I would have been able to drive straight back to the caravan (if we were talking ideal world, I'd have my own house) and cry a bucket of tears over my first encounter with Brodan. Not only had he ignored me, he'd turned his back on me. His bloody monosyllabic friend was more chivalrous! Was picking up spilled groceries beneath the almighty Brodan Adair?

Arsehole.

But no. In my shitty, emotional mood, I had to spend time around Mum.

"I said last time that I hate this kind of bread," Mum snipped at me as she hovered in the kitchen doorway.

"You should be off your feet," I reminded her.

When she fell down the narrow stairs in the house and broke her hip, Mum's healing didn't go as the doctors had hoped. She was now scheduled for a hip replacement, which meant I was stuck playing nursemaid for goodness knows how long. The thought made me want to scream.

"That's the wrong soup," she sniped, picking up the can of lentil. "I hate this brand."

"It's cheaper," I murmured.

"Och, well, I'm paying for it, so just buy the bloody brand I like."

I sucked in a breath. "Actually, I'm paying for it. You haven't given me any money for your groceries." She'd promised she would, but I'd bought her groceries for six weeks now, and she hadn't coughed up a penny.

"Oh, so now I'm a scrounger!"

I winced as she raised her voice, but continued to put away the food. "What do you want for dinner?"

"A grateful daughter," she snarled. "I paid for your food until you were eighteen, lass. Surely a few weeks of returning the favor is little to ask."

Well, technically, it's a parent's job to feed their child, but who could argue with that logic?

"Dinner?"

She made a sound of disgust and turned away. "Doesn't matter. It'll taste like shit, anyway."

Tears threatened again, but I allowed my indignation to fight them back as I hurried to unpack the rest of the food and prepare Mum's dinner. Curiosity got the better of me, and I googled Brodan's name on the off chance it might explain his return to the village.

And yup, there it was.

Articles detailed how Brodan had pulled out of several film projects, and it was believed he was recuperating from exhaustion at his brother Lachlan's famous Ardnoch Estate.

Brodan was home.

Indefinitely.

Fuck.

Brodan was also recuperating from exhaustion.

A bit of concern lit through my panic, but I shoved it straight back out. The man didn't care if I existed, so why should I care about him at all?

Pushing the thought to the rear of my mind, I took dinner out to Mum and changed the linens on the single bed we'd put in the living room to save her from having to walk upstairs.

"Have you heard from Dad lately?" I asked, the words spilling out before I could stop them. I'd asked her numerous times over the last few months if she'd heard from my father, but she always said no. She did so again, with a grunt of annoyance, but still I pushed. "Do you know how to contact him?"

"No," she snapped. "Now let me eat in peace."

It was worth a try. I'd searched the internet to find him, but nothing. I could hire a private investigator, but I didn't have the money for that. Something bothered me about the way Mum always evaded eye contact whenever I asked about him. My gut told me she knew something. I'd just need to try again later.

I left with her criticism of the baked potatoes and salad dinner I'd made ringing in my ears.

I'd needed to make her something quick so I could get the hell out of there.

My mum was the last person I wanted to be around after the horrible, empty encounter with Brodan.

Driving to the caravan park nestled above the dunes of Ardnoch Beach, I let the misery of it all wrap around me. Just for a few seconds.

As I stepped inside the caravan and felt that prickly chill of fall in the evening air, I clung to the misery for a little longer. This place would freeze come winter.

Worry churned in my gut.

Mum's nastiness echoed around my head.

Then I thought of Brodan.

He was home.

Why the hell did I come back here?

2

MONROE

THE PAST

Ardnoch Academy catered to not only Ardnoch but the surrounding villages. It was still tiny compared to most high schools. As an academy, along with normal classes, you could learn subjects for specific jobs, such as construction, early education and childcare, and rural skills. I didn't mind its smallness—I quite liked it. In fact, unlike Brodan and Arran, I enjoyed high school. I got to focus on classes that would take me into teaching. However, I didn't only like the learning part. I liked the being anywhere but at home part.

At the academy, I was safe.

Last month on the third of January, Brodan turned fourteen, and I was just about to. After the summer, we'd be fourth years. The thought made me feel good. I hated being considered among the babies of the school. At my height, a lot of adults still treated me like a kid. I'd stopped being a kid a long time ago.

I most definitely didn't want Brodan to see me as a kid, especially as there were only six weeks between us.

Pondering whether I might ever get up the courage to tell my best friend I had a massive crush on him, I was in a daydream as I wandered the hall toward one of the exits. Last bell had rung, and most pupils were rushing toward the doors as if escaping hell.

"S'cuse you." Harry Grant threw his weight against my side, and my books and papers tumbled everywhere. My upper arm ached where I'd taken the brunt of his shove, and I glowered up at him as I lowered to my haunches to collect my things.

Harry gave me an evil smirk and turned away. Something made him stiffen, and then he dove out of the side entrance in a blur of movement.

Straight ahead stood Brodan, glowering after him.

Then my best friend was suddenly on his knees before me, helping me pick up my stuff.

"Thanks," I muttered, taking them from him.

"Are you all right?" Brodan asked as he took hold of my elbow and helped me up.

I glanced down at his hand on me and tried not to flush like an idiot. It was Brodan. We'd been best friends since we were five. Just because I'd started getting butterflies in my stomach when he smiled at me didn't mean I needed to act like a blushing moron around him. "I'm fine."

When people described someone's eyes as piercing, they were talking about Brodan. His were pale-blue and he could look right into you with them. His wee sister Arro had the same color eyes, and yet they didn't seem to search a person's soul like Brodan's did. Mind you, she was only ten.

Brodan was fourteen and already six feet tall. People, even teachers, mistook him for being older all the time.

Thankfully, I'd grown used to that piercing look over the years. Kind of. "I'm fine," I insisted.

My friend looked over his shoulder to where Harry had disappeared. Then he took my backpack from me, even though he had his own to carry. I tried to take it back the first time he'd carried it for me, but Brodan ignored me. To be fair, there were so many books in that backpack, my friend carrying it was a relief.

We were quiet as we walked outside, but then Brodan said with a gruff annoyance, "You know Harry fancies the pants off you. That's why he's a dick to you."

This time, I couldn't help the blush that stained my cheeks red.

Brodan's eyes narrowed on my face. "But you already knew that."

That was the problem with being friends with someone as long as I'd been friends with Brodan. We could read each other like a book. Trying to be casual about it, I shrugged. "He asked me out at the start of the year." And had been a little shit ever since I turned him down.

"Why didn't you say anything?" He scowled. "How come no one told me?"

Probably because they knew you'd act like an overprotective big brother. Ugh. I shrugged again. "Because I don't fancy him, and it didn't matter."

The frown between Brodan's brows didn't ease as we walked toward the school gate where Arran waited by the bike rack.

A devil nudged at me, and I blurted out with a breeziness that belied my jealousy, "Anyway, I thought you'd be off snogging Michelle Kingsley right about now." Brodan had been sneaking away whenever he could to get off with

Michelle these past few weeks. Michelle was in the year above us, and there were rumors she was letting Brodan do way more than just snog her.

The thought made me sick.

Brodan nudged me gently. "When have I ever not walked you home?"

Never. He always walked me home. Only times he didn't were on the rare occasions he was at home, unwell.

Arran came into view, standing with some mates at the bike rack. He was in second year and was hitting a growth spurt. He was a cutie. All the Adairs were unfairly blessed with good looks, but cursed with heartache and a crumbling old castle that might one day sink them into poverty. Not that I'd ever let anything happen to Brodan and his family if it was in my power to help.

"I'm glad you said no to Harry," Brodan suddenly confessed.

I swear my heart somersaulted in my chest. "Why?"

"Because he's a wee dick. You're too good for him." He looked down at me, his expression fierce. "You're too good for anybody here."

Pulse racing, I could only gape at him, wondering if he counted himself among *anybody*.

"Bro! Roe!"

It broke our intense eye contact as Brodan turned toward the call.

Fergus, Brodan's friend who was in our year but looked like a first year, ran toward us, his massive backpack bouncing almost comically. Poor Fergus got terribly bullied because his family didn't have a lot of money and also because of how small he was. The Adairs might not have money, but no one dared mess with them, mostly because the three eldest, Lachlan, Thane, and Brodan, were built like they had Viking blood. Also, their family had standing in Sutherland as landed gentry. They lived in a bloody castle on one of the biggest estates in the country. No one cared if they were technically low on funds.

Fergus was not so lucky, but Brodan tried to protect him as best he could. That was who Brodan was and probably one of the many reasons I'd started to have feelings for my best friend.

Sometimes I wished we could just be kids again.

Life was way less complicated then.

So were feelings.

"Don't let Arran hear you calling us that," Brodan grumbled good-naturedly as Fergus caught up to us.

Fergus grinned at me, and I smiled. I didn't mind the Roe and Bro nicknames Arran had given us. It made me feel like our connection was so strong, everyone else could see it too.

Arran peeled himself away from his friends, and he and Brodan unlocked their bikes from the rack. Ardnoch Estate was a good ten-, fifteen-minute drive from the village, so the boys had to bike it most of the time. There was snow on the ground last month, though, so their dad, Stuart, drove all the Adairs to school. Come November, Lachlan would turn seventeen, and he'd be old enough to drive them. When he graduated, that duty would fall to Thane.

The boys chattered about some football game they were arranging for the weekend, and I walked quietly at Brodan's side. He always slowed his long stride so I could keep up.

We said goodbye to Fergus first, and then Arran got on his bike and rode slowly ahead of us. He looked back over his shoulder at his brother. "I'll get you on the road."

Brodan frowned. "Don't go too far ahead."

"Just go with him," I said.

He shook his head, and I rolled my eyes, even though I loved it that he wanted to walk me to my house.

"How are things?" Brodan asked as we approached my narrow street of row cottages.

I tried not to tense at the question. With my dad gone, things were somehow just as awful. Mum didn't raise her hands to me, but her cruel words hit with enough force to leave a mark. But I didn't want my friend worrying about me. "They're fine."

He didn't look convinced. "Sunset."

"It is what it is." I smiled brightly up at him. He'd given me the nickname *Sunset* when we were twelve, and when I asked him about it, he just grinned that boyish grin as he replied, "I think of your hair every time I see the sunset." I didn't think he realized how romantic that sounded to me now.

At my smile, Brodan's gaze dipped to my mouth, and his frown deepened.

Sensing he wanted to push the subject, I changed it. "I was thinking we could jump on a bus and go to Inverness this Saturday. I phoned Ness Island Vinyl, and they have the US import in for The White Stripes album." We couldn't get the album any bloody where because it hadn't been released in the UK yet. "They said they'd put it aside for me, if I can guarantee coming in for it this Saturday. I've been saving up." My paternal grandmother sent me Christmas and birthday money every year, and I'd saved almost every penny. Now that Dad was gone, we were even more strapped for cash than before. Mum was a nurse at the hospital in Golspie, about twenty-five minutes north of here. Let's just say she saved all of her bedside manner for her patients.

At Brodan's silence, I looked up at him. He seemed preoccupied.

"Or not." I shrugged, like it didn't bother me if he didn't want to spend Saturday with me. Of course, it bothered the heck out of me.

He glanced down. "No, aye, sure. Saturday."

"We can go another time if you're busy."

He shook his head. "I can cancel the other thing."

Jealousy scored through me as we came to a stop at my front door. I turned to my friend, forcing myself to meet his gaze as I smirked through the pain. "If you have plans with Michelle, we can go another time."

Brodan searched my face for a few seconds and then the corner of his mouth tilted up as he bent his head toward me so our noses were too close for my comfort. "Roe, she's not my girlfriend. I can cancel." He straightened but tugged on a strand of hair that had fallen out of my ponytail. "I'd rather go to Inverness with you. I'd *always* rather spend time with you."

He rubbed my hair between his fingers before he released it and settled his hand on the other handle of his bike, his smile boyish. "Inverness, Saturday?"

I nodded, my heart thumping so hard, I was sure the pulse in my neck must be visible. "Saturday."

He handed me my backpack and I almost dropped it, it was that heavy.

Brodan chuckled under his breath and then abruptly muttered, "Oh, aye, before I forget." He slid his backpack off and unzipped it. Rummaging through the books, he pulled out a small black brick.

My mistake.

A mobile phone.

"What's that?"

"Dad's got a contact at Nokia." He shoved the phone toward me. "I asked him to get you one. We're paying for the minutes and texts, so you don't need to worry about that."

Most everyone at school had turned up with a phone first term last year. There was no way I could ask my mum for one, so I'd felt like the odd man out. During break, everyone

23

was always texting one another, even though they were right bloody next to each other.

"I can't take that." I pushed his hand away.

Brodan frowned. "Take it for me. I got it so that if you …" His gaze moved to my front door. "If you ever need me, you can just call and I'll come get you."

"Brodan, I'm fine."

His expression darkened, his eyes flashing with something a bit like panic. "For me, Roe. Take it for me so I can feel okay. I can't … I never want to go through what we went through in first year."

As difficult as it had been for me to endure the beating my dad had rained down on me in first year, a beating that changed our lives, I knew by how watchful and even more protective Brodan had grown that finding me like that had traumatized him. He was my ultimate protector during the gossip in the following weeks. He fought people who made snide comments and tried to hide me from pitying looks.

Because he cared about me.

I'd always loved Brodan. Since we were kids.

But at that moment, as he held out the phone to me, I *fell* in love with him.

And as I took the phone that he wanted me to have for his peace of mind, I wished we could be kids again. Because I was pretty sure if Brodan was falling in love with me back, he wouldn't be snogging Michelle Kingsley behind the school every day.

3

BRODAN

PRESENT DAY

It was some view from Lachlan's suite in our family's renovated castle. With Robyn pregnant, he never stayed on the estate overnight these days, so he'd offered me his room until I figured out my next move. The windows overlooked the North Sea, and on a perfect September evening, the sun set across the water in spills of red, orange, and gold. Not even a drop of pink or purple to soften the fiery sky.

So naturally, all I could see was the long, red-gold hair of Monroe Sinclair.

The woman had barely changed in almost eighteen years.

It really had been like staring into the face of a ghost.

And like one, I'd treated her as if she didn't exist.

Watched her fumble with those groceries and sent my bodyguard to help her.

Very mature.

"Prick," I muttered to myself.

25

SAMANTHA YOUNG

I couldn't get those big gray eyes of hers out of my head.

Almost eighteen years.

We'd now been apart longer than we'd been friends. I rubbed my chest where it ached.

A knock at the door drew my head around, and Walker Ironside stepped into the room. He'd been part of my private security team for four years, and, much like my brother Lachlan with his ex-bodyguard Mac, when two Scotsmen find each other in foreign lands, they tend to bond. Walker was more than my bodyguard—he was my friend.

"Still heading to the Gloaming?" Walk asked, hovering near the door.

When I finally decided I'd done enough running and for once, I'd let my high-handed big brother take over managing my career, most of my security team took jobs elsewhere. Not Walker. Lachlan offered him a place on the security team here at Ardnoch, the private members-only club that catered to film and TV industry people. Walker took the job, but he made it clear his priority was still protecting me.

"Aye." I nodded and stepped away from the sunset that reminded me too much of a ghost. "Leaving now." I'd promised my eldest and youngest brothers I'd meet them at their newly renovated (but not quite finished) pub, restaurant, and hotel for a drink.

"I'm coming with you."

It was not said with the tone of a friend, but in the tone of a bodyguard. "Walk, I told you, I'm safer here than anywhere."

"You've just moved back, and the news of it is everywhere. There could still be a threat, and until I determine the village is safe, you're not going anywhere alone."

It was the most Walker had said in one sentence in a while. Lips twitching, I slapped him on the back. "Then let's go."

To my further surprise, as Walker drove us out of the estate toward the village, my friend spoke again. "Do you want to talk about whatever has you in a strange mood?"

I flicked a look at him. Walker knew more about me than anyone did, even my family. He even knew about the best friend who'd slept with my brother and then left, never to be heard from again. "The redhead today."

"Aye?"

"That was Monroe."

"I know." He looked at me before staring back at the road. "She gave me her name."

Scowling, I replied, "You didn't say anything."

"I was waiting for you to say something. Anyway, I knew she had to be someone because I've never seen Brodan Adair give up the chance to rush to the aid of a gorgeous woman."

My frown deepened.

He huffed. "Don't worry. Even if she was my type, and she's not, I wouldn't go there."

"I don't care," I lied.

Walker made a quiet sound of disbelief, but I let it sit.

Honestly, I was still too fucking tired to deal with anything I was feeling. Collapsing at Thane's and Arrochar's double wedding was a big wake-up call. I'd been pushing and pushing.

Running.

I was too tired to even fake my famous charm and humor.

One reason I let Lachlan cancel film projects I'd signed on to was because I had no fuel in the tank. No passion. The thought of shrugging on someone else's persona exhausted me.

I missed my family.

I missed the Highlands.

I missed who I used to be, and I wasn't even sure I knew who that was anymore.

"I'm thirty-seven years old, and I'm bloody lost," I admitted hollowly.

"You'll be all right, Bro," Walker offered quietly. "Life's about choices. Just have to be sure you take time to think about things before you make your next move."

At Walker's sound advice, I turned toward him. Over the years, I'd cracked him open a bit. He was more loquacious with me than anyone, but he usually only opened his mouth when he had something important to say. And everything he said always made sense. Something occurred to me. "I've got an idea."

"Okay."

"From now on, you make all my choices. All my decisions." I grinned, feeling free of the burden already. "Aye, I'll even pay you a bonus for doing it."

Walker shot me a disbelieving look. "You want me to be the boss of you?"

"Who better?" I sat up, my mood lifting as I got into the spirit of the idea. "Walker Ironside is a wise man."

"You're second-naming me?"

"With a name like Ironside, people should second-name you all the time."

He grunted because it pissed him off when he found out I'd actually hired him partly based on his cool-as-fuck surname.

"C'mon, Walk. I'm floundering. I'm fucked. I don't know what the hell I'm doing. But you are a man of common sense and a perceptiveness bordering on the occult."

"Bro—"

"I've been making some really stupid decisions over the last few years. I know you're my mate, but even you can agree with that."

"Considering you exhausted yourself into the hospital, aye, I can agree with that."

"So … *you* decide what I do with my days. For the next … three months. Three months of bossing me around. It'll be a nice turnabout for you, I'm sure." That was sarcasm. He was a bossy bastard.

Walker looked like he was considering this. "I get to make all your decisions from now on?"

"Aye."

"For three months?"

"Three months. My life is in your hands." I reconsidered that, since my life was in his hands daily. "More than usual."

"And you have to do *everything* I tell you to do?"

"Everything."

"What happens if you don't do what I tell you to do?"

Hmm. "I'll wash your clothes for a month."

He snorted at that. "Pathetic."

"I'll, uh … buy you a very nice watch."

"What the fuck do I care about very nice watches?"

I frowned. "Well, what do you want?"

Walker pulled into a parking spot outside the Gloaming and switched off the engine. He turned to me with the devil in his eyes. "To make sure you take this seriously … I want your Black Shadow."

"Get to fuck," I guffawed. I owned one of the few 1950 Vincent Black Shadow motorbikes still in existence, and it had cost me six figures.

My friend shrugged. "If you want me to do this, give me a reason to believe you'll take my decision-making seriously."

"Has anyone ever told you, you're an intense moth-erfucker?"

He stared at me with a cool look that either meant he was bored or preparing to kill me.

See?

Intense.

"Fine," I agreed. "If I fail to follow through on your decision-making, you get my Black Shadow."

With a nod, Walker slid out of the SUV. I noted him checking our surroundings, always in work mode. I got out, and we walked into the Gloaming together, looking forward to familiar faces.

Being around my family was a balm. I felt a bit out of it, having missed so much of the amazing changes that had happened in their lives over the last few years, but just being near them was enough.

I'd barely taken in the pub's transformation when a stranger popped out of nowhere, inches in front of me. She stared up at me with unbridled awe.

"It said online you'd be here, but I never actually thought I'd get to meet you," she said in an accent that sounded Welsh. "I'm Angharad, and I'm such a fan."

Discomfort and more than a twinge of annoyance surged through me. I shoved it down as I caught sight of Lachlan, his pregnant wife Robyn and my youngest brother Arran, and his girlfriend Eredine sitting at a table with banquette seating at the rear of the pub.

My attention returned to Angharad as I felt Walker hover just over my shoulder. She'd barely even looked at him, which was shocking since Walk was hard to miss. "Hi, Angharad, nice to meet you," I said as patiently and pleasantly as possible.

"I came all the way up from Cardiff just to see you and wondered if you could sign me." She yanked down the collar of her T-shirt, almost exposing herself. "I'm going to have it turned into a tattoo." With her other hand, she held out a marker.

It wasn't the first time someone had asked me to sign cleavage. Remembering our deal, I glanced at Walk. "Well?"

He grunted and lifted his chin.

So I scribbled my autograph where Angharad from Cardiff wanted it and said, "Have a nice evening."

She grabbed hold of my arm to stop my departure, and I heard Walker clear his throat in warning. Angharad dropped her hand quickly. "Can I buy you a drink?"

I looked at Walker in warning. He shook his head, just like I knew he would.

"I'm here to spend time with my family, so not today, but thanks."

"Oh, okay." Her disappointment made her smile tremble, but she held up her phone determinedly. "Will you take a selfie with me, then?"

"Nope." Walker put a hand between me and the phone. "No selfies."

She stared wide-eyed up at Walker as if she'd just noticed my hulking bodyguard. Then she looked at me. "No?"

I gave her an apologetic shrug. "He's the boss."

"Oh." She frowned in confusion.

"Nice to meet you, though. Have a good night. Safe travels back to Cardiff," I added, feeling a tiny bit bad she'd come all the way up here and Walk wouldn't let her take a selfie. I asked him why as we neared my family's table.

"You're at home. You need normality. We don't need her posting your face online and reminding everyone where they can come to get a selfie with Brodan Adair."

Like I said.

Wise.

Most of my face-to-face encounters with fans went fine. Sometimes overzealous fans tried to touch me inappropriately, but the worst fan encounters actually came in the mail. All of my fan mail arrived at a PO box we set up, and I'd eventually hired someone to sort through it so I didn't have to see the nasty stuff. Men and women's unclean underwear wrapped up like presents. Hair clippings. Toenail clippings. Lovelorn letters proclaiming we were meant to be.

The only mail on the darker side I ever saw were the threats. We had to make the police aware of those, and thankfully, they were few and far between. Though, we've been vigilant since two years ago when threats I'd received turned out to be from my old school friend Fergus. He'd stabbed my sister's husband in the gut, killed a guard at Ardnoch Estate, and kidnapped Lachlan and Robyn with the help of Hollywood starlet Lucy Wainwright. Lucy killed Fergus and was now doing a life sentence for her crimes. Lucy was a psychopath obsessed with Lachlan.

Fergus's apparent reasoning for his part in it was that he resented me for leaving him behind and hated my sister Arrochar for breaking up with him when we were younger.

So, aye, we took those kinds of threats seriously.

And while Angharad was no such threat, I appreciated Walker protecting my privacy.

"Fans found you already, then?" Arran asked, standing up and gesturing to two empty seats. I met Lachlan's gaze as I took a seat across from him.

"You all right?" my big brother asked.

I nodded. "Fine. You know what it's like."

Lachlan was actually the one who got me in the door in Hollywood. He'd started making a name for himself as a young action star, and after being on set with him a few times, I caught the acting bug and took up drama at university. However, Lachlan had never truly enjoyed acting and retired to turn our family's neglected castle and estate into the esteemed private club it is today.

He met Robyn two years ago, the estranged daughter of Mackennon "Mac" Galbraith, Lachlan's head of security. Mac had Robyn when he was only sixteen and living in the States. They'd reconnected when Robyn came to Scotland to find him, and she and Lachlan fell in love after a very rocky start.

I smiled at her in greeting, my attention dropping to her neat but prominent bump. She looked ready to pop. "How are you feeling?"

Robyn smiled wearily as she smoothed a hand over her belly. "Tired, mostly. Ready to meet her."

"How long to go now?"

"Three weeks, give or take."

In a bizarre twist of fate, my sister Arrochar fell pregnant at the same time and was due a couple days after Robyn. Even more complicated, she was married to Mac, Robyn's father. My siblings were determined to make our family tree a talking point for generations to come.

"Get you anything?" Arran asked.

Walker slid into the seat beside me and nodded silently in greeting to my family.

"I'll have a pint," I said. "Walk?"

"Driving."

I nodded and then turned to Eredine as Arran disappeared across the room behind the bar. Her gorgeous hazel-green gaze met mine. "How are you, sweetheart?"

She smiled her pretty smile, and it surprised me I didn't feel the pang of attraction I once did. I guess now that she was firmly with Arran, I'd psychologically made the switch that she was off-limits. "I'm good."

I knew that was an honest answer because for the first time in the seven years I'd known Eredine Willows, she actually seemed good. The air of sadness and worry had drained from her entire being. She glowed in such a way it was almost like looking at a new person. That probably had something to do with the fact that for years, she'd been in hiding from her twin sister's murderous ex-boyfriend. He'd finally caught up with Ery, but Ery had fought back and won, and now the bastard was where he was supposed to be—rotting in jail, awaiting his trial, not just for the murder of Ery's sister but for several counts of sexual assault. Several other women had come forward since his incarceration, including a US senator's daughter.

The bastard was fucked.

Good riddance to him.

I gave her a quick one-armed hug. "Glad to hear it. My brother's taking good care of you, then?"

"You know it."

Looking at Lachlan, I gestured around to the pub that had been brightened with new plasterwork and furniture. It very much looked like the interior designer for Ardnoch Castle had been in here, and I had no doubt that was true. "It's looking good."

"It is," Lachlan agreed. "Arran is doing an amazing job. There's just a few more renovations to do upstairs, and then it'll be done. On schedule, no less."

"What are we talking about?" Arran placed the pint in front of me before taking his seat next to Eredine and draping his arm around the back of her chair.

"What a fantastic job you've done on the Gloaming." I was proud of my brother, but I had to admit, I was also jealous. Not that long ago, Arran had been the lost one, drifting farther and farther from our family. I'd done what I could to keep him with us, and when he returned, he proved himself he was not only capable of looking after his family, but of being a bloody good businessman. There was nothing but contentment around him, and as happy as that made me … aye, I was a bit envious too.

Arran grinned. "Thanks, Bro. How's recuperating going?"

"Well"—I took a gulp of my lager and then relaxed back in my chair—"I made an important decision today."

"Oh?" Robyn asked, seeming genuinely interested.

"This man here"—I clapped Walker hard on the back, and he glowered at me—"is making all my decisions from now on. Except for when I eat and take a piss, of course."

"Charming." Eredine wrinkled her nose.

"I live to be so." I smirked at her, and she rolled her eyes.

"You are joking, right?" Lachlan asked wearily.

"Nope. And my Black Shadow is Walk's if I fail to go through with whatever he tells me to do, so I have a vested interested in being an excellent employee."

"You bet your Black Shadow?" Arran gaped at me.

I grimaced. "It was the only thing that would get the bastard to agree." And they all knew I never backed out on a bet. Walker was using my sense of honor against me.

"I think you and I need to get to know each other better, Walker." Arran chuckled. "You sound like my kind of people."

Walker tipped his head toward Arran in silent agreement.

"A man of few words," Robyn surmised.

Walker just stared at her.

And she stared right back, big, gorgeous hazel eyes unblinking, completely unintimidated.

Christ, Lachlan married a sexy woman.

I could tell by the way the corner of Walker's mouth twitched as he continued to stare at her, he thought so too.

"So, the gossip mill was whirring today," Arran said, drawing my attention. He was frowning, all humor gone. "Word is you bumped into Monroe in Flora's and ignored her. What's that all about?"

"Arran," Lachlan murmured in warning. Eredine nudged her boyfriend with a frown.

My wee brother raised an eyebrow, not letting it drop. "Well?"

"It's none of your business." This was a reminder of how Ardnoch protected its celebrities behind the gates of the estate, but gossiped about each other like it was an Olympic sport.

"She's our friend, or have you forgotten that?"

Whoa, where did that come from? *"Was*, not *is."*

"She has no one. Do you care?"

An ache speared my chest, and I ignored that too. "I guess I stopped caring when she fucked my brother."

Tension crackled around the table as Eredine murmured under her breath and Arran leaned toward me, eyes flashing. "One, that's not polite to mention in front of Ery. Two, I didn't sleep with your girlfriend, Bro, and I'm done acting like it was that kind of betrayal … unless, of course, you finally admit you wanted Monroe for yourself."

"Arran," Lachlan snapped.

Arran shook his head, gaze still on me. "Nah, I'm sick of carrying around that guilt. He doesn't get to treat me like I betrayed him if he doesn't actually give a shit about Monroe. Either he cares or he doesn't."

Heart racing, I pushed up from my chair, yanked money out of my pocket, and threw it on the table. "I couldn't care less about her."

"Sit."

At the rumble from my left, I turned to gape at my bodyguard. "Are you kidding me?"

Walker shrugged casually. "I make all your decisions, and I've decided you're finishing your pint."

"While this wee prick antagonizes me?"

"Sit."

With my Black Shadow on the line, I slowly sat and took a lengthy chug of my beer.

Lachlan grinned from Walker to me and back to Walker. "I think I like this new arrangement."

Robyn visibly choked on her laughter, and I glowered at them.

"So, we're good, then?" Arran leaned past Ery. "Since you don't care."

"Aye, we're fine." I'd like to kick his antagonistic arse, but we were fine.

"What are you planning to do while you're home?" Eredine asked, breaking the tension.

"Rest," Lachlan answered for me.

"I can't just rest. I need to do something."

They all looked at Walker, surprisingly way too okay about my bodyguard making all the decisions on my behalf.

Walker sighed. "I'll think of something productive."

Thankfully, Eredine the angel switched the subject to the fact that more locals had shown up at the pub tonight than usual. It was taking the villagers a little longer to get used to the idea of Arran and Lachlan running the Gloaming with all the changes they'd made.

Later, as Walker and I got into the SUV to drive back to the estate, I felt a black cloud hover over me. Sometimes alcohol, even in small amounts, depressed me, which was why after I got drunk and started a fight at a club in LA a few years ago, I'd mostly steered clear of the stuff.

"Maybe your next decision for me should be for us to leave. We could go to an island somewhere with exotic beauties serving us food in coconut-shell bikinis."

Walker sighed as we pulled away from the Gloaming. "No. You're where you're supposed to be."

I raised an eyebrow. "You really think so?"

"Aye. Problem is, there are things you've kept hidden from your family. And you've been absent. They miss you. They're worried about you."

He was a talkative bugger tonight. "So that gives Arran the right to be a dick?"

"It just means things are probably going to be bumpy for a while until you work out all those old resentments."

Walker the Wise, I thought humorlessly.

"What the hell am I going to do here for months? I'm knackered, but the thought of doing nothing makes me restless."

"Maybe we'll start with your family. See if they need help with anything."

"Arran clearly needs help with a smack to the face. Cheeky shite."

Walker's lips twitched. "Typical brother. Pushing all the right buttons."

Indignation suffused me. "No buttons were pushed. *She* isn't a button." She was a ghost.

And I had enough ghosts haunting me.

I didn't need another.

4

BRODAN

THE PAST

That was it. I was never getting serious with a lassie, ever. Okay, so I already knew that, but Michelle Kingsley had one hundred percent sealed my fate as a bachelor for life.

And I was barely fifteen.

I was not the only guy Michelle had been messing around with for the past year. She was not the only girl I had. But a few months ago, she *was* the first lassie I'd had sex with, and even though it wasn't her first time, she was acting like it was and suddenly, we were supposed to be boyfriend and girlfriend.

Moving onto Laura Bannerman as my casual go-to had made things nice and clear.

Which was why I was spending my lunch break with Michelle in my face and an embarrassing audience of our classmates to witness her meltdown.

39

"You think you're hot shit, but you're not!" Michelle yelled, her face purple with anger.

It was difficult at that moment to remember why I'd ever fancied her. "We both knew the score," I reminded her quietly.

"The score?" She gaped. "The score!" She shoved me so hard, I lost my footing and nearly fell.

I righted myself, blood rushing to my face as the crowed oohed and tittered. My fists clenched at my sides as I scowled at her. Clearly satisfied by my reaction, Michelle shoved me again. I braced against it, my chest aching where she jammed her fingertips into me.

The problem was, she knew I'd never lift my hand to stop her. So she kept shoving me and screaming insults in my face.

Still, I kept my hands to myself and let her have at it.

I'd seen what happened when a man lifted his hands to a girl.

Images of Monroe's pretty face swollen, bruised, and bleeding filled my mind. That day I'd found her on the road to our estate still haunted me. I'd never been so scared in my life.

As if I'd conjured her, Roe appeared out of nowhere and shoved Michelle away from me with a force of strength I didn't know she had. She also wore an expression I rarely saw—one of pure fury.

Michelle had barely righted herself from the shock of Roe's appearance when Roe shoved her again. "How do you like it, eh?" Roe shouted, and my eyebrows flew up in surprise. My Roe was a pacifist.

Not today, apparently.

She shoved Michelle again. "You think you can hit him because he won't hit you back, aye?" Roe braced herself in front of me, and I could see the lines of her body trembling with anger. "Well, *I* hit back, and it might not look like it, but I hit really bloody hard."

Pride and gratitude filled me as my best bud stood up for me. Most guys would probably be embarrassed as fuck to have a girl stand up for them. But I wasn't most guys. I approached Roe's side as Michelle glanced around at her audience. Even though she had a few inches on Roe, she swallowed hard and backed up as she sneered, "You're pathetic hanging around him, waiting for him to notice you."

Indignation churned in my gut, and I slung my arm around Roe's shoulder. "She's not the pathetic one here, Michelle. You got what you wanted." I gestured around at everyone and the spectacle she'd made. "I tried to do this the nice way, but since that didn't take … fuck off. For good."

Hurt lit her features, and I actually felt guilty. "I hope Laura gives you a disease." She turned and nodded to her posse, and the four of them flounced away.

The crowd broke, and the quad became a normal hangout space again.

Monroe turned to me with a sigh, her gray eyes even bigger than usual.

I laughed at her expression and reached out to tuck a strand of hair behind her ear to appease my constant need to touch her. "Are you my bodyguard now?"

My friend gave me an admonishing look. "Well, if you keep messing around with lots of girls, you're going to need one."

I frowned, not liking that I might have disappointed her. "She knew the score."

"Still, as much as I dislike Michelle or what she just did, people have feelings, Brodan. Why can't you just pick one girl to date for real?"

The thought made me antsy. "I don't want to be anyone's boyfriend, Sunset. I'll *never* be anyone's boyfriend."

She stared at me in disbelief. "Ever?"

"Ever," I promised.

"Why?"

My gut twisted. "Just because."

"That's not an answer, Brodan."

I grinned cheekily at her to cover my racing heart. "It's the only answer you're getting. Now, Bodyguard, where should we go next? And bear in mind, wherever we go, chaos follows."

She laughed reluctantly. I ignored the swooping sensation in my stomach, just as I'd ignored it the first time I felt it a little over a year ago.

It happened these days anytime my best mate smiled at me.

5

MONROE

My last job had been at a primary school in the suburbs of Glasgow, and there were some nights I didn't get home until six o'clock, even though the last bell rang at three fifteen. However, since moving back to Ardnoch, I had no choice but to be out of the classroom by three thirty because of my current caretaking duties.

Passing by Ellen Hunter's P6 class, I bid her good night as she sat at her desk marking jotters. She waved at me absent-mindedly, and I hurried out of the school. To my surprise, I saw two kids lingering forlornly at the gate and was even more surprised when I realized the boy was in my class.

Lewis Adair.

He stood with his little sister Eilidh, who I knew was in P3.

He was a quiet, intelligent boy with an athletic side that made him popular with his peers. I liked him. His father was

Thane, and I remembered Thane being a bit of a scrapper when we were younger. He was always the one Brodan and Arran looked to for protection, because the other boys were afraid of Thane. By all accounts, he'd grown into a civilized gentleman, but he'd sadly lost Lewis and Eilidh's mum a few years ago. He'd since remarried and had caused quite the scandal since his new bride was his twenty-seven-year-old nanny—who also happened to be his brother Lachlan's wife's sister.

Keeping it in the family, those Adairs, I thought wryly as I walked across the car park to make sure the kids were all right.

"Lewis!" I called to him, and the children turned.

Lewis had his sister's hand gripped tightly in his.

Adorable.

Something like relief flashed across his face when he saw me, and my heart stumbled. "Ms. Sinclair."

"Are you all right?"

"You're Lewis's teacher," Eilidh announced brightly. She was a beautiful child with big blue eyes and dark curly hair.

I smiled. "I am."

Suddenly, she frowned. "You're very pretty."

My lips twitched, wondering why this would cause her to frown. "Thank you." My attention drifted to Lewis. "Everything okay?"

Considering all the other kids had been collected and these two were still standing here, I had to think not.

"Who's picking you up today?"

"Mum," Lewis answered, his brows pinched together. "It's supposed to be Mum."

I vaguely noted he called his stepmum *mum* and how lovely that was before I nodded. "Okay, let's go back inside and see if we can call her."

"Ms. Sinclair!"

Turning around, it shocked me to see our head teacher, Mrs. Anita Cooley, hurrying across the car park. I'd never seen her move at anything but a sedate pace.

"Ah, thank goodness," my boss said as she slowed to a stop. "I'm so glad you're waiting with the children. Mrs. Adair just called. The children's uncle Arran is on his way to pick them up, as Mrs. Adair had to rush her sister to the hospital. She's in labor."

Oh my.

"Where's Uncle Lachlan?" Lewis stepped forward, concerned. Eilidh leaned into his side.

"He was on the estate," Anita said. "He's on his way to the hospital, too, but your mother was with her sister at the time."

Just then, we heard the telltale sound of an engine and a black Range Rover skidded to a stop outside the gates. Arran jumped out of the driver's side, and I ignored the unease I felt at the sight of him. I knew Arran wanted us to be friends again, but it was too complicated for me.

Arran's relief upon seeing the kids was palpable, and then our gazes met and gratitude filled his expression. "Thank you for waiting with them."

"Of course. I hope your sister-in-law is okay."

"Robyn is a warrior," Arran said, just as Eilidh threw herself at him. "It's okay, sweetheart." He lifted her into his arms and she clung to him like a little monkey. "Aunt Robyn's tough, isn't she?"

"She's tougher than you, Uncle Arran," Eilidh agreed with a serious nod.

Anita snorted behind me, which made it hard to stifle my laughter.

Arran grinned, completely unabashed. "You haven't met Robyn. Eilidh only speaks the truth."

"It's true." Lewis nodded. "Aunt Robyn used to be a police

officer, and she's been shot and she taught every girl in the family martial arts."

I knew a lot of this from village gossip, but to hear it confirmed made me want to meet Robyn Adair in person. She sounded like quite a character.

Of course, if I met her, it would only be in passing. I'd never have the chance to get to know her.

"Anyway, we better get going. Thanks again." Arran gave me an intense look. "Hopefully, I'll see you soon."

I tried not to blush. I knew *he* knew I was avoiding him. Arran had tried to get me to rent a cottage owned by the Adairs at a discounted rate, but I'd turned him down, and we hadn't seen each other in weeks.

I gave a noncommittal smile and waved them off.

"See you tomorrow, Ms. Sinclair," Lewis said before he followed his uncle and sister.

"See you tomorrow, Lewis."

Once they drove off, I turned toward my car and almost squeaked with fright at the sight of Anita. I'd forgotten she was there.

She looked like she was struggling not to smile, as if she knew quite well I'd forgotten her presence. "Rumor has it you used to be quite close to the Adairs."

Anita Cooley was a transplant from Aberdeen. She'd taken on the position of head teacher at the primary school ten years ago, so Brodan and I were before her time here. "Years ago, yes."

"Parents' evening is coming up. I take it that won't be an issue for you."

"Not at all," I promised. And it wouldn't be. Thane Adair probably barely remembered me, and it wasn't like Brodan would stay in Ardnoch much longer. It had been a few weeks since he'd ignored me on Castle Street, so surely his feet were itching to leave by now. Besides, even if he didn't leave soon, I'd never have to be around Brodan simply because I was teaching his nephew.

~

The good thing about driving a small car was that I could squeeze into small spaces. I grabbed the last parking spot near my mum's cottage, but she wasn't my first stop. Hands filled with shopping bags, I had to settle them on the ground to unlock my neighbor's door.

Flora's mum, Belle, had given me a spare key once I started insisting on doing her shopping for her. Unlike my mum, Belle gave me money every week for my help. Flora used to do it for her, but since I was already bringing Mum hers, I didn't see any point in Flora stressing herself out trying to run the café and look after Belle. I knew Flora's husband was a police officer and had little free time either. So I helped. It was why Flora wouldn't let me pay for coffee.

"Belle, it's me!" I called as I stepped inside, lugging her groceries.

"Hullo, Monroe!" she called from the living room. The kitchen, like ours, was at the front of the cottage, so I dropped the bags off first before I headed into the sitting room at the back.

October had brought with it the first signs of winter chill, and Belle looked cozy, settled on her lounge chair with a blanket over her lap and a book in hand, walking stick nestled beside her.

"Look at you." She rested her book on her lap. "Cheeks all pink with the cold. You're pretty as a picture."

I smiled at her compliment. "Flattery will get you everywhere, Belle. How are you? Can I get you anything before I put your shopping away?"

"Do you have time for a cuppa?"

Of course I did. "Let me put the shopping away, and then I'll bring some tea and biscuits through."

Not longer later, I sat across from Belle on her floral sofa, sipping tea and munching on shortbread. I knew the longer I waited to go next door to take care of Mum's dinner, the snarkier she'd be, but Belle seemed to delight in my visits. I knew Flora loved her mum dearly, but despite her sometimes sunny demeanor, Belle focused on negative articles she read online or in the newspaper. I'd noticed many elderly people did this. I understood it could be tiring, and I think Flora didn't quite know how to deal with it without getting frustrated or depressed.

But everyone needed someone to talk to, so I listened as Belle chatted away to me about corrupt governments, conspiracies against the elderly, and how climate change was devastating us already and everyone was burying their heads in the sand.

Once we finished our tea, I gave Belle a kiss on the cheek, and she smiled at me fondly before I left.

I found Mum in the kitchen, fumbling around, pain etched on her features.

"What are you doing?" I asked.

"What am I doing?" She glowered at me. "I'm starving. Where have you been?"

"I'm sorry you're hungry, but I had to drop off groceries for Belle."

"I'm your mother, not that old witch." She stepped into my space, her face almost touching mine. "You remember who took care of you."

I pulled my head away from hers. "Funny, this coming from someone who didn't even want me here looking after her in the first place."

"Then fuck off," she snapped, stomping her walking stick

angrily as she tried to hurry from the kitchen. "You're not wanted."

Apparently, I never had been.

Ignoring how my chest caved in a way I thought would've disappeared with age, I removed my coat and got to work making Mum's dinner.

6

MONROE

THE PAST

I spent most of my days on Ardnoch Estate. Brodan's family owned acres upon acres of land, and growing up, we'd made it our life's mission to explore every inch. They even owned a private, golden-sand beach, and on those rare gorgeous summer days, we'd hang out there. Most of the time, Arran was there, sometimes even Fergus. When we were much younger, Lachlan and Thane would have joined us too. Yet today, the skies above the castle estate were brooding, the clouds' mauve bellies threatening a downpour. It was humid, though. So bloody humid that my hair stuck to the back of my neck, and I'd braved wearing a short summer dress even with the threat of rain. My mood mirrored it as we walked across the wild lawn toward the castle.

"Tell me what's going on, Sunset." Brodan nudged me. "You've been off for days."

I gave him a tight-lipped smile. "Nothing's wrong."

My friend scowled and stared straight ahead. It had been his suggestion to hang out at his place today, and though I wasn't the best company, I'd do anything to get away from Mum. She was part of the reason for my shit mood. Thankfully, it was only poor Brodan being infected by it today. Fergus had to work, Arran was off with some girl, and Lachlan should have been home for the summer from his second year at St. Andrews University, but by fluke, he'd ended up as an extra in a movie and grabbed the attention of the producer who'd gotten him an audition for another film. And he'd gotten the part! It was crazy. Right now, he was filming a proper Hollywood action movie in Canada. I still couldn't get my head around the fact that we'd be able to go to the cinema to see Lachlan in a movie. It was mind-boggling. His whole family thought so too.

Thane Adair was back from his first year at Glasgow Uni, but he had a summer job at an architectural firm in Inverness, so we saw little of him.

As for Arrochar, she was thirteen now and had a group of friends she spent the summer with, biking around Ardnoch. It surprised me Brodan was allowing his wee sister so much freedom. They were usually all over the poor lass. To my shock, Brodan had been pretty attentive to me the past few weeks. Not that he wasn't an involved friend, but during last term, between his many casual hookups and the fact that I had a boyfriend, we'd definitely spent less time together.

Brodan seemed determined to change that this summer.

Since I no longer had a boyfriend, I had no reason not to spend the days with my best friend.

Another reason I was in a shitty mood.

Just wait, I thought as I followed Brodan into the castle. In a year's time, I'd be graduating from high school and on my way to university, where surely I'd meet a boy who could make me fall out of love with my best friend.

As Brodan took a left instead of a right, I frowned. "Where are we going?"

Ardnoch Castle was too big for the family to afford to use the entire place. In fact, they only used a few rooms. The rest of the castle was dank, dark, and a bit creepy. As kids, we'd explored every inch too.

Brodan threw a smile over his shoulder and then grabbed my hand, pulling me along after him. I wanted to tighten my fingers around his, but forced myself not to. To my surprise, he led me to the door to the castle's only turret.

"What are we doing?"

"C'mon."

We climbed the narrow stone staircase within, up to the next door, and when we stepped out, I sucked in a breath.

As children, we played in the turret. It was our place, where we'd tell each other all our secrets. It was the place I'd finally told Brodan that my dad hurt me and where he'd begged me to tell someone. I'd pleaded with him in return to keep my secret, and he had until that fateful day almost five years ago.

Brodan had turned our place into a campout. He'd strung fairy lights everywhere, so it didn't look so cold and gloomy. He brought in multiple sleeping bags, duvets, and a large picnic basket filled with snacks.

"What is this?" I asked him in wonder.

My best friend looked down at me. He was now taller than Thane, almost as tall as Lachlan. That put him exactly a foot taller than me. Not a comfortable height difference, and one of the many small reasons I compiled to remind myself that Brodan and I would never be more than friends.

I'd started dating Phil in December of last year because I knew it was time to move on from these feelings for Brodan. Sometimes, however, when he looked at me the way he was looking at me now, he made it really hard to forget that I was in love with him.

"I thought maybe if I brought you here …" He shrugged, looking around at the place filled with memories. "You'd talk to me."

"Brodan—"

"Don't." He gave me a wounded look. "Don't say you're fine. I know you're not. Did I do something? Is that why you won't talk to me anymore?"

I shook my head, feeling guilty for shutting him out. "No, of course not."

"Then why?" Those blue eyes were so hurt and troubled. "We haven't even graduated yet, and I feel like I'm losing you. That fucking kills, Roe."

This was the problem when you were as close as Brodan and me. We'd always told each other exactly how we were feeling. Never afraid to be vulnerable. Until I fell in love with him and closed down communication. Things between us had not been the same for a few years, but I'd acted my arse off so Brodan wouldn't feel that distance.

I guessed I'd just grown tired of pretending.

That wasn't his fault, though.

He didn't ask me to fall in love with him.

"Talk to me," Brodan pleaded.

With a sigh, I walked over to the bed of blankets and sleeping bags, kicked off my trainers, and sat, legs out, leaning back on my hands. Brodan took this in and approached, eyes glued to my face as if searching for something. He kicked off his trainers and sat beside me, mirroring my body language.

"Mum has been particularly shitty lately," I told him quietly. "She keeps trying to talk me out of uni, telling me it's a waste of my time, that I'll fail. And everything I do around the house isn't enough. My weekend job at the store isn't enough." I'd been working at the general store every weekend for over a year. "Never enough." Apparently, that was a theme in my life. Sometimes it seemed impossible that I could feel so much for Brodan and not have him feel it back. Other boys found me attractive, so it really bloody stung that he didn't.

Mind you, he was Brodan. He was the best-looking guy in Ardnoch. Maybe even the entire county. Not that his looks were the primary reason I was in love with or even attracted to him. I loved Brodan's openness with me when he was so closed off with anyone outside of his family. I loved that I knew things about him no one else did, like how he still enjoyed eating Chewits and ready-salted crisps at the same time. A "delicacy" he'd discovered when we were kids. Yuck. I smiled to myself at the thought. I loved how loyal he was to me and his family. He was popular, but he wasn't a bully. He treated everyone with the kindness they deserved until they proved otherwise, but even then, he wasn't mean. If you were a shitty person, he just wouldn't give you his time.

But yeah, I was attracted to him.

My body reacted to his in a way that it never reacted to Phil's.

I didn't feel that deep tug of need in my belly when I looked at Phil, the way I did when I focused on Brodan's hands or his broad back and shoulders. I didn't get butterflies when Phil smiled at me, but I sure as hell did whenever Brodan gave me his boyish grin.

"I can't wait for you to get away from that woman." Brodan brought my thoughts back to the confession about my mum. He turned his head to look at me. "You know she's wrong, right? She's just scared of being alone, so she's saying anything to make you stay."

I shrugged, as if I didn't care. "It's only pushing me further away."

"I'm sorry." He nudged me with his arm. "You deserve so much better."

I gave him a sad smile.

"So, is she the only reason you've been quiet lately? You haven't spent much time with Phil …," he said with an uncharacteristic tentativeness. However, the truth was Brodan didn't talk to me about Phil unless he had to. I think it was weird for him that I'd started dating. I think maybe he wanted me to stay in a place where he didn't have to acknowledge I was a girl.

"We broke up." I smoothed the hem of my dress, even though it didn't need smoothing. When I glanced at Brodan to see his reaction to my news, I found his attention on my hemline. Or my legs. Sensing my stare, his eyes jerked to mine.

"When did you break up?"

"A week ago."

"Why didn't you tell me sooner?"

"I was processing."

Brodan scowled. "Please don't tell me you're upset about it. He wasn't good enough for you, Sunset. I'm fucking glad you broke up."

Indignation roared through me. "Nice."

He sighed. "I'm just being honest. The guy is a prick."

"There is nothing wrong with Phil. If anyone wasn't good enough for anybody, I wasn't good enough for him."

Scoffing, Brodan shook his head. "He's lucky you gave him the time of day. I still don't know why you did."

"Because he was nice. And funny. *I* didn't treat *him* right. Brodan, I just … I didn't … I'm not like you. I can't just have sex with someone and be okay about it if I don't have genuine feelings for them."

My friend shot up, drawing his knees to his chest and wrapping his arms around them. He gaped out of the small turret window, sounding choked as he asked, "Did you ... did you have sex with Phil?"

At his disbelieving tone, I felt a mix of anger and hurt. "That's so hard to believe?"

Brodan swallowed hard, still not looking at me. "No, 'course not. I just didn't realize you were that serious about him."

"It wasn't that I was serious about him. I wanted to have sex, so we had sex."

"Right."

At his refusal to look at me, hurt won over, and I felt myself retreating. "I'm going to go."

He whipped around, his hand landing on my knee. "No. No, don't."

My skin tingled where he touched me. Brodan used to touch me casually all the time. It never used to bother me. Now it was like being hit by a jolt of electricity. "Can you handle talking about this? I'm not Arro, you know."

Brodan wrinkled his nose as he removed his hand from my leg and wrapped his arms around his knees again. "One, Arro is never allowed to have sex, ever. Not happening. Sex does not exist for Arrochar Adair."

I giggled, and Brodan's expression lightened.

"Two"—his gaze drifted over my face and quickly swept my body before he looked away—"you're not my sister, Roe. We're best buds. We can talk about anything." He met my eyes again. "I promise."

"I can talk to you about this?"

"Of course." Suddenly, his countenance darkened. "Did he hurt you?"

"No." I grimaced. "But it was bad." So bad, it might have put me off sex for good if I wasn't so sure that there was something missing.

Brodan ran a hand through his hair, something he did

when he was uncomfortable. "Uh … well, the first time is supposed to be weird."

Now that he'd promised I could talk to him about this, I wanted Brodan's advice. Even though I hated the thought of him with other girls, he was experienced, and his opinion mattered. "We did it more than once, and it didn't stop being weird. I think maybe we skipped some parts. Like … fore-play." My cheeks burned, but I was proud of myself for being bold enough to put it out there.

Brodan's head whipped around, and my cheeks only burned hotter at his aghast expression. "He didn't even … did he not …" His eyes dragged down my body again, and he looked away, shoving that bloody hand through his hair once more as he gritted out, "Please tell me he didn't just … that he …"

"Wow, choke it out, Brodan. I thought we established I'm not Arro. You said we could talk about this stuff."

His glower could have incinerated me. "I fucking know you're not my wee sister."

What did that mean?

My eyes widened, but feeling something shift between us, I pushed. "Okay, so tell me where Phil went wrong, or I'm giving up on sex for good and never talking about *anything* with you ever again."

Brodan's eyes narrowed at my challenge, and he turned his body toward me. "Fine. Did he just stick his dick in you without getting you ready?"

I was pretty sure my entire body flushed beetroot. "Do you have to be so blunt?"

"You asked for it." He smirked, delighted by my reaction.

Fine. Challenge accepted. This was just like when we were kids and Brodan kept teasing and daring me to ride my bike down the highest point of a quarry north of Ardnoch. When I'd made a move to take on his challenge, he roared in panicked outrage and then physically hauled me away from the quarry. He was so mad and frightened, I felt awful afterward. But he'd learned never to dare me to do something he didn't really want me to do.

Or so I'd thought.

"No. He didn't 'get me ready,'" I air-quoted, making him scowl. "He pushed into me a few times and came. All four times we did it."

At that, Brodan shook his head, scowling. "What a selfish prick."

Emboldened by our forthrightness, I moved a little closer to him. "What ... what was he supposed to do?" I had some idea from movies and the things I'd heard people say at school, but I'd experienced none of it. And of course, I'd touched myself and had wondered maybe if Phil had touched me where I liked to touch me, maybe things would have gone better.

Brodan's eyes widened at my question, but then they dropped to my mouth, and not for the first time, I had hoped that Brodan might actually have more-than-friendly feelings for me. Sometimes I'd catch him looking at my mouth or my legs or my breasts, proving that he was, in fact, aware of me as an actual girl and not just his best friend. My insecurities allowed me to forget those moments until they happened again.

Like now, as Brodan's breath hitched and his attention moved to my cleavage and then drifted down to my bare thighs. The crests of his cheeks turned pink in a way I'd never seen before, and he wrenched his gaze away. "Like you said"—his voice was gruff—"foreplay."

"Like what?"

He shot me a pissed-off look. "You know what."

"I think we've established I don't, since Phil was selfish."

Brodan didn't laugh or smile at my teasing. Instead, his

gaze was suddenly intense in a way that made my heart race. "It's a complete waste that he was your first time. Remind me to deck him the next time I see him."

"You'll do nothing of the sort, Brodan Adair. I think ..." Guilt suffused me, and I dropped my eyes in shame. "I think I really hurt his feelings when I broke up with him."

"Well, that's what he gets for not treating you properly. Fuck. Don't feel bad for the arsehole."

Phil had gotten teary-eyed when I broke up with him, so I felt bad. "He just ... I don't think he meant to be selfish. I think he was just inexperienced."

"Bullshit. He had three girlfriends before you, and I know for a fact that he used to shag one of them because she told me."

I wrinkled my nose as I guessed that she'd told Brodan this after she'd shagged him too. "So, Casanova, what should he have done? Seriously. I'm curious what has all the girls from here to Inverness willing to put up with your shite for a chance to shag you?"

Brodan grinned at my teasing. "I'm very, very giving."

My pulse raced, and I pushed through my awkwardness. "What does that mean?"

"We're not talking about it, Sunset."

"I thought you said we can talk about anything. Best friends talk about their sexual exploits, you know. C'mon." I gave him a little shove. "I have my very own Don Juan to turn to for advice. Don't get all shy on me."

His eyes narrowed again as he offered bluntly, "I usually go down on them before we have sex."

Do not blush, do not blush, do not blush. Unfortunately, the image of Brodan's head between my legs caused a deep tug low in my belly, and my skin flushed accordingly. I saw him studying my reaction with a smugness that made me push through my embarrassment and arousal. "Do you ... do you like doing that?"

Brodan's breath hitched at my question, and his chin tilted stubbornly. "Aye. Not all girls like it, though. One girl didn't want me down there with my mouth. So I got her off by rubbing her clit."

His deliberate crudeness wasn't pushing me away from the subject but rather spurring on my curiosity—and turning me the feck on, awakening the desire to have him take care of the tension I could never seem to get rid of. I squeezed my thighs together against the pulsing sensation between my legs, and Brodan's gaze dropped to the movement. His nostrils flared, and there was the flush on the crests of his cheeks.

Was Brodan ... turned on?

Hope and recklessness clashed within me, and before I could stop myself, I blurted out, "Show me."

Brodan glowered, but there was heat in his eyes.

"Show me," I repeated.

Surely if he didn't want to, he'd have immediately protested?

Instead, he was breathing hard, and his hands clenched into fists. Before I could pull myself out of the moment, before I could lose my courage, I took hold of one of his hands and waited for him to resist.

Brodan visibly swallowed, but didn't pull away.

Not when I slowly rested it against my inner thigh.

In fact, his fist uncurled, and his hand flattened, his fingers tickling the sensitive skin there. I let out a little gasp, and the muscle in his jaw ticked as I slid his hand under my dress. The throbbing between my legs intensified.

"Show me," I whispered and spread my legs.

Brodan inhaled sharply, and he gripped my thigh hard. "Fuck ... Roe." His eyes flew up to meet mine. "If I do this ...

it changes nothing. I'm just …" He licked his lips almost nervously. "I'm just showing you what it should be like, right? It changes nothing between us. Our friendship means too much. Promise."

My hormones, unfortunately, were totally in control of that moment. Because I thought, as I laid there with the possibility of Brodan Adair touching me intimately, that it would be enough. That if it was all I could have from him, I'd take it. "I promise."

He shuddered and then this fierceness took over his expression as he suddenly straddled me. Looming above, his shoulders so broad, his body so big, I'd never felt the differences between us more. I'd never felt more fragile and feminine.

A glance down his body revealed he was not unaffected.

His hard-on was clearly visible through his sweatpants.

My breasts swelled at the knowledge he really wanted me, and my nipples hardened. Brodan noted this as I wasn't wearing a bra with this dress, and his grip on my thigh tightened.

Then his fingers slipped beneath my underwear, and his thumb found my clit.

"Brodan," I gasped, my hips arching into his touch.

He braced his free hand at the side of my head and leaned over me, his eyes holding mine as he rubbed his thumb over the sensitive bundle of nerves between my thighs. I reached for him, needing something to hold on to, my fingers gripping his back, drawing him closer. Our breaths met, our faces so close as he played me.

And then he pushed his fingers inside me at the same time, and shivers cascaded down my spine. "Brodan."

"Roe," he panted against my lips. "Roe. So tight. Fuck. Roe."

In some part of my brain, I couldn't believe this was

happening, but forefront of any thought was chasing the sensations rioting through me. At every thrust of his fingers, I arched my hips, riding his touch. The tension inside me grew tauter and tauter with each thrust, my heartbeat rushing and pounding in my ears.

Then suddenly my body locked, and Brodan slammed his mouth down over mine a second before that tension shattered into a million glorious pieces. My inner muscles tightened so hard around his fingers, it drew him further inside me, and Brodan grunted against my mouth. His kiss was suddenly ferocious. His fingers pulled out of me and then his hand was on my breast, squeezing and shaping it as he ground his hips between my legs. He nudged his arousal into me, and I could only hold on to him as he kissed me with a thrilling sexual hunger.

A chill blasted over my body as Brodan practically threw himself off.

I blinked at the abrupt distance between us and sat up on my elbows to find Brodan panting and staring at me as if he'd never seen me before.

Dread filled me, and I sat up, drawing my knees tight to my chest.

Brodan took in the move, and something like pain shot through his expression before he reached out to draw one of my hands to his mouth. He kissed my knuckles and squeezed his eyes closed. "Nothing changes," he said hoarsely. "Promise me, nothing changes." When he opened his eyes, he was no longer hiding his pain or his fear. "I can't lose you, Roe."

I didn't understand.

He clearly felt about me how I felt about him, or the last blissful minutes wouldn't have happened.

Whatever he saw in my eyes made him clasp my hand between both of his and plead, "Please."

"You enjoyed it. I know you did," I whispered feebly.

"Roe." He hung his head, still gripping onto me.

When he said nothing else, I tugged on my hand, wanting to run as fast and far from him as possible. Because clearly his enjoyment wasn't about me. He'd just reacted like a typical horny teenage boy. *Fuck!*

Brodan's head whipped up as he held tight to me. "No. Don't. Look …" He took a breath before he confessed, "If I wanted something serious with a girl, it would be with you, Monroe."

My heart soared—

"But I will never want that with anyone."

What?

"It's not in me to want that. I won't become my dad. He lost Mum and just stopped living, Roe. He barely exists. I won't become like him because I'm stupid enough to get serious with someone. I decided a long time ago that my life would be a series of casual fucks." He leaned toward me, his eyes light with emotion. "You will never be a casual fuck. So we're friends. You're my best friend. And I cannot lose you just because I think you're gorgeous."

For the last five years, I'd wanted nothing more than to hear Brodan Adair tell me he thought I was pretty.

Now part of me wished he never had.

But as he begged, "Don't leave me because of this. Please. I can't lose you, Roe, so please just pretend with me. Pretend like this never happened. It should never have happened," he ended in a pained, rough whisper.

And because I could see the genuine turmoil and fear in his expression, I put Brodan's feelings above mine and murmured, "It never happened. I promise."

However, as I let myself into the house I hated coming home to after Brodan walked me back into town, I couldn't help that little bloom of hope that sprung to life inside me.

ANTHA YOUNG

Brodan had said if he could be serious with anyone, it would be me.

So ... I just had to play the waiting game.

I just had to wait for the day that Brodan Adair grew out of his trauma, out of his fears.

I could be patient for the one I loved. Especially after experiencing a tiny moment of what it would be like between us.

When he was ready, I'd be the one he chose.

7

BRODAN

PRESENT DAY

It was a copout. Asking Walker to make all my decisions for me. It was a bloody copout, and I knew it.

I wasn't particularly proud that I was so fucked in the head I couldn't see clearly enough to make decisions about my own life. However, I couldn't deny that as much as it wasn't admirable that I'd handed the reins over to Walk ... the results were worth any wounds to my pride.

It had been a long time since I felt like I was exactly where I was supposed to be.

The water of the North Sea was a brooding gray blue today, almost indistinguishable from the livid sky above. It should be raining on a day this sullen. But not a drop fell from the sky as I sat at my desk. I'd moved the piece of furniture to the bay window in my suite on the estate, so I had a view while I wrote.

This morning I'd braced myself against the blustery

65

October winds to take Eredine's morning mindfulness and yoga class. Walker ordered me to take the classes three times a week. I thought he was doing it to mess with me, but the sessions with Ery helped. Where the gym was a place I poured out my frustrations and worries, and also where I had to be to maintain the physique Hollywood found so desirable, Ery's classes were different. Yoga stretched me, and so did the mindfulness meditation. My mind had been like a muscle knotted from tension and stress, and the meditation allowed me to stop overthinking everything in my past, present, and future and just think about the moment, to be fully aware of existing in the moment. To my shock, it helped me feel less overwhelmed.

Then Walker found a way for me to be productive. For years, I'd been telling him I wanted to be behind the camera. That I wanted to write the scripts. Writing wasn't a passion that had always been with me. It snuck up on me over the years. I started reading scripts and then, between takes, I started devouring books. Acting had given me a thirst for storytelling.

So what did Walk order?

For me to sit down in the afternoon and work on a script.

It took days before words actually came. Another surprise: I think I was writing a fucking love story. A tragic one. But one, nonetheless.

My phone vibrated beside my laptop, drawing me out of my thoughts, and I hoped it wasn't one of the women I counted among my fuck buddies, or my agent, Anders. Now and then, I'd get a text or a call from a woman I had a previous casual thing with, asking for a hookup. While I'd quite like to get laid, the thought of fucking some woman I didn't really care about left me feeling weirdly (and worryingly) empty.

As for Anders ... well, after Lachlan (the high-handed

bastard) fired my manager for overworking me, I'd cooled down enough to realize he was right. The manager stayed fired, but I kept my agent. Anders, however, was freaking out about my indefinite vacation from acting and called at least once a week. When I told him about the scriptwriting, it settled him a bit.

Thankfully, my caller wasn't a fling or Anders. It was Regan. It would be naive of me to ignore the fact that being around my family, celebrating two momentous occasions, hadn't had an effect on me. There was still a disconnect—I couldn't bridge years of distance in just a few months. But we were getting there. I'd forgotten how much I needed *them* to be content within myself.

"Hi, gorgeous."

"Hey, yourself. I'm just checking you haven't forgotten about dinner?"

I glanced at the clock on my phone. I still had time. "No, I haven't. It's not until six, though, right?"

"Right. And Walker is more than welcome. You two seem to be a package deal these days."

"Meaning?"

"You remind me of Mac and Lachlan. Anyway, let him know he's invited."

"He's working, but I'll be there. See you soon."

"Is Uncle Brodan coming, Mum?" I heard my niece Eilidh in the background.

"He is, but what did Mom say about interrupting people when they're on the phone?"

"It's rude."

I chuckled at Eilidh's beleaguered reply.

She then yelled, "Tell Uncle Brodan I'm sitting beside him at dinner!"

An ache flared across my chest. "Tell my favorite niece I can't wait."

"You can't say that anymore." Regan chuckled. "Because now you actually have nieces, plural."

It was true. Two weeks ago, Robyn gave birth to a wee girl called Vivien Stacey Adair, named for our mother and Robyn's mum. While visiting Robyn and Vivien in the hospital, Arrochar went into labor. Hers was a little longer and nerve-racking for all, none more so than Mac, but finally they welcomed their daughter and, in a grand tradition of naming people in our family after places in Scotland, they named her Skye Robyn Galbraith.

I was an uncle four times over now.

Eilidh's desire to spend time with me made me feel great, but it also filled me with guilt that I'd missed her and Lewis's early childhood.

No more. Not that long ago, I was determined to avoid Ardnoch. Now, after spending only a few months there, I never wanted to leave. The mindfulness, the peace, the time to reflect, had brought me that one clarification. Home was what I'd been missing for years. It was time to stop missing it.

"Well, tell one of my three favorite nieces that I can't wait to sit beside her at dinner." I grinned and surveyed the dull afternoon as it darkened toward an early-winter evening.

"I will. See you soon, Uncle Brodan," Regan teased.

William's Wine Cellar just off Castle Street carried a varied and impressive collection of alcohol and stayed open later than most stores. I drove into Ardnoch alone, realizing that part of the reason I felt great was my sense of freedom. Walker had deduced some weeks ago that I was safe enough now to wander Ardnoch alone. He didn't want me going anywhere else without a security detail, but he was satisfied I had privacy and respect here, now that most of the tourists had departed. The October break always brought a fresh gaggle of them, but that had ended and schools were now back in session.

While whisky was my drink of choice (it was the one alcoholic beverage I could enjoy at a leisurely pace and it didn't depress me), I knew the ladies of our family were wine drinkers. Deciding to pick up a nice bottle of wine for dinner, I swung the Range Rover I'd borrowed from Lachlan's estate fleet into a space outside the Gloaming. Arran wouldn't be there—he was probably already with the family. Although it was Regan who called me, Sunday dinner was at Robyn and Lachlan's. Everyone would be present, including my brand-new nieces.

Maybe three bottles of wine, I thought as I strolled down the cobbled lane between the old jail turned museum and Chen and Wang Lei's Chinese restaurant. The lane was lit by Victorian-style lampposts and protected me from the icy wind.

The swanky wine store lit up like a beacon in the dark lane, and I hurried inside out of the cold. I gave the owner a polite smile and nod, then rounded the shelves and shelves of whisky to check out the massive wall of wine at the back. The expensive stuff was in a locked wine cellar, the cheaper stuff on the adjacent wall on open shelving.

I halted at the sight of a woman.

She stood with her back to me, perusing the cheaper wine.

Tumbles of familiar red hair fell down her narrow back from beneath a dark green beanie. She wore a short puffer jacket. Tight, dark blue jeans perfectly hugged her pert, wee arse. On her feet she wore the local fashion — hiking boots.

My pulse raced, and I was just about to turn quietly and

leave when I saw her back straighten abruptly. As if she felt me, she slowly turned around.

Monroe Fucking Sinclair.

Her cheeks were flushed from the cold, her big gray eyes bright beneath the store lights. She looked so young, nowhere near the thirty-seven I knew her to be. Monroe was a natural beauty. The kind of beauty I hadn't come across since, and I'd worked with and met some of the most beautiful women in the world.

She really hadn't changed. It was like staring into the face of nineteen-year-old Roe. My best friend.

Who had abandoned me.

Aye, this was the woman who taught me a very valuable lesson.

I scowled at her, deciding at that moment I wouldn't be chased out of the store, or Ardnoch, because she'd decided to come back.

Ignoring her, I strolled over to the large wine cellar and perused the expensive stuff.

Yet I could barely take in the labels. I could feel her attention on me. My hands clenched into fists at my sides as the cheek facing her grew hot. At the sound of her footsteps drawing near, I glanced sharply at her.

Monroe stared up at me and licked her full lips nervously. My eyes narrowed on her mouth. I hated she could make me feel so much, even after all these years.

"I ... uh ... I felt ... I just wanted to acknowledge you." Monroe shrugged wearily. "We live in the same town, Brodan. People talk. I just wanted to say hello and be civil to you."

Hearing her voice after all these years was a punch to the gut. My throat felt thick with emotion and I was afraid if I spoke, she'd hear the roughness. She'd know being in her presence affected me beyond bearing. There was no way I'd reveal that to her.

So, I looked right through her and turned my back on her. As I strode toward the exit, I caught sight of her reflection in the store window. Monroe clamped her teeth down on her lower lip, something she'd always done when she was fighting back tears.

Jesus Christ.

I would not feel guilty I vowed, as I marched out of the shop. *You have nothing to feel guilty about*, I reminded myself.

I wasn't the one who left her.

She left me.

She'd ignored me when I reached out to her.

Almost twenty years of the strongest bond I'd ever felt with someone, and she left me like it was easy.

Crying babies had a way of making you forget anything but the sound of crying babies.

My nieces were apparently already best buddies because as soon as one started crying, the other wailed right along with her. Fuck, my head was nipping. I had no idea how my siblings were coping with this.

Despite dinner being hosted at Robyn and Lachlan's, Regan was cooking. She'd smiled gratefully at me when I deposited three bottles of wine I'd bought from Morag's on the island in front of her, and Eredine had swooped in to pour those of us drinking a glass before dinner even started.

It might have had something to do with the cacophony of infant indignation.

Though Christ knew what they had to be pissed off about.

"They're so loud, Mum!" Eilidh stood at Regan's side, her cute face scrunched up in horror.

"You were loud once too," Thane reminded his daughter as he grabbed two glasses of wine and walked over to our sister to offer her one.

Arro shook her head, waving the wine away, as she watched Mac sway their daughter from side to side. He murmured words I couldn't hear, but Skye's crying petered off.

Vivien's, not so much.

Robyn held her while Lachlan hovered over them, looking as if he hadn't slept in ten years.

To be fair, they all looked like they hadn't slept in ten years. All four of them had taken maternity leave. Lachlan had even hired a new hospitality manager at Ardnoch. Aria Howard, the efficient and very attractive daughter of legendary director Wesley Howard. He was a member of Ardnoch Estate's board and owned one of the multimillion-pound homes on the estate's coastal land. Lachlan had introduced me to Aria before Robyn gave birth. He was a control freak, so he was nervous about handing over the reins, but I'd promised I'd keep an eye out for him. So far, Aria was running the place as efficiently as Lachlan would. Even more so because she wasn't distracted by a newborn.

"Let's try putting them down again," Arro suggested loudly to be heard.

Robyn nodded, and Lachlan leaned in to take his daughter. "I'll do it."

With Vivien in his arms, he and Mac tread upstairs to the nursery to try once more to get the girls to fall asleep.

My sister-in-law shared a weary smile with my sister.

"It's going well, then," I teased, raising a glass to them.

"It's worth it," Arro said, even as she rested her head against the armchair and closed her eyes.

"Oh, aye, it looks it."

At my sarcasm, Robyn quirked an eyebrow. "Just you wait until it's your turn. You'll understand then."

"Never going to happen," I said with absolute conviction. Fatherhood was not in the cards for me. Ignoring the pang of loss at the reminder, I searched for distraction elsewhere.

As my siblings talked about nappies and bath times and all that shit while Eredine sat on Arran's lap and they happily listened, I zeroed in on my nephew. Lewis sat on the farthest-away armchair, his headphones on and a tablet in hand.

Smart man.

I sauntered over to him, and he looked up at me as I sat down on the armrest. Lewis removed one side of his headphones.

"What are you playing?" I glanced down at his screen.

"All Star Tower Defense."

Never heard of it. "Right."

Lewis smirked at me. "It's on *Roblox.*"

He was speaking a foreign language. "Of course it is."

My nephew grinned. "You want to see?"

"Sure."

And so until dinner was ready, my nephew played and explained to me what was happening with his anime character and the mission he was on. I'd never been a gamer, but I could see the appeal.

To everyone's relief, Mac and Lachlan got the girls to sleep just as Regan and Thane delivered dinner to the table. We talked quietly (although Eilidh had to be reminded to lower her voice multiple times) to not wake the babies. All in all, I thought I was doing a grand job of shaking off the encounter with Monroe ... until Eredine asked the kids how school was going.

Eilidh gave us a full five-minute rundown of life in

primary three. By the way she told it, she was the benevolent leader of her class and champion of the underdog. No bully was getting past Eilidh Francine Adair. The kid was so bloody cute, it killed me. I grinned down at her the entire time she talked, watching her gesticulate with her little hands. Her stepmum gently hushed her anytime her voice rose with excitement.

Then it was Lewis's turn. "School's good." He shrugged. "Ms. Sinclair is the best teacher I've had."

My gut clenched, and I stuffed a piece of roast chicken in my mouth so I didn't have to look at anyone.

I felt their attention on me, anyway, but waited patiently for someone to change the subject. Lewis wasn't particularly talkative, so I was sure we were done with it.

"Why is she the best?" Robyn asked.

Fuck, thanks, Robyn.

"Uh … I don't know. She just is." Lewis shrugged again.

Eilidh grinned at her brother. "Lewis fancies her."

Lewis went beetroot. "I do not, Eilidh. Shut up!"

Nearly every single adult at the table hurriedly shushed him. Thane gave his son a warning look. "Don't tell your sister to shut up."

"Well, tell her to stop lying."

Eilidh grinned wickedly at her brother. "I only speak the truth."

Before Lewis could launch himself across the table at his sister, Lachlan leaned his head toward our nephew and said something quietly that made Lewis relax. From there, thankfully, the subject of Ms. Sinclair was dropped.

But it was too late.

I kept seeing her expression in the window reflection when I'd walked away as if she'd never spoken. And not for the first time, I wondered why she was still Ms. Sinclair. Why hadn't she married? Why on earth was Monroe still single? It made no sense. All Roe had ever wanted was a simple life. She'd told me she wanted a job she cared about, a husband who loved her, and children they'd adore, breaking the cycle of abuse and loneliness in her family.

Yet she was still alone?

Needing some air, I excused myself after dessert and stepped out into the back garden, closing the sliding doors behind me so I wouldn't let in the chill. Outdoor lights illuminated the deck and a small portion of the garden.

The moon, mostly obscured by clouds, danced in broken shards across the black water beyond the cliffs. I could hear the sea crashing below, and though I shivered against the cold night, I closed my eyes and focused on the present.

Slowly, my tension eased.

Then the door opened behind me, and I turned to find Arran stepping outside to join me. He closed the door and shoved his hands into his pockets. "It's fucking Baltic. What are you doing out here?"

"Just needed a minute."

"William McLoud supplies the bar at the Gloaming with its more expensive alcohol," Arran said abruptly. "We've become friends."

Shit.

Arran glowered. "Got a text from him that you ignored Monroe when she approached you in his store tonight. That you walked out without a word. Will said Monroe looked like you'd slapped her."

Wee prick. "Got your spies watching me?"

"You know what this place is like, Brodan. Don't pretend you don't. Someone is always watching."

"Well, isn't that creepy?" I drawled.

Arran sighed. "I thought you and I were past this. I thought you weren't pissed off at me anymore about what happened all those years back, but what you said a few weeks ago at the Gloaming has really been bothering me. You're still holding that drunken night with Roe against me."

I cut him an annoyed look. "I am not. Aye, there's no denying I was angry at the time, but it was only because you fucking Monroe was like you'd fucked my sister." Lie. Bloody lie. "I'm not angry now. I'm over it." Honestly, I didn't know one way or the other if that was the truth.

Arran scoffed. "If that were true, you'd still be talking to Monroe, not treating her like she doesn't even exist." I heard the censure in his voice and looked away. "Fergus slept with Arro behind our backs when she wasn't even legal, and we all forgave him and her. Of course, that was before we knew he was a sociopath."

Flinching at the reminder that my friend had turned on my family, had taken his beef with me out on them, I glared out at the dark sea. "Is it possible to catch up with my brother without him bringing up people who don't matter anymore?"

"If she didn't matter, you wouldn't be so furious with her."

"Arran ... leave it."

"She's not had it easy." My brother pushed. "Right now, she's looking after her mum, and from what I remember, that woman was a witch to Monroe."

I remembered. I'd wanted Monroe to move out as soon as she turned eighteen. Dad had even agreed to let her stay at the castle, but Roe was too prideful to do it.

"She's living in Gordon's caravan and winter is rolling in. She'll be freezing her arse off out there, but she won't accept a better place to live. I've tried."

So she was still too prideful. I refused to picture her in a caravan by the water during the harsh Highland winter.

"Why do you care so much?" I asked lazily, as if I didn't care that Arran cared.

My brother yanked on my arm, drawing my gaze back to

his. He stared at me incredulously. "Because she's my friend. I've known her my whole life. Because she's a good person. And once upon a time, you would have died before letting anything happen to her. Do you even remember that?"

Rage flushed through me, but I controlled it. I turned it to ice in my veins. "Things change," I told my brother flatly. "I haven't thought about Monroe Sinclair in almost eighteen years. She means nothing to me. I couldn't care less where she's living or what she's dealing with. She could fall off the face of the planet, and I wouldn't notice."

Arran curled his upper lip, and I tried not to wince against his disdain. "When did you turn into such a callous bastard?"

He walked away, slipping inside the house, before I could say another word.

Teeth grinding, I turned back to the sea and closed my eyes, listening to the waves crash, trying to find the peace I'd had before my youngest brother pushed my buttons.

I couldn't.

All I could think about was the cold trying to burrow through my long-sleeved tee. And then all I could think about was Monroe, freezing and unprotected in a caravan anyone could break into. Only a few years ago, Fergus had broken into the one Robyn was staying in and attacked her with a knife.

The thought made my chest tighten.

Robyn had survived.

And Roe would survive a winter alone in a caravan.

She was made of stern stuff.

She'd be fine.

8

BRODAN

THE PAST

As much as I was enjoying my time in St. Andrews, I had to admit I missed the hell out of Ardnoch. I didn't know if it was being away from the Highlands in general, or if it was missing the people who made home *home*. That included Monroe. It hadn't gotten easier.

We'd both just started our second year at uni, and leaving her again after weeks of hanging out was utter rubbish. So I was excited as fuck to come home for the weekend and see her. Being apart from her for weeks on end was rough. Not knowing how she was or what she was getting up to agitated me. We checked in all the time, we texted daily, and we called each other every week, but it wasn't the same. She and I had been joined at the hip since we were five years old. Being away from her was like missing a limb.

Arran and I were as close as any brothers could be, and I

missed him, too, but it was different with Roe. At least I knew Arran was there, keeping an eye on her.

He wasn't the only one, though.

I sipped at my beer, looking casual to the outside observer, when, in fact, my heart was fucking racing, every nerve end screaming. All because Monroe had invited some friends of hers from the University of Highlands and Islands where she studied in Inverness. One of them was all over her. Roe wore jeans and a tight-fitting Killers T-shirt that molded perfectly to her body. My girl might be short, but she had curves that had been driving me crazy since we were fifteen. Everything about Monroe was beautiful. Not just her body, her masses of red hair, or those gray eyes … but her soul. She was the kindest, strongest, most loyal person I'd ever known. Too good for me, or anyone, for that matter.

Including the arsehole she'd brought from uni who kept touching her hip, even though Roe stepped away every time he did.

"You sure you two are just friends?" Arran's voice yanked my attention from Roe and the arsehole.

I frowned at my brother. "Of course," I lied. Well, it wasn't really a lie. Was the day I'd made her come in the castle turret burned in my brain? Aye. Every bloody detail. It had taken every ounce of control two summers ago not to make love to her that afternoon. Sometimes, that day plays like a masochistic film over and over in my mind. Sometimes I fantasize we had sex.

But I hadn't lied to Roe that day. I couldn't be with her like that. If I thought it was painful to be away from her now, imagine what it would be like if she was mine completely, and then something took her away.

I rubbed my chest at the thought.

"You sure?" Arran pushed. "Because you're staring at Luca like you want to rip off his head."

"Who?"

"Luca. The bloke she's talking to."

I studied Arran. I forgot he knew all of Roe's friends because he got to spend more time with her. To our dad's displeasure, Arran had decided against university and was instead flailing, directionless. To be honest, I was worried about him. But at least he had Roe in his life. I had hoped she'd keep him from getting into too much trouble. "Roe and I are just friends," I reiterated. "Christ, I've known her since we were five. It isn't like that between us." The image of her flushed, her eyes bright as they stared up into mine in wonder as she climaxed around my fingers, flashed through my mind. My skin heated at the memory, and I chugged back more beer.

"So why do you want to kill Luca?"

"I know Roe." I shrugged. "She doesn't want this guy's hands on her. I'm keeping an eye. I would do the same for Arro."

"You have done the same for Arro and worse," Arran reminded me, chuckling.

It was true.

Thane had put me and Arran in charge of intimidating our wee sister's would-be boyfriends when she started dating. One, we thought she was too young to date, but since we couldn't be hypocrites and stop her from dating at the age we started having sex, we took the other path. We didn't want her seeing anyone who wasn't strong enough to stand against the disapproval of her four big brothers. I grinned. "Anyone new we need to intimidate?"

"Nah. She seems to have given up for a while. Focusing on school."

"Good." My gaze drew back to Roe. I hadn't seen her in weeks. I wanted her over here with me. She said something to Luca the Arsehole and then disappeared out of the room.

Probably to use the bathroom. The urge to follow her was real, but with Arran watching me, I didn't want to give him proof that I'd lied earlier.

Instead I turned to talk with him and the group of friends he'd invited to the castle. Our dad never cared when we had people over, and even though he hadn't seen me in weeks, he'd barely made an appearance. He greeted me last night when I showed up and then fucked off.

I couldn't say it didn't hurt, but I was used to it.

I knew my dad loved me. Loved us all. He just … it was like this huge part of him died when Mum died, so only half of him was here with us.

That was messed up.

Which was exactly why I planned to avoid that ever happening to me.

I felt it the moment Monroe came back into the room, and I willed her to come over to me. When minutes passed and she didn't, I chanced a glance over my shoulder and searched the crowd. Luca had her practically pinned in the corner.

Was she seeing him, then?

Was that why she hadn't come near me?

A rush of red-hot indignation and hurt flushed through me.

Jealousy.

Aye, it wasn't the first time I'd felt the burn of that emotion.

In fact, it was jealousy that had driven me to touch Monroe when we were seventeen. When she told me she'd lost her virginity to Phil Forrester, I honestly wanted to hunt him down and rip off his goddamn head. It was bad enough she'd been dating the prick, every second torture, but to know that she'd slept with him …

I was still impressed with how calm and cool I'd acted

when she told me, considering the turmoil going on inside me.

Then, when she explained how he'd treated her, I was pissed off for a different reason. I wanted to show her that sex was supposed to be great. The problem was, I'd learned a huge lesson I couldn't seem to shake—I'd never been with someone I loved before. It was better than great. With Monroe, it was a rush unlike anything I'd experienced. She was all I could see, feel, think about. It was the sexiest moment of my life. In fact, it had taken more willpower than I knew I had to pull myself away from her.

I had no right to be jealous of anyone Monroe slept with, considering I was pretty much the opposite of a monk. But I was jealous, nonetheless.

She'd always feel like mine.

Even if she'd never be mine.

Fuck.

I chugged back more beer and was about to look away from her for good when I saw her push Luca's hand away. He pressed her into the wall, and fury overtook me. One second I was standing cool and collected with a beer in my hand. The next I'd shoved the beer at Arran, jumped over the couch, and crossed the room in seconds to pull the fuckwit off my best friend.

"You want him touching you, Roe?" I asked, shoving him so hard he had to stop himself from falling.

Monroe's face was flushed, her eyes glassy with alcohol and bright with irritation. "That would be a no."

"Problem here?" Arran appeared at our side.

"Aye. This prick needs an escort off the property."

~

82

We walked Luca and one of his buddies off the estate. The arsehole tried to taunt me into a fight by saying sexual shit about Roe. If it hadn't been for Arran, I probably would have buried the bastard.

To say my adrenaline was up by the time we returned to the small party was an understatement. Arran strolled back into the room and over to the girl he was chatting up, while I immediately sought Roe. She wasn't here.

Frowning, I checked the bathroom and couldn't find her. Then the kitchen at the back of the castle downstairs, though I doubted she was there. The only other room on this floor she was as familiar with was my room, so I headed in that direction.

Sure enough, light poured from under the crack in the door. Our bedrooms in this wing of the castle were pretty massive. They were also difficult to heat, so I knew it had to be bloody cold in there.

Stepping inside, I paused at the threshold to find Monroe sprawled across my bed on her back, her long, loose red curls spread across my sheets. Swallowing hard at the thrumming in my blood, I crossed the room to her. Her tee had risen, showing off her flat stomach. Little freckles scattered sporadically across her skin.

I wanted to kiss every single one.

Dragging my gaze to hers, I found her staring at me through low-lidded eyes. Her cheeks flushed. I smirked. "Had too much to drink, Sunset?"

"Maybe," she murmured and then giggled.

I loved that sound.

Clenching my hands into fists, I sat beside her and patted her knee. "Maybe you should sit up before you pass out."

With a groan, she did, but then rested her head on my shoulder. Her perfume tickled my nose, and I rubbed my hands on my thighs to force them to keep to themselves.

"Sorry about Luca."

I tensed at the reminder. "Just tell me if you have anymore problems with that guy, okay? I know I'm not here all the time, but Arran is."

"I know." She sighed heavily and then slurred her words a little as she confessed, "I miss you so much."

Taking her hand in mine, I laced our fingers together. "I miss you too."

Lifting her head from my shoulder, she looked up at me, and I turned to meet her gaze. My fingers tightened on hers at the adoring expression on her face. "I love you, Brodan."

Panic suffused me for a split second until I chuckled, forcing myself to play dumb. "I love you too, Roe."

Her brow puckered, her nose wrinkling in that cute way of hers. "Nooo."

"No?" I teased, trying to keep the moment light.

"No." She rested her chin on my shoulder now, her eyes huge. "I'm *in* love with you."

Fuck.

My heart hammered hard, racing toward her all while speeding away, as euphoria and dread filled me in equal measure.

"And I know you're not ready for that, but I want you to know that I haven't forgotten what you said ... and I'm waiting for you. I'll wait for you to be ready. To work through what loss has done to you until you're ready to be brave. To be with me. One day, loving someone like your dad loved your mum won't scare you, Brodan. And I'll be here. I want to be the someone you love like that."

Pain cracked through my chest.

That was what I got for telling this girl everything.

And it hurt that she thought time would conquer my fears.

Before I could say anything, she reached up, cupping my cheek tenderly, before she pressed her soft mouth to mine.

For a moment, I was weak.

Because I loved Monroe Sinclair more than I loved anybody in this world.

I kissed her back. *Just one more taste*, I told myself.

But then I felt her chilled hands slide under my T-shirt, jolting me back to reality.

In my panic to end this, to stop her from wasting her life waiting for me, I immediately blurted out the lie, "I met someone at uni. I have a serious girlfriend."

Monroe jerked back in shock, expression wounded and horrified.

Then she promptly threw up at my feet.

9

MONROE

PRESENT DAY

I always got butterflies on parents' evenings. When I first started teaching, I didn't. But over the years, I discovered you really never know what you're going to get when a parent walks into your classroom to discuss their child. Unless, of course, they were a helicopter parent and were constantly phoning the school to catalogue their child's needs as if I didn't have other children in my classroom. I wanted to give all the kids exactly what they needed, but that was impossible when I was one person teaching twenty children all at once. I did my best, and I was proud to say that I really gave them everything I had.

When a child wasn't succeeding in my classroom, I made it my personal mission to help them because I felt like I wasn't succeeding right along with them.

Perhaps the butterflies for tonight, however, had more to do with the fact that I'd be interacting with parents that *I* went to school with. I'd also see Thane Adair for the first time in eighteen years.

My first parent was, lo and behold, Michelle Kingsley. It was clear from her frosty demeanor and nitpicking that she'd not forgotten our high school altercation over Brodan. Fortunately, her son was a sweet kid, and I had nothing but good things to say about him. He must have taken after his father, whom I knew had divorced Michelle a few years ago.

Thinking Michelle would be the worst of the lot, I tried to relax as the evening wore on.

I caught sight of Thane and his wife Regan waiting outside my classroom with the other parents and took a deep breath as I welcomed in the mum of a new student.

"It's nice to see you again, Ms. Harrow," I said as I gestured for her to take a chair opposite my desk. We actually met a week ago when her daughter Callie enrolled at the school. Sloane Harrow was a very young mother. It would surprise me if she was older than twenty-five, making her a teen when she had her daughter. I knew from our first meeting that she and Callie had moved from Los Angeles on Sloane's work visa. She'd gotten a job at Ardnoch Estate as a housekeeper. It was all a bit mysterious to me why Sloane would leave the States for a remote village in the Highlands, but it was her business.

Sloane smiled as she sat down, and I noted not for the first time how pretty she was. She had a sweet look, a natural attractiveness that wasn't overdone, but her smile was glamorous. I wondered if all LA people were born with that certain star quality. Sloane's sun-streaked, shoulder-length blond hair fell around her face in beachy waves, her skin glowed with a tan that would disappear after a few months in a Highland winter, and a reassuring warmth filled her large, dark brown eyes.

"I know Callie only started a week ago, but I wanted to let you know how it's going."

"I really appreciate that." Sloane nodded, clasping her hands in front of her. "She really likes you, and it's made all the difference that she has a teacher who makes her feel safe and comfortable. I wanted to thank you." She reached into her large handbag and pulled out a Tupperware box. "I bake. I hope you like cupcakes."

Some parents were thoughtful and had their kids bring me gifts at the end of the year, but I'd never gotten baked goods on parents' evening. Taking the box with a gracious thank-you, I gasped when I opened them. Inside were the most beautifully decorated cupcakes. Pink buttercream frosting piped on in three different nozzle styles with pink edible pearls and little hearts scattered over them. They looked professional. "You baked and decorated these?"

She grinned, pleased by my reaction. "Baking is my passion."

"Well, these are beautiful. Thank you so much."

"You're welcome. So, like I said, Callie seems to be fitting in, but I wanted your opinion. And to see how she's coping with her schoolwork."

"She's doing very well," I promised, and she slumped with relief. I loved dealing with parents who really cared. Unfortunately, there were some parents who never bothered to show and others who only showed because it looked bad if they didn't. It was clear, however, from the sincerity in her expression that Sloane Harrow loved her kid. "She made friends on day one." With none other than Lewis Adair. I'd kept an eye out for Callie during the break this past week, and I'd spotted her on the playground with Lewis and his friends. "They've spent every break together, and they're good kids."

"Lewis." Sloane nodded. "She's been talking a lot about him."

"Lewis Adair, yes."

Her eyes rounded. "As in … my boss Adair?"

I nodded, hoping she wasn't uncomfortable with that because I didn't think it would be wise at this juncture to ask Callie to stop being friends with Lewis. "Yes. He is Lachlan Adair's nephew."

"Oh." She considered. "Okay."

"As for Callie's schoolwork, it seems her American classes already covered a lot of what we're doing. There are some differences in mathematic styles for her to get used to, and spelling and language differences are a little frustrating for her, but Callie is very bright, and I think she'll be spelling favorite with a *u* in no time."

Sloane chuckled. "That's such great news. It's … it's been a lot moving here, and I'm very lucky I have a daughter who's up for an adventure, but I worry. I worry about her. It's a relief that she's doing well."

Even though I shouldn't, I wondered how *Sloane* was coping with the big move. There was just something so endearing about her. I wanted to make sure she was okay. "Are you adjusting to the emigration?"

She seemed surprised by my question. "Uh … I'm … it's … uh." Her smile faltered. "It's strange, but it'll get easier."

There was no rule that you couldn't teach a friend's child, but it was considered appropriate to recuse yourself from teaching any child you might have bias toward. That very hard to do in a village school, and I knew what it was like to be lonely. I *was* lonely. Despite my history here, I had no true friends. My closest friends had been the Adairs, and I'd forsaken all others for them. Now I had nothing but a handful of acquaintances. No one to truly talk to. Maybe that was why I offered, "If you ever want to grab a coffee, I'm here."

Her eyes brightened. "Really?"

"Of course. I'll give you my number."

"I'd like that. Callie is right. You're the nicest."

Sloane left with my number, and I hoped to have discovered a new friend. It had almost, but not quite, distracted me from Thane and Regan Adair.

I held the door open for them and closed it. I'd met Regan at the start of school, and she'd been lovely. According to village gossip, she was thirteen years younger than Thane.

We shared the red hair gene, but that was about it. Regan was taller, elegant, and intimidatingly beautiful. Thankfully, she was friendly and down-to-earth, so it wasn't her I was worried about.

My eyes met Thane's as I gestured to the seat across from the desk.

But he surprised me by taking a step forward, his gaze searching, as he held out his arms. "Would it be inappropriate to hug you?"

The question was like a trigger on my emotions, and a choking sensation squeezed my throat, rendering me unable to speak as I fought back tears. I stepped into his embrace, and his tight hug reminded me of Brodan. All the Adair men gave the best hugs. Like they really meant them.

"It's nice to see you, Monroe. It's been too long."

I squeezed him back, grateful for his kindness. I'd assumed all the Adairs hated me after what happened between me and Arran. It was nice knowing at least Arran and Thane did not. I definitely knew Brodan despised me after the way he'd walked out on me at William's without uttering a word. He'd looked at me like I was a stranger. An irritating bug of a stranger. But I couldn't think about that.

As for Arro, she hadn't reached out, but she'd also just given birth to her first baby, so she was a bit preoccupied.

Thane released me and flashed a handsome smile surrounded by a thick but neatly trimmed beard. "Are you well?"

I nodded, a little dumfounded by his warmth. "You?"

"Aye, very." He stepped back to smile adoringly at Regan. "I know you've met my wife."

"I have. It's nice to see you again."

Regan beamed, pretty dimples appearing in her cheeks. "You too. Lewis loves you."

I blushed at that, delighted. "That's always lovely to hear." Taking my seat at my desk, I faced them as Thane sat down too. "He's a wonderful boy."

Taking them through Lewis's schoolwork, his strengths, and his weaknesses, I noted both parents listened attentively. They also engaged, asking questions about how *they* could help at home to improve where work still needed to be done. I gave them some advice and then we moved on to his behavior. "Lewis is quiet and respectful. I have a few children in this class who are always the ones answering my questions and are loud about it." I smiled. "So, it's not often easy for my quieter children to put themselves forward to answer questions. But I would like to see more of that from Lewis."

"He's quiet at home too," Regan said, taking a hold of Thane's hand and resting their clasped hands on her lap. I felt a pang of envy at their obvious closeness. "His sister is very gregarious and loud in the best way, but I do think, perhaps, he's just used to stepping back. Letting her shine. Perhaps that's why he is like that in class too."

"Possibly. But interestingly enough, there is one thing that Lewis gets very chatty about. Perhaps it's in the Adair genes." I teased, and they leaned in, intrigued. "Lewis is very enthusiastic about our upcoming Christmas play. It was announced this week that there will be two plays this year, one organized by the lower school, P1 to P4, and another by the upper school, P5 to P7. Lewis is excited about it. We got together with the other classes on Friday to discuss ideas because we enjoy having the kids' involvement, and Lewis was brimming with suggestions." I leaned toward them now. "And he told me he'd not only like to help with set design but that he'd like a part, too, and wondered if he could do both."

Regan grinned from ear to ear as she nudged her husband. "Part architect, part actor, huh?"

Thane chuckled but appeared surprised. "The set design part doesn't shock me. Lewis has always been interested in my work. But the acting takes me aback."

"It's good, though, right?" Regan studied him. "It could bring him out of his shell a little. Give him confidence."

Thane nodded, contemplating it. "Aye, aye. I'm just surprised he wants to. But that's great." He looked at me. "Can he do both? Set design and acting, I mean."

"I aim to make sure my kids can follow their passions, whatever that may be. We'll give him space to do both."

"Good. Thank you, Roe—I mean, Ms. Sinclair." He gave me an affectionate look.

"You can call me Roe."

Regan chuckled. "Then you have to stop calling us Mr. and Mrs. Adair."

A few minutes later, I bid them goodbye, turning to my last parent of the night and catching words I don't think Regan Adair meant me to hear.

"Okay, my curiosity is killing me now. You have to tell me how you all know her."

My stomach flipped at the thought of Thane telling her my story.

"Ms. Sinclair."

The parent standing before me drew me from my

panicked thoughts. Staring into his dark eyes, I searched my befuddled mind for his name. "Mr. Barr?"

"Call me Haydyn, please." His grin was almost flirtatious.

Shaking off the idea, I gave him a tight-lipped smile and led him into the classroom. When I glanced over my shoulder at him, I found his eyes on the sway of my arse.

Okay, maybe his smile had been flirtatious.

Unfortunately, it wouldn't be the first time a dad had flirted with me. I'd even had a dad flirt with me in front of his wife. Classy.

"Take a seat, Mr. Barr," I offered.

"Haydyn, please." He unbuttoned his stylish wool coat and sat down, crossing one leg over the other. Now that I wasn't thinking about the Adairs, I noted that Mr. Haydyn Barr was attractive. I knew from his son, Michael, that they lived in one of the outlying villages and that Haydyn was a professor at the University of Highlands and Islands. A professor of what, I did not know. From Michael's lack of chat about a mum, and the fact that a nanny picked him up from school, I guessed Mr. Barr was single. How a professor could afford a nanny and the designer coat he wore, I did not know. "So, how is Michael's progress this year?"

Michael was one of my brightest pupils, and I told his father so, relaying his achievements over the first term.

"Wonderful. I hope he'll follow in my footsteps into engineering, and you need to be well-rounded for that."

"You're an engineer?"

"I teach civil engineering at the Inverness campus of UHI."

Smart and attractive.

Stop noticing his attractiveness. "I'm sure *if* Michael has an interest in engineering, he'll grapple the subject easily."

"If?" Mr. Barr smirked. "Michael's nine years old. I'm not

going to *force* him to follow in my footsteps. I just would like it. That's all I meant."

Realizing he'd caught my slight admonishment, I tried not to blush. "Of course."

"He talks about you. I was looking forward to meeting the teacher he enjoys so much, and I have to say, I understand completely now."

Oh, boy. "That's very nice."

"Here." He slipped his hand into his coat and pulled out a business card. "If you ever need to discuss Michael."

I took the card. "Thank you."

"Or ..." He leaned into me, his smirk definitely inviting. "If you'd ever like to grab a drink. Usually I'd ask for your number, but I'm pretty sure that wouldn't be appropriate ... so I'll leave it in your hands." He stood as I gaped at him in shock at his forthrightness. "I hope you call about that drink."

I licked my lips nervously because I was going through the world's longest dry spell, and a woman had needs. Remembering exactly why I was going through the dry spell, however, shook me out of my stupor, and I gave him a soft smile. "That wouldn't be appropriate."

Haydyn Barr grinned and walked toward my classroom door to pull it open. "Keep the card for next year. When you're no longer my son's teacher."

Wow.

I bit back a smile and he chuckled, nodded, and strolled out.

Turning his card over in my hand, I stared at the embossed words: *Dr. Haydyn Barr, Professor of Engineering.* Below were his contact details at the university.

He was tempting, but one, I would never jeopardize my job by dating a parent; and two, I never wanted to date again. My romantic history wasn't loaded down by many men. After I'd fled Ardnoch and struggled to make rent living as a student in Inverness, I'd avoided dating for almost two years. No one was Brodan, so I didn't want them.

When I moved to Edinburgh for teacher training, I met Nick through a uni friend. He was a few years older, a fireman, and he reminded me of Brodan. Not in looks, but just his cocky charm that hid a sweetness. I thought I might even love him a little, but after four years of dating, he fell in love with a colleague. She was my opposite in every way. They fucked around behind my back for six months until I caught them together. All my friends were his friends, so I lost them and had to start over again.

Then I moved to Glasgow to teach. I dated a little, but nothing serious, and then I met Steven when I was twenty-seven. Steven … a disaster of epic proportions. It had taken me three years to get myself out of that situation.

I'd been single for the seven years since.

All my dreams of being a wife and a mum went up in a puff of smoke.

Because as painful and lonely as it was to be alone, at least I was safe.

10

MONROE

THE PAST

The last few weeks had been excruciating. I could barely concentrate on my tutorials and lectures. Mum was always on me for being absentminded in the house, and I was constantly checking my phone for texts from Brodan.

We used to text every day and call every other day.

I hadn't heard from him in a few weeks. A few days after that night at the castle, I'd texted and asked him how he was doing, and he'd replied that he was good but busy. Brodan always asked me how I was doing, but there was no reciprocation this time, no eagerness to continue the conversation.

And he hadn't called.

He'd been distant ever since he told me he had a girlfriend.

Part of me really wanted to believe that he was lying to push me away. I'd been drunk that night, but not so wasted that I didn't remember telling him I was in love with him.

96

My cheeks burned with embarrassment every time I thought about it. Either he was lying about the girl, or he was distant because of what I confessed.

I'd prefer to believe he was lying. Obviously.

Arran didn't know about any of it. He and I had grown closer since Brodan left for uni. But he was oblivious to my true feelings for his brother. That was also why he was the best source of factual information. We'd been in touch, but I hadn't seen him until now because he was busy last weekend.

Butterflies swarmed in my stomach as I drove the piece-of-shit car I'd saved up for. It was honestly a miracle that the ancient Brava could get me back and forth to Inverness. And as much as it was a piece of shit, I also loved it. She (my car was definitely a girl) represented my freedom.

She chugged to a stop outside the castle, and as I got out, the double doors opened and Arran stepped out with a bottle of beer in each hand, his arms spread wide as he yelled, "Let's get fucked!"

I laughed at his nonsense and rounded the bonnet. "Aye, give me, give me."

Grinning, he held out a beer. "Don't tell Brodan I'm corrupting you while he's gone."

The mention of his brother caused that familiar pang, and the urge to burst into tears was real. I forced myself to roll my eyes instead and took the beer. "I was corrupted long before you, Arran Adair."

"Oh, aye?" He waggled his brows. "Who was the lucky bastard?"

Wrinkling my nose, I huffed, "No one worth mentioning."

"That bad, eh?" Arran snorted.

Shoving him toward the house, I replied, "None of your business. I hope there are snacks in here."

Arran led me to his bedroom, and I asked if anyone else was home this weekend.

"Dad's in Skye for the weekend again for who knows what. I wonder if he has a fuck buddy there."

"Is that all you think about?"

"Pretty much. Anyway, Lachlan is filming in Canada, and Thane's at uni. And so, of course, is Brodan."

"Speaking of," I led casually, "is it true, then? That he has a girlfriend? We haven't spoken much lately."

Arran flopped down on his bed with a frown. "The big shit isn't dropping the ball on your friendship because he's got a fucking girlfriend, is he?"

My breath caught as my gut twisted painfully. Letting my hair hide my face as I settled into his comfy armchair, I asked, "So, it's true?"

"Aye. Who would have thought?" Arran gestured to the pile of snacks on his bed. "What delicacy would you prefer with your beer, my lady? Pringles, peanuts, chocolate?"

I shrugged, and he tossed a bag of chocolate buttons at me. I caught them, even though my mind was screaming at him to tell me more.

Thankfully, Arran spoke with no further prompting. "Brodan brought his bird home last weekend."

"Don't call her a bird," I admonished.

He grinned. "Apologies. He brought his *lady* home last weekend."

Brodan brought her here.

"Thane and Dad were both home, so he wanted us all to meet her. I can't believe he's finally getting serious about someone." Arran wrinkled his nose. "She was fit, don't get me wrong, but she kept giggling at everything Bro said. It was fucking annoying."

"Are they serious?"

Arran sat up to take a chug of his beer, his eyes narrowing on me. I tried not to squirm under his regard. Swallowing his mouthful, he asked, "Brodan really hasn't told you about her?"

No.

Brodan had not only lied when he told me he'd never be serious about anyone (insinuating that if he could be serious, it would be about me), but he'd cut me out of his life.

Without exaggeration, the pain in my chest was excruciating. I felt like I was going to fall into a million pieces or float away from myself, untethered for eternity. Both thoughts panicked me.

"Roe? You okay?"

Don't let him see. Don't let any of them see.

And never let Brodan Adair see what he'd done to me.

Wanting to be numb, I chugged back my beer until I was gasping for breath.

"Roe?" Arran leaned toward me, concern on his handsome face.

"It's stupid … I just … I never thought he'd drop me when he got a girlfriend." I fudged the truth so he wouldn't see. Wouldn't see that I was in agony.

"That shithead." Arran looked furious. "Has he really not spoken to you?"

"Not in a few weeks. He used to text every day and call every other. He didn't say anything to you about me, did he?" I prodded, hoping like hell Brodan hadn't told Arran that I was in love with him.

He shook his head, scowling. "Not a bloody word. But *I'm* going to have a word with him. He can't just drop you because he has a girlfriend. And Vanessa better not be the reason."

"Vanessa?"

"Aye, that's her name."

Vanessa.

He'd abandoned me for someone called Vanessa.

Brodan had abandoned me.

He was the only person on the planet who knew how alone I felt because of my shitty parents. Even so, he'd abandoned me. Just like they had.

At that moment, I hated him. Truly. I let that hatred creep through me and miraculously, it stifled my growing anxiety. "Don't say anything to him." My voice didn't sound like mine. It was flat, cold. "I don't want Brodan's friendship just because his brother reminded him to give a shit."

Arran sucked in a breath. "Roe ... I'm sorry."

Not wanting his pity, I threw back the rest of my beer, finishing it. I held out the empty bottle and waggled it. "Got anything stronger?"

With a sigh, Arran pushed up off his bed and crossed the room to take the empty bottle. His fingers wrapped around mine instead. "You're my friend, Roe. And no bird—I mean, *lady*—will ever make me forget about you."

Tears threatened, so I pulled back my hand and gave him a lopsided smile. "Good to know, Arr. Now, do you have anything stronger?"

He chuckled and backed up. "Turn up the music while I go hunt for the good stuff."

As soon as Arran left the room, panic tried to force its way back in. I lunged across the room, opening the ancient bloody window that offered little protection against the cold, and sucked in a lungful of night air. I noted my hands trembled and realized my whole body was too.

"Calm down," I whispered to myself. This was not a normal reaction, right?

But Brodan had abandoned me.

Just like everyone else who was supposed to love me.

STOP!

I didn't want to think about it. I didn't want to think about anything. It hurt too fucking much.

Cranking up Biffy Clyro on the fancy desktop Lachlan had bought Arran, I wandered around his room, looking for a distraction. Thankfully, he returned not too long later with a full bottle of whisky.

At first, everything was free and clear of the cognizance-destroyer that was alcohol.

We chatted about my time at uni and about his job as a waiter at a fancy restaurant north of Ardnoch. We reminisced about school and talked about the places we wanted to see. He told me Lachlan had offered to bring him and Brodan out to his film set next summer. But I couldn't remember much of our conversation after a certain point.

I honestly didn't know who reached for who first.

The moment would be forever fragmented in my memories, flashes of kisses, of sensation.

Everything came crashing back into clear, painful, focused reality at the sound of someone roaring, "I'm going to fucking kill you!"

Not someone.

Brodan.

Arran was above me. Inside me.

We were naked.

Shock suffused Arran's face, and he twisted his head around to look over his shoulder. Then he was scrambling off me, revealing Brodan, who gaped at me in abject betrayal, his look cutting me to the core.

The room swayed as I whispered his name.

He flinched, and then his gaze shot to Arran, who was pulling up his jeans. "Look, Bro, just—"

Brodan cut him off by lunging across the room at his brother. I sobered up quickly. Practically falling off the bed, I hurried to pull on my clothes as I heard the telltale smack of a fist meeting flesh.

"No!" I cried out, yanking down my sweater to see Brodan on top of Arran.

Arran struggled beneath him, trying to avoid his brother's fists.

"Brodan, stop!" I yelled.

But he wouldn't.

He wouldn't stop.

He was pummeling Arran.

Punch after punch, the smack of flesh turning my stomach.

Terror propelled me to them, and I yanked on Brodan's arm, but he shrugged me off with such force, I flew back and hit the foot of the bed. Pain ricocheted up my lower back, and I cried out as I landed hard on my wrist.

Brodan whirled around, horror on his face. "Roe." He looked back down at Arran, who was a bloodied, groaning mess. Brodan heaved himself off his brother. Tears swam in his eyes, a million tortured emotions within.

And I couldn't face him.

I couldn't face what I'd done to them.

So I ran.

Not thinking clearly, I got to my car, threw up on the gravel beside it, and then got in where I drunkenly cried and recklessly drove all the way home.

I'd never been so drunk that I couldn't remember details. But over the next few weeks (and years), I tried desperately to remember how Arran and I ended up having sex ... and I couldn't. We'd finished an entire bottle of whisky and started on his pack of beer. I was ill for days with the worst hangover of my life.

I wasn't in my right mind when I had sex with Arran. Neither was he.

There were only flashes of memories, everything coming into sharp focus upon the moment of Brodan's appearance.

It was a night that I could barely remember … and yet it had ruined everything.

11

MONROE

PRESENT DAY

Leaning against my desk, I tried not to laugh at the sight of Ellen Hunter and David White, P6 and P7 teachers, sitting in the small chairs that belonged to my pupils.

Instead, I concentrated on the task at hand.

It was lunchtime. The kids were in the cafeteria or out on the playground, and we'd inhaled our own lunches so we'd have time to discuss the upcoming Christmas play. Unfortunately, I had to rush to Mum's as soon as the school day ended to take her to a late appointment with her physical therapist. So this was the only time we had this week to choose a musical among a very small list we could legally get a license to perform.

"I don't know about you two, but I am completely out of my depth as a stage director."

They chuckled, and Ellen nodded. "I've done it a time or

two, but I'm warning you both, it will be stressful on top of everything else we have going on."

That's what I was worried about.

"And," David said, leaning forward, his gaze flicking between me and Ellen, "Cooley is determined to make Ardnoch Primary's reputation as stellar as Ardnoch Academy, so she wants the plays on social media, and she wants it to have potential to go viral. No pressure."

I frowned. "Why? We're a tiny village in the north of Scotland. Also, Ardnoch Academy is a secondary education facility that provides learning in a specialized field. It's not an ordinary high school. I should know, I went there."

He smirked. "All I know is, Cooley reckons that if we make the school adored by the public, she might get more in her budget next year from the council. Like the academy."

"Ardnoch Academy is given its budget based on its success rates, and it has a pretty high success rate of sending its pupils on to higher learning. Cooley wants us to traipse the kids out like zoo animals on social media to get a bigger budget?"

"Don't look at it like that." Ellen gave me an admonishing look. "We can still make this fun for the kids and give *Anita* what she wants. Stop calling her Cooley, David. You're not one of the children."

He scowled at her like one of the children, and I inwardly sighed. I'd worried when I realized the three of us would have to work together. While I got on individually with both of them (so far), I'd noticed within only a few weeks of working at the school that Ellen and David often clashed in the staff room.

How were the three of us going to write and direct a play?

"Any favorites on that list?" I nodded to the paper in Ellen's hands. We'd been told that while we had to organize the entire school to open show night with a medley of

Christmas songs, the plays themselves did not need to be Christmas themed. The lower school had already chosen *The Nutcracker*.

"We did *Guys & Dolls* in high school," David offered with a shrug. "Is that on the list?"

I grimaced. "No. And it's a little mature, is it not?"

"There's something called *Everybody's Talking About Jamie*." Ellen squinted at the paper.

"Again, a bit mature."

She looked at me blankly, suggesting she didn't know the content of most of the plays on her list.

Wonderful.

I sighed. "I was thinking … *The Wizard of Oz*."

"Let's do it," David replied.

"Just like that?"

"We need to apply for the license now or there will be no musical."

"Agreed." Ellen surprised me with her emphatic nod.

"Okay. *The Wizard of Oz* it is. Let's apply for that today. Now." I grinned a little hysterically at them. "Assuming we get the license… how do we direct a musical?"

"My uncle could help."

I startled at the young voice.

Lewis Adair stood just inside my classroom, his big eyes round and eager.

Unfortunately, I hadn't processed his words. "Lewis, what are you doing here? Lunchtime isn't over."

"I left my apple in my backpack." He gestured to the wall of hooks where the children hung their bags.

"Okay, grab it and go, please."

"Wait, wait." Ellen stopped him. "Lewis, which uncle could help us with the play?"

What?

Panic shot through me, and I sat ramrod straight.

Lewis gave her a small smile and stepped forward. "My uncle Brodan. He's a movie star."

He said it like we didn't already know that.

"Talk about making the school go viral," David murmured, his eyes huge with excitement. "Brodan Adair directing."

No.

No. No. *NO!!!!!!*

"We have to direct it ourselves," I answered hurriedly, trying not to snap for Lewis's sake. "We can't have outside help."

"Not true." Ellen shook her head. "Last year, the P7s did the Christmas play, and a parent directed it. Brodan Adair is Lewis's uncle. That's like a parent."

"No. That's like an uncle. Plus, we can't impose on Lewis's uncle because I'm sure he's not staying in Ardnoch permanently."

Lewis stepped forward again, his breathing a little faster with enthusiasm. "I can ask him. I'm sure he'll say yes."

"That would be wonderful, Lewis." Ellen beamed. "Could you ask your uncle this week and give us an answer by Friday?"

"Yes, Mrs. Hunter."

"Thank you!"

"Nice." She and David shared an ecstatic smile.

Fuck. My. Life.

BRODAN

"How did the writing go today?" Walker asked as I drove us to Thane's for dinner.

"It's going good. I think I'll have the first draft finished soon." I still couldn't quite wrap my head around the fact that I was writing and actually enjoying it. "You're good at this life management shit, you know. You could take it on as a second career."

Walk grunted as he stared out at the passing scenery. "Managing your life is enough for now."

"To be fair, you haven't had to make many decisions lately."

"Aye, because the ones I already made are keeping you busy."

I smirked. "True." I shot him another look. "You're not bored working security for the estate, are you? I know it's not the jet-setting life you're used to." Walker had been a bodyguard to several celebrities before he became head of my security detail.

"If I were bored or unhappy, I wouldn't be here."

Fair enough.

My not-so-loquacious friend characteristically didn't speak for the rest of the ride. Thane and Regan had invited us over for Monday night dinner—we missed Sunday because of the chaos my new nieces had rained down upon my siblings. The new parents and their adorable but very loud daughters were not attending tonight. I made a note to look in on them this week. To make sure they were all okay.

I hugged Regan as she welcomed us and tried not to laugh as she held out her arms to Walker and he scowled at her in warning and patted her shoulder awkwardly in greeting.

"He's not the cuddling type," I murmured in her ear as we walked into the main living space.

Her dimples popped as she nodded. "Duly noted."

"Uncle Brodan!" Eilidh jumped from a stool at the island

and rushed me. She was getting too big to haul up into my arms, I realized as I hugged her back. The thought made me feel shit about missing out on so much, so I threw it away.

I was all about the present these days.

No dwelling allowed.

Eilidh released me with a cheeky grin and stepped over to Walker, tilting her head back to look up at him. "You're as tall as Uncle Mac."

Walker's expression softened the tiniest bit. "Is that so?"

"Yeah. He's my Aunt Robyn's daddy, but he's married to my Aunt Arro. That must be really confusing for Skye and Vivien."

I coughed into my fist to cover my laugh, my eyes meeting Arran's across the room. Eredine had turned her head into Arran's shoulder to stifle her own amusement, but Arran was blatantly chuckling.

Walker, however, kept a straight face. "You just have to explain it to them when they're older."

"Explain it how?" Eilidh wrinkled her nose. "I don't think you can explain that."

Thane coughed loudly, most definitely covering a laugh as Regan turned her back on the lot of us and busied herself in the kitchen, definitely trying not to bust a gut.

"Well, let's see," Walk said patiently. "Skye and Vivien are first cousins because Lachlan and Arrochar are brother and sister. But Skye is not only Robyn and Lachlan's niece, she's Robyn's half-sister. Vivien is not only Mac and Arrochar's niece, she's Mac's granddaughter, so that makes Skye Vivien's half-aunt."

Eilidh's hands flew to her hips in indignation. "And you don't think that's confusing?"

Laughter burst out of me before I could stop it, and Walker's lips twitched with amusement. "I suppose it is."

"I love this kid." I bent down to press a quick kiss to

Eilidh's temple, grinning as I straightened, eyes on Thane. "Good job, Bro."

Thane raised his hands. "I can't take credit. She came out like that."

Thundering footsteps on the stairs drew my attention, and Lewis suddenly appeared at the bottom of them. "Is dinner ready yet? I'm starving." His eyes widened at the sight of Walker, and then he swung his gaze around the room as if searching. At the sight of me, my nephew beamed in a way that tugged at that gnawing ache in my chest. "Uncle Brodan!"

Lewis was usually so quiet, it was gratifying to see him show enthusiasm about my presence. "Hey, bud, how's it going?"

He hurried across the room, slipping slightly in ill-fitting socks.

"Pull up your socks, Lew, before you break something," Thane said from the couch, taking the words out of my mouth.

"Uncle Brodan, I need to ask you something."

"Lewis, let your uncle eat before you ask him for favors," Regan called from the kitchen.

His face fell, and he trudged to the table with an "Okay, Mum."

Christ, he was a good kid. Curious, I turned to Thane and mouthed, "Favor?"

Thane gave me a strange look, almost wary. His lips parted as if to say something, but then he just gestured to the table.

Soon we were all seated and helping ourselves to toppings for the chicken fajitas Regan had cooked. It was messy and delicious because the woman had the magic touch, but my focus was on my nephew. Once I'd inhaled one fajita and was piling toppings on the next, I said, "Okay, hit me with it, Lew. What's up?"

Fucking great kid that he was, he looked to Regan first for approval.

She smiled and nodded.

Lewis turned back to me, his expression pleading.

What the hell …

"Uncle Brodan, my class and the P6s and P7s are doing *The Wizard of Oz* for our Christmas musical."

Understanding dawned. "Did you get a part, bud? Do you need some pointers?"

"Well, yeah, but also I overheard the teachers freaking out about how they don't know how to put on a play, and I said I'd ask you if you'd direct it. So … will you direct it for us?"

Fuck.

I had not been expecting that.

But looking down at his cute wee face, eyes begging me to say yes, I couldn't say no. Directing small kids in a musical didn't exactly sound like an ideal job for the next few months, but I would get to spend more time with Lewis. Maybe make up some lost time.

"Before you answer," Thane interjected, and there was that wary look on his face again. "Remember that Ms. Sinclair is Lewis's teacher."

Fuuuuuuuuuucccccck.

Oh, hell no.

There was no way in fucking hell I was spending weeks with that woman.

Shit.

I stared at Lewis, trying to think of gentle words to let the wee man down.

"He'll do it," Walker announced decidedly from across the table.

I glowered at him. *Repeat that, and I will eviscerate you.*

The bastard didn't even flinch. He just took another bite of his fajita.

"Will you, Uncle Brodan?"

"Look, Lewis—"

Walker cleared his throat loudly, and I turned back to the motherfucker. He held my stony gaze as he wiped his mouth with a napkin and said, "Two words: *Black. Shadow.*"

And he was supposed to be my friend.

What a prick. I silently promised retribution. But with the word *fuck* reverberating in my head, I turned to my nephew and acted my arse off as I promised enthusiastically, "I'll do it."

12
MONROE

Usually, an early-morning walk on Ardnoch Beach would wash away a dreadful night or shitty morning, but enjoying the golden sands was now relegated to afternoons. It was too dark in the morning during autumn as it was still twilight when I left for work, so I arrived at school in as rubbish a mood as when I'd awoken.

Not that I woke up exactly, considering I'd barely slept a wink. The first thing I did was order an electric fireplace from the internet. Arran had warned me autumn and winter in the caravan would be freezing. Last night was Baltic, and I'd worn layers before sliding under my duvet. Come winter, I could see myself wearing a hat and gloves to bloody bed.

I wish I could say it was just the cold that had kept me awake, but my mind wouldn't shut down either.

In fact, I was currently staring at the cause of my insomnia.

Colm, our young school receptionist, had seconds ago led Brodan into the gymnasium where I waited with Ellen, David, and the children. Ellen and David hurried over to greet Brodan while I held back, feeling like a deer trapped in headlights.

Pain swamped me as I watched him greet my colleagues with the famous smile that crinkled the corners of his eyes. He had a short beard, the scruff sexy on him. In a navy peacoat, light gray sweater, fitted dark jeans, and dark shoes, he was effortlessly stylish. He was beautiful beyond bearing, and his clothes were expensive. Everything about him screamed unattainable.

Factor in our previous encounter, I was pretty certain I was the last person on earth Brodan Adair would ever save from a burning building, never mind actually find attractive.

I allowed the pain of our history and my feelings to linger for a second, and then I conjured up my own hurt and hatred toward Brodan. I'd been determined to let it go, to put the past behind us, but if he wanted to revel in his disdain for me, then I'd happily return the favor.

Shrugging on those negative feelings like armor, I turned away to survey the children, my gaze moving toward Lewis. He sat forward from his spot on the gym floor, attention trained on his uncle. There was no denying the hero worship on Lewis's face. I could only hope Brodan was a good uncle and worth it. But then, he had to be if he'd agreed to this.

Today was Brodan's first day meeting the kids at the school as acting director for our Christmas musical.

When Lewis told us Brodan had agreed to direct, I'd wanted to vomit. Why on earth would Brodan agree to this? Didn't he have a Hollywood film to run off and make? Didn't he realize I was Lewis's teacher? Just the thought of having to spend two mornings a week with him for the next six weeks sent me into a downward spiral.

I pulled myself together enough to ask Ellen to be a liaison to Brodan. If Ellen thought it was strange that I didn't want to be the liaison, considering Lewis was my pupil, my colleague didn't say a word. She was too busy being ecstatic that she got to be Brodan's go-to person at the school. Ellen and David had met with Brodan prior to today to discuss the script and songbook. I'd used my caretaking duties for Mum as my excuse not to be in attendance for the meeting.

Of course, the news overjoyed Anita. She hoped for some social media gold because of Brodan's presence. The teachers of the lower school were not so happy. They grumbled about us using outside help. However, Anita reminded them they could use someone else to direct as well. Still, I didn't think it was our using outside help as much as it was us using a famous Hollywood actor as said outside help. If it were up to me, it wouldn't be happening, but apparently, I had very little control over my life at the moment.

At least, that's the way it felt sometimes.

We'd been given a schedule for when we could use the gymnasium. The back wall of the gym folded away to reveal our large cafeteria, which would become the seating area for the audience on show night. The gymnasium was also a stage and backstage area and a great place to rehearse. Ellen, David, and I had gathered the children there to wait for Brodan.

The kids' excited chatter had died down at Brodan's arrival, and I met Lewis's gaze now.

"Can I go over to say hello, Ms. Sinclair?" he asked quietly.

"You *may*." I gestured toward the Hollywood star without looking at him.

Lewis grinned and shot to his feet. My gaze reluctantly followed him as he hurried over to Brodan. My chest squeezed as Brodan's entire face lit up at the sight of his nephew. He pulled Lewis into his side for a hug, bending his head to ask him something I couldn't hear. Lewis craned his head back, grinning up at his uncle as he nodded and replied.

Whatever it was made Brodan chuckle and bend down to press a kiss to the top of Lewis's head. So easily affectionate. He was the same when we were kids—always taking my hand, hugging me, kissing my temple.

Bringing me to orgasm in the castle turret.

My cheeks flushed at the inappropriate memory, and thankfully, the kids distracted me. Their chatter rose with their growing impatience, so I hushed them as Ellen and David strolled over with Brodan and Lewis at their backs. To my horror, I noted the way Lewis's eyes locked on me, and he tugged on his uncle's hand, drawing him toward me.

The memory of Brodan ignoring me in William's flashed through my mind, and I forced myself not to wince. My anger resurged.

"Uncle Brodan, this is my teacher, Ms. Sinclair," Lewis introduced us as they drew to a stop beside me.

Harnessing all my professionalism, I nodded at Brodan, whose eyes rested anywhere but on me. "Hello, Mr. Adair."

A muscle flexed in his jaw as he gave me a chin lift in greeting and turned away, drawing Lewis with him.

"Everyone, we'd like to introduce you to our director, Mr. Brodan Adair. Say hello to Mr. Adair." Ellen beamed from ear to ear. Honestly, I'd never seen her so happy.

"Hello, Mr. Adair!" the children chorused.

Brodan grinned. "Hi, everyone."

"My mum fancies you," a boy from Ellen's class called out. "She told my dad she'd dump him for you if you asked."

David covered a snort with a cough while Brodan tried not to laugh. Ellen, however, scowled at her pupil. "None of that, Max Kristofferson." She glanced at Brodan and noted his hands resting on Lewis's shoulders. "Lewis, return to your seat, please."

A few seconds later, everyone but the adults were seated, and the children were quietly waiting for direction. Ellen hurried over to the chair where she'd placed the pile of scripts and brought them over to hand out.

"Mr. White plays the piano, so we're fortunate that we don't need to wait for the music teacher to join us to rehearse the musical numbers. I thought we could start there," Ellen offered.

Brodan nodded, but I noted his frown.

"Perhaps," I offered quietly, "we could choose parts today. See which of the children would like a main part and audition them."

He didn't look at me. Instead, he said, as if I hadn't spoken a word, "I think it would be better if we chose the children's parts today." He smiled at the kids. "Raise your hands if you'd like a lead role in the musical."

Both Ellen and David frowned, their gazes bouncing between me and Brodan.

Several hands shot up, including Lewis's.

We asked the kids who wanted a lead role to stand up and over to the side. I reluctantly stepped toward Brodan and my colleagues. "We should probably start with the roles of Dorothy, the Wicked Witch, the Tin Man, the Lion, and the Scarecrow."

Brodan tensed beside me and perused the newly condensed script like I hadn't spoken.

Ellen's brows drew together as she noted my lips pinch in frustration and embarrassment. She cleared her throat. "Yes, perhaps we should ask those wishing to play Dorothy to read and sing first?"

Brodan nodded. "Excellent idea."

I couldn't meet my colleagues' gazes.

As David sat down at the piano and Brodan made the children laugh to relax them a bit, Ellen sidled up to me. "Pen mentioned you two have history," she murmured under her breath.

Pen was a P3 teacher who had been in Lachlan Adair's class at school. She was also a gossip.

"It's nothing."

Ellen sighed heavily. "I'm thinking it's something. If there's animosity between you two, you should have said something. This could be a terrible idea."

"No. The kids love him." I gestured across the room where he had them laughing at who knows what. "You help him audition the kids. I'll keep the others quiet." And stay far, far out of the immature bastard's way.

∼

BRODAN

I knew I was being an immature arsehole.

But every time Monroe got near enough for me to smell her perfume, I wanted to bare my teeth like a savage animal. It didn't matter if she was an inch from me or thirty feet away. I could feel her in the room. Every bloody second.

I'd spotted her as soon as I strolled into the gym.

She wore a dark green dress with long sleeves and a high neck. The hem came to just above her knees to reveal dark tights on her short but great fucking legs. The green made her hair look like copper as it spilled down her back in natural waves.

None of *my* primary school teachers had looked like Monroe Sinclair. Christ, she was thirty-seven and still looked like she'd barely graduated from uni. I knew women in my line of work who would kill for Monroe's perpetual youth. Looking at her made holding back the memories difficult, so I'd stopped.

In fact, I was adamantly not acknowledging her.

Like a prick.

I didn't know how else to get through this.

Forcing myself to focus on the kids, I zeroed in on my nephew. I'd noted he'd grabbed a girl's hand to come join him to audition. She was a cute wee thing with blond pigtails and big blue eyes. Callie was her name, and she had an American accent. It had shocked me and Thane that Lewis wanted to audition for the musical since he was a bit of an introvert compared to his sister.

But Lewis further surprised me by stepping forward with determination to audition for the role of the Scarecrow. My shock was even greater to discover that my nephew was a wee comic. He delivered the lines with humorous nervousness and his clumsy physicality had me laughing out loud. I guessed acting was in the genes, after all.

His American friend, Callie, was clearly shy and probably coerced by Lewis to audition for Dorothy, but she delivered the lines with a cuteness I knew the audience would find adorable. After we'd had all the kids run lines, we asked them to sing any song they wanted a cappella.

Lewis didn't have a fantastic singing voice, but he didn't need one. Callie, however, had a soft but sweet voice that, with a bit of work on projection, would do nicely for Dorothy.

As soon as we stopped to discuss quietly, however, my attention drew away from Ellen and David to Monroe. The back of my neck tingled, and I wondered if she was watching me. If she was as hyper fucking aware of me as I was of her.

Giving in, I casually turned to peruse the kids and let my gaze linger on Monroe.

She wasn't looking at me. She kneeled down by a small girl, listening attentively to whatever she was saying. Her expression was soft and kind as she nodded and then gave the girl a reassuring smile.

I watched her take the girl's hand, and they stood together. My heart thudded in my chest as Monroe walked across the room, murmuring with the child as she gripped her hand. She said something to Ellen, who nodded, and then I watched as Monroe led her from the room.

My chest ached like I'd been struck.

A throat cleared, and I turned to find Ellen staring at me in curiosity. She'd caught me watching Monroe.

Damn it.

This was torture.

And Walker Ironside would pay for putting me in this position.

13

MONROE

I bumped into Arrochar Adair Galbraith in Golspie, of all places.

After spending all of Friday morning with Brodan, I'd been desperate to flee Ardnoch and everything it represented. So I drove up the coast Saturday morning and walked around the quaint neighboring town of Golspie. I considered driving just a bit farther out to spend the morning at Dunrobin Castle because I hadn't been there in years, but I'd situated myself in a coffee shop just off Main Street and was enjoying my latest book too much to leave. The proprietor happily kept my coffee filled, not caring if I'd glued my arse to one of her small bistro chairs.

It was peace.

A lovely distraction.

So imagine my surprise when the bell tinkled above the door and in came Arrochar, pushing a pram. My pulse raced as our eyes connected. I didn't know how Arro would respond to my being home. In fact, it was a miracle we hadn't bumped into each other yet. Now here we were, in another village, staring at one another.

To my shock, Arro's face split into a beautiful smile. "Roe!"

My eyebrows sprung upward. "Arro."

She pushed the pram toward my table, and my eyes dropped as I heard a baby making gurgling noises from within. Arro's wee girl. My goodness. Sometimes it felt like time hadn't passed, and then I was reminded that it absolutely had. Arro pushed the pram into the corner by my table, and I stood to greet her as she wrapped her arms around me. The smell of her perfume enveloped me, and tears sprung to my eyes as she squeezed me hard.

"I've missed you," she said, sounding a little hoarse.

I cleared my throat. "You too," I whispered.

When she pulled back, she didn't release me. Arro stared down at me, studying my face as I studied hers. She hadn't changed much. In fact, she glowed, her blond hair lighter than it used to be, her eyes that same striking pale blue as Brodan's. Happiness radiated from her, and I was glad. When I'd first discovered she was married to her sister-in-law's father, I didn't know what to make of it. Then I saw Mackennon Galbraith in the village one day, and I could certainly see the attraction. He'd had Robyn very young, so the age gap between him and Arro didn't seem so drastic in reality. Especially considering Arro was a mature woman in her thirties.

Still, what a complicated family tree the Adairs were growing.

"I can't believe we bumped into each other here. Since I heard you were back, I have been waiting to see you. I actually called the school for your number, but they wouldn't give it to me."

Shocked by this revelation, I had to force back fresh tears. I was so sure Arro was mad at me. But no. "They wouldn't? I'm sorry." I blushed with frustration at myself. "I ... I just assumed you didn't want to hear from me. That's why I never …"

Arro gave my arms another squeeze and stepped back. "It's all water under the bridge. Do you mind if Skye and I join you?"

It was on the tip of my tongue to reject her, just as I'd rejected Arran the numerous times he'd tried to engage in friendship. But after the way Brodan had treated me in rehearsal—in fact, since that first day in Flora's—I was done acting like I had done something wrong. I was sick and tired of hosting all the blame for the deterioration of our friendship. Why should I make myself miserable for someone who didn't exist anymore? Brodan wasn't the kind, protective boy of my childhood.

He was a complete and total wanker.

My attention moved to the pram, to the adorable baby girl inside staring up at her mum. "Oh, Arro, she's beautiful."

"Thank you. Let's settle in, and you can hold her if you'd like."

An ache tore through my chest. "I'd like that."

"Can you watch her while I order a coffee?"

"Of course."

"Do you want anything?"

"I'm good." I was reeling. This felt surreal on so many levels.

As Arro waited to be served, I leaned over the pram. "Hullo, Skye," I greeted the baby softly.

Her blue eyes moved to me and she raised her fists, giving me a smile in return.

The pain of longing intensified.

I thought I'd have children, plural, by now. Maybe even one already in high school.

Life didn't turn out how I'd expected. I wondered if it did for anyone.

When Arro returned to her seat, I asked, "What brings you to Golspie?"

"They needed Mac at the estate for some security system update today." She shrugged before taking a quick sip of coffee. "And honestly, I just wanted to have a gander with Skye without bumping into someone every five seconds." Realizing how that sounded, she placed a hand over mine. "Not you. This is different. I'm so glad we bumped into each other."

"No, I get it. Why do you think *I'm* here?"

Arro chuckled and then shook her head as she held my gaze. "You haven't changed a bit."

"Neither have you."

"You're too kind." She smoothed a hand over Skye's blanket. "I've changed since this wee drop of stardust fell into my life. I haven't had a full night's sleep since, for a start."

"Well, you would never know. You look beautiful."

Arro gave me a soft smile. "Forever kind, as always, Roe. Goodness, I can't tell you how wonderful it is to see you." Her smile dropped. "Though Arran tells me you're staying in Gordon's caravan. That won't do, Monroe. Not over the winter. One reason I wanted to bump into you was to offer you Mac's cottage on Castle Street. We've been renting it as a holiday let, so there's no current tenant. We can rent it to you for the same as whatever Gordon's renting the caravan."

Which would be a crazy discount. I flushed at her generosity and the fact that I required it. Pride made me shake my head. "I appreciate that, but I'm fine, really."

She opened her mouth as if to argue, so I hurried to ask, "May I hold Skye?"

A minute later, I had a warm, sweet-smelling baby in my arms. "How old is she now?" I asked as she made little baby sounds and blew raspberries at me.

"Six weeks, nearly seven. I don't know where the time

has gone." Arro stared adoringly at her daughter. "Other than waking up through the night, she's so good. So chilled out."

"She must get that from you." I always remembered Arro being laid back.

"And Mac. He doesn't look it, but he's very chill."

"Are you happy?" I blurted out.

Arro met my gaze and answered sincerely, "I wish everyone could have what I have. The world would be better for it."

Emotion stung my eyes. "I'm glad for you, Arro."

Concern wrinkled her brow. "Are you happy, Roe?"

I knew what she was thinking. She was one of the few people who'd known my simple dreams of the future. Teaching, marriage, babies.

At least I had one of those.

"I will be," I answered, hoping it was true.

~

BRODAN

Never google yourself. Rule number one.

I broke the rule.

Now, as you'd imagine, what I found pissed me off.

Not at the rumors swirling about my whereabouts, my retirement, "the end of Brodan Adair" as we know it, but at some lying scummy social media influencer called Harriet Blume. She had five million followers, and while I wasn't the focus of all her gossip and lies, she certainly seemed taken with me. She'd wracked up millions of views on a video of me with a pregnant Robyn that she'd taken while in

Ardnoch. Blume had insinuated nothing. She'd let the video do the work.

People thought I'd gone home because I'd gotten someone pregnant. Thankfully, folk who paid attention had rushed to the comments to fact-check and tell others that Robyn was my sister-in-law. But it was obvious the brat had posted this for views.

I tried not to let it get to me.

Blume was no longer in Ardnoch. She could post nonsense about me and other celebrities, and it should not bother me one whit.

A text message dropped onto the screen, so I tapped out of the platform, vowing to delete the apps, and opened the message.

It was from Rachel Wilde, an actor I'd made my first big movie with. We'd slept together during the making of the movie and whenever she wasn't in a relationship. According to rumor, she'd just broken off her engagement to some nephew of a billionaire businessman.

Apparently, it was true.

In Paris in December for a week. Could use some company.

I would quite like to get laid sometime soon with no complicated strings.

To my indignation, an image of Roe's face flashed across my mind.

Strings? She was a fucking museum of strings.

Before I could answer, a knock sounded on my door. Perhaps it was housekeeping. "Come in."

To my surprise, my sister strolled in, her cheeks flushed with the November chill. And she was alone.

I frowned as I stood. "Where's my gorgeous wee niece?"

"Downstairs with her dad. I just thought I'd pop up and see you before we leave." Arro looked around my suite, a frown furrowing her brow. "I wish you'd move out of here and in with one of us."

"This is still home to me, Arro." I sat on the edge of the bed. "It might be filled with strangers, but this is where we grew up."

Sighing heavily, Arro sat in a chair across from me. "Speaking of … I bumped into Monroe in Golspie today. We had coffee."

My pulse picked up. "And?"

Arro studied me carefully. "I didn't get a lot out of her. It's hard to catch up on eighteen years over coffee with a baby in hand, but I saw enough."

Curiosity pricked at me. "I'm not interested."

"Aren't you doing the school musical with her?"

I shrugged. "We're not really interacting."

Concern filled my sister's eyes. "She didn't say it, but she's not happy, Brodan. I'm worried about her."

"You speak to her for all of five minutes, and you've deduced that much?"

Arro scowled. "We talked for an hour, and she was very good at being vague about her life and her feelings. Something you two have in common."

"Arro," I warned.

"Don't you care? She used to be your best friend in the entire world."

"Christ." I pushed off the bed, walking away from her toward the window. "You sound like Arran."

"Well?"

"Well what?" I spun on her. "Arro, I don't know that woman anymore. She's nothing to do with me, and I wish my family would stop trying to make it into something it's not. I couldn't care less about her. She's a stranger to me now."

My sister stood up, glaring at me. "I'm going to pursue a friendship with her."

"Do what you like."

She scoffed and shook her head. "It's funny you should say Roe's a stranger to you now … Because, honestly, I feel that way about you."

Her words hit hard. They fucking hurt. "What does that mean?"

Arro shrugged sadly. "Just that I don't know you anymore. My funny, charming, affectionate, loving brother came back this autumn a guarded, aloof man hiding behind a false smile. I see it, even though you think I am too busy as a new mum to notice. You're not happy, Brodan, and you won't admit it. You won't talk to me about it."

I smirked to hide the way her words struck a nerve. "You said it yourself—you're busy with Skye."

"Not too busy to talk if you need it."

"I don't."

Arro sighed. "That's what I mean. You're lying to me right now."

"What do you want me to say?" I snapped. "That my fucking life is in the toilet? That I don't know what I'm doing or what I want? That life didn't turn out the way I thought it would and seeing fucking Monroe Sinclair every fucking where takes me back to a place that kills me!"

The words rang through the spacious room, shocking us both.

Arro took a step toward me. "Yes, Brodan. I want you to tell me those things."

"I can't," I said between gritted teeth. "Because if I don't keep it together, I'm afraid …"

"Afraid of what?"

"That I won't be able to pick up the pieces."

My sister rushed me, throwing her arms around me. I hugged her back, holding on to her slight frame as if she were a lifeline.

"Talk about the things that bother you, Brodan. Or it'll all explode out of you one day in a way you don't want it to."

I nodded. Though I wasn't ready to talk, I shuddered, holding her tighter.

Arro rubbed my back. "It's okay, big brother. Just know I'm here when you're ready to let it all out."

14

MONROE

I'd never wanted to kill an Adair more in my life. It was no surprise that Brodan could make a placid, nonviolent person turn bloodthirsty. How had I never realized what an annoying arsehole he really was? Seriously.

However, I chose to look at it this way: being enlightened to Brodan Adair's true self was good for me.

The day had not started well. I had to drop Mum off at a doctor's appointment, so I was late to rehearsals for the musical, and not just late but in a foul mood. I'd tried asking Mum about Dad again on the way to the hospital, and she'd bitten my head off.

"He never loved you, so I don't know why you're so determined to find him," she'd spat venomously.

I'd tried not to let her see how much the words cut, but as soon as I sped away from that hospital, the tears fell. Furious that I'd let her get to me, I'd pulled over, fixed my makeup, and strolled into work trying to knock that chip off my shoulder.

Unfortunately, David also had a doctor's appointment that morning, and Ellen had scheduled the school's music teacher to help us with rehearsal. Two weeks of rehearsing, and Brodan had ignored me at every opportunity, to the point where Lewis was picking up on it and it felt as if he was acting distant with me.

Anyway, if two weeks of his dismissive behavior wasn't bad enough, Brodan had ramped things up by flirting with our music teacher.

Ms. Ava Reid was barely out of teacher training college and giggling like a wee girl at everything Brodan said.

I rolled my eyes for the hundredth time as Brodan leaned over Ava where she sat at the piano. They murmured together while the noise level among the kids increased in tandem with their growing impatience. I caught Ellen's gaze.

Her lips pursed, unamused. "Mr. Adair, perhaps we should continue."

Brodan straightened and threw Ellen his boyish smile. "Ms. Reid and I were just discussing changing the tempo of 'We're Off to See the Wizard'. Give it something a bit different and unexpected to the audience."

I tensed. "Unfortunately, we don't have time for changes at this stage. We need to forge ahead with what we have."

The son of a bitch didn't even acknowledge me. He turned back to Ava, murmured something in her ear that made her giggle, and pointed at the songbook on her piano.

My cheeks burned with frustration, and my heart ached. When I glanced along the rows of children, I noted Lewis staring at me with a frown between his brows.

"Mr. Adair," Ellen's voice snapped like a whip, and Brodan straightened again.

"Yes, Mrs. Hunter?" he drawled.

"I'm not sure if you couldn't hear Ms. Sinclair over Ms. Reid's simpering," Ellen said pointedly, throwing Ava a sharp look, "but we don't have time, nor the legal right, to make changes to the musical. Let's put our attention on the children, please."

Chastened, and amused by it, Brodan gave Ellen a militant nod, laughter on his lips. At that moment, I didn't find anything about him charming. He was an immature man-child, and I was beginning to think I'd made a lucky escape when he abandoned me all those years ago.

Half an hour later, more flirting was exchanged, but at least we were getting somewhere with the children. However, when I asked Lewis to stand in a certain place, he ignored me. I had to repeat myself, and Brodan's gaze narrowed on his nephew as Lewis pretended not to hear me.

Patience thinning, I hardened my voice. "Lewis, please respond when spoken to."

He looked at me, shifting on his feet, hesitating.

"Lewis," Brodan warned.

Lewis gave his uncle a confused look but followed my instructions. Irritation thrummed through me, and I had to stop myself from spearing Brodan with angry eyes. Didn't he realize he was the reason Lewis was acting up? He watched his uncle like a hawk, and what he saw was Brodan disrespecting me at every turn. So, clearly, he'd deduced there was a good reason.

While the children were preoccupied, I strode toward Brodan and stood directly in front of him so he couldn't dismiss me. His gaze flickered over my face before dancing above my head.

"Mr. Adair, I'd like a word in private, please."

"I'm busy."

"A word in private. Now."

He sighed heavily but nodded and followed me to the other side of the gymnasium. Still, Brodan wouldn't look at me, his attention on the kids. I saw Ava watching us curiously. Poor girl. She had no idea she was being toyed with.

"Two things, and they're both about your professionalism. I'm sure you've had to work with other actors who you didn't like very much, just as I'm sure that you sucked it up and were a professional. This is no different, Brodan. Lewis watches your every move, and he's learning from you."

His head snapped toward me. "If Lewis doesn't like you, that's not my problem."

Anger swelled in my throat, almost choking me. "Lewis and I got on wonderfully before you arrived, and you know it."

"I know nothing."

Was he always this obnoxious?

Brodan's expression tightened at whatever he saw in my gaze. "Anything else, Ms. Sinclair, or may I return to my duties?"

I stiffened at the disdain in his voice. "Yes. Stop flirting with our music teacher. First, she's barely out of school, and second, it's highly inappropriate in front of the children, and the only person who'll end up looking bad is Ava. So stop."

His expression remained flat, unemotional. "I can flirt with whoever the fuck I feel like flirting with. You, however, should really do a better job of hiding your jealousy."

"Jealous?" I scoffed, hating him at that moment. "Sorry to deflate your ego, Adair, but immature, obnoxious man-children don't really do it for me."

Brodan's eyes narrowed. "Or maybe you're just jealous because Ava's a young woman in her prime, and you're a middle-aged spinster."

I stared at him as if I'd never seen him before—because I hadn't. Whoever had returned to Ardnoch, it wasn't my childhood friend.

Noting my reaction, the muscle in Brodan's jaw ticked and then he hissed out, "Fuck," and marched away from me.

Hot tears built behind my eyes, and I turned away,

pressing my forefinger and thumb to my nose to stem them. *I hate him*, I decided. I truly hated him.

"Ms. Sinclair, are you all right?"

I jumped a little at the sound of my head teacher's voice and blinked back the tears as I turned to her with a bright smile. "Ms. Cooley, what brings you here?"

Anita searched my face, concern evident. "I thought I'd drop by and see how rehearsal is going." She repeated, "Are you all right?"

"A bit of a headache," I lied. "I was just taking a moment."

"If you're certain." Anita turned toward the children. "I'll observe from here. I don't want to distract them." Her gaze moved to Brodan, who was back at the piano, chatting with Ava. "It's all very exciting, isn't it?"

However, it wasn't long before Anita's excitement died in lieu of disapproval. Brodan had returned to flirting with Ava at every opportunity, and while rehearsals were moving along, I could see Anita's irritation building.

And unfortunately, just as I knew would happen, her annoyance was not directed at Brodan.

Finally, with a huff, Anita strode across the gymnasium. As much as Ava's unprofessionalism peeved me, I worried about her as Anita led the young teacher from the room. I moved toward the children as Ellen had Callie repeat some lines she was struggling with. Ava returned a few minutes later, eyes downcast, cheeks bright red … and she wouldn't even look at Brodan.

Aye, she had been well and truly chastened.

Brodan spoke to her, and she just gave him a tight nod without looking at him. He frowned and moved away to direct the kids.

I couldn't help myself. As soon as everyone was fully engaged elsewhere, I sidled up to Brodan's side. I could sense him tense at my proximity and I smirked, feeling a vindictiveness rise in me that no one had ever provoked. "Ava was reprimanded by her boss. That's the world we live in, Brodan. Fair or unfair, it's a fact. You know quite well that you're untouchable here. A powerful man. So what does it matter if you make a young woman look bad in front of her boss as long as you're having fun? But then, looking back, you always were a selfish prick." I strode away before he could speak and joined Ellen on the other side of the stage.

My heart raced from the confrontation, but satisfaction numbed a little of the hurt he'd caused.

15

BRODAN

Monroe was done playing nice.

I'd say I preferred her being honest over her fake bullshit "professionalism," but there was no denying she'd pissed me off yesterday.

Mostly because what she said was true.

I'd been so busy trying to make sure she knew how little I cared about her I hadn't taken Ava Reid's position into consideration. I'd put her in a bad spot with Anita Cooley. It was selfish.

I fucking hated that it had given Monroe an opening.

Then again, after the way I'd treated her, I deserved it.

This whole situation with her had me off-balance. One second I was seething, channeling every shitty thing that had happened that weekend I found her with Arran into my fury. Then once I'd made it clear how little she mattered to me I'd swirl in a clogged drain of guilt. Her face yesterday when I'd said that about her being a spinster ...

I had a feeling she really, truly hated me now.

It was for the best.

Even if the knowledge of that was pressure crushing my chest.

During the break in Friday morning's rehearsal, a bake sale would open for business. We had bake sales back when I was a kid at Ardnoch Primary. Every term, the kids and parents baked cakes, sold them at break time, and the money helped fund the school.

So as soon as the break bell rang, the kids took off for the cafeteria behind the gym for the sale. Monroe disappeared too.

Lewis caught up with me. "You coming to the sale, Uncle Brodan? Mum's there with Eilidh."

"Of course, wee man. I'm going to fill my belly with whatever she's baked." Regan had proven herself awesome in the kitchen.

Tables and parents and kids packed the cafeteria. It smelled amazing. I wasn't really a cake guy, but now and then, I liked a treat. I was unsurprised to see Walker stride into the cafeteria behind us with a visitor's badge hanging around his neck. He'd insisted on having access to the school in case I needed him for security. Regan had talked about the bake sale at dinner last night, the dinner to which we invited him, and despite his muscular physique, Walker Ironside had a sweet tooth. He had tight control over it, but once a week, he bought pastries for breakfast and then ran a few extra miles to work them off.

"What are you doing here?" I teased.

My bodyguard scowled at me. "The place is packed. Thought it best I be here for you."

"Sure. That's believable."

He cut me a dark look before a nearby table of cupcakes stole his attention.

"None of that." I wagged my finger at him. "If you're

buying, you're buying from the Adair table. Regan's going to kick everyone's arse."

"It's not a competition, Uncle Brodan," Lewis informed me.

I frowned. "It was when I was a kid." We always bragged about whose table got cleared first. It was never me. Dad didn't bake, so it was left to Lachlan and Thane to put something together after Mum died, and let's just say they weren't natural bakers.

Following Lewis through the crowded room, Walker at my back, we reached Regan's table only to discover she was sharing it. Apparently with Callie, our Dorothy's mum.

Callie's mum was a very attractive, very young blond.

"Brodan, Walker," Regan greeted us with that dimpled smile as she rounded her table to hug Lewis into her side. She looked down at her stepson. "How was rehearsal?"

Lewis shrugged.

Guilt pricked me. He'd been off the last couple of rehearsals, and I was worried Monroe might be right about him picking up on the animosity between us.

"Uncle Brodan, I helped Mummy make scones!" Eilidh drew my attention to where she stood with Callie and the blond.

"They look amazing," I complimented, rubbing my tummy for emphasis.

Regan pulled Lewis behind the table with her as she gestured to Callie and the blond. "This is Sloane Harrow and her daughter Callie. Though, Brodan, you know Callie already from the musical."

"I do. She's our wonderful Dorothy." I reached across the table and held out a hand to Sloane. "Nice to meet you."

People reacted one of two ways to meeting me: awkward starstruck delight or deliberate indifference as some manner of "putting me in my place." Sloane, however, reacted normally. She gave me a pretty smile and shook my hand like I was just the guy next door. "It's nice to meet you too," she said, her American accent unsurprising. "Callie is having a lot of fun, aren't you, baby girl?"

Callie nodded shyly. Apparently, she was one of those kids who came out of her shell on stage but turtled back inside as soon as she was off it.

"This is Walker Ironside." I gestured to Walker, who was eyeing the cakes in front of Sloane like a starving man. To be fair, the cupcakes were decorated to perfection. They looked professional. As did the pie and madeleines she'd baked.

Sloane's eyes lit up with interest at the sight of Walker. It wouldn't be the first time a woman had thrown me over for Walk, the handsome bastard that he was.

"You work security at Ardnoch, right?" Sloane asked.

Walker looked up at her, his gaze searching. "I know you … you're the new housekeeper."

"You're a housekeeper at Ardnoch?" Regan asked.

Sloane nodded, still gazing up at Walker. "We started around the same time, I think."

"Right." Walker's attention dropped back to her cakes, oblivious to how her eyes raked his shoulders and chest.

Or he was ignoring her interest.

It was hard to tell with him.

I sighed under my breath. "Walker is my bodyguard but is working at Ardnoch while we're here."

"Oh." Sloane's gaze ran down his body and back up again, a tinge of pink cresting her cheeks.

I grinned at Regan, who smirked knowingly. Aye, she'd caught it too.

"What's funny?" Eilidh asked loudly.

"Life, princess," I answered, and then rubbed my hands together. "Okay, how much for one of those delicious scones?"

"Would you like to try a cupcake?" Sloane asked Walker as I handed over the money to my niece.

"Aye, how much?"

"Two pounds."

Walker frowned and pulled out his wallet. He handed her a five-pound note. "Keep the change. You're not charging enough."

"Oh. I'm still getting used to what everything should cost here." She reached down and plucked a cupcake with white buttercream icing and held it out to Walk.

"Thanks." He peeled back the paper to bite into it. His eyes widened as he chewed. "Holy fuck," he murmured, as his attention dropped to the other cupcakes.

Regan glowered at Walker. "There are children present."

He wasn't listening. He inhaled the rest of the cupcake and retrieved his wallet again. "I'll take a box."

Laughing, I considered betrayal of the Adair bake stand at his reaction. "That good?"

"Try one," he answered while Sloane beamed as she boxed up four more cupcakes for Walker.

"Do you want to try my madeleines too?" She gestured to the seashell-like cakes.

"Aye, throw in a few of those." Walker nodded to the pie, already sliced. "What's in the pie?"

My shoulders shook with amusement as Regan snorted. "Sloane does kick my ass in the baking department."

Sloane flushed. "The pie is chocolate and salted caramel."

"You baked it?" he asked.

"Yes. I baked everything here."

"My mom is the best baker in the world," Callie offered quietly.

Walker's gaze moved to the wee girl and softened. "Is that right?"

She nodded, pushing into her mum's side. "You should try the pie."

"Then I will. Slice of pie."

"You'll go into a sugar coma at this rate," I warned him.

He cut me a look and answered belligerently, "If you'd try her cupcakes, you'd understand."

Chuckling, I looked at Regan. "Do you mind, sis?"

"Have at it. Callie does not lie. Eilidh and I had a cupcake before you arrived, and it was …" She made a chef's kiss.

"Oh, Ms. Sinclair!" Sloane suddenly called behind us, and I stiffened as Monroe came into sight. It surprised me when Sloane enveloped Monroe in a hug, like they were friends. My ex-best friend noted me and quickly looked away toward the array of baked goods.

"I've been meaning to tell you that my neighbor and I devoured the cupcakes you gifted me, Sloane. Best cupcakes ever. Seriously. In fact, I need more." Monroe opened her purse. "How much for one?"

"Five quid," Walker answered around a mouthful of madeleine.

Sloane shot him a surprised look, her lips twitching. "I think we can discount for Callie's favorite teacher."

He grunted.

Monroe chuckled, and it set off a sharp pain near my heart. I hadn't heard that sound in eighteen years. "I'll pay the fiver. It's for the school, and your cakes are worth it."

"Try a madeleine." Walker picked up the tray and held them out to Monroe.

"Oh. Okay. I'll take one of those too." Monroe reached for one. "How much?"

"One—"

"Two pounds fifty," Walker interrupted Sloane.

I could hear Regan choking on her laughter, and despite Monroe's presence, amusement filled me at Walker's proprietary reaction to Sloane Harrow's baked goods—and the fact that the gorgeous young woman was staring up at him like he was a god and Walk was oblivious to it.

"The pie's fuc— is amazing too," Walker added.

Monroe's gaze dropped to her purse, and I saw the slight pinch around her lips before she waved him off. "A cupcake and madeleine will more than see me through."

Was cash a problem for her? Is that why she was in Gordon's caravan, freezing her arse off?

It shouldn't bother me, the idea of Monroe struggling.

"You must take a scone, Ms. Sinclair," Regan called to her. "Eilidh and Lewis helped me bake them."

"Really?" Monroe's face lit up, and she moved around the table, passing me to get to them. I caught a whiff of her perfume, and my gut tightened, my eyes dropping to her tight arse as she sashayed past me in a skirt that molded to her body. A short split in the back was annoyingly tantalizing.

The clothes she wore to school switched between young at heart and playful and sexy receptionist.

"These look so good. Well done, Eilidh. Well done, Lewis."

"Thanks, Ms. Sinclair." Eilidh beamed.

Lewis scowled at the table.

Fuck.

Monroe's face fell while Regan stared at her stepson in surprise. "Lewis, what do you say to Ms. Sinclair?"

He shrugged.

Double fuck.

"Lewis, do not ignore Ms. Sinclair."

His eyes flicked up to me and then to Monroe. "Thanks."

Shit. Fuck. Shit.

Monroe was right again.

Regan caught my eye and looked between me and Monroe, a warning in her expression for all to see. Great.

Now my sister-in-law was catching the vibe, and it wouldn't be long until Thane heard about this. My big brother would not be happy I was causing his son problems at school.

I wasn't happy.

Because this meant I was going to have to act like I could stand to be around Monroe for Lewis's sake.

"If you'll excuse me," Monroe said quietly and strode away.

I forced myself not to watch her leave and engaged in conversation with an exuberant Eilidh who tried to get me to taste everything she, Regan, and Lewis baked. More people came to our table, and Walker became my entertainment, distracting me with the gruff and almost aggressive way he sold Sloane's cakes for her. What brought an American to Ardnoch as a housekeeper, and how did she get the job in the first place? Curiosity reminded me to ask Lachlan.

"I helped Mom with the pie," Callie said to Walker during a quiet moment.

"Aye?" he asked. "You a good baker, too, then?"

Callie smiled shyly. "I like it. Mom wants to open a bakery, and I could help."

Walker looked at Sloane. "Bakery?"

She sighed. "Pipe dream."

"I don't know about that. You can *bake*, woman."

Her eyes grew heated at the growled compliment, and I shot Regan another look. My sister-in-law watched Sloane and Walker as if they were the best soap opera on telly.

"You should try my lemon meringue pie sometime," Sloane offered with a hint of flirt. Not too obvious, but enough for a man to hear the invitation in her words.

Walker Ironside nodded. "That would sell well here. Next time."

Regan looked at me, rolling her eyes in exasperation.

Walker was a perpetual bachelor. Either he genuinely was

unaware of Sloane's attraction to him or he didn't want to lead her on. Could be either.

As Callie talked to Walker about the best flavors of buttercream (a topic I'd never thought I'd hear Walker actively engage in), my attention wandered. Like a magnet, I got stuck on Monroe.

Annoyance flared through me at the sight of her laughing with some good-looking bloke and his son. I recognized the kid from our rehearsals. He was in the chorus and one of Lewis's friends. Martin or Michael or Mason or something with an M.

The good-looking bloke held out a cake toward Monroe, and she flushed.

He gestured with it, and she rolled her eyes before taking a bite right out of his hand. She nodded, making big eyes at him, and the bastard leaned over and slowly wiped a crumb from her lip with his thumb. Then he licked the crumb off his thumb. Fury swirled in my gut as Monroe blushed, murmured something, smiled sweetly at him, and strolled out of the cafeteria.

Jealousy licked up my spine as I glared at the guy. He was staring after Monroe with determined satisfaction.

Not thinking straight, I excused myself. Walker was too busy listening to Callie to notice me leave, but I could feel Regan's watchful gaze on me. Ignoring her, I hurried through the crowds, hearing my name murmured among them and not even bothering to offer them a friendly Hollywood smile.

It was like I was possessed.

My boots echoed off the shiny corridor floors as I turned left at reception and hurried through the double doors toward the classrooms. I ducked my head into every doorway until I found her in her classroom, halfway up the corridor.

Monroe stood at her desk, staring out the window, as if in a daze.

Because of the fuckwit dad who just practically licked a crumb off her lip? Was something going on between them?

I'd meant to discuss Lewis.

To promise to be more professional, so he would go back to treating Monroe with respect.

But it was like a devil took over my body and my mouth.

"You know you've got some cheek slapping me on the wrist for flirting with a music teacher when it looks like you're fucking a pupil's parent."

Monroe whirled on me.

I saw my words sink in.

"Excuse me?" she seethed, her eyes narrowed.

"Everybody caught the show," I drawled, strolling with a casualness I did not feel toward her.

To my astonishment, Monroe retreated physically.

That pissed me off, her acting like she had something to fear from me.

My devil made me keep moving and she suddenly registered she was backing up and stopped.

"What do you want, Mr. Adair?" She tilted her chin defiantly.

I huffed at her formality. "I want you not to be my nephew's self-righteous, pain-in-the-arse teacher. But here you are."

"Self-righteous?"

"Sticking your nose in the air." I searched her face, fully looking at her, and realizing there were more freckles on her forehead than there used to be. There was a new one at the corner of her right eye too. "Admonishing me and Ava for harmless flirting, while you let your pupil's father practically lick your mouth." Said mouth drew my attention, and a perverse heat flickered through me. Roe had a full, pouty mouth that had driven me mad as a teenager and made me feel guilty as hell anytime I fantasized about doing something sexual to it.

I could still remember how well she kissed. How soft her lips were.

Goddamn it.

My eyes flew to hers to find her glowering at me. "Step back, Mr. Adair."

See? There it was again. The insinuation I'd hurt her.

"Afraid to be too close to me? Too tempting?"

Monroe sneered, and I felt her disdain like a slice across my gut. "I'd sooner fuck a cactus."

Ironically, her words pricked my vanity. "Quite the potty mouth for a primary school teacher."

"I think you need to stop obsessing over my mouth and leave me alone, Brodan. I preferred it when you were ignoring me."

I didn't move away. I moved closer, determined to see that heat in her eyes she used to give me when we were teens. Don't ask me why. Call it a masochistic need to play with fire. "I didn't come here to argue with you, *Ms. Sinclair*. I came to let you know that from now on, I will be professional and acknowledge you during rehearsals, for Lewis's sake. But I don't want you mistaking it for me being interested in forgiveness or friendship."

Her gray eyes searched mine. Then she curled her upper lip. "I would never mistake it for that, *Mr. Adair*. You can choke on your bitterness for all I care, as long as it doesn't interfere with my relationship with Lewis. You're nothing to me anymore."

Fury and other feelings I couldn't quite admit to churned in my gut as I pushed my face into hers, making her gasp. "You should never have come back here. No one wants you here."

True torment flashed in her eyes, and suddenly I remembered her parents.

All the pain they'd caused.

All the hurt they probably still inflicted upon her.

My thoughtless jibe suddenly took on a monstrous quality. What the fuck was wrong with me?

Self-hatred slammed through me, but before I could say anything, take back the words, a familiar deep voice whipped into the room. "Brodan."

I looked over my shoulder to find Walker glaring at me. "What?"

"Out here. Now."

I raised an eyebrow at his demand but turned back to Monroe. Her gaze had dropped to the floor, the color drained from her cheeks.

What did I care, though, right?

My gut wasn't in knots because of her.

I opened my mouth to speak—

"Brodan, now."

At Walker's clipped tone, I muttered a curse under my breath and pushed off the wall.

I waited for Monroe to look at me, but she just kept staring at the floor. My eyes dropped to her fisted hands. Her knuckles were white with strain.

Anguish filled me. A thousand apologies and a thousand accusations swirled inside. I turned and stalked out of the room, glowering at Walker as I stormed past him. "What the fuck is it?"

He caught up with me quickly, but remained silent until we neared the cafeteria doors and the noise of the bake sale beyond. "Brodan."

I stopped and looked at him. Something in his expression rendered me silent. There was a menacing air around my friend that I'd only ever witnessed when fans were getting too close to me.

"I'll say this once and only once," Walker warned. "If I ever hear you intimidate or talk to a woman like that again, I don't care if you fire me, I will knock your teeth out myself."

It was like he'd punched me. Indignation stole my breath. "I wasn't intimidating Monroe."

Was I?

"I saw you towering over a woman half your size and talking to her like she was shit on your shoe. Is that who you are, Brodan? Because if so, tell me now, and you won't need to fire me. I'll see myself out."

Bile rose in my throat.

"You should never have come back here. No one wants you here."

Self-directed disgust floored me. I felt so lost. So detached from myself. This wasn't me. This wasn't the man I wanted to be. The last few weeks rolled through my mind, and I stood outside myself, seeing the way I'd treated Monroe. Even if she had abandoned me when I needed her most ... did I really want to be the man who acted like this? Someone I hated? Someone my friends no longer respected?

I scrubbed my hand over my face, exhausted. "Fuck. Fuck, fuck!"

Walker stared at me stonily.

Flinching at his disappointment, I apologized, feeling like a wee boy. "I'm sorry, Walk. I ... it won't happen again."

"It's not me you need to apologize to."

The very thought of being vulnerable toward Monroe shriveled my balls. "I can't." I looked at the cafeteria doors, the noise behind them increasing beyond bearing. "You don't understand. And I can't go back in there. Will you tell them I felt unwell and had to leave early?"

"What the fuck is going on, Brodan?"

148

Monroe's downcast face flittered across my mind. "She takes me back to a terrible time in my life. But you're right." I rubbed my chest, trying to soothe the sharp pain. "It's no excuse. Eighteen years ago ... well, if I'd seen someone treat Monroe the way I've been treating her, I'd have laid them out. I don't know what the fuck is wrong with me."

"You know ..." Walker shifted uncomfortably. "You can talk to me if you need to."

I appreciated that and said so. "But I just want to forget it. I don't want to dredge it up."

"I don't know if that's working for you. And while I thought me making your decisions for a while might be a good thing, I see I was wrong. Your life is yours again, Brodan. Keep your Black Shadow. It's time to make your own decisions."

I nodded, understanding. "My first decision is ... to not be here." And with that, I turned and walked away before Walker could say anything else.

The truth was, I wasn't sure if I was angry at Monroe, or if I was just using her as a punching bag. But no woman, no person, deserved that, and if I couldn't fix my head enough to be around her, then I couldn't *be* around her.

But not being around her meant letting Lewis down.

So all that was left to do was bury the anger and move on.

16

BRODAN

It was the first time in a few weeks that the Adairs found themselves all in one place. Thane's house was filled with my siblings, their partners, and their children as I strolled into the living area. My nerves had been torn to shreds the last few days, but while standing there, taking them all in, a sense of peace calmed me.

This was what I needed.

My family.

The room smelled amazing, rich with Regan's cooking. The island was laden with ingredients for chicken tacos. Nice.

"Uncle Brodan!" Eilidh yelled before jumping off the couch.

Pure love filled me as I lifted my niece into my arms. Her long legs dangled comically. "Hi, princess. How are you today? Treating your royal subjects well, I hope."

Eilidh wrinkled her nose as she wrapped her arms around my neck. "They make it hard sometimes. Especially Mum."

"Eilidh Adair," Regan, who was nearest to us in the kitchen with Robyn, admonished half-jokingly.

I snorted as Eilidh grimaced and whispered, "Oops. Forgot she was there."

"What did I ever do to you?" Regan huffed, hands on her hips.

"You know what you did," she said like a forty-year-old.

Shaking with laughter, I lowered Eilidh to her feet, and she gave Regan a raised eyebrow and stalked off to throw herself back onto the couch beside Arran and Eredine.

"I have no idea what I did." Regan looked at her sister in confusion. "Do you?"

Robyn shrugged. "No, but if you're already getting that kind of sass from her, you're screwed when she's a teenager."

"You gave birth to an Adair, so good luck when Vivien starts talking."

Leaving the sisters to tease each other, I wandered farther into the room, greeting everyone. "Where are my other two favorite nieces?"

"Napping upstairs," Lachlan answered. He sat in Thane's armchair, eyes closed.

I chuckled as Mac nodded from where he sat at the dining table with Arro. "The girls sleep whenever they're together."

"Aye, I think we'll all have to move in together," Arro cracked.

Lachlan's eyes opened. "It's sad that I almost want to do that."

I patted my big brother's shoulder as I passed. "Sleepless nights?"

"Vivien is going through a nocturnal phase right now," he murmured, his eyes already closing again.

My gaze shot to Robyn, who studied her husband with

affectionate sympathy. She looked tired too. Christ, I didn't envy them. But then she crossed the room and eased herself onto the arm of the chair. She pressed a kiss to Lachlan's temple as she tenderly brushed his hair back from his face. His eyes opened, and he smiled softly before pulling her onto his lap.

Okay.

Maybe I did envy them a wee bit.

I also worried for Lachlan. If something ever happened to Robyn or Vivien, it would destroy him.

It would destroy Thane to lose Regan or the kids. Arran to lose Eredine. Arro to lose Mac or Skye.

Growing up and losing what we had, my siblings had to have known what they risked. They were just braver than I was.

The thought attempted to sour my mood, so I pushed it away and wandered over to Lewis, playing a game on his tablet. He hadn't said hello, and I wondered if it was because I'd bailed on the rehearsal.

As if she'd read my mind, Eredine said from her spot at the other end of the large corner sofa, "Are you feeling better, Brodan?"

I frowned.

"Regan told us you left the bake sale early because you were sick."

"Oh. Aye. I had a headache come on." Feeling guilty about the lie, I lowered to my haunches by Lewis, drawing his attention from the game. "Hey, bud."

"Hi, Uncle Brodan." He stared at me impassively.

"Can we talk?" I jerked my head toward the sliding doors, gesturing to outside.

"You'll need jackets for that," Regan called from the kitchen, proving she had bat ears. She moved toward the hallway. "And don't be too long. Dinner will be ready soon."

As I stood, Regan returned with Lewis's jacket. He

lowered his tablet to the couch and got up to shrug it on, still not looking at me or saying a word. More guilt consumed me. It was a wonder I could function with the amount of it I carried daily.

Leading Lewis to the sliders, I heard Regan ask Eilidh, "Now, what's this about me doing something to you?"

"You know what you did," Eilidh repeated in a huff.

"Eilidh, don't cheek your mum," Thane admonished gruffly.

I opened the slider door, the biting November air blasting through us.

"She ruined my favorite shoes. She said she was getting them fixed, but I found them in your closet!"

"She has a name," Thane said with his authoritative dad voice. "And what were you doing in our closet?"

"Um ..."

"Eilidh."

"Looking for Christmas presents."

I closed the slider behind me and Lewis as the room erupted into noise as everyone chimed in on the conversation. Except for Lachlan and Robyn, who I think might actually have fallen asleep.

Turning to Lewis, the deck light illuminating us, I grinned. "Your sister is something else."

Lewis smirked as he rubbed his chilled hands together. "Her friends told her that Santa only brings one present and the rest is from our family. Then they told her all the good places to hunt for them."

"Did you join in the hunt?"

He shook his head. "I'd prefer to wait until Christmas."

Nodding, I turned and stared out at the blackness beyond. Clouds obscured the moon tonight, and I couldn't make out the sea. But we could hear it crashing against the coast. Despite the cold nipping at our skin, the fresh sea air was awesome. Not for the first time, I considered that plot of land waiting for me along the coast from my siblings' architect-built homes. Thane had designed each one to maximize the spectacular view.

"It's freezing," Lewis reminded me.

"Right." I glanced down at him. "I just wanted to chat with you about something. First, I'm sorry for leaving early on Friday."

He dropped his gaze. "It's fine."

"No. It's not. I haven't been acting … I haven't been the best uncle to you, and I'm sorry."

Lewis frowned. "You're helping with our school musical. The other kids think I'm lit."

"Lit?"

The wee shit smirked. "It means cool, Uncle Brodan."

Right. I knew that.

"Anyway, some of my friends have even seen your movies."

My lips twitched. "And they think you're lit because of me?"

He nodded seriously.

Grinning, I reached out and hugged him to my side. "You're a good kid, Lew. But … I noticed that you've been a bit rude to Ms. Sinclair lately, and I think I know why."

My nephew stiffened against me but didn't pull away.

"You know, a long time ago, Ms. Sinclair and I were best friends. A bit like you and Callie."

"Really?" He stared up at me, shocked.

"Aye. When we were your age. Younger, even. We became friends in P1 and never looked back." A hollowness gaped in my chest. "But life happens, and stuff that I won't get into because it's private occurred between us. I think you're old enough to understand that. That some things are just between two people."

Lewis nodded, solemn.

"But all you need to know is that my behavior has been wrong." I'd had two days brooding alone in my room at the estate, Walker's threat ringing in my ears, to really step outside myself. To see myself for the prick I was. Guilt and fear had warped me. And I vowed to stop letting them control me. "I've been rude to Ms. Sinclair, and it's going to stop. I don't want you thinking she's wronged me somehow and acting accordingly, as much as I appreciate your loyalty. Ms. Sinclair is a good teacher, and I know you like her. She deserves to be treated with respect."

He relaxed, the tension seeming to drain out of him. It made me feel like an even bigger selfish bastard.

"Okay, Uncle Brodan."

"You're a good kid," I repeated.

"Am I a good actor?" He grinned.

Chuckling to see the Adair charm I'd used in my career shining back at me, I nodded. "Aye, you're that too. But if I have my way, you'll follow in your dad's footsteps. You know he's way more *lit* than me, right?"

"You think so?" Lewis seemed chuffed about that.

"Oh, aye. Your dad is the very best of men. I can only hope to be half the man your dad is, Lew."

My nephew puffed up his chest with pride and nodded. I might be an uncle that Lewis admired, but Thane was the dad he hero-worshipped. The man he loved and most wanted to be like.

An ache splintered in my chest as I stared down at my nephew, filled with more love for the boy than I'd ever anticipated. That ache, I realized, was longing. Perhaps even something like envy toward Thane. It shocked the shit out of me. But I couldn't deny I felt it.

That pull a man might feel when he wanted children of his own.

SAMANTHA YOUNG

Fuck.

Off-balance, I shrugged off my confused feelings with a smile. "Come on, let's go eat tacos."

Stepping back inside, delicious heat hit us at the same time my family's curious gazes did. I was sure Thane would ask me later what all that was about, but the rest of them could just wonder. Nosy buggers.

A short while later, all of us seated around the dining table, we created a cacophony of noise that Lachlan kept wincing at, his attention on the baby monitor beside his plate. Finally, our conversation died down as we dug into the tacos Regan and Robyn had put together.

"I just wanted to give you a heads-up," Regan said, breaking the verbal silence, her eyes on me. "That social media journo, Harriet Blume, who was here annoying everyone this summer, is gossiping about you on her platform."

Ignoring my irritation, I swallowed a bite of taco. Wiping my chin with a napkin, I replied, "What's new? The gossip rags will gossip."

"Well, she's posting frequently about you and how you're here hiding because Celia Bergstrom broke your heart."

I snorted. I'd worked with the attractive Swedish actor on a film last year, we fucked once, and it was barely memorable for either of us. Sometimes, even if you had good chemistry on screen, it did not translate to the bedroom. "Let her write whatever nonsense she wants. As long as she's not here, that's all I care about."

"I don't know how you cope with people making up stories about you," Arro said, her brows pinched together. "It would drive me nuts."

"Which is why you're not an actor."

"Do you miss it?" Thane asked seriously.

I felt Lachlan's eyes on me now.

156

"Aye and no," I answered. "It's complicated."

Thane nodded, seeming to understand.

"You should start thinking about finding somewhere more permanent to live," Regan advised. "Now that you're staying."

"Am I staying?" I teased.

She scowled at me. "Why wouldn't you want to stay here surrounded by the people who love you?"

"Point well made." I bit into the rest of the taco, feeling my family watch me, waiting for me to say more. Swallowing the bite, I chuckled. "I'm staying, okay. I have no plans to leave anytime soon. But I'm not rushing into buying a house."

"Or building one?" Arran raised an eyebrow.

"Or building one. Just yet."

That seemed to appease them.

"You know who needs a house." Arro shot me a quick look before addressing Arran. "Monroe."

My stomach dropped.

"Gordon told me yesterday that he accepted a delivery for a freestanding electric fire that Roe's putting in his caravan. He's not thrilled about it because he's worried it's a fire hazard, but I asked what else he expects her to do. The caravan is twenty years old and bloody Baltic."

"That I can testify to." Robyn nodded. "And I didn't stay in it in the winter."

"What can we do?" Eredine asked, her worry for a stranger evident. "Arran has tried talking to her about moving out of there, taking help from us, but she won't listen."

"I know. I offered her Mac's cottage at a discount, but she turned it down." Arro shared an exasperated look with her husband.

I felt that exasperation rise in me.

Why the hell wouldn't she just accept help from someone?

The rest of the evening was a blur. I barely checked into the ever-moving conversation and excused myself early, much to the chagrin of Regan, who'd bought a chocolate pie from Sloane Harrow for dessert.

I hugged the women goodbye and when I wrapped my arms around Robyn, I whispered, "Which caravan?"

She stiffened in my arms and eased back, studying my face. Then decisively, she whispered in return, "The last one on the beachfront."

I squeezed her gratefully, even though I wasn't quite certain why I'd asked. Until I got in the Range Rover I had permanently borrowed to drive toward the castle and at the last second, I took the road leading to the beach. To Gordon's caravan park.

There were very few lights on in the caravans as I followed the road toward the beachfront properties. The SUV turned onto gravel, the stones crunching beneath the tires as I glided it slowly toward the end. I parked the car, facing the water, my eyes drawn to the last caravan. Sure enough, Monroe's old car was parked outside, the caravan lit up like a beacon.

Like a target.

She wasn't safe here.

Stubborn woman.

Angry at her stupidity and pride, I jumped out of the SUV and marched across the gravel and up the steps of the caravan. I could hear the murmur of a TV show coming from inside and raised my fist to bang impatiently on the door.

Hearing a muttered curse, anticipation thrummed through me, heating my blood.

A curtain on one window near the front of the caravan moved, and a shadowed face peered out.

Then footsteps thundered toward the door.

It flew open, and there she was.

Monroe Sinclair.

Her long hair was piled on top of her head in a messy bun, her face wiped clean of makeup, and she wore a thermal top and bottoms as pajamas.

"What the hell are you doing here?" she snapped.

I took that as an invitation and barged in, slamming the door shut behind me. Tugging on my scarf, I stared around at the tight surroundings. A laptop was open on the bench sofa at the front of the van, and we were standing in the middle of a galley kitchen. At the other end, I saw a narrow hallway that led to a double bed at the back. The bathroom must have been in a door behind the kitchen. A tiny electric fire was on the floor near the couch.

Fuck.

"Are you taking the piss?" I whirled around to glare at her as I threw my scarf down on her kitchen counter.

"Are you?" she yelled, her face flushed with indignation. Her gray eyes were bright under the awful aluminum lighting.

It should be a crime for a woman to look as beautiful as she did in blue thermals without a scrap of makeup on.

"Look at this place, Monroe. What the fuck is wrong with you that you can't accept help from my sister? You'd rather freeze your arse off in a caravan than give that fucking pride of yours a rest."

"Stop swearing at me!"

I gritted my teeth. "Anything could happen to you here. You do know Robyn was *fucking* attacked by Fergus in this very caravan? Difference is, Robyn can take care of herself."

Monroe's eyes blazed. "*I* can take care of myself. Believe you me, I have been taking care of myself since I could crawl, Brodan Adair! How dare you barge in here, yelling at me, when you couldn't give a shit if an entire army of Dothraki kidnapped me!"

"I thought that was every woman's fantasy."

Her nostrils flared. "Fuck you! And get out!"

"Not without you. Grab your shit, we're leaving." I strode toward her bedroom. "Is your suitcase in here?"

"Stop!" she snarled behind me.

I ignored her, searching the tight space. Where the fuck did she keep anything? There was no storage.

"Stop!" Monroe grabbed my arm, tugging me toward her. "Stop this craziness right now. Stop pretending like you care. You've made it quite clear that you don't. I don't need this or want this in my life, Brodan."

"And what is *this*?" I crowded her, forcing her backward until her legs hit the bed.

Heat swirled in my gut.

"Your myopic behavior!"

"My myopic behavior?" I raised an eyebrow. "You're the one who came back."

"Because I thought you were gone!"

Hurt flared through me, and I stepped closer until my body pressed to hers. "So you did factor me in, in your decision to return?"

She glowered up at me. "God! What do you want from me?"

I glared back at her, not knowing what the fuck I wanted anymore.

Before I could decide, Monroe let out a sexy growl of frustration before she reached up and yanked my head down toward hers, crushing her lips over mine.

17

MONROE

One minute, I was shocked at Brodan's arrival. I'd done my damnedest to exorcise him from my mind that weekend after Friday's altercation. He'd been so cruel to me, I felt something die inside. There had been nothing but pain since. I'd avoided my mum's phone calls because I just couldn't bear someone else treating me like I was *nothing*.

So for Brodan to show up, to pretend like he cared, even as he glared at me like he hated me, was too much.

All my rage and frustration became a fire inside of me I didn't know how to expel. Apparently, my body had decided exactly how it wanted to release all that pent up anger.

Part of me needed this. To feel anything but sorrow. Another part wanted to brand myself on him, to ruin him.

So I kissed him. And he kissed me back.

Lips, tongue, hunger. Ferocious, biting kisses that stole our breaths. I pushed at his peacoat, shoving it down his arms without breaking our kiss, and then we fell upon the bed. Hands pawing while lips and tongues searched for any naked spot they could find. He squeezed my breasts just hard enough to shoot pleasure pain through me as he ground between my legs. Then his fingers curled around the elastic waist of my thermals and underwear and he shoved them both down to my knees.

Impatience darkened Brodan's expression as he glowered down at me seconds before his mouth found mine again and his thumb slid over my clit. I moaned as he massaged the bundle of nerves. His kisses grew more ravenous as I fumbled to pull the zipper down on his jeans.

His fingers prodded inside me. The wet he found there made him grunt into my mouth. He tore his lips from mine, and my chest rose and fell in frenzied breaths as he reached into his back pocket and tugged out his wallet. Brodan's hands shook as he flipped it open impatiently and removed a foil package.

Anticipation made me squirm beneath him as he threw away the wallet and tugged the zipper on his jeans down the rest of the way. He never broke eye contact as he shoved down his jeans and boxers just far enough to release his thick, swollen erection.

A tiny voice in the back of my mind tried to warn me this was a terrible idea. That the momentary bliss of sex would never be worth the torment of the aftermath.

Yet I shoved the voice out.

Desperate for something. Anything but the pain between us.

Brodan held my gaze as he rolled on the condom and fell between my legs, his elbows braced on either side of my head as he kissed me.

I let my legs fall open, wide, and as he nudged, I breathed heavily into his mouth.

Brodan pushed into me. Hard.

My desire eased his way, but he was thick, and that over-whelming fullness I'd been desperate for shot electric sparks of pleasure down my spine.

I needed more.

"Brodan," I gasped, sliding my hands down his ass, pushing his jeans further out of the way so I could curl my fingers into his silken, hard muscle.

"Say it again," he growled against my lips, holding still inside me.

"What?" I murmured in a daze.

"Say my name."

"Brodan." I reached for his lips, but he pushed up onto his hands and moved his hips.

If rational thought ever had a chance, it was lost as my whole being, my entire existence, centered on the hot, fast, hard drive of Brodan Adair inside me. My hips rose in shallow thrusts to meet his, my cries filling his ears as his groans filled mine.

My fingernails dug into his arms as I held on to him, taking his thrusts with pleasured moans.

The tension inside me tightened, tightened, tightened every time he pulled out and slammed back in. So full. So overwhelmingly full.

Brodan was inside me.

Above me.

Surrounding me.

It was perfect.

And it took me to the edge so quickly. Too quickly.

"I'm close," I moaned.

He reached for my thigh, wrapping his big hand around it, and pulled it up against his hip, changing the angle of his thrust. There was a slight pain in it, but a good pain. It was too much. Just the right amount of too much. Hard and possessive and all-encompassing.

His jeans scratched deliciously against my bare thighs. The drag of his cock in and out of my tight muscles caused a

SAMANTHA YOUNG

rush of tingles to tighten the tension deep inside me. My heart raced so hard. My skin flushed hot. More.

Give me more.

Brodan's expression was harsh with desperation, his groans and huffs and fierce need fueling mine.

The tension inside me shattered, lights flickering behind my eyes, and I yelled his name as my inner muscles clamped hard on him and throbbed like a tight fist around his cock.

Brodan grunted, shock slackening his features. "Fuck!" His hips pounded faster against me and then momentarily stilled. "Monroe!" he groaned, his grip on my thigh bruising as his hips jerked with the swell and throb of his release.

As his climax shuddered through him, he let go of my thigh and slumped over me. I felt his warm, heavy weight and closed my eyes, disbelieving what just occurred.

Our labored breathing filled the tiny bedroom.

My pulse practically jumped in my throat.

Finally, the blood rushing in my ears calmed, and I became fully cognizant of our situation.

I sprawled on the bed with Brodan on top of me, between my legs, still inside me. We were both fully clothed, my thermal bottoms around my ankles and Brodan's jeans around his hips.

It had been frantic.

Aggressive.

Fucking.

And the best orgasm of my life.

Brodan stiffened and raised his head to look at me. Something tortured in his gaze made me freeze like a deer in headlights. Then his expression shuttered, and he pulled out of me, the muscle in his jaw flexing before he rolled off and sat up. I pushed onto my elbows, fear cooling my pleasure-heated skin as I watched him brace his elbows on his knees and his head in his hands.

The posture of despair.

What every woman wanted to see from the man who'd just thoroughly fucked her.

"Brodan?"

He tensed and then looked over his shoulder at me. His gaze dropped to between my legs, and I suddenly felt incredibly vulnerable. I pulled my thermals and underwear back on. Brodan pushed off the bed and shoved open the door in the hallway to the tiny bathroom. Inside, I heard some rustling and deduced as he came back out, zipped up, that he'd disposed of the condom.

The condom.

Because we just had sex.

I did not see that coming.

"Brodan?"

He shot me an unreadable look before he bent down to pick up his discarded coat. His eyes came back to mine as he shrugged it on. "So ... how did I compare to Arran?"

Pain so extreme sliced through me, he might as well have stuck me with a knife.

Realization dawned.

He'd kissed me back ... and fucked me for revenge.

To hurt me even more.

A chill crawled through me. I needed it. I needed to feel nothing but cold because otherwise, I'd break in front of him. And I wouldn't give the bastard the satisfaction.

"Get out. Now."

For once, he listened.

Brodan spun on his heel and marched out of the room and through the small caravan. The door slammed shut behind him seconds later, and a minute after that I heard the crunch of gravel as his car left.

I crawled off the bed, clutching my stomach like I'd actually been gutted, and I pushed into the tiny bathroom. With the shower on as hot as it would go, I stripped out of my thermals, promising to burn them later, and stepped under the hot spray. I scrubbed at my skin, trying to wash him away, my sobs filling the small room like a thunderstorm breaking the heat.

18

BRODAN

I t was official.
   I was a selfish fucking prick.

The words on the page of my book blurred every five seconds.

Monroe.

I couldn't get the woman out of my head.

Her breathy moans, the scent of her perfume, the feel of her tight and throbbing and hot around me.

Then the look on her face at the words even I couldn't believe had come out of my mouth.

Betrayal.

I'd never seen her wear that brittle expression before. Like every warm feeling she'd ever had for me died with just a few words.

All because I'd been scared shitless of what I felt as I moved inside her.

Like I was finally home.

That was terrifying, so I'd lashed out.

I wasn't even angry about her sleeping with Arran

anymore. I'd let go of that years ago. It was what came after that had wrecked me. Because Monroe Sinclair had abandoned me when so much shit was going on in my life, proving what I'd always feared.

The Adair men were cursed to lose the women they loved.

But every time I punished her for breaking me, I hated myself a little more.

I had to forgive Monroe or leave her behind for good.

This morning I'd taken another of Ery's yoga and mindfulness classes, but even that didn't help. Ery had watched me, concern wrinkling her brow, and I hurried from the class as soon as she called its end.

At the knock on my suite door, I dropped my book onto the bed and crossed the room to answer it.

"Lachlan?" I stared at my eldest brother, his eyes bloodshot with exhaustion. "Come in."

He gave me a closed-mouth smile and patted me on the shoulder as he passed. Closing the door, I turned as he took in the suite that used to be his.

"Feeling nostalgic?" I teased.

Lachlan threw a smirk over his shoulder as he moved about the room. "Only for the times Robyn and I shared in here without interruption."

Grinning, I sat down on the edge of the bed as he lowered himself into an armchair. "No sex for the new parents, then?"

He scrubbed a hand down his face. "We're honestly too exhausted."

Sympathetic, I assured, "I've heard it passes. Things will get easier."

Lachlan nodded. "I know. And believe it or not, it is worth it."

Aye, I was beginning to think maybe it was. "What brings you here, then?"

"I was checking in with Aria and Mac. Everything looks good, though."

Remembering my curiosity over Walker's admirer, whom I'd since seen around the castle, I said, "You've got a new housekeeper. Sloane. American."

He frowned. "My staff are off-limits, Brodan."

Annoyed, I held up my hands defensively. "Not interested like that. She just ... I was curious because she's American and I think she has a thing for Walk."

His frown deepened. "She was a hire of Aria's. Some connection to the family, so I agreed to house her and her daughter in one of the lodges on Loch Ardnoch."

"A connection to the Howards?" I raised an eyebrow.

Shrugging, Lachlan sighed. "I trust Wesley and, by default, Aria, so I'm not seeking answers to information they haven't provided themselves. Aria is doing an excellent job as hospitality manager and making my life easier, so this is the least I can do. Fuck, I'm so tired."

I gave my brother a piercing look. "You sure marriage and fatherhood are worth it?"

Lachlan sat forward in his seat, elbows to his knees. "Are you asking for a specific reason?"

Taking a breath, I opened a topic of conversation neither of us probably wanted to dive into. But I needed to. For Monroe's sake. "Arran told me you both got drunk at the anniversary ceilidh this year. You got blootered because you feared something happening to Robyn during childbirth ... because of Mum."

My eldest brother's scowl deepened. "That's true. Why do you mention it?"

Heart racing now, I exhaled slowly. I never wanted anyone to see me as the coward I saw myself as, but I had a feeling Monroe already did, so I supposed it didn't matter if Lachlan thought so too. "I'm ... uh ... I'm a-afraid to get close

169

to anyone. To a woman. I … I think that you're right. That we're cursed."

Lachlan gave me a grim nod of understanding. "To lose the women we love. You know I used to think the same. And I gave Robyn a hellish time because of it. I'm lucky she forgave me and took me back."

Blood rushed in my ears as I leaned toward my brother. I'd known that Lachlan had felt that way, and that Thane had felt so the opposite he'd gotten a tattoo that meant 'curse-breaker' on his shoulder. Thane's sense of control over life was just another reason I envied the bastard.

However, to admit my fears out loud to Lachlan—to know he truly understood something I'd kept bottled up inside for so long—was such a relief. "How did you get rid of it? The fear?"

My brother gave me a bolstering look. "You don't get rid of it, Brodan. It lives inside you all the time … But for the sake of the woman I love, I overcome it. Every day. I remind myself that a moment with Robyn is worth any pain I risk in the future. I slipped a bit when she was pregnant, but I had to get over that, too, because she needed me to be strong. She has her own fears, and I have to be the one who makes her feel safe. I have to put her well-being before my demons. Loving someone is to be selfless, Brodan."

Emotion clogged my throat, and I dropped my head.

Every shitty, selfish fucking thing I'd said to Monroe bounced around in my mind. "What if you've hurt the person you love? Damaged them. Can you come back from that?"

Lachlan was silent for a few seconds and then asked, "Is this about Monroe?"

My head came up, meeting his gaze. He flinched at whatever he saw in it.

"You'd be fucking ashamed of me, brother, if you knew half of what I've done to her to push her away."

"Do you love her?"

"She left me. She abandoned me."

"Do you love her enough to forgive her?"

Hot tears burned in my eyes. Embarrassed, I looked away.

"Brodan?"

I nodded, unable to speak as I forced down the tears.

"Do you love her enough to be selfless?"

I nodded again.

"Then you need to fix whatever is broken between you. *You* need to make amends, and her amends might follow."

Swallowing the lump, I asked, voice hoarse, "Is that how you got Robyn back?"

Lachlan nodded, a glint of humor in his eyes. "That, and a fuck ton of groveling."

My nose wrinkled at the thought. "Seriously? Groveling?"

Laughing at my expression, Lachlan stood and pointed at me. "Just you wait. She'll have you on your hands and knees, begging for her, before the year is out."

"I think I've got more pride than that."

"Fine. But unless you flush that pride down the toilet in the name of the woman you love, you'll have to make do with pride being the only thing in your bed to keep you warm at night."

I nodded, feeling like I was about to wade into a battle I might not win. Panic flickered through me. "Right. Say goodbye to my pride. Got it."

The very thought made me restless inside my bones. I muttered a curse under my breath and stood up. "I think I need a run."

"Robyn runs, too, when she needs to sort out her head."

"You're obsessed with that woman." Maybe giving into love was a terrible idea after all.

"Tell me," Lachlan drawled mockingly, "when was the last time you didn't think about Monroe Sinclair?"

Fuck.

I glowered at him. "Point taken."

1 9

MONROE

It had been two days since Brodan metaphorically gutted me. School was a much-needed distraction. But in the hours before and after class, the memory of him tormented me.

Coming home had been a huge mistake. I couldn't wait for the school year to pass so I could get the hell out of there.

Another distraction came in the form of Mum. On top of her hip issues, she'd developed osteoarthritis. She had an appointment with a specialist, so I'd taken the day off school to drive her to and from Inverness.

It was around one o'clock by the time we returned to her cottage. She'd been quiet and docile the entire morning, a reprieve from her acerbic tongue. In fact, it made me brave enough to bring up my dad again in the hopes of getting some answers this time.

I finished making tea in the small kitchen and took a cup and some biscuits to Mum, who sat at the dining table.

Sucking in a breath, I decided to say it before I lost my nerve. "I'm going to track down Dad. Arro says Mac could find him." It was true. We'd had coffee again last week, and when I'd told Arro about my father, she'd offered Mac's expertise.

Mum froze for a second, holding the cup in midair before her lips pinched tightly together.

Trying not to heave a sigh of exasperation, I walked into her small kitchen to wash the dishes she'd let pile up last night.

"Why?"

I glanced over my shoulder at the sharp word. "What?"

"Why would you want to find that auld bastard?" Venom tinged every word.

So much for her docile mood.

This woman had treated me like crap my entire life because of Dad's abandonment, but she hated him just as much as she resented me. "To make peace."

Mum gave a snort of disdain. "Well, it's too late for that."

"It's never too late." At the hard glint in her eyes, my stomach dropped. "What is it?"

"He's dead."

My heart missed a beat in fear. "What are you talking about?"

Taking a casual sip of her tea, she waited to reply calmly, "He called me about six years ago to tell me he was dying of cancer and wanted to get in touch with you. I told him he could rot in hell." She took another sip of her tea like she'd just told me Morag's was out of fresh bread.

I wanted to slap that cup out of her hand.

My skin felt suddenly cold. "You're lying."

Mum's eyes flashed in rage. "Why would I lie? Look up his death in the registry. He died rotting from the inside out, just as he should have."

No.

No, no, no.

"He wanted to talk to me?"

She shrugged. "Said he wanted to see how you were doing. Said he had things to say. I told him he was getting nowhere near you after he abandoned us."

Had things to say?

Had Dad wanted to apologize?

To make peace?

To give me peace?

To give himself peace?

And she'd stolen that from us.

Tears of fury brimmed over my lids. "Tell me you're lying."

Her eyes widened. "Och, don't give me that after everything that man did. I was protecting you."

I laughed in disbelief, and it was such an awful sound, even she flinched. "You've never protected me in your entire life. You did this out of spite. You never told me my dad was dead. For six years!"

"He was never a father to you!"

"No, he wasn't. But maybe we could have talked." A sob burst out of me, a wail that didn't sound like me at all. "We could have made peace."

She scoffed. "You're living in a dream if you think that would have happened. Look at you. Melodramatic girl."

"You know, you've always been a shitty mum, but you're also just a terrible, horrible human being!"

"How dare you speak to me like that! And over that man!"

"That man broke me in so many ways, Mum ... and I needed that last talk with him. I needed that. I needed to forgive him. And you stole that from me!"

"Some people aren't worth forgiving," she hissed.

In an instant, something snapped inside. A calm came over me as I grabbed my purse and keys and stood over her to lean in and hiss back, "You remember you said that."

I turned and strode for the door.

"Where are you going? I need help with my tea."

I stopped and looked back at her. "Help yourself. I won't be back."

"Monroe!" she yelled as I marched out of the room toward the front door. "Monroe!"

I yanked it open.

"You selfish, ungrateful wee bitch!"

Closing my emotions to her screaming, I slammed her door and got into my car.

Every muscle in my body ached as I forced myself to remain in control. I drove from her house to the caravan, parked, and stepped out to feel a blustery, icy breeze sweeping up the sand dunes from the water.

I pushed into it, eager for its swift caresses through my hair as I stumbled down the dunes and onto the beach. My strides were quick as I walked across the sand toward the shore. As if the universe knew I needed the solace, there was no one else here.

My feet hit the shoreline, the water soaking my boots as all the emotion I'd pushed down boiled up inside me. My chest heaved, my shoulders lifting as I struggled to breathe through the magnitude of it.

A scream tore from my lungs, turning into a sob as my knees gave way and I hit the wet sand. Pain so old and deep had finally ripped its way out, and I couldn't have stopped my body's wracking cries if I tried.

"Roe!" I heard the voice like a memory in my mind and ignored it.

"Roe!" It sounded louder now.

Then I jolted as strong arms wound around me, and my chin was forced upward.

Brodan.

"Roe, what the hell happened?"

I couldn't speak, couldn't think. Just collapsed against him as the sobs spilled out from that corner of my heart I'd locked up for so long.

His arms tightened around me, and I felt his chin on my head. "Fuck, Sunset, you're scaring the hell out of me." When my crying didn't ease, he squeezed me tight. "I'm here, Roe. I've got you. Shh, it's okay. I've got you."

I didn't know how much time passed in Brodan's arms on the cold beach, but eventually my sobs eased, even as the pain circled my ribs like the past was holding on far too tightly.

Then realization sunk in.

Who was comforting me.

Someone I did not want or need comfort from ever again.

I shoved Brodan away and stumbled to my feet as he fell on his arse in surprise. He gaped up at me, looking so much like the young boy I used to love that I felt my heart breaking all over again.

"Sunset?"

I flinched at the nickname. "Don't," I seethed. "Don't you dare."

"Roe ..." Brodan got to his feet, towering over me again. He wore nothing but a T-shirt and joggers, the T-shirt stretching over his impressive shoulders, making me feel small in his shadow. "What happened?"

"Nothing."

"Is it ..." Something like fear flickered across his face. "Is this about us?"

I scoffed, "No. It has nothing to do with you. When you left on Sunday night, I showered and scrubbed my body until my skin was raw."

He winced.

"And vowed to never give a damn about you again. So ... this has nothing to do with you, and I definitely don't need you, of all people, comforting me right now." I turned to leave, but then Brodan was in front of me. He held up his hands in a gesture to stop me.

"Please. Roe, let's talk. I have so much to say."

"I think you made yourself very clear. It was a revenge fuck, right?"

Horror slackened his expression, and I faltered a little. "No," he said hoarsely, taking a step toward me, but he stopped when I retreated. "No, it wasn't that. I don't know why I said that to you, and I'm not even angry about you sleeping with Arran. I know you were both wasted that night ... it was what came after. You abandoned me, Monroe. That's what I'm angry about."

Disbelief renewed the rage I had only seconds ago been determined not to feel toward him. "I abandoned you?" I stared at him incredulously. "I was humiliated, and you made me feel guilty, as if I'd cheated on you when you'd made it perfectly clear that you were in a serious relationship with someone else. A relationship, I might add, you told me you'd never be in, which was a lie. You just didn't want to be in a relationship with me!

"You messed with my emotions for years. But *I* was made to feel like the bad guy. And you never came after me. You threw me away at my first mistake after thirteen years of friendship. You were the one who was supposed to come after me. But you didn't. *You* were all I had. *I* wasn't all you had." Tears, stupid, frustrating tears, stung my eyes. "*You* weren't the one who was abandoned, Brodan."

He opened his mouth to argue, but I cut him off.

"I was so in love with you, it almost killed me."

Despair, genuine or manufactured, tightened his expression.

178

I sneered at myself. "I even thought of ending it once."

Brodan looked as if I'd stuck a knife in him. "Roe."

"Don't worry. It was just the melodramatic musings of a young woman who realized that almost everyone I'd ever loved couldn't love me back. I wanted to blame myself, which was why I contemplated jumping off the top of a college building. But as I stood there on the edge, I searched and searched for reasons, for actions so horrible they'd make the people I loved treat me like shit, and I couldn't find anything that warranted the cruelty. I was mad at my parents for not loving me, but I wasn't mad at you for not loving me the way I wanted. I was mad at you for messing with my head and for just not loving me, even as a friend.

"But I know I'm not a bad person. That I'm worth something. That the fault laid with my parents and with you. So I decided in that moment to step back from the ledge and promised myself that even if it took a lifetime, I wouldn't let bitterness consume me. I wouldn't stop searching until I found someone who loved me the way everyone deserves to be loved. Someone kind and protective and loving.

"Here's the sad thing, and this might even make you laugh at the absurdity of it, but I don't think I realized until these last few months that part of me still hoped that person could be you. And this occurred to me because I finally realized on Sunday night that the person I'm looking for will *never* be you."

Tears brightened Brodan's eyes. Real? Who knew?

Everything I'd bottled up inside was set free. Recklessly free. "I had an ex, someone I tried to love. He beat the shit out of me, just like Dad."

Shock, fury, passed over his face. Was that real too?

"What is it about me that makes the people who are supposed to love me want to hurt me?"

"Monroe," he whispered, as if in agony. "I'm so sorry."

I shrugged, brittle, cold, almost numb from what had transpired. That Dad was gone and I'd never get closure with him. That Mum had stolen that from me. That the only man I'd ever loved my whole fucking life was as bitter a disappointment as the people who raised me.

"You never lifted your hands to me, but I'm your punching bag all the same."

"Monroe, no—" He stepped toward me, but I raised my hands, my expression a stark warning for him to stay back.

"It doesn't matter. I'm leaving Ardnoch. For good. Once the year is up, I'm taking a job in the Lowlands. There's too much pain here." I looked at him, gesturing between us. "Even this place that was once so safe … it's all pain now. You have no idea how it feels to live your life with no one who truly loves you, Brodan. No idea how lonely that is. But I refuse to give up on finding someone. To give up hope, because without it, what's the point? So I need to let this place go. I need to let you go. Or I'm afraid I'll just disappear."

Sobbing, I turned my back on him and on the years spent and lost between us.

20
BRODAN

Years ago, when I first lost Monroe, I didn't think I could ever feel as bad as I felt in those months afterward. They were the reason I sought out acting. I wanted to lose myself in other characters, in other lives, so I didn't have to dwell on all I'd lost in mine.

Then a few years ago, I'd received a letter that fucked with my head, and I didn't think I'd ever feel guiltier, or more of a failure, as I had at that moment. Though the damage Fergus wreaked upon my family because of me certainly did its worst.

Nothing in my life, however, could prepare me for my current state of agony.

Once upon a time, Monroe Sinclair was so vital to me, I would have protected her against anyone who tried to hurt her, no matter what it took to make her safe and happy.

How was it possible that *I* could be the source of so much of her pain?

I think I'd allowed myself to believe that she hadn't loved me like I loved her. It had made it easier to let her go.

But as she tore me to shreds with her confessions, realization dawned.

Stunned, I let her leave me on that beach. I'd given her that space. Because I had a truth to uncover first before I spoke to Roe again.

I was like the walking wounded as I banged on Mrs. Sinclair's door the next afternoon. Waiting, I could feel my fury building, as if I needed that emotion to cope with how much everything bloody well hurt. I didn't sleep last night. I'd forced myself to stay away from Monroe's mum's door until I couldn't anymore. Answers were required.

They were essential.

She took a while to open, but finally Mrs. Sinclair appeared before me, looking as if she'd aged forty years in the eighteen since I'd last seen her. If she'd done what I was pretty certain she'd done, I'd blame her black soul for her physical decline.

She squinted at me, and then recognition slackened her wrinkled face. "What do you want?"

"We need to talk." I barged in, brushing past her as she blustered and gawped like a goldfish.

Finally, with a beleaguered sigh, she closed the door and followed me in, her walking stick thumping on the carpeted floor. Standing in her cottage was like going back in time. Barely anything had changed since the last time I was here. Speaking of which ... I turned to face her as she eased herself into an armchair.

"The letter I left for Monroe all those years ago ... you didn't give it to her, did you?"

Her lips pinched together, and then her eyes narrowed. "Are you the reason Monroe has been behaving like a petulant child recently? I thought you were off in Hollywood with your Hollywood sluts to keep you company. What do you care about Monroe?"

"Answer the question."

"Oh, you think because you're rich and famous, you can come into an old woman's home and interrogate her? I don't think so."

"The letter?"

She sneered at me and, for the first time, I saw pure malice on that woman's face. It destroyed me knowing this was what Monroe had been subjected to her whole life.

"You didn't give it to her." It wasn't a question. I already knew.

Fuck.

Stupid fucking arsehole for trusting this negligent cow to do one good thing for her daughter.

Before I could lose my temper, the front door slammed, and footsteps sounded down the hallway. Suddenly Monroe was there, clutching two grocery bags. Her eyes widened in shock, and her gaze moved from me to her mum.

Mrs. Sinclair huffed, "I thought you weren't coming back."

"I only came by to drop off one last shop and to ask you where Dad is buried." She glanced between us again as I froze at the news her father was dead. "What's going on?"

"This boy was just leaving, that's what's going on," Monroe's mum snapped.

"Monroe, put the bags down. Please," I requested.

"Get out!" Mrs. Sinclair snarled.

I glowered at her. "Not before she knows the truth."

"Oh, God, what now?" Monroe dropped the bags, as if she couldn't hold them anymore, groceries spilling onto the carpet at her feet.

I took a tentative step toward her, drinking in her beautiful face, wishing I could hold her as I told her the truth. Knowing that I might never hold her again. Swallowing hard against that thought, I said, "I never abandoned you, Monroe."

Her chin jerked back. "What do you mean?"

"That's enough!"

I pointed a finger at Mrs. Sinclair and clipped out, "You shut up."

Her lips slammed together like she couldn't believe I'd spoken to her like that. Auld witch.

Turning back to Roe, I explained, "When you ran off that night, you left your phone. I couldn't get in touch with you. And honestly, I didn't know if you'd want me to, so I came here."

Monroe shook her head slowly.

"I came here with your phone and a letter. In the letter, I apologized for how I reacted and I told you I just wanted to know you were all right. That you were"—emotion thickened my voice—"that you were still my best friend, and if I was still yours, then just to call me."

Tears brimmed in Monroe's eyes as she turned them accusingly on her mother. "I never got that letter or my phone."

"Which would make sense since I tried calling you for weeks after that." I took another step toward her. "I let my stupid pride stand in my way because I should have just come to you at school. But I convinced myself you were done with me."

"That *I* abandoned *you*." A tear slipped down Monroe's cheek, and I felt her torment like it was my own. Bloody hell. We were a fucking Greek tragedy.

And she wasn't wrong. Most of it was my doing.

Well, we wouldn't end as a tragedy. As much as she scared the shit out of me, life with her had to be a million times better than life without her.

Her tear-filled gray eyes flew to her mother. "Why?"

Mrs. Sinclair lifted her chin in arrogance. "You weren't meant for the likes of an Adair. I always knew that boy would hurt you. I was protecting you."

"Like you were protecting me when you didn't tell me my dying father wanted to see me?" she seethed.

What the fuck?

Yesterday, on the beach, when I'd been running and saw Monroe up ahead, it had felt like the world gave way beneath my feet at the sound of her scream tearing through the skies. That sound terrified me. Her agony haunted me. Now I think I knew what had caused the pain.

Rage churned in my gut as I glowered at her mother. "You didn't."

"I will not be talked to like this in my own home!"

"Fine." Monroe shook her head. "Never mind about Dad's grave. I want nothing from you ever again. I'll find out for myself. You can rot in isolation for all I care. *Never* call me again." Monroe turned and stalked out of sight.

"Just like your father! Abandoning your family! You horrible wee bitch!" Mrs. Sinclair screamed after her.

"Enough!" I barked, and she slammed back in her chair like she was frightened. That furious part of me found a perverse satisfaction in her fear. "You heard Monroe. Never contact her again."

"Or what?"

"I didn't protect her from you when I should have … but I won't make that mistake again. If I have to, I'll drive you out of Ardnoch to keep you away from Monroe."

"You can't do that."

"You'd be surprised what an Adair can do."

"You're threatening me? An old lady? Pathetic."

"No, what's pathetic is a woman so filled with spite and self-loathing she isn't even capable of loving her own child." I bent my head toward her, voice thick with promise, "Cross

Monroe again, and I'll make you a fucking pariah in this town. Understood?"

She scoffed, "So that's what's hiding behind that fake charm of yours. You're a bully."

"Takes one to know one." I cut her one last dark look and marched from that cold cottage. Outside, I searched left and right for Monroe, and relief filled me to find her sitting in her car. I hurried over and got into the passenger side.

Monroe startled, turning to me, face pale, eyes haunted, cheeks tearstained. I wanted to touch her, to wipe the tears from her face, but I knew it was too soon. "Brodan. I thought you left me."

I knew she spoke of eighteen years ago. "I didn't. But I did."

Monroe shook her head. "But I thought you threw me away because of Arran, and I was so angry at you. And all this bloody time, she kept your letter from me. I had to get a new phone, and they wouldn't transfer my number because you owned it."

"Shit." Of course. Technically, Lachlan owned it. He'd obviously stopped paying it and didn't bring it up because Monroe was not a topic I let anyone discuss.

"All that time," she whispered, grief-stricken. "All that time lost. And now all that's left between us is resentment and hurt."

Her words sliced through me. "That's not all that's between us, Roe."

"Yes, it is." She turned away. "It doesn't change the past. It doesn't change how you've treated me. Who you've become. I've been your target practice, Brodan. But … my heart can't take it anymore."

Panic suffused me, and I reached for her hands, gripping tight. "Please give me a chance to prove that's not who I am. I will never treat you that way again."

She eyed me incredulously. "I don't believe you. I loved you once in a way I have never loved anyone."

Emotion stung my nose and thickened my throat.

"But I love the boy I left behind. I don't love the man. I could never love someone who has treated me as you've treated me."

Fuck, that hurt. I released her hands and a strained huff escaped as I tried to suck back tears.

"I'm sorry," she whispered, sounding as lost as I felt.

I shook my head. "You've nothing to be sorry for," I told her gruffly. "Goodbye, Monroe." I got out of her car, the cold late-November air whipping across my skin like a slap from the universe. It made me halt before closing the door.

Monroe was right. There was no way she could love a man who'd treated her like the enemy for the last few months. Who had fucked her and then taunted her.

That was not the man I wanted to be. Ever again.

A man driven by his trauma and his fears.

Someone I was ashamed of.

Yet a man could change, couldn't he? A person could become better than they were before?

I turned around and bent down into the car.

Monroe's wide eyes held mine.

"No."

She raised a brow. "What?"

"Not goodbye." Determination filled me. "I've spent my life running from anything that might hurt me, but I'm done. I know with my very being that I will never intentionally hurt you again."

"Brodan—"

"You don't believe me. I know. I understand why. But you *will* believe me, eventually. I'm going to prove it. Just give me time."

"For what purpose?" She looked so exhausted I wanted to take her in my arms and keep her there forever.

However, patience was required for that outcome.

"To be with you," I answered honestly.

Her lips parted in shock.

"I want what I could have had if I hadn't acted like a frightened wee boy when we were kids. I want you." Deciding she'd had enough shocks for one day, I gave her a small smile and stood up to close her door.

The memory of her stunned expression made me smile sadly to myself as I walked toward my SUV. Patience wasn't one of my virtues, but for Monroe, I'd have all the patience in the world. Fear lingered in the background, just as Lachlan had warned, but I was done letting it win.

21

MONROE

I still wasn't quite sure how this had happened.

One minute I'd been sitting in the caravan, marking my kids' jotters, watching the sky darken before four thirty. And in what seemed like the next minute, I was standing in Mackennon Galbraith's cottage.

The knock landed on the door after the grind of kicked-up gravel drew me to the caravan window. To my surprise, two SUVs had parked beside my car, and then two very tall men jumped out of them. The security light outside the caravan door revealed them, and I drew in a breath at the sight of Brodan and Mac.

What the hell were they doing here?

The last few days had taken their toll. I was emotionally and physically drained by what had been revealed, still reeling from Brodan's pronouncement that he wanted me.

As much as I hated to admit it, a small part of me still belonged to the girl from the past, and *she* experienced a flare of relief and exultation. However, grown-up me didn't believe him. He was guided (or misguided) by guilt, and soon enough he'd realize what a mistake the two of us were together. We were from different worlds now. I was a primary school teacher, and he was a famous Hollywood actor. We made little sense. But the most important roadblock between us was my lack of trust in him.

I'd promised myself after the relationship with Steven turned violent that I'd never again allow a man to treat me like his punching bag, emotionally or physically.

Brodan's vow to never mistreat me felt like an empty pledge in the face of his past actions.

Which was why I was genuinely surprised to see him the evening after our moment in my car, now standing on the caravan steps with Mac.

I opened the door, licking my lips in nervousness, and Brodan stared at me wide-eyed for a second. Mac nudged him and cleared his throat. Brodan blinked rapidly and then walked right in.

Huffing in exasperation, I stepped back to allow Mac in too. They dwarfed the caravan as they looked around the small space. "Uh ... can I help you?"

Brodan turned to me, his expression granite with determination. "It's Baltic in here, and you're not staying in this death trap any longer."

"Excuse me—"

"He's right," Mac cut me off. "Gordon's caravan is old. It's not built with the proper insulation like the newer models in his park. You can't stay here in the winter, Monroe."

I raised an eyebrow at their bossiness. "You must be Mac."

He held out his hand. "Apologies. Mac Galbraith. Nice to officially meet you."

Shaking his big hand, staring up close into his ruggedly handsome face, I could *certainly* see the attraction. Brodan and Lachlan were the tallest of the Adairs, but Mac had height even on them. I was tiny next to him, and he was overwhelmingly masculine. "You too. Though I'm still confused by what you both expect to achieve here."

Brodan grinned at my schoolteacher voice, and I grew still at the affection in his smile. I hadn't seen that look in eighteen years. "We're moving you out. Right now."

Flabbergasted, I threw my hands up. "To where?"

"My cottage on Castle Street," Mac supplied, his gaze darting around the caravan again. "I have a tenancy agreement in the car you can read over. For now, let's get you packed up. Any of the kitchen appliances belong to you?"

I shook my head, too flustered to speak.

"Okay. I don't think we'll need too many boxes, but I'll grab some from the car." Mac disappeared out of the caravan.

I whirled on Brodan already walking toward the bedroom. "What are you doing?"

"Do you have a suitcase in here?"

"Under the bed," I answered without thinking. "Brodan! You can't just barge in here and take over."

"I can when your stubborn pride is keeping you in this shithole," he threw back. "I should have gotten you out of here weeks ago."

"It's not your place—" I cut off abruptly at the sight of him on his knees by the bed. "What are you doing?"

He reached under it, and my suitcase appeared, along with a shoebox. My cheeks flushed, my heart racing.

"What's in—"

"Don't!"

But it was too late.

He'd taken the lid off the shoebox.

Nosy bugger.

Feeling hot all over, I watched Brodan glance up from the contents with laughter on his lips and the mischief I remembered so well in his eyes. He lifted my pink vibrator out of the box. "Are you sure it's big enough?" he teased.

I lunged over the bed and snatched it out of his hand. "Put that back!"

"It's an honest question. I mean, I'm feeling a wee bit inadequate after seeing that."

"Shut up." I shoved it in the box, slamming the lid back on. "You can't just come in here and start nosing around in my things."

"Why? Do you have more sex toys lying around I should know about?" He peeked under the bed. "I'm surprised they'd fit with that thing taking up so much room."

"I'm going to kill you."

He stood up, chuckling. "Don't be embarrassed, Roe. Masturbation is perfectly natural, even if your choice of toys is not."

"You're a bastard."

Brodan's laughter filled the caravan as I grabbed the suitcase out of his hand and threw open the small wardrobe. I pulled clothes off their hangers and tensed as Brodan hovered near my back.

"Is that all you've got with you? Where're the rest of your clothes?"

"These are all of my clothes," I gritted out between clenched teeth.

He grunted, sounding agitated.

Embarrassed, I turned to glower at him. "Not all of us are made of money and can afford a house-sized wardrobe filled with clothes."

Those pale eyes locked onto mine. "I'm not judging *you*, Sunset."

The nickname tore through me. "Brodan—"

"I should have been taking care of you," he said with gruff self-reproach.

I stiffened. "I take care of myself. And anyway"—I turned to the closet—"I'm not yours to take care of."

There was a moment of silence and then I felt his heat score along my back. His breath tickled my ear as he leaned in, scattering goose bumps down my spine. "You've always been mine to take care of. And today is the day I stop failing at it."

"Got the boxes!" Mac called from the other end of the caravan, and I let out a breath as Brodan moved away.

It took less than half an hour to pack up my life, and I think I found that more depressing than anything. Ultimately, I let Brodan and Mac move me out of the caravan, because I knew they were both right. Living there in the cold autumn had been miserable, and I could only imagine winter would be horrendous.

Trying to exorcise Brodan's words to me in the bedroom, I followed them in a bit of a daze, driving my car out of the park and down the country road toward the center of the village. I parked in the allocated parking spot behind the row houses, and because there was no back door, I walked around the building to Castle Street where Brodan and Mac had parked out front of the cottage.

Touring the row house, I decided I didn't care if the whole situation was a sting to my pride. The cottage was lovely. It was comfortable and inviting. The front door led into the sitting room, with the staircase against the wall directly opposite the entrance. A wood burner (heaven!) sat in the corner of the living room, and of the two dark, worn leather sofas, one pointed toward the fire, the other toward the huge TV mounted on the wall. An actual television. It felt like forever since I'd had one of those. There were tartan cushions and throw blankets, footstools, and a battered wooden coffee table.

A doorway at the back of the room led into a small kitchen. It had been renovated and was very modern with sleek white cabinets, white tile flooring, and a gray quartz countertop. Lovely. A door off the kitchen led to a small downstairs bathroom.

Upstairs was a tidy guest bedroom and a primary bedroom. The main bedroom wasn't massive but cozy. An original fireplace must've been used by the prior tenants because there was ash in the grate and a basket of fresh firewood next to it. A fire in the bedroom too? This really was heaven. The bed took up most of the space, and the frame was made of solid dark oak. A pile of decorative cushions over plump, luxurious pillows made me want to dive right into it.

Yup, definitely worth my pride, I decided as I signed the tenancy agreement. I knew for a fact Mac and Arro were charging me way less rent than what the place was worth. That stung, too, but I was also incredibly grateful and told Mac so. He shrugged uncomfortably. "By Arro, Arran, and Brodan's account, you're family. We take care of our family."

Emotion clogged my throat, and I met Brodan's searching gaze.

"I told you," he said quietly. "I'll do whatever it takes to make this right."

Trepidation filled me. "The cottage is lovely, Brodan, but you must know that it's not enough. I can't be bought."

"I know that." His gaze moved to Mac.

Mac gave him an abrupt nod before informing me, "There's some food in the fridge, some milk. Here are your keys and my number." He held out said keys and a card. "You give me a shout if you need anything."

I took them. "Thank you again. Tell Arro I'll call her."

"I will do." He nodded at me, turned, and patted Brodan on the shoulder before walking out of the cottage.

As soon as the cottage door closed gently behind him, Brodan stepped toward me.

I tensed warily.

A flash of pain crossed his expression, but he halted. "If you're not too tired, I wondered if we could talk? There are some things that happened all those years ago that I want you to know."

To be honest, I wasn't sure my heart could take much more, but I'd spewed all my hurt at him on the beach, only to learn he had tried to reach out to me. Only my mother stood in my way. Again. I hadn't had time to fully process the wounds my mum had inflicted, but it eased me somewhat to know that Brodan hadn't just walked away.

So maybe, even if it changed little between us, it was only right I give him a chance to tell his side of the story.

"All right."

He was surprised by my capitulation but nodded grimly. "Shall we sit?"

I glanced down at the comfortable sofas. A place I could sit with the TV on, marking the kids' work in comfort. A place I could take a nap on lazy Saturday afternoons while the wood burner crackled warmly in the corner.

It reminded me of a little cottage I had when I worked in the Lowlands. I could have that again and be able to afford it myself almost anywhere but Ardnoch. So it mattered little what Brodan confessed tonight. I'd still be leaving next year.

Why did I need to remind myself of that?

A warning bell rang in the back of my mind, but I shut it off. "I could check to see if there's coffee or tea in the kitchen."

He nodded, nervously. "A cup of tea would be great."

Worried that Brodan seemed anxious when I didn't think he ever got nervous, I shot him a wary look and wandered into the kitchen. What I hadn't noticed before was that Arro had left me a hamper filled with tea and coffee, biscuits, crackers, cheese, and all different snacks. Warmth filled me. She was a good 'un, that Arrochar Galbraith.

A few minutes later, I returned to the living room to find Brodan had shrugged out of his jacket and was sitting on one of the sofas. I set down the tray of tea and snacks, took hold of my cup, and sat on the opposite sofa.

"Help yourself to some snacks. Arro left me a hamper."

Brodan smiled. "She's very mothering under that no-nonsense facade."

"She's been lovely to me." I met Brodan's gaze. Before, I hadn't thought him entitled to know, but after hearing about his letter, I decided to put the information out there. "I don't remember most of that night with Arran. I was so drunk … all I really remember is you showing up. And I got so drunk because Arran confirmed you were serious about Vanessa."

He studied me with such a neutral expression I didn't know what to think. Then Brodan sighed heavily. "I told you the truth—I'm not angry about that night anymore. Arran and I got over it. Besides, as Arran has reminded me many times, you weren't my girlfriend. I made sure of that."

I wanted to ask why, but I was afraid he'd misinterpret my need to know the truth as evidence I could be won over again.

Brodan settled back against the sofa, the shadows of sadness in the back of his eyes pushing to the forefront. I didn't want to feel sympathy for him, but my love for the boy he'd once been still existed. Still made me feel things I didn't want to.

"I loved you so much, Roe," he confessed hoarsely.

Every muscle in my body tensed as my heart leapt in my chest.

I saw the ghosts in his eyes haunting him. And I realized I was one of those ghosts. All this time … I had mattered to him once.

"I was terrified. I *am* terrified."

"Of what?"

196

"Losing you." He shrugged wearily. "We lost Mum and then my aunt. Watching Dad become this half person without Mum, I never wanted to let loving someone do that to me. When we were kids, it was fine. I feared losing you as I would be of losing anyone I loved, but as we got older and I realized I was *in* love with you, I tried to bury the feelings."

Compassion and hurt mingled. "Did you know I was in love with you?"

"I suspected it. Then you told me when you were drunk."

My cheeks heated, remembering it. "It was mortifying."

Brodan shook his head. "Never be mortified. It made me so happy, but it scared me shitless more. So I lied to you. I told you I had a girlfriend."

I jolted. "You lied about Vanessa?"

He nodded, shamefaced. "I thought if you thought I was dating someone else, you'd move on." He laughed harshly. "I just wasn't prepared for what that would look like. What it would feel like. When I saw you with Arran ... fuck, Roe, it was like someone tore out my guts. Is that what I did to you? With the girls? With Vanessa?"

I didn't want to go back there. I didn't want to relive it. "Brodan ..."

"Never mind." He exhaled. "I lied to Arran about her, too, to sell the lie. But I never lied to her. Vanessa ... we were just casual. But bringing her back to the castle sent mixed messages."

"She thought you were getting serious about her?"

"I made it clear that we weren't." He looked agonized now, and my heart raced with trepidation. "I swear, Roe, I made it clear. I've gone over and over all the moments together I can remember, and I made it clear."

"What happened?"

"It wasn't just on a whim that I came home that night. Something had happened the night before and ... I just ...

needed you." His eyes brightened. "I've told no one this story."

Blood whooshed in my ears. "Brodan ..."

"A group of us went to Vanessa's house. It was meant to be a casual hang. She lived in a big house in the country just outside Anstruther. Her parents were supposed to be down south for the weekend, but they came home that night. Vanessa left the room to talk with her parents, and we could hear her dad shouting. When she came back, her cheek was bright red, and I knew the bastard had hit her, but she wouldn't talk about it. She told us that her parents agreed we could stay the night, but we had to leave in the morning. An hour passed, and then her dad came into the room we were all hanging out in, and he had a shotgun."

My whole body chilled as Brodan's voice deepened with the memory.

"Oh my God."

"He was wasted and easily antagonized. Well ... he wouldn't let us out of the room. He held us at gunpoint, laughing like it was a big joke one minute, foaming at the mouth in rage the next. The girls were crying, even a few of the lads. The bastard didn't care he was traumatizing us," he sneered.

"What happened?"

"He eventually let us leave, but one of the guys called the police, despite Vanessa begging him not to. For Vanessa's sake, I refused to give a statement. And because of Lachlan's fame, they all agreed to keep my name out of it, otherwise it would blow up in the press. As it was, it made local news, and her dad was arrested. He did six months for it. I broke off the casual relationship with Vanessa that night. It was one of the shittiest things I've done. I was young and scared, and I didn't want to get tangled up in her mess when I wasn't serious about her. I know it was selfish. No one could berate me for it more than I already have."

"I'm so sorry," I whispered, hating that he'd gone through that ... and then come home for comfort only to find me with Arran. Suddenly, his violent reaction that night made more sense. He was already on the edge, and we'd flipped him right over it.

"The weeks after it, she texted me. She showed up at my classes, practically begging me to take her back ... to help her get away from her dad. I told her I would help her with the latter, but that I couldn't be her boyfriend. She didn't want one without the other." He shifted forward in his seat. "I was impatient with her."

Though I'd seen his impatience now for myself, I couldn't imagine nineteen-year-old Brodan that way. He'd always been so patient and kind.

As if he read my mind, he whispered, "I'd lost you, Roe. Something scary and shitty happened to me, and I needed you, but I'd lost you. You were gone. And it felt like there really was a curse on the men in my family. I couldn't help her because I was fucking drowning without you."

At the jagged emotion in his words, tears sprang free before I could stop them. I swiped at my cheeks to rid myself of their trails.

"I'm not telling you this to make you feel bad ... I just needed you to know where my head was at. How messed up I was. I thought you'd abandoned me. I was angry at you because I missed you so bloody much. Then ... a few years ago, something happened. Something that really fucked me up, and I've had a hard time dealing with it. I thought I'd dealt with it ... until you. Do you know about Fergus? About Lucy Wainwright?"

I nodded. "I saw it in the news. And Arro filled me in on a little more."

"About a year before Fergus went off the deep end, I got word through a friend from uni that Vanessa committed suicide."

Sympathy for her and for Brodan caused a deep pang in my chest. "I'm so sorry."

A muscle flexed in his jaw. "A few weeks later, a few of us from that night received letters. Vanessa wrote them before she killed herself. She left them for those of us she felt were to blame for that night and the consequences. In my letter, she ... she told me she'd loved me and I'd made her feel like I loved her too, only to abandon her. To leave her to her father. That she'd wanted me to protect her, and I'd failed."

Horror suffused me, and I reached for him, squeezing his hand between mine. "Brodan, no. You are not to blame for the actions of that man. And clearly Vanessa was not in her right mind when she wrote that letter."

I watched him fight back emotion, and I hated it could still gut me to see him in pain. "I know that." He covered my hand with his free one. "Logically, I know it. But it messed with my head. I fell off the edge. Starting fights, acting like an arsehole on movie sets. The tabloids loved it. Then Fergus and Lucy went after Lachlan, Robyn, and Mac, and it shook me out of my spiral. But it also compounded it. I started seeing a therapist. No one knows. But I had weekly sessions with him for just over a year. It helped a lot. So I thought I'd dealt with it. But seeing you again triggered it all." He pulled me toward him, remorse haunting his gaze. "Roe ... I channeled all that anger and fear and hurt into you, and I am so fucking sorry. I cannot even tell you how sorry I am. Every time I think about what I said, what I've done, I feel sick to my stomach."

Searching his face, every tortured feature, I saw only the truth. "I believe you. And I forgive you."

Vivid relief slackened his features. "Really?"

I nodded but gently extricated my hands and sat back. He watched my movements with the intensity of a hunter. Disappointment glimmered in his eyes before I even said the words, "But that doesn't mean I can be with you."

Brodan swallowed hard.

"I appreciate you telling me all this. It makes sense of so much. And while I think I can try to be friendly ... I ... that you can hurt me so deeply terrifies me, Brodan. We are not the same people we were back then, and we're holding on to the love between two kids who don't exist anymore."

"I don't believe that," he whispered.

Needing to guard myself against him, I stood up. "I can offer you friendship, but nothing more."

Brodan slowly stood too, towering over me, so goddamn handsome it hurt. "I can accept friendship ... but if we're going to be honest with each other from now on, I should tell you I intend to make you fall back in love with me."

A bubble of surprised, nervous laughter slipped out. "W-What?"

He nodded, deadly serious. "I'm staying in Ardnoch. I have no real clue what I'm doing with my life, but the one thing I know is that I've missed home beyond bearing ... and Ardnoch isn't truly home without you, so I'm going to prove to you I can be a better man. For myself. For my family. For you. And you are going to fall back in love with me."

I crossed my arms over my chest at his arrogance. "You're so sure of yourself?"

Determination gleamed in his eyes. "I know that when I put my mind to something, I rarely fail. Prepare yourself, Monroe Sinclair, because I'm putting my mind to making up for the last eighteen years so we don't spend the next eighteen without each other."

22

BRODAN

Glancing back at Arran and Eredine's house, I waved to Ery as she stood in the doorway watching me and my brother walk down the drive.

"The place looks great." I turned to Arran as we made a right. The house Thane designed for him had been completed a few months ago, and my brother wasted no time asking Eredine to move in with him.

"We love it." Arran flashed me a quick smile. "Your plot is waiting for you."

Anticipation filled me at the thought of putting down roots. "Aye, I'm planning on talking to Thane about it."

Arran raised an eyebrow. "You're going to build?"

I nodded.

"Is that why you wanted to talk this morning?"

We passed the plot of land that belonged to me, and I pictured a house there with big windows overlooking the sea. I also pictured Monroe there with me. At the end of the property we Adairs owned in Caelmore was a path that led down through the fields and into sand dunes before hitting a small public beach. That's where I led Arran.

"Brodan?"

"Let's talk once we hit the beach. I'll be too busy avoiding sheep shite to concentrate on conversation," I cracked. It was true. Our land abutted a local farmer's, and he used his for grazing.

My brother shot me a curious look but remained silent. Ten minutes later, we'd traversed our way downward, through fields and dunes and onto the golden sands of the beach.

Despite the winter chill, there was only a slight breeze, and the water lapped gently at the shore for this time of year. Not another soul walked along the small beach, which was what I'd been counting on.

I walked, gesturing for Arran to follow me.

Then I talked.

After I'd shared the story of Vanessa and her dad with Monroe, I realized the world did not, in fact, end. Better yet, Roe's forgiveness made me feel less ashamed. For years, I'd felt like the most disloyal coward for leaving Vanessa behind in the aftermath of that night, knowing that the small moment I'd experienced at the hands of her father was nothing compared to what she'd gone through with him. I'd told myself that because I didn't love her, it was none of my business.

But really, I was young and too devastated by my own loss that I couldn't see past my selfish fucking nose. The letter she'd sent me a few years ago had made me step outside my own actions, and I hated what I saw in myself. I was a fucking coward. Those feelings were only compounded by the fact that the world saw me as some kind of hero.

The world had no idea who I was.

My therapist had tried to show me reason and rationale, to help me move past it. I thought I had to some extent. But I hadn't.

Not until Roe had forgiven me.

If she could forgive me, then I knew I could be a better man going forward.

If she could forgive me, I knew suddenly that my family would too.

So that morning on the beach, I told Arran everything.

When I was finished, my brother didn't say a word for what felt like forever. Agitated, I wondered if I'd overestimated the situation. But then my brother stopped, pulling on my arm to draw me to a halt.

Worry creased his brow as he glared at me. "Why the fuck didn't you tell me years ago, Bro? You knew about Colin's death and how much guilt I carried because of it. Don't you think that I, of all people, would understand?"

Years ago, while Arran was in Thailand, he'd gotten drunk and took a swim in the ocean. His friend, Colin, had thought he was in trouble and ran in to save him, only to drown himself. "Your guilt was misplaced. Mine isn't."

"Funny, but that's what I think—that yours is misplaced, but mine isn't. Because that's how guilt works."

"I fucked up," I whispered roughly.

My brother cursed under his breath and then hauled me into his arms. I held on to him like he was a lifeline, relief easing the tension within. "You can tell me anything," he said gruffly, "and it'll never change us, brother."

Emotion thickened my throat and I nodded, patting his back with an appreciative thump that he reciprocated. We pulled away, giving each other a reassuring look, and then turned around to make our way back down the beach.

"You should tell Lachlan, Thane, and Arro," Arran said. "They've been worried about you for years. Knowing the truth will give them some peace."

"I will," I promised. "But it's not the only reason I wanted to talk to you."

"Monroe," Arran surmised. "You said the incident with Vanessa's dad happened that same night you found us. Now I get why you lost it so completely."

"Well, I was definitely on edge, but make no mistake, most of my rage was at finding you with the girl I was in love with."

Arran looked tortured as he hissed hoarsely, "You should have told me."

"I know," I assured him. "And I'm not blaming you. For the first time in my life, I want to be honest about it. Don't think I haven't noticed you trying to antagonize me into admitting it."

My brother gestured between us. "I think it might have worked."

"Being around Roe worked. But I've been a total and complete prick to her since I got back."

My brother cut me a dark look. "So I've heard."

"It's worse than what you've heard." I told him about the night in the caravan.

Arran gave me a look so fierce, I thought he might hit me.

"You don't have to say or do anything." I held up my hands defensively. "I hate myself enough for it, believe me."

He grunted.

"Arran, I'm trying to make it up to her."

"For what purpose?"

At his suspicious tone, I replied honestly, "To win her back."

He considered this, then shocked me by asking, "And you're sure this isn't just a whim? Not too long ago, you were pissed off at me for dating Ery because you had a thing for *her*."

I'd thought often about how easily I'd gotten over my

feelings for Eredine, and after some self-analysis, I came to a surprising conclusion. "She reminded me of Roe."

Arran's eyebrows rose.

I chuckled dryly. "I know they don't seem alike, but behind her smiles, Roe always had this haunted look in her eyes. Because of her fucking parents. And every time I caught that look, I wanted to make it better for her. I wanted her to know that someone loved her, thought about her, wanted to be with her. Even if I could only do it through friendship. I saw that look in Ery's eyes, and I think I was drawn to her because of it. I love Ery," I promised him, "but I was able to let go of the idea of her too easily for it to have been anything more than platonic. And I know that because every time I see Monroe …" I looked away, fear rising in me that it was too late. "It feels like I've been sleeping for years, and then suddenly she's there, and I'm awake. I'm fucking terrified of losing her, Arran. What do I do?"

My brother rested a hand on my shoulder and squeezed it in sympathy. "You grovel like you've never groveled before."

A bark of laughter burst out of me. "Lachlan said the same."

"Our big brother should know. I hear he groveled his arse off to get Robyn back. Even flew to Boston for her."

I chuckled at the thought because my big brother, especially during his Hollywood days, was an even bigger ladies' man than me. "How the mighty have fallen."

"Look who's talking. On that note"—Arran frowned—"have you really thought this through? Just because you've had some peace and quiet here the last few weeks doesn't mean you should forget that you're famous, Brodan. The world will be very interested in Monroe if you choose to settle down with her here. Do you think she can cope with that kind of scrutiny? Can you cope? It's different putting up with that shit for yourself, but when it affects someone you love, it'll be ten times harder."

I had thought about it. Of course, I had. "I have to try, Arran. I can't live the rest of my life regretting not trying to be with her. She's the one." I shrugged helplessly. "She always has been. It scares the absolute shit out of me, but continuing to live an empty life without her terrifies me more."

Arran blew out a breath. "Fuck, when we Adairs fall, we don't do it by half measure, eh?"

"Aye, maybe that's why it's so bloody scary."

"Well, if you're sure Roe is who you want, then it's simple. Words won't work with Monroe. Actions. Let your actions speak for you."

"She's closed off to me. Not just because of what I've done, but because of what others have done. There was a bad previous relationship."

Arran scowled. "Is there someone we need to kill?"

I nodded grimly. "Most likely."

"Fuck." He shook his head. "Life is so unfair sometimes. She's had it harder than most."

"I want to make it better."

"Then that's what you do. Make Roe's life better, for her, not for you, and without taking her choices away as you do it."

I considered this as we walked up the dunes toward the fields. Pride swelled in my chest. "You're a good man, Arran."

He looked at me seriously. "You are too, Bro. I promise."

23

MONROE

I t was quite the novelty being able to walk out my front
door and stroll toward Flora's in just a few minutes.
Living in the cottage was life changing. I hadn't realized how
miserable I'd felt coming home to that caravan every evening
and waking up in it every morning.

Now I couldn't wait to get home and throw some wood
on the fire, pour a glass of wine, and check my kids' online
homework with the TV playing in the background.

That I had the Adairs (i.e., Brodan) to thank for it was a
bit awkward, but I could deal with that to have a lovely place
to rest my head at night. Not that I found falling asleep easily
these last few nights. The culprit was, of course, Brodan.

He was being *nice* to me.

At the musical rehearsals over the last two days, he'd
been kind and attentive and respectful toward me. He
wasn't overtly flirtatious or unprofessional. Just nice. There
was something different about him. Something ... lighter.
Like a burden had been lifted. Even Ellen and David
commented on the change in his demeanor. I couldn't help
but wonder if his confession and my forgiveness had

effected such a change. Could my opinion really matter that much to him?

Ugh.

I was in turmoil.

As much as I appreciated his newfound attitude, I couldn't let go of how he'd treated me previously.

When he asked me to meet him for coffee on Saturday, I was relieved to tell him honestly that I already had plans with Sloane Harrow for brunch at Flora's.

The truth was, I needed a friend who wasn't an Adair. As much as I loved Arro, she'd no doubt root for whatever made Brodan happy, and if she thought that was me, there would be pressure. Regan would be the same.

An impartial friend who I might talk to about this stuff once we got friendlier sounded like a solution. Therefore, I called Sloane and asked her to brunch. Luckily, Callie was spending the day at Lewis's. He'd invited her over to play his new video game. They'd become like two peas in a pod in class, and my chest ached every time they reminded me of how Brodan and I were as kids.

That's all it was, I told myself continuously. Brodan wasn't in love with me now. He was just confused by our long history and the love we'd shared as children. He'd realize that soon enough, and who would end up hurt again? Me. Thus, I was standing strong against whatever plans he had to make me fall in love with him again.

I even googled him last night.

I knew it was a bad idea.

But I was weak and needed some armor against him.

Seeing images of him with one stunning beauty after another and reading articles about his dating history helped. I was nothing like those women. For a start, they all seemed comfortable in the spotlight. I most certainly was not. And being in a relationship with Brodan Adair would change life as I knew it. My face would be plastered over tabloids and the internet, and jealous people would make nasty comments and question why he'd chosen me. The speculation would make me feel trapped in my own skin.

Um, no thanks.

"That's a serious look." Sloane's voice interrupted my thoughts.

I blinked, realizing I'd been so lost in my musings, I'd walked into Flora's on autopilot. I turned to find Sloane at a table by the window. "Hi." I laughed wryly at myself. "I'm so sorry. I was in dreamland."

She flashed her glamorous smile and gestured to the empty chair. "No worries. I visit there often."

Chuckling, I took the seat. "How are you?"

"Still having 'pinch me' moments that Callie and I live in the Scottish Highlands now, but otherwise, good."

I wanted to ask what had brought them here, but I sensed it would be better to leave it to Sloane to tell me. "But you like it here?"

"What's not to like? Everyone is so friendly. Callie's found a new best friend, and I have a stable job and a nice place to live."

"It's not strange wandering that castle, seeing all those famous faces?"

She shrugged. "I'm from LA. I grew up seeing a famous face or two."

"Right."

"Have you ever been to the castle?" Sloane asked. "It's something to see."

Nostalgia seized me as memories of running through the halls filled my mind. "I used to be quite familiar with it before they renovated. It used to be the Adairs' family home, but they only lived in a small portion."

"Really?" Sloane leaned forward, her chin on her fist. "So you're friends with them all? I did sense that at the bake sale."

Melancholy threatened. "I used to be best friends with Brodan. When we were kids. Much like Callie and Lewis. It's wonderful she's found a good friend." I attempted to change the subject.

Sloane's whole face lit up. "I'm so relieved. And Regan is a sweetheart. She's been telling everyone about my baking, and I got a few orders for birthday cakes."

Flora stopped at our table. "What can I get you, ladies?"

I greeted her warmly before she took our orders, and she rested a hand on my shoulder and squeezed. I met Flora's eyes, and she offered a grim smile, and I knew she knew. Last evening I'd popped in to see her mum, and I'd told her I wasn't helping my mum anymore. I'd even told her why. Belle understood. She hadn't known my dad had died either. Apparently, Mum had told no one. Belle was so sad for me, and I'd tried my best to assure her I was okay. She'd obviously told Flora.

I think I'd been ignoring my feelings about Mum. It was easier to be distracted by Brodan than to contemplate my mother's lies. To contemplate searching for my dad's resting place.

I couldn't think about it just yet.

Sloane and I fell easily back into conversation. While we dodged personal details about our pasts, we were comfortable with each other, and I sensed that one day we could confide the hard stuff. I'd always had a gut instinct about people, about whether a person would be a casual acquaintance or a friend I could have a fun but shallow relationship with—or someone with whom I could share a deep, genuine friendship.

I hadn't felt the latter in years, which was why I moved back to the Highlands without it upsetting anyone's life back in Glasgow. Sure, I got a text now and then from teachers I was friendly with down there, but that was it.

Sloane Harrow was the first person in a long time, outside of the Adairs, who I felt so comfortable with that it was like we'd known each other for years.

It wasn't ideal that I taught her daughter, but Ardnoch was a small place, and these things couldn't be avoided.

Sloane was in the middle of telling me that Regan had already invited her and Callie to spend Christmas with the Adairs, since they were alone here, when her attention drifted outside and she paused midsentence. A flush crested her cheeks, and I glanced out the window.

I tensed in my seat.

Brodan and Walker were strolling toward the café.

Shit.

Butterflies fluttered to life in my belly.

Seeing Sloane's suddenly bright eyes, I shifted uncomfortably. "I thought you were used to famous people."

Her gaze flew to mine. "Oh. Oh no, yeah, I am. It's not … I have a little crush on Brodan's bodyguard."

I relaxed and hated myself for the reaction. "Ah."

"He's just so …" Her dreamy stare drifted back out the window. "Rugged and sexy and tall. He works on the estate, too, you know. Every time I catch a glimpse of him at work, I swear my knees turn to jelly. What is that? I've never reacted like this to a guy. And that accent … yum. And he likes my baking a lot." Sloane's lips pinched together for a second. "But he doesn't seem to know I exist beyond the baking. Not that I need to be in a relationship. In fact, I need a relationship like I need a hole in the head." She leaned toward me and whispered, "It would be nice to get laid, though."

I chuckled, nodding. "Aye, I know that feeling."

Sloane grinned. "And I could climb that man like a tree."

I burst out laughing just as the bell above Flora's door tinkled.

"What's so funny?"

Tensing, I looked over my shoulder to see Brodan smiling at me. Walker stood by his side. The two of them, as always, filled the small café. I shrugged. "Just girl talk."

He studied my face like he was memorizing every feature before he looked at Sloane. "Nice to see you again."

"You too." She smiled prettily at him, immediately turning it on Walker. "Hi, Walker."

"Sloane." He nodded at her and then at me. "Monroe."

"Hi."

"Flora, my love, how are you?" Brodan called across the busy café. "Any extra seats so we can join these lovely ladies?"

Flora tittered like a schoolgirl as she nodded, and Walker followed her into the back to grab the folding bistro chairs.

Fuck.

Sloane practically squirmed with delight. "Looks like we have company."

Of course, it was thrilling for her to sit with her crush. Not so thrilling for me to sit with Brodan.

It pissed me off.

I'd told him I had plans, and he'd deliberately crashed them.

Narrowing my eyes on him, I let my displeasure emanate from me as they tried to squeeze their too-tall bodies into the small chairs. Brodan, of course, sat beside me. He leaned his elbows on the tiny table, so his arm touched mine. His grin was wickedly boyish and sexy as hell. "Well, this is cozy."

I glowered at him.

The bastard grinned harder.

"Oh, sorry," Sloane suddenly said, her cheeks flushed as she shot Walker a look.

He waved her off. "I'm the one who kicked you." He

scowled at Brodan, but his friend and boss wasn't paying attention.

"You look beautiful," Brodan said sincerely.

Determined not to be swayed by flattery, I stared stonily at him. "You look squashed. So does Walker."

Walker grunted in the affirmative.

"I'm definitely not squashed." He pressed his leg against mine under the table. "I'm just right."

"You're no' right in the head, more like it," I replied.

"I think I am for the first time in years."

I sighed. "What are you doing here?"

"Joining you for brunch."

"No one invited you."

"I did."

"That doesn't count."

He smirked. "I just assumed you were too shy to invite me."

"I have never been shy around you, Brodan Adair."

"Oh, don't I know it." He wiggled his eyebrows suggestively.

I was going to kill him. "So ... this is the way you've chosen to die?"

He smiled so big it almost broke me. "I'd prefer to be under you in that moment, but a man takes what he can get."

"Brodan!" I shoved him, glancing around to make sure no one beyond our table heard him.

Sloane choked on her laughter as Brodan threw his head back and let his go. It drew stares, and I wanted the ground to swallow me whole. "You're making a scene."

His laughter quietened as he searched my face. "I'll make you laugh again someday, Sunset."

Pain lashed through me, and his eyes darkened as if he saw it.

Sloane cleared her throat as she pushed back from the

table. "Actually, I just remembered I have things to do, so I really should be going. Walker." She looked down at him. "Would you walk me out? I baked some cupcakes for Regan and Thane since they've been so welcoming, and I have extra. They're yours if you want them."

If Walker was a man that pounced on an excuse to leave a situation, I think he would have. Instead, he nodded casually and stood slowly, stepping back to allow Sloane past him.

"Sloane—" I gave her a pleading look.

She smiled apologetically. "We'll catch up later. I'll call you."

I nodded, trying to not be sullen about her departure.

"Walk." Brodan said his friend's name as a goodbye.

"Brodan." Walker smacked him so hard on the shoulder, Brodan flinched. I decided I really liked Walker Ironside. "Monroe."

"Bye." I gave him a weary wave.

Then they were gone.

And everyone in the café was trying not to look at us ... and failing.

"You can go too," I said under my breath to Brodan.

But Flora approached with a tray of food. "I take it this is for you two now?"

"We can't waste Flora's efforts," Brodan answered with faux innocence.

I smiled sweetly. "I hope you choke on a sandwich."

Flora choked on a snort as she laid the plates out. She winked at me. "Enjoy."

Staring at Brodan, I huffed, "If you're staying to eat, you can move."

He smirked. "Is my proximity too much of a temptation?"

"To stick this butter knife in your thigh? Aye. Far too tempting."

"I walked into that one," he murmured congenially, but he got up to take Sloane's empty chair.

I could breathe a little now that I wasn't enveloped in his heat and aftershave. "What are you really doing here, Brodan?"

His expression turned serious. "I wanted to spend time with you, and I knew that you wouldn't agree to it."

"So, you *forced* it?"

"I … I'm … fuck." He sank back in his chair, scrubbing his hands down his face. "I'm sorry." He pushed up from the table. "I'll leave."

"Sit down." I sighed in exasperation. I shouldn't have capitulated, but he looked so much like that lost wee boy I still held in my affections.

He sat down so quickly it was almost comical. "I promise I won't do it again."

"Don't make promises you can't keep, Brodan Adair."

"I love when you second name me," he teased. "It does things to me."

"Don't flirt with me either." I pointed my fork at him in warning.

Brodan shook his head. "No, can't promise that."

I rolled my eyes and dug into a sandwich so I didn't have to deal with him for a few seconds. Then, still feeling as if we had an audience, it reminded me to ask, "No calls from Hollywood, then? No film sets awaiting your arrival?"

He swallowed his bite of pastry. "I think I'm done with acting."

My breath caught, but I didn't let him see this news affected me. "Think?"

He shrugged. "I used to see this therapist."

"You mentioned that." It still shocked me, but I admired him for it. "I'm glad."

"Aye, well, we talked about how acting was my escape. I

216

wanted to get lost in other people's lives because it was easier to deal with than my own. Especially after my dad died."

I'd heard from my mum about Stuart Adair's death. At the time, I grieved him, and I grieved for his children, for Brodan. I'd wanted to go to Brodan. To stand at his side for the funeral, but I'd believed then that I wouldn't be welcome. Now I knew differently.

"I'm so sorry about your dad, Brodan. I'm sorry I didn't come to his funeral. I regret it."

Brodan reached across the table and curled his hand over mine. "I understand. And thank you." He released me and sat back in his chair. "I was so angry when he died because I felt like I hadn't gotten a chance to really know him. That I'd pushed him away as much as he'd pushed us away. We had a complicated relationship, and it left me with lots of regrets. So I buried myself in acting. I realize how true that is now. How empty I was in between takes. I don't want that to be my life, Roe. To turn into my father and be so crippled by fear and grief that he held the people who loved him at arm's length. *I* want to come home. I want to see my nieces and nephews grow up. Maybe," he paused for a second, "maybe have kids of my own."

My gut twisted at that. "Oh."

"So, no, I'm not going back to acting. But I still like the world of storytelling, you know. I've, uh, I've been working on a script."

Surprise suffused me. "Really?"

Brodan nodded, seeming almost shy. "I don't know if it's any good. I actually … I wondered if you might read it."

"Me?" I pressed a hand to my chest. Surely, he was mistaken. "Brodan, what do I know about scriptwriting?"

"You read more books than anyone I know and I come from a family of readers. But I don't want their opinion as much as I want yours. You know a good story. That's all I want to know. I want your honest opinion, if you think it's a good story. I trust you."

Well … damn it.

"Brodan—"

"Please."

Sighing, I nodded. "Okay. I'll read it for you."

"Great." He smiled. "I'll come over to your place with it. I'll bring wine. The good stuff."

I narrowed my eyes. "You opportunistic bastard."

Brodan chuckled and shrugged unapologetically.

"You'll bring it to school next Thursday. I'll read it in my own time, and I'll get back to you. Now shut up and eat some of these sandwiches."

"I like this bossy side of you." His gaze smoldered. "I'd quite like to see how it translates in the bedroom."

I stiffened, arming myself against his flirty, cocky charm. Not meeting his eyes, I said quietly, "The last time you were in my bedroom, you humiliated me, so you'll never be back there again."

Once more, Brodan reached across the table to curl his hand around my wrist. Tortured sorrow darkened his countenance. "If I could take back those words, I would. But know that I did not intend them to humiliate you. I said them to push you away because I was so scared of how fucking amazing it was to be with you." His grip tightened. "I would never lie about this, Monroe. And I would never say these words to win you over. I'm saying these words because they're the truth. Until I ruined it … that night with you was the best night of my life, second only to our afternoon in the castle turret."

Heat flushed over my skin as his words caused a deep flip low in my belly. I squeezed my legs together under the table and yanked my wrist out of his hold. All the outrageously beautiful and experienced women he'd been with, women from all over the world, and he expected me to believe that our rushed fuck in the caravan and inexperienced fondling in the turret were the best of his life?

"Talk to me, Sunset."

I looked him straight in the eye. "I *don't* believe you. And I want you to stop. It hurts me, Brodan."

"Why don't you believe me?" he almost pleaded. "Monroe?"

"Because," I hissed, leaning over the table. "I've watched on, with the rest of the world, as you moved from one extraordinary woman to another, and you expect me to believe that I'm special." I snorted and pushed back from the table. "The only thing special about me, Brodan, is I'm the first woman to say no to you. I'm a challenge, and you'll grow bored. Like always." I stood and yanked my wallet out of my bag, fumbling for some notes. I threw them on the table as he glowered up at me. "Just leave me alone."

I hurried out of the café, no longer caring if I stirred up a hornet's nest of gossip, and strode quickly toward the cottage.

"Roe!" Brodan called after me.

Fuck!

I whirled around. "Do you not understand English?"

Determination and anger etched his features as he marched toward me and only drew to a stop when inches separated us. "Aye, I've been with a lot of women. And every single one of those encounters was empty because I wanted nothing more from them than the quick relief of sex."

Jealousy soured my gut. "Brodan—"

"I don't know what makes someone the person who fits you." He shrugged in exasperation. "But you have been that person since I was a wee boy. First as my best friend."

"Brodan—"

"Then ..." He breathed hard, like he'd been running.

219

"Then one day, we were walking along the beach, and you turned to smile at something I said, and I felt your smile here." He placed a fist to his lower belly. "You gave me butterflies. I'd never had butterflies in my fucking life." Brodan stepped closer. "We were fifteen, and it had been warm that morning so you were wearing this blue strappy summer dress. But the weather changed as we walked on the beach. The wind kept whipping your hair and dress. You weren't wearing a bra, and your dress was molded to every inch of you … and I wanted to lay you down on the beach and make love to you."

Shocked, I gaped at him. I remembered that afternoon. Brodan had gotten cool and distant with me, and it was so unlike him, I'd worried.

"Ever since that day, I couldn't separate loving you from wanting you. And I knew that if I gave into those feelings, you would become everything to me. Because you just fit, Roe. You fit me. I refuse to be that scared wee boy who didn't realize what you meant to me … you were already everything to me. You always will be. Eighteen years apart just numbed the empty ache you left behind. But now you're here, in front of me, and I know that you're my missing piece. No one will ever fit me like you do. No one."

My tears spilled free before I could stop them.

Brodan reached out to cup my face and brush the salty drops with his thumbs. He bent to rest his forehead on mine. "One day you'll believe me," he promised before pressing a gentle kiss to my forehead.

Then he was gone, walking back down the street toward Flora's.

Leaving me there in a confused state of a million emotions.

24

MONROE

Before I knew it, it was December 1. Like every year since my early twenties, the weeks had melted into the next until another year was almost over.

Standing back from the kids and watching them rehearse, pride filled me. The musical was coming together. Callie had grown more confident over the past few weeks and was a wonderful Dorothy, with the sweetest voice. Lewis was hilariously bumbling as the Scarecrow, and one of David's tallest pupils, Andrew, was over-the-top dastardly as the Wicked Witch.

"They're doing great," Brodan murmured as he stepped beside me.

I tried not to tense as his upper arm brushed my shoulder. He was so much bigger than me. Big men made me wary. Brodan did, too, just not physically. "They are," I agreed.

Yesterday at rehearsal was my first time seeing him since he crashed brunch the weekend before. Since he'd said those heartfelt words that kept running around and around in my mind. I didn't want them to seep into me as they had. I wanted to forget them, in fact. But every time I tried, his anguished face flashed in my mind, and my stupid, neglected, battered heart clung to his declaration.

In my need to protect myself, I hadn't exactly been warm to him yesterday, but Brodan was immune to my aloofness. It reminded me that when Brodan Adair wanted something, he got tunnel vision. There was no one as determined as this man. That much hadn't changed about him. The thought exhilarated as much as it frightened me. My frustration with myself and him was at explosive levels. It was another reason I was wary of being around him at school. I was afraid I'd detonate all over him one of these days, and I didn't want witnesses.

"I have my script with me. I wondered if I could pop round to yours after school with it?"

"Just post it through the letter box," I murmured.

"Monroe."

At his tone, I looked up at him. He stared down at me, expression almost vulnerable. "I'm being serious about the script. It's not a ploy. It means something to me. And I know I don't deserve for you to care about anything that means something to me … but I want you to."

Goddamn it!

Sighing heavily, I looked back at the class. "Fine. But only if you'll be quiet during rehearsal."

I actually felt his body deflate with the release of tension. "Thank you."

Bloody hell. I was such a soft touch when it came to this man.

After class, I drove directly home, now that I didn't have Mum to look after. The thought of her was abruptly shoved out because I still wasn't ready to deal with my feelings.

Walking around the corner to the cottage, I found Brodan's SUV parked out front, him leaning against it. The village streetlamps had come on as the short day darkened to twilight, casting a yellow glow over Brodan. His gaze locked on mine as I approached, and he pushed off the SUV. I noted the A4-size leather envelope in his arm.

"Thanks for doing this," he said.

"You could've just given it to me at school," I grumbled as I shoved my key in the lock.

I felt his heat at my back and then his breath on my cheek as he bent his head to say softly, "You could have insisted I did."

Goose bumps scattered down my neck and spine, and I cursed him under my breath as I pushed open the door. He was right, of course. There was no reason for me to allow him to follow me home.

Other than abject loneliness.

Rubbing the ache in my chest, I stepped aside to let Brodan into the cottage. Thankfully, the heating was on a timer, so it was nice and toasty for me coming home. Brodan wandered in, his gaze darting around the room, taking in the space.

"You haven't changed or added anything," he noted. "Come to think of it, where are all your books?"

Closing the front door, I bent down to pick up my mail. I left all my books behind in Glasgow long ago. "I have an e-reader."

"What about *stuff*?"

"You did help pack me up," I replied dryly as I flipped through the mail.

"So, that's really all you have in the way of belongings?"

"It's all I—" I cut off as I flipped to the end of my small stack of mail and found the Christmas card. I knew it was a Christmas card before I even opened it because I recognized

223

the handwriting on the address label. My cheeks flushed as adrenaline coursed through me, my hands shaking as I flipped over the card to check for a return label.

There was none.

How did he find me here?

"Not possible," I whispered frantically, dropping my mail to rip open the card.

It was an illustrated image of a loving couple sitting before a fireplace decorated for Christmas with a tree in the corner. No. No, no, no. I opened the card and my stomach dropped.

There's nowhere you can go where I can't find you. Merry Christmas, Monroe.
Yours always, Steven

"Monroe?"

Finding me in Ardnoch was easy enough … but how did he know I'd moved to the cottage? I'd only been living here a few weeks. Surely, he should have sent the card to Mum's. How did he know I was here?

"Roe?"

Had he come here? Had he been watching me?

Was he going to step out of the shadows one day? Maybe when I least expected it.

This is what he wants! Every birthday and every Christmas … he did this to mess with my head. Because he was a fucking coward!

"What is going on? Give me that."

Brodan snatched the card out of my hand, bringing me crashing back into the room. "Brodan—"

His face darkened with fury, those pale-blue eyes like ice chips as he raised them from the card to me. "What the fuck is this? Who is Steven, and why is he threatening you?"

Part of me wanted to tell Brodan to bugger off and leave me to my shitty existence. But an even bigger part was so tired. So alone. I needed someone to talk to … and he was there.

"Steven is my ex." I dropped my handbag on the side table and stared wearily at Brodan. "You're not the only reason I don't trust you."

The muscle in his jaw flexed. "Tell me. Please."

I nodded. "I think I'd quite like a spiked coffee first, though. You?"

His impatience was obvious, but he controlled it, nodding. Like he was afraid I would disappear in a puff of smoke, Brodan trailed me like a puppy dog into the kitchen and watched me make coffee spiked with the whisky I'd found in the back of a cupboard. He then followed me back into the sitting room and we sat together, the mug warm between my cold palms.

"Sunset?" he prompted quietly.

I couldn't quite look at him as I spoke. "It took me a long time to get over you. There were disastrous attempts at uni, casual sex that left me empty."

Glancing at him, I noted he was white-knuckling his mug, his own gaze on the drink as if he was afraid to look at me too. It bothered him? The thought of me with others? For some reason, that hurt. There was no satisfaction.

"When I moved to Edinburgh for teacher training, I met a firefighter called Nick. He reminded me a little of you."

Brodan looked at me now, his anguish clear. "What a fucking pair we are, Sunset."

Pain warmed my chest in a bright flare, and tears burned my eyes. I fought them back with a grim smile as I nodded. It took me a minute to be able to speak around the sudden lump in my throat. "Nick and I were together for four years until I discovered he was sleeping with a colleague behind my back. They decided to be together, and I left. Most of our friends were his, so they chose him and the new woman."

"Fuckers," Brodan bit out. "The lot of them."

I harrumphed in agreement.

"Roe ... you should know I have never cheated on anyone, and I never would."

"I know. You were always very honest when you grew tired of a girl and moved on to the next."

He flinched.

Remorse hit me unexpectedly. It wasn't Brodan's fault that Steven liked to torment me, and I didn't want to do to Brodan what he'd done to me. I didn't want to keep taking hits at him. "Sorry."

He waved off my apology. "Just tell me about this other guy. This Steven person."

"Steven Shaw. I met him when I moved to Glasgow to teach. He was ten years older than me, charismatic, intelligent, and he worked in the financial industry. I still don't know exactly what his job entailed, but I knew he was successful because he showered me with expensive gifts, and I allowed myself to be swept off my feet by him. Fancy dinners, fancy holidays, fancy flat in the West End of Glasgow." I smirked bitterly. "But it wasn't the lifestyle that pulled me in. It was him. It was me. He was looking for someone like me."

"What does that mean?"

"Someone vulnerable. Someone desperate to be loved. After you, after Nick..." I glared into my whisky. "Steven must have smelled it on me like a shark smells blood."

"Roe." My name seemed to be dragged out of Brodan, rough and ragged.

I looked at him and saw his self-recrimination.

I shook my head. "No one is responsible for anyone else's life or their choices."

"But I loved you, and I walked away from you because I didn't think you cared anymore. It was easier to let the fear win. My cowardice left you thinking no one loved you. I can't forgive myself for that."

"You're not to blame, Brodan. No one is to blame but Steven. He's a piece of shit. You might not forgive yourself, but I forgive you. I forgive us. You need to forgive us as well."

His expression softened. "You were always wiser than me." Then, just as quickly as he'd softened, his features hardened. "Now tell me what that bastard did to you."

I took another swig of coffee before continuing. "Steven pulled me in with how passionate he was about me. How much he wanted me and how quickly he fell for me. He told me he'd never fallen for someone so fast. I felt special because he made me feel that way. He made me feel loved. And even if I didn't love him back in the same way, I was addicted to how much he wanted me.

"However, a year into our relationship, he lost his job, and he started to take it out on me. Steven turned out to be just like my father." The thought of Dad threatened to open a volcano of emotions, so I continued quickly, "Every time I tried to leave him after he'd hit me, he would apologize and make me feel loved again."

"Jesus fuck," Brodan bit out, letting go a shuddering sigh that seemed to rattle his insides.

I couldn't look at him as I confessed, "I try hard not to be ashamed of the fact that I stayed with him for so long. It was part fear, part manipulation, and a wee part of me had begun to believe that maybe it was me. Maybe there was a reason this was how people 'loved' me."

"Roe, no," Brodan whispered harshly.

"I know." And I hated that there was ever a point in my life when I'd believed that. "I know better now. I talked to a counselor behind Steven's back, and she helped me a lot. It took me a long time to break the cycle, but eventually, I left him and got a restraining order. By then, I was thirty years old. It took me three years to be free of him. For the past seven years, he's sent me a card on my birthday and at Christmas. He's made no other move. After all this time, I reckon he's just a coward. He has no plans to actually do anything to me, but he likes me on edge. He doesn't want me to forget him. I just ... don't know how he knew to send one to the cottage, considering I've only been forwarding my mail here for a few weeks."

Silence fell between us, and eventually, I forced myself to look at Brodan.

His whole body trembled with rage.

Then he said with quiet fury, "I'm going to find him, and I'm going to fucking end him."

Fear jolted through me. "No, you will not. Please, Brodan. Don't do anything. Like I said, he just sends the cards to mess with me. He has no intention of doing anything. It's been seven years."

"Seven years too long." Brodan stood to his feet. "This stops now."

"Brodan—"

"I won't kill him. Even though it'll take every ounce of self-control I have. But Walker and I are going to find him, and we're going to make sure he knows you are now off-limits. No one fucks with you again, Monroe. And I will ruin anyone who tries."

Even though my heart beat frantically at his words, I stood and forced myself to remind him, "I can take care of myself."

"Aye, you can, and you do it very well, my love. But that doesn't mean I can't take care of you too."

My love.

My mind reeled at his endearment and butterflies fluttered to life in my belly, betraying me. I'd be a fool to believe him.

But exhausted, I didn't protest as he called Walker to give him Steven's full name, and I provided his last known address. Brodan wanted him found, he told Walker, but he'd explain everything later when he saw him. After the call, Brodan insisted I put my feet up to read his script while he cooked. If it surprised me that the man knew how to cook, I hid it. Just as I hid my bemusement.

Just as I hid from the truth.

That as I sat there in my sitting room, reading a wonderful script that made me laugh, cry, and swoon, written by the man making dinner in my kitchen … I felt something close to safe for the first time in eighteen years.

25

BRODAN

There was no snow on the ground, but it didn't matter. Ardnoch was like a Christmas postcard. I surveyed the street fair that had been set up in the dark hours of the morning and took in the strands upon strands of fairy lights, the faux snow–dusted, red-and-green stall coverings, the winter-bundled customers, and the smell of crisp, smoky air, mulled wine, and hot doughnuts. Waiting outside Monroe's door, I experienced a contentment I hadn't felt in a long time.

I was a small-town boy who'd been trapped in a traveling man's body for too long.

The door behind me opened, and I spun around to find Monroe stepping out of the cottage. Her gorgeous hair glinted copper in the low morning sunlight, the strands falling around her shoulders from beneath a green beanie that looked adorable on her. She locked her door and turned to me, her eyes filled with a light I hadn't seen in a while.

My heart beat a bit faster.

Ever since the night I cooked dinner and she read my script, things had shifted between us. Roe was still wary, a bit

230

guarded, but there was no more animosity. I hadn't slept that night. I wanted to be thrilled by her assessment of my script. She'd loved it. She had a few notes on my female characters, which were great.

But it wasn't my script that kept me awake. I tossed and turned, denying myself the urge to jump in a car and drive to Glasgow. Steven Shaw was very lucky I'd made a promise not to turn him into a dead man. Walker didn't exactly help. In fact, *I* had to rein *him* in. My bodyguard had zero tolerance for violence against women. It was the one thing that transformed him from my cool, sensible head of security into a hot-tempered weapon.

We wanted to send Shaw a message and both agreed it would be better that neither of us did it because we'd probably maim the bastard. Therefore, we'd sent some guys Walker knew to calmly but forcefully explain that Monroe Sinclair was officially off-limits, and if he so much as breathed in her direction, he'd be breathing through a tube next.

The thought of him hurting this precious woman was a vise around the beating organ in my chest.

"Are you okay?" Roe's smile of welcome dimmed a bit.

I grinned. "You're just too fucking cute in that hat. Lost my ability to speak for a minute."

She rolled her eyes with a snort of disbelief that made her even cuter and turned to take in the Christmas street fair that had made driving down Castle Street a no-go for the day. "I wish they'd had this when we were kids." Roe stepped off the pavement toward the hubbub.

I followed and gently took her arm to thread it through mine, tucking her into my side. Our height made it a wee bit awkward, but I couldn't care less. The heat of her, the scent of her perfume, were worth anything.

Roe gave me a look as if to say, *I know what you're doing,* but she didn't pull away. That was definitely an improvement. My optimism rose.

"Let's check out Sloane's stall first. It was so nice of Regan to get her a stall last minute."

It was actually Lachlan. Regan had tried and failed to get the town committee to allow a last-minute seller to join the fair, especially an "outsider," so she spoke to Lachlan, who was on the committee as a prominent business owner. He'd not only convinced them, he had a friend on the local council fast-track a permit for Sloane.

Following Roe through the crowd, I noted some people doing a double take when they looked at me. I gave them a nod but hoped the influx of tourists outside of Ardnoch would not be a problem. Spotting a young woman I didn't recognize surreptitiously trying and failing to take a photo of me on her phone, I tried not to tense. Who knew where that photo would end up on the abyss of the internet. We'd become a society repulsively comfortable with taking images or videos of strangers in private moments and posting them online for entertainment, a culture that had surely developed from our treatment of celebrities.

Glancing down at Monroe, I noted she was too preoccupied with perusing the wares at the stalls to have noticed. Thankfully.

"There's Sloane and Callie. Her stall is so busy already." Roe sounded thrilled for her friend, and affection flooded me.

I let Roe lead me to the stall, chuckling as she shoved our way to the front. Sloane and Callie both looked at us with beaming smiles. "You made it!"

"We did," Roe said, eyeing all the baked goods. "How did you guys pull this off? Look at all this!"

"I'll have two gingerbread men, four cupcakes, and four

mini Santa cheesecakes!" the woman next to Roe *shouted* at Sloane.

Sloane gave us an apologetic look, but Roe waved her off and then slapped my chest dramatically as she cried, "Brodan, look at the Santa cheesecakes. Those are adorable!"

Her easiness with me reminded me so much of what it used to be like. I grinned like a madman. "They are adorable." It was true. Sloane had piped cream cheese and added sugar-dusted strawberries to the top of each cake and then piped a dot of cream cheese on top of that, so the strawberries looked like Santa hats.

"Ooh, I don't know what to get." Roe bit her lip as her gaze darted over the stall like it was the most important decision of her life.

"How about we get a couple of everything?" I suggested.

Her eyes flew to mine. "We can't do that. Who'll eat it all?"

"You've met my family, right?"

Monroe laughed, her eyes crinkling at the corners, the sound and look of her so sweet, it took everything within me not to kiss the laughter right off her lips. She must have caught the heat in my eyes, because she flushed and she glanced away quickly. "Won't your family visit the market themselves?"

"Aye, but at this rate, Sloane will be sold out before they get here."

She considered this. "Maybe we should get a couple of things."

A few minutes later, the stall had cleared a bit and I told Sloane, "Give me four of everything."

"Four!" Monroe gasped. "How will we carry that?"

"I'll keep it behind the stall for you," Sloane offered. "You can collect it after."

"See?" I grinned at the solution.

"I want a Santa hat now, though," Roe murmured, looking like a wee kid.

I chuckled. "Don't worry, you can have your Santa hat, my love."

Sloane shot Roe a wide-eyed look before she began boxing up the treats. "This will be our biggest sale of the day."

"I'll help, Mom," Callie said, reaching out to box more of the treats.

"Do you want to be a baker, too, Callie?" I asked. "Or have you caught the acting bug?"

She smiled at me. "I like being in the musical, but I think I like baking more."

"That's understandable. I'm an actor, and I like eating baked goods more."

Callie giggled, and I felt Roe's attention on me.

"What?" I asked her.

Roe snorted. "You don't look like you like baked goods more."

"And if I did?" I asked, a hint of seriousness in the question. It took a lot of dedication to stay in shape. Without my personal trainer on hand, I was hitting the estate's gym hard every morning with Walker before anyone else was awake. When we had time, we swam laps in the glass-roofed pool afterward.

Monroe gave me a tender smile. "Then you'd still be Brodan. Just cuddlier."

I grinned, relieved, and leaned in to murmur in her ear, "I'm cuddly now, and you're welcome to explore just how cuddly I am. Anytime."

When I pulled back, her cheeks were pink, and I recognized desire when I saw it. However, she replied, "I already have a *toy* to cuddle with."

An image of her with the toy in question flashed through

my mind, and heat flooded my groin. *Fuck*. I glowered at her in frustration. "Play nice."

She appeared far too smug for my own good.

"Mom, there's Walker," Callie said loudly, reminding me we were not alone.

I glanced over my shoulder to see Walk strolling stiffly through the market while the woman he'd come back to Ardnoch with last night clung to his arm. He'd told me this morning at the gym that he'd hooked up with someone from a pub two villages north and brought her back to the bungalow he'd rented now that we knew we weren't leaving. Walker liked it here as much as I did, so he'd decided to stay too. He was a man, however, who liked separation of work from living space, so he'd found a place near where Arro used to live. Walker had left the house this morning with the woman still sleeping in his bed, hoping she'd be gone by the time he returned.

Obviously, that hadn't happened.

Feeling Roe's arm tense around mine, I glanced down at her and found her staring worriedly at Sloane. Sure enough, the pretty blond appeared crestfallen at the sight of Walker with another woman.

Shit. I'd forgotten Sloane had a thing for Walk.

I wished I could tell her that the other woman probably meant very little to Walker, but it wouldn't matter, anyway. I'd known the man for half a decade, and in that time, he'd never gotten remotely serious about a woman.

A fake, cheery smile graced Sloane's face as Walker approached the stall. He gave her a nod and then greeted her daughter. "How's it goin', Callie?"

She beamed. "Great! Mr. Adair just bought four of everything."

Walker scowled at me. "You didn't buy everything, did you?"

I snorted. "Relax, Sweet Tooth, there is plenty left for you." I looked at his companion, not wanting to be rude. "Hi."

She gaped at me. "You're Brodan fucking Adair!"

I winced at how loud she was and watched Walker's face darken.

"I love your movies." She fluttered her eyelashes at me. "You're an awesome actor. I particularly loved *Redemption Road.*"

Of course she did. It was the movie where I was filmed naked in the shower. No full frontal, but arse and all. Many a meme had been made from that scene.

"Thanks," I murmured as I gently pulled Roe tighter against my side.

The woman didn't take the hint. "You know, I'd love to sit down and have coffee with you, talk about your movies."

I glowered at Walker.

He had the decency to look apologetic. Then he turned to her. "I'm sure you would, but as his bodyguard, that's a hard no from me."

"No need to be jealous," she purred.

"Aye, okay, this is done," Walker muttered and then handed Sloane a few notes. "Put aside a box for me, whatever this gets me. I'll come back for it."

Sloane took it, not meeting his eyes. "Sure."

"Right, you, let's go."

"But I wanted to see the rest of the fair," she grumbled as Walker led her away.

Roe grimaced. "Was she for real?"

I shrugged. "Happens."

"That was rude to you and to Walker."

Sloane snorted, but it wasn't a cheerful sound. "Walker wasn't exactly Mr. Manners either. He didn't even introduce her to us. Is that how he treats women?"

Looking at Callie, I hedged my words, not knowing how

to say this in front of a nine-year-old. "She, uh … is a casual acquaintance he made last night, and I think she invited herself along today."

"Then he should use better judgment." Sloane stuffed the money into her apron and angrily placed cakes into a box for Walker.

More people crowded around her stall, and she was clearly in a bad mood, so Monroe told her we'd circle back and we strolled away. As Roe bit into her Santa cheesecake, I said, "So, Sloane has a thing for Walker."

Roe squeezed my arm and swallowed a bite. "She told me it was just a crush."

"Seems like it's more than that."

She shrugged. "I couldn't tell you."

"You wouldn't even if you could."

Roe grinned up at me, a dollop of cream cheese on her lip. "Girl code."

I smiled fondly down at her and wiped the cream cheese off her lip with my thumb before sucking it into my mouth. Her eyes widened, and then she swallowed. Hard.

Very, very good.

"She's lucky to have you as a friend. Anyone would be," I told her.

Roe shoved me playfully. "Should I expect to be flattered all day, Brodan Adair?"

"That was my plan."

"I have a better one." Her expression lit up upon seeing a burger van. "It's almost lunchtime, and that cheesecake wasn't enough. I'm starving."

"Well, we can't have that." I tugged on her arm, pulling her into the queue for the burgers. "What do you want?"

She studied the menu board, and I could practically see her salivating. "What are you having?"

"Preferably you, but I'll take a cheeseburger in the meantime."

She let out an exasperated laugh. "You are indefatigable."

"Ooh, good word, Ms. Sinclair." I wrapped my arms around her waist, drawing her back to my chest as I murmured in her ear, "And you have no idea just how indefatigable I can be."

Tilting her head back, Roe snorted. "Oh my God, stop it."

I shook with laughter against her. "I can't help myself."

"Holy shit, you're Brodan Adair." The male voice cut through my moment with Roe, and she pulled out of my arms.

Facing the intruder, it took everything within me not to snarl at the young man. He stood with a young woman, and they blinked at me like two deer in headlights. Swallowing my irritation, I nodded hello.

The guy raised his hands to his head and then spread his fingers as he made an exploding noise. "How cool! I mean, we knew we might see someone famous while we were here, but Brodan Adair!" He pulled the woman at his side tight to him. "You're on both of our lists."

I didn't ask because I already knew what they meant. This wasn't the first time someone had said it to me.

Still, he acted like I asked. "Our sex lists," he explained.

Shit.

I shot a look at Roe. She stared in astonishment at the couple.

"You know, like, if we met you, we give each other permission to fuck you."

"Excuse me?" Monroe stepped forward, anger staining her cheeks red.

The young guy looked surprised by her reaction. "Oh, oh, like, it's a compliment."

"Is it?" Roe said sarcastically, crossing her arms over her

chest. "It's a compliment to tell a complete stranger that you have permission to fuck them? Because in my world, that's called sexual harassment."

"Roe," I murmured, tugging her gently back. "It's fine."

The couple stared at Roe like she was insane. She was right. But some people thought because they'd seen me in a bunch of movies that they knew me. Boundaries they normally wouldn't cross no longer existed for them. Not wanting the situation to become an ugly anecdote online, I said to the couple, "Would you like an autograph?"

They grinned broadly. "Can we get a selfie with you?" They shoved a phone at Roe before I could comply.

Roe stared at it in her hands like it was a bag of dog shit.

I rubbed her back. "It's fine," I repeated.

Thankfully, she took the photo without another word, but the easiness between us was gone. Once we'd grabbed a couple of burgers, it became obvious that any privacy we might have was blown. The tourists at the fair had gotten word I was here. We stood to the side, eating our burgers, but we both felt public attention on us.

"How can you be okay with them talking to you like that?" Monroe asked.

Shrugging, I explained, "It's easier to ignore it, give them a photo or autograph, and just walk away. It comes with the job. To them, I'm not a stranger."

"But you are. And they talked to you like you were some inanimate sex toy."

I snorted at her words. "You are very sexy when you're angry. That might be a problem for me."

"Shut up," she said without heat.

"You've always been like this."

"Like what?"

"Just as protective of me as I am of you. Remember when

239

Michelle Kingsley kept shoving me in the quad? You came running to my rescue."

"She's lucky I didn't break that perfect nose of hers," Roe muttered, clearly still agitated by the young couple at the burger van.

"Admit it." I nudged her. "You still care about me."

Monroe eyed me seriously. "It was never a question of that, Brodan."

Fuck, I wanted to kiss her so badly.

"Mr. Adair."

I squeezed my eyes closed in frustration but pasted on a smile as I turned to face our latest interrupters. It was a family of four, all staring at me with shy excitement. I widened my smile. "Hullo."

The mum said, "Mr. Adair, we're such big fans. Could we bother you for a photo?"

And so it began.

By the fourth group that asked for a photo, I turned to see if Roe was okay and found the space where she'd been standing empty.

My gut twisted. I conjured my acting skills to smile for the camera with the fan. Just as he nodded his thanks and walked away, two older women eyed me like they wanted to approach. Just as they got up the courage to do so, my phone vibrated in my pocket. I pulled it out and found a text from Roe.

Sorry for leaving you. Just feel a bit sick and didn't want to interrupt. Have a good day.

I scowled at the formal tone of the text.

This was what I'd feared.

That even if I could convince Roe to give me another chance, my fame might be too much for her to handle.

Giving the approaching women a quick nod of hello, I hurried past them to Sloane's stall. She was cleaning up for the day. Word had obviously gotten around about her amazing baking. "Hi," I said.

"Oh, hey. We've got your boxes. Can you carry them all?"

"Pile them up." I held out my arms.

Sure enough, they towered right up to my nose. I could just see over the top, and I left with Callie giggling at how ridiculous I looked as I tried to walk carefully down the street. The upside was that the boxes disguised me as I slowly made my way down Castle Street to Monroe's. I had to kick her door in lieu of a knock.

What felt like forever later, she opened it.

"What on earth?" Roe asked from beyond the boxes.

"Grab your stuff and come with me."

"Brodan—"

"I know you're not sick, Roe. I'm sorry about the fair." This was ludicrous. "Look, I can't talk to you when I can't see you. Just get your stuff. Please."

To my utter relief, Monroe did as I asked. "Now to my car."

"Let me take a few of these."

"Nope. They're hiding me."

She chuckled as we skirted the fair to get to my SUV that I'd parked outside the Gloaming. It was a miracle I hadn't dropped any of the boxes. Once they were loaded, I pulled out a bunch of notes from my wallet and handed them to Roe. "I'll wait here. You go back and buy some mulled wine and as many hot chocolates as you can carry."

"Where are we going?"

"My family hasn't shown up yet, so we're taking the market to them."

"Brodan—"

I stepped into her. "It'll be like this for a while. But the fame will die down now that I've retired. It won't be as bad as this."

Roe sighed. "Brodan—"

"Just … today we were supposed to spend time together as friends. I don't want it to be ruined. So let's just go bring a wee bit of Christmas cheer to some very exhausted new parents."

She considered this and then nodded. "Okay."

I deflated with relief, watching her walk away before I climbed into the Range Rover. Then I called Regan to tell her to gather everyone at her place. She loved the idea because she loved being surrounded by family. The two of us had that in common.

Not long later, Monroe returned with an impressive load of mulled wine and hot chocolate. "Your family knows we're just friends, right? And they're good with that? Eredine is good with that?" Monroe fired at me as I swung the car out of the space and took the side road that would lead me out of Ardnoch.

"They know, and they're good with it. Eredine is good with it. She just wants me to be happy, and being your friend makes me happy."

Roe groaned. "You are a silver-tongued devil, Brodan Adair."

I grinned. "Oh, there's—"

"Do not make an innuendo about your tongue."

Laughter shook through me. Because damn, she knew me so well.

26

MONROE

There was only one week of rehearsals left before the kids put on their Christmas musical for friends and family. That meant that soon there would be no real excuse to see Brodan twice weekly.

I would be lying if I said I didn't feel myself softening toward him. That I didn't enjoy that familiar feeling of camaraderie and affection between us. When we'd taken the baked treats, hot chocolate, and mulled wine to Thane and Regan's, the Adairs swept me up in their easiness and good humor, despite two sets of parents' exhaustion. They were grateful we'd brought the fair to them.

Thane lit the firepit in the back garden, and we all bundled out there with the sea as our view, this spectacular home filled with an extraordinary amount of love. I was happy that Brodan had this and felt a bit melancholy for myself that I didn't. But I enjoyed being welcomed by the Adair family. Arran swept me up in a massive hug, seeming genuinely delighted to see me. Lewis was watchful at first, trying to make sense of my relationship with his uncle, I think. Soon, he relaxed and enjoyed a game of football with his uncles, sister, and stepmum while I chatted with Arro, Robyn, and Eredine.

Eredine, whom had been stiff and unwelcoming in the past, was like an entirely different person. She was reserved but kind and seemed truly interested in my job. I also got to hold Arro's and Robyn's baby daughters for a while and tried very hard to hide my abject longing.

Looking up at one point, however, I caught Brodan watching me with a thoughtful expression on his face. Did he sense what it felt like for me to hold a baby, believing I'd probably never have a child of my own? My kids at school would have to fulfill that emptiness.

Despite the sadness I kept to myself, it was a lovely afternoon that turned into a fun evening. We ordered takeout, and I got tipsy on the mulled wine. Brodan drove me home, teasing me the whole time, and then the opportunistic bastard carried me into the cottage and upstairs to bed. He'd taken off my jacket, hat, and scarf, then my boots, and tucked me into bed. I remembered his kiss on my forehead before I passed out.

So, yes.

The idea of letting myself fully give in to a friendship with Brodan definitely intrigued me. However, the vibe between us was plagued by a sexual tension much more potent than what it was when we were hormonal teens. Just when things started to feel comfortable between us, Brodan would look at me like he wanted to eat me alive, and I knew I was teetering on the edge of control.

Despite my tumultuous emotions around him, the dominating one was disappointment in knowing that next week would be our last rehearsal. Which was why, when he approached at the end of our penultimate week of rehearsal, a mixture of relief and fear swirled within me when he asked me out on a date.

"I thought I told you, if I can give you anything, it will just be friendship, Brodan," I'd said, my voice shaking.

He'd given me this arrogant, cocksure look and replied, "We both know that's bullshit. It will always be more than friendship between us. Let's finally stop lying about that."

And since he was annoyingly bloody right, I'd sighed and told him honestly, "I don't think I'm ready."

"You'll never be ready unless you give me a chance." He'd taken another step toward me. "I'm not asking for promises. I'm asking you to go on one date with me. We'll see what happens from there."

Memories of what had happened the morning before our lovely afternoon at Regan and Thane's remained with me, and I'd whispered apologetically, "I'm not sure I can handle the fame thing."

Brodan nodded in understanding. "I'll promise not to hold it against you if it becomes too much."

"Brodan—"

"Monroe, give me a chance. Let's not waste another eighteen years."

That was why I was currently a mess of nerves, even unable to eat breakfast, as I waited for Brodan to pick me up. For our first-ever date.

"How did I get here?" I murmured to myself as my knee bounced rapidly. How had I gone from vowing to guard myself against this man to promising a date?

It's just a date, I told myself. No promises. Just a date. Don't kiss him. That will definitely complicate things and fluster you and seduce you into forgetting all the reasons you don't quite trust him yet.

You should tell him that. No kissing or hanky-panky, I ordered myself. *Make your boundaries clear from the start.*

The doorbell rang, giving me a jolt, and I stood, taking a

deep breath. I couldn't remember the last time I'd been this nervous about a date.

It's just Brodan, for goodness' sake.

Smoothing down my fitted winter jacket, I summoned inner calm and strode across the room to open the door.

Brodan stood on the pavement, beautiful in his wool peacoat and gray scarf, his cheeks flushed from the cold. Those famous pale-blue eyes glinted with delight at the sight of me. "Morning, Sunset."

I'd long given up on telling him not to call me that. I smirked. "Morning, Adair."

He held out a hand. "Ready to go?"

I stared at his outstretched hand, then his face. "There have to be rules first."

Brodan lowered his arm, his expression wary. "Okay?"

Licking my lips, I drew myself up and ordered primly, "There will be no kissing on this date. There will definitely be no sex. Physical desire will be ignored so that we have all of our faculties about us."

"Why? Will we be solving equations on this date?" he teased.

"I'll be solving the puzzle that is you, Brodan, so yes, as a matter of fact. I will need to be clearheaded so I can decide what I want, and I can't do that if I have lust gumming up the works."

His lips twitched with amusement. "Don't you think our amazing sexual chemistry is an important deciding factor?"

Typical man. "Unlike some people, I'm not led around by my vagina."

"Oh, really?" He took a step toward me, challenge blazing in his gaze. "Fine. I'll bet I can hold out longer than you."

Surprised, I gaped. "From what? Kissing me?"

"Kissing, fucking … the lot."

I snorted long and derisively. "I'd like to see you try."

"And you will. I'll wager if you break first, you have to agree to date me for at least three months."

"What?"

He nodded, anticipation clear in his expression. "And if I break first … it's just a month."

"Pfft. If you break first, I don't have to date you at all."

"No, I'm not taking that bet."

"Ha, because you don't trust yourself not to break first."

"Fine." He scowled. "If I break first, you don't have to date me at all."

I held out my hand, feeling pretty certain I was going to win this bet, and trying not to think about why that filled me with unease. "Shake on it."

Brodan shook my hand, still glowering. When he released me, he gave me a look of such longing, I felt a crack across my heart. Looking away, I reached inside to grab my keys and bag off the sideboard and then stepped out to lock up. "Okay, let's do this."

When Brodan drove us south and we were crossing the firth, I was worried for a second that he was taking us to Inverness. I was pretty sure we'd never get a moment's peace in the city, if the Christmas fair had been anything to go by.

"No. We're going to Portmahomack," Brodan explained.

"Really?" The tiny harbor town sat on the coast, looking back across the water toward Sutherland, including Ardnoch and Caelmore. Although postcard picturesque, there wasn't a lot there except for a small, lovely beach.

"Thought we could grab a quiet lunch at the pub. Away from the prying eyes of Ardnoch. And I reckon it's one of the few places no one will interrupt us."

I reckoned he was right. It was mid-December. Most

tourists had gone home for winter, and Portmahomack should offer us some privacy.

"Does it bother you?" I asked as we drove along the frosted coast.

"What?"

"Strangers asking you for selfies and intruding on your privacy everywhere you go?"

"It didn't use to. Now that I actually want my life back, I think I might have a harder time dealing with it. The fair wasn't fun for me, just so you know."

I could understand that, and I hated it for him. Yet, we both knew it was the consequences of the choices he'd made. "I'm sorry for leaving like that."

"No, I get it. It's a lot." His knuckles tightened around the wheel despite his understanding tone.

Changing the subject, I asked, "Have you let anyone else see your script yet?"

Brodan relaxed and shot me a smile. "I did. I got up the courage to send it to my agent, Anders. He's been pestering me for weeks, so the script made his day. He's not happy I'm retiring, but I think he thinks I'll change my mind, so he's letting it go and shopping the script out to people—actors, producers, et cetera—to see if anyone bites. I would like to be a producer on it, see it through, but we'll just need to wait."

"Would that mean being on set?" Would that mean him traveling constantly again?

"Sometimes. Not all." As if he sensed my apprehension, he added, "It wouldn't be like before. I wouldn't be gone all the time. I don't want to be. A movie a year would satisfy."

Doubt hounded me. "After exhausting yourself into the hospital, Brodan, I can't imagine you being happy sticking around Ardnoch for most of the year."

"I told you," he said, his voice gruff with emotion, "I was running from a lot of things. But I always missed home.

And being home for the past few months has only made me realize how much I want to be here. I was going to tell you later, but now that you've brought it up, I've been thinking how much I've enjoyed teaching Lewis and Callie and the kids about acting. The truth is, I didn't know I had it in me to explain the craft and to explain it in a way that kids could understand." He laughed a little self-consciously, reminding me of the Brodan of my childhood. "Do you think it would be ridiculous of me to consider teaching drama?"

My pulse raced. "Seriously?"

He frowned.

"No, I don't mean it like that," I hurried to assure him. "I'm just surprised you would want to do that. I think you'd be wonderful at it."

"Aye?"

I nodded. "Of course."

"The University of Highlands and Islands have a drama course. They've asked me a few times over the years to guest lecture, and I haven't. But I think I might like to change that."

As wonderful as that would be, considering my alma mater was only a forty-minute drive from Ardnoch in Inverness, I felt obliged to tell him, "Brodan, you're one of the best actors of your generation. I'm not just saying that. You could guest lecture at the best acting schools in the country. In the world."

He was quiet a moment. Then he replied, "As much as I appreciate that, and I do, Roe, more than you know … none of those schools are within touching distance of you or my family."

Blood rushed in my ears, and I swallowed my fear to remind him, "I don't know if I'll be here next year. I've put feelers out for a job in the Lowlands. You shouldn't decide based on where I'll be."

His head whipped toward me. "I didn't realize you were serious about that."

We entered Portmahomack, following the signs to the beach car park. Only a few cars were there, and Brodan glided the SUV into a spot, switched off the engine, and turned to me. His eyes searched my face. "Roe?"

"I wasn't lying when I said there's a lot of pain in Ardnoch for me. I know you and I are working toward fixing that, and I'm grateful we are, Brodan, but you're not the only person who's hurt me."

"Your fucking mother," he bit out angrily.

"Mrs. Waddle scolded me in Flora's the other morning for abandoning Mum when she needed me." I shook my head, indignation burning in my chest.

"Mrs. Waddle?"

"She lives a few doors down from Mum. Remember, she used to tell us to get off her stoop anytime we were standing outside her house on the *public* path?"

Recognition lit Brodan's eyes. "Arran and I subscribed her to a porn magazine."

I burst out laughing, remembering it. "You were wee buggers, so you were."

He grinned. "She deserved it." Then his smile dimmed. "Especially for saying that to you in Flora's. She hasn't got a fucking clue what your mother has put you through."

My lips twitched. "Flora gave her an earful before I could. But that's what living in Ardnoch is like. Everyone in your business and everyone thinking they have a right to it."

"That's just the negative parts. Mrs. Waddle isn't the problem. You not talking about your mum and your dad is the problem."

"I can't." I pleaded, "Please, Brodan, I can't. Every time I let myself think about it, I feel like something inside me will shatter again."

Emotion brightened his eyes. "I won't push. But I want you to promise to come to me the moment you're ready to face it."

I looked away, staring out at the water. "Let's not make any promises to each other."

Feeling his cool fingers touch my chin, I allowed him to turn my face back to his. "We have a problem here, Sunset. Because I want to make *all* our promises to each other."

"How can you be so sure?" I whispered. "About me? I'm not sure of anything, Brodan."

He shrugged helplessly. "I once convinced a director to let me do my own stunts, including base jumping from one of the tallest skyscrapers in Europe. And yet, nothing has made me feel as alive as I've felt the past few months being home … with you."

The man was determined to make me melt all over him. "Brodan …"

Then his words penetrated, and anger at his recklessness filled me. I smacked him hard across the shoulder.

"Ow." He rubbed the spot. "What was that for?"

"For throwing yourself off a bloody skyscraper." I unbuckled my belt in my fury and launched out of the car. The salty, brittle sea air hit me hard, but I needed it.

To my surprise, the bastard got out of the car, grinning from ear to ear, as he rounded the bonnet to get to me.

"What have you got to smile about?"

He bent his head to mine and brushed his lips across my ear. "Because you really like me."

I jerked away. "Keep those lips to yourself, or I'll consider the bet over."

Brodan had a spring in his step as we walked down the harbor street. "You really, really like me."

"I do not."

"Do too."

"I do bloody not. You're a pain in my arse, Adair."

"But you care I threw myself off a building."

"If you want our date to continue, I wouldn't keep reminding me."

"You like me."

"If you don't stop, *I* will throw you off another building."

He grinned boyishly to himself.

I couldn't help the smile that tugged at my lips.

"I'm going to hold your hand because it wasn't stipulated in the bet," he announced.

"Touching was implied."

"Aye, like my tongue on your clit kind of touching? Not holding hands."

I swear my clit throbbed at his words. Stopping in the middle of the quiet street, I gaped at him. "You did not just say that."

Brodan searched my face, delighted by whatever he found there. "Oh … oh, this is good."

I spluttered a nonresponse.

He practically did a jig. "We never stipulated there could be no sex talk, right?"

"Brodan—"

"And look at those rosy cheeks just at the mention of me going down on you."

"Brodan—"

"This is going to be fun." He rubbed his hands together gleefully. "As will fucking you on your hands and knees until you see stars, but that can wait."

"Brodan!" I glanced around frantically to make sure no one was around to hear his filthy words.

"And you'll keep saying my name like that every time I thrust into your sweet, tight pussy."

My whole body flushed hot as I throbbed with need, gaping at him in desire and horror.

"Fuck." He scrubbed a hand over his face. "This is making *me* hard."

"Good," I snapped, stalking toward him. "Then maybe you'll think twice about talking to me like that in public."

"I have," he agreed, hurrying to catch up. "I'll save it for when we're alone."

I squeezed my eyes closed in despair.

This was going to be the most torturous bet of my life.

Brodan reached for my hand, and I glowered at him.

He smiled back. "I think the date is going well so far."

27

BRODAN

Dating Monroe Sinclair was exquisite torture.

We'd only technically been dating for a week, and my self-control had been pushed to its limits. Yet, I was determined I would not be the one who broke. There was too much at stake. Plus, it stung a little that Roe really thought I'd jeopardize our future for a kiss. Did she think I was some prepubescent hound who couldn't control his hormones, for fuck's sake?

However, trying to tempt her into breaking first was a form of self-torment. Whispering dirty things in her ear made me long to be inside her, but outwardly, I tried to appear as calm as possible. Mostly because it pissed her off that she was so flustered, and I was cool and collected. And Roe pissed off was a glorious sight. She was like the physical embodiment of fire.

It made it difficult for me to believe that any man had manipulated her the way Shaw had, and knowing that he'd crushed her for a moment in time made me want to kill him. However, I'd have to be satisfied with warning the bastard off. Walker's contacts had paid him a visit last week, and Walk said the bully almost wet himself at the threat and promised to leave Monroe alone. Our guys were assured Steven Shaw would not be sending anymore threatening postcards.

One job ticked off the "Make Monroe Sinclair's Life Better" list.

Now I just had to convince her that giving me a real shot would make her life better too. I'd see to it.

"You've got a look on your face," Walker said as he accompanied me into the primary school.

After another rehearsal yesterday and one today, tonight was finally the night the kids performed the musical. I was looking forward to it for them. They'd worked really hard, and it had come together nicely.

"What kind of look?" I asked, avoiding parents' gazes, hoping we could stroll right past them toward backstage.

"The same look you always get when you want something."

"Oh, that look. Aye, I'm wearing that look."

Walker grunted. "Good luck."

"Do you know what I want?" I grinned.

"Everyone paying attention knows what you want."

"Good." I spotted the dad who'd flirted with Roe at the bake sale. "Then they'll back the fuck off what's mine."

"You sound like a prick," Walker said blandly. His expression, however, was fierce enough to cut a path through the parents.

I laughed. "Wait until you find a woman you can't stop thinking about. You'll turn into a prick too."

"Never going to happen." Suddenly, his eyes narrowed ahead of us near the doors to backstage. "Sloane." His voice boomed, drawing even more stares our way.

The blond in question startled at his voice, and she

255

turned toward us. Sloane offered a small smile, though her eyes darted away from Walker. "Hey."

"Do you want in there to be with Callie?" Walk asked, reaching for the door to backstage.

"Oh, I don't think I'm allowed inside." She looked edgy. "But Callie was really nervous, and I feel bad I'm not with her."

"Come on," Walker urged. "We'll take you in."

"Are you certain?"

"Aye."

She looked at me.

"If you being there will calm Callie, then you should be there." I gestured for her to go ahead of us, and she smiled gratefully.

Backstage was a clamber of noise as the kids milled around in costume, laughing, shouting, and chasing one another. Adults moved around them, trying to get organized, while David practiced on the piano in the corner. Monroe told me they were starting with the upper school (our musical) and ending with the lower school who were performing *The Nutcracker*.

Red hair glinted under harsh lights, and I spotted Monroe talking with Callie. My heart beat faster upon seeing Monroe in her element, and I wondered if that would ever go away. Would there come a day when I could look at this woman without feeling my whole body vibrate with life?

Sloane hurried ahead of us to get to Callie, and Monroe seemed glad to see her. Then, as if sensing me, she tensed and turned slowly to look in my direction.

Our eyes held, and she gave me a slow, gorgeous smile.

Everything else stopped around us.

It was just Monroe. Smiling at me like I was all she wanted to see too.

My pulse thundered as my fingers itched, and a panic set in at the thought of her walking away from me one day.

Fuck, I was terrifyingly in love with this woman.

~

MONROE

I should've been in a great mood.

The musical had gone great. There were only a few lines flubbed, and the audience seemed to find it adorable, so we were good. The kids got a long-lasting standing ovation from the parents and were full of energy as we tried to hustle them as quickly as possible to the seats at the front of the audience, now vacated by the lower school.

Attempting to keep jazzed-up kids quiet through the nativity wasn't easy, but everyone was in high spirits and feeling very Christmassy. It was a natural mood booster.

However, the plays ended, and the parents were offered teas and coffees with baked treats before they left. During this reception, mums (and several dads) accosted Brodan.

They touched his arm provocatively and smiled and batted their eyelashes up at him. I was irritated.

Now and then, he'd find my gaze and give me an apologetic smile, but he never removed himself from the situations, so clearly, he got off on all the flirting and attention. Or … or he was deliberately trying to make me jealous to force me to lose the bet.

Well, wasn't that an awful thought?

Was I right to guard myself against this man? Or was I blowing the whole thing out of proportion? Why did he have the ability to twist me up inside like this?

I whirled around so I didn't have to see it anymore and almost collided with Haydyn Barr. "Oh, apologies."

He smiled down at me. "No need. I quite enjoy beautiful women running into me."

Flushing at the compliment, I laughed nervously and glanced around. "Where's Michael?"

"Backstage with some of the other kids. I think they need to blow off steam after the big night. You did an amazing job. Michael actually enjoyed himself." Haydyn chuckled. "I thought the only thing that boy enjoyed was Nintendo. Wonders never cease."

A genuine smile teased my lips. "I'm glad."

He reached out suddenly and touched my hair, tucking it behind my ear. I stiffened as he gazed into my eyes. "Stray hair," he explained.

I patted the place he'd touched, feeling uncomfortable. Deciding it wasn't fair to lead him on or allow him to think he could touch his son's teacher without permission, I opened my mouth to tell him it wasn't appropriate (especially in front of other parents) when I jolted at the feel of a large hand on my waist. Heat spread up my side as familiar aftershave filled my senses.

Brodan slid his hand possessively down my hip, leaning into me as he stared stonily at Haydyn. "I don't think we've been introduced." There was more than a hint of menace in his tone, and I stiffened against him.

Haydyn blinked rapidly. "Uh … no. Right. Brodan Adair. Pleasure to meet you." He raised his hand to shake Brodan's. "I love your movies."

Brodan stared at Haydyn's appendage like it was a bug. "That's nice." He looked back up at Haydyn, who suddenly registered how Brodan was holding on to me.

"Oh." He took an unconscious step back. "You two …"

"Aye, we're together."

"I didn't realize." Haydyn gave a thin-lipped smile. "Sorry."

"Now you know." Brodan turned us away from my pupil's father and muttered under his breath, "Prick."

Seething at his side, I choked out, "Excuse me." Then I pulled out of his hold and tried my best not to storm out of the cafeteria because I didn't want to get tongues wagging. Giving parents a pained smile, I hurried as quickly from the room as possible, up the stairs, and along the corridor to the quiet of my classroom. I hadn't yet made it to the room when I heard footsteps behind me.

Glancing over my shoulder, I saw Brodan following. I glowered and then marched into my classroom, whirling to face him.

He appeared a few seconds later, expression wary.

"How dare you?" I blurted out angrily.

He scowled. "You want that arsehole flirting with you?"

Gut churning with indignation, I tried to fry him with a look alone. "I was just about to tell Mr. Barr it was inappropriate for him to touch me without my permission. It was up to me to do that. I didn't need you to come and pee all around me like I'm some possession to be fought over."

Brodan exhaled slowly and then squeezed the bridge of his nose.

I trembled as I waited for him to annoy me by trying to justify his actions.

Instead, he shocked me.

"You're right. You're absolutely right." He gave me a pleading look. "I'm sorry, Sunset."

Stunned, I deflated. "You're sorry?"

"Aye, I'm sorry." He took a step toward me. "I have never been territorial over women … just you. And I'm not proud of it and promise to do better to curb the possessive arsehole within. I'm just … I'm afraid you'll change your mind about me. That you'll walk away. Maybe even find someone else."

I wanted to be angry with him, but as I thought about my

own jealous reaction to the parents flirting with him earlier, I'd be a hypocrite. Still, it was a good reminder. "I haven't decided about us, Brodan. And watching your fans"—I gestured toward the door, indicating the legion waiting for him in the cafeteria—"fawn all over you isn't exactly making me want to give us a shot."

Brodan frowned, taking another step toward me. "They have nothing to do with me. I can't help what other people do, Roe."

"You didn't exactly extract yourself from the situation."

"I directed the musical their kids were in." His voice rose with exasperation. "They wanted to thank me, to talk about it. I can't help if they flirt while they do that, but I wasn't flirting back, and you know that. Other people's actions are not my responsibility, Roe, and you holding them against me isn't fucking fair." He looked devastated all of a sudden. "And I can't live my life in fear that you'll walk away from me because of it."

So instead, *he* walked away from me.

Panic seized my chest with an unexpectedness that made my knees wobble. How had this discussion turned into something so devastatingly final?

I'd let my jealousy get the better of me.

Just as he had.

Damn it.

The entire time we'd become friends again, not once had he held that night with Arran against me. He'd shown me compassion and understanding for my lost night, despite it being the catalyst that ruined us.

I still didn't know if I could fully trust my heart to him, but I knew I wanted to try, and our relationship wouldn't survive if we held things against each other.

Hurrying out of the room, I slammed the classroom door

shut behind me and locked it. I could see Brodan marching down the corridor, almost out of sight.

"Brodan!" I yelled, hurrying after him.

He kept walking.

"Brodan!"

To my relief, he halted and turned around. As I neared, I saw the muscle flexing in his jaw, his expression wary.

I didn't stop until we were almost touching, tilting my chin to hold his gaze as I laid my hands gently on his chest. His heart beat fast beneath my palm. "I'm sorry," I whispered.

As he remained guarded, I continued, "Brodan, I'm sorry. We were both jealous. We're both on edge as we work this thing out. I promise to do better."

His entire body sagged with relief, and he reached for me, wrapping his arms around my waist as he bent to rest his forehead against mine. "I promise to do better too."

28

MONROE

"You're sure your family doesn't mind me crashing Christmas Day?" I asked, feeling more nervous about approaching Thane and Regan's home than I had the afternoon of the Christmas fair.

Christmas Day was for family. Mum and I hadn't spent Christmas Day together in well over a decade, so there was really no change in that department. I'd always called her, even though I'd end up feeling like shit after the call. No, over the years, I'd spent Christmas Day with friends and other people's families. When someone heard you were spending it alone, the offers poured in. It was the season of generosity, after all.

However, I'd spent my thirties alone at Christmas. After Steven, I'd moved out of Glasgow and started over in Renfrewshire. I felt ashamed to tell my new work colleagues and friends that I was spending Christmas alone, so I'd lie about going home.

This would be my first Christmas with a family again. A tantalizing tease of what could be.

"Of course, they don't," Brodan assured me as we turned

down the country lane toward the two homes that belonged to his eldest brothers. "Sloane, Callie, and Walker will be there too."

I nodded in relief at the reminder and then studied the house as we pulled in behind a line of cars cluttering the driveway. In the covered entrance of Thane and Regan's was a large Christmas tree, accompanied by a massive lit wreath on the door. It looked beautiful and warm and inviting.

"I've spent every Christmas alone since I was thirty," I confessed suddenly.

Brodan switched off the engine, not saying a word.

Afraid of what he might think of that, I reluctantly dragged my eyes off the front entrance and looked at him. Brodan stared at me, half anguish, half guilt.

"Don't do that," I practically whispered. "I didn't have to be alone, Brodan. I made choices that led me to that too."

"If you'd had a family worthy of you, you'd have never spent a Christmas alone." He reached over and caressed my cheek. "I want to give you this"—he gestured to the house— "for the rest of your life ... but if you decide you don't want that, promise me ..." Pain flared in his eyes. "Promise me you'll find it with someone else. Because I'd rather suffer through the agony of knowing you love someone else than ever suffer the pain of knowing you're out in the world alone. You deserve so much more than that, Monroe."

A sob escaped before I could stop it, and the fear I'd held deep within me burst forth. "What if I don't deserve *you*?"

Brodan's eyes widened, shock at my question evident. Confusion too. He opened his mouth to reply, but we both jumped at a rattle against the driver's-side window. I'd been so lost in our moment, I hadn't even noticed Regan come out of the house.

Cursing under his breath, Brodan hit a button, and the window lowered to reveal Regan and her beaming, dimpled smile. "Merry Christmas, you guys! Can you move—" She cut off at the sight of me wiping my eyes, and her smile fell. "Oh my God, I'm sorry. Did I interrupt something?"

"No." I gave her a fake smile. "Merry Christmas, Regan. Thank you for inviting me."

"Of course." Her worried gaze moved to Brodan. "You okay?"

"Aye. Merry Christmas. What was it you needed?"

"Never mind. Arro and Mac might not even drive, so it's a possible parking nonissue. Come on in."

I unclipped my seat belt, refusing to meet Brodan's probing stare. "Better not forget the presents in the back." I jumped out of the SUV and opened the rear passenger door. Thankfully, my invitation came early enough for me to buy a little something for everyone. I especially wanted to give Arro and Mac a wee thank-you gift for letting me stay in the cottage.

Regan hurried up the front porch but waited for us to follow. Brodan grabbed his bags of gifts for everyone and rounded the car. His eyes flicked to his sister-in-law before coming back to me. "Don't think this discussion is over," he murmured.

Wonderful.

"Come in, come in." Regan waved us into the house, and for the first time, I noticed she wore a reindeer headband, Christmas baubles hanging from her ears, and her dress was red and green. She made me smile.

Until we stepped inside and she said, "Ooh, stop," as she closed the door behind us.

Brodan and I did as she asked, me assuming she wanted us to remove our shoes. The sound of laughter and chatter accompanied by low-level Christmas music and the scent of delicious cooking drifted toward us. Anticipation fluttered in my belly, and I was relieved for its distraction.

Regan ruined my moment by grinning devilishly. She pointed a finger skyward. "No couple may pass beneath the mistletoe. It's an entry requirement."

My pulse skittered. Brodan, to my surprise, had been a very, very good boy this year. He was sticking to the requirements of the bet. Sometimes it felt like he had more self-control than me, especially when he whispered dirty nothings in my ear. That meant our lips had not touched in weeks. And after my vulnerable moment in his car, I wasn't sure I wanted this to be the time it happened.

"Our bet," I murmured.

He shrugged, eyes glittering with amusement. "I want my Christmas dinner, so I reckon we call a temporary ceasefire."

"Fine." I drew up on my tiptoes and pressed my lips to his briefly before settling back down. "There."

Regan pouted with disappointment. Voyeur. "That wasn't a kiss. You're disrespecting the mistletoe."

Brodan searched my face. Whatever he found there made him ask Regan quietly, "Let's let her off the hook, sis, eh?"

"Fine. You know I put that mistletoe there, so Thane is forced to kiss me before he leaves for work every day." She grinned cheekily.

"Somehow I doubt my brother feels forced," Brodan observed, taking the thought right out of my head.

"No, he does not," Regan agreed. "This way." She sashayed ahead of us, leading us into the main living space. The room was decorated beautifully, a large tree in the far corner surrounded by gifts the kids had already opened and others that remained wrapped.

The room was a flurry of activity. Eredine was in the kitchen, a glass of wine in hand, and Arran sat at the island. Lewis sat with Thane on the couch, looking over what I assumed was a shiny new laptop. Eilidh and Callie huddled together in the large armchair, giggling over whatever they were doing on a tablet computer. They were both dressed in the cutest Christmas dresses, Callie in green, Eilidh in red, and looked like a perfect postcard. Searching for Callie's mum, I found Sloane seated next to Robyn and Baby Vivien, while Walker stood chatting with Lachlan near the dining table.

The only folks missing were Arro, Mac, and Baby Skye.

"Look who's arrived, everyone!" Regan announced.

Eyes flew toward us, and smiles and cries of "Merry Christmas" met our ears. Regan gestured for us to put down our bags, and Arran was the first to approach to hug us. With the moment in the car still on my mind, I tried not to tense as Arran hugged me tight and kissed me on the cheek. "Merry Christmas, Roe. So happy you're here."

I wanted to look at Brodan. To see his expression. I wanted ... to know. But the coward I was, I kept my attention fixed on Arran and replied, "Merry Christmas. Happy to be here."

Eredine rounded the counter, smiling brightly as she hugged Brodan, then me. We exchanged hugs and handshakes all around (and received a nod of greeting from Walker, whom I wasn't sure knew how to crack a smile) before we shrugged out of our jackets and settled in.

Arro, Mac, and Skye arrived not long later, and then we were a full house. Brodan and I offered to help in the kitchen, but Regan and Eredine assured us they had it under control. They'd yell if they needed us.

After a glass of wine, I relaxed a bit, chatting away with Sloane and Robyn, and while Brodan had gotten involved with whatever Thane and Lewis were up to, I could feel his inquisitive eyes on me now and then.

"So, your parents couldn't come to Scotland for the holidays?" Robyn asked Sloane after Lachlan came over to take

Vivien. He and Mac had disappeared to put the girls down upstairs.

Sloane looked uncomfortable as her gaze flew to Callie, and she shook her head. "We're on our own."

Robyn, being a smart cookie, left it at that. "Yeah, well, sometimes I wish we were on our own."

Regan, she of the bat ears, called over, "Amen to that!"

Her sister snorted, and I asked, "You don't get along with your parents?" Maybe we had that in common.

"Yes, and no. Regan's dad, my stepdad, is the best. But our mother is ..."

"The Queen of Passive Aggression," Regan supplied helpfully.

My lips twitched as Robyn grimaced. "She's not wrong. Mom wanted us to come out to Boston this year for Christmas since they've been flying here. But it was just the worst year to ask us to do that because of Vivien. And now Regan and I have been treated to not-so-subtle guilt-tripping for the last few months, and she refused to fly here. Even though we offered to pay for it. My stepdad won't leave my mom alone, so Merry Effing Christmas."

Her words made me wince. "I'm sorry. I know what it's like to have a difficult mother."

Sympathy filled Robyn's expression. "Well ... let's just forget about it for today and enjoy Regan's awful cooking."

"Hey!" the cook in question yelled, and seconds later, a raw brussels sprout flew across the room and bounced off Robyn's head.

Robyn chuckled, leaning down to pick it up. "You do have good aim, though."

"No dessert for you, Robbie."

"Oh, come on. Everyone knows I'm kidding," Robyn huffed and got up to stride across the room toward her sister. "I am very grateful you are cooking a delicious

Christmas dinner for our horde, and I'm sorry for teasing you. Even though you make it really hard not to when you're wearing those antlers on your head."

Sloane and I chuckled at the sisters' banter. "This is nice," Sloane said quietly as we stared around the room. "This is how it should be."

Our eyes met, and I saw a sadness in hers that mirrored my own. A moment of deep connection thrummed between us, and I reached out to squeeze her hand. "Merry Christmas, Sloane."

She squeezed my hand in return. "Merry Christmas, Roe."

"What whisky is this?" Brodan asked, frowning as he smelled it.

Gifts had been exchanged before dinner, and I was almost brought to tears by the Adairs' generosity. Not only had every couple given me a gift, they'd given Sloane, Callie, and Walker something too. I now had everything from perfume to a spa voucher to take home with me.

My gifts of a book about screenwriting and a bottle of his aftershave had delighted Brodan. He was impressed I'd guessed correctly what he'd worn. I'd nearly burned my nose off in a fragrance store trying to find the damn scent, but it was worth it to see that boyish smile.

However, he'd told me he wanted to wait until we were alone to give me his gift, so I was stuck in anticipation throughout dinner. As for dinner, it had been a tasty, raucous affair. Skye and Vivien interrupted it a few times, their parents jumping up from their seats mid bite to run upstairs to check on them. Eilidh and Lewis squabbled over who had the most mashed potatoes while Callie watched on in bemusement. Arro had one glass of wine and almost crash-landed in her dinner from tiredness, so Regan got up to make her an extra-strong coffee.

There was teasing and conversation among the Adairs, and they pulled me, Sloane, and Walker into it as if we'd always belonged there. I learned Regan was studying to get a business degree so she could open a preschool in Caelmore, an excellent idea since we were sorely lacking in that department. Arran regaled us with the latest stories from the Gloaming. I saw Sloane eyeing Walker a few times, especially as he was seated on Callie's other side. He was soft with Sloane's daughter in a way he wasn't with anyone else, and I had to admit I could see why that might intensify Sloane's crush on him.

It was chaotic and joyful, and I'd never had a Christmas dinner like it.

Now the adult after-dinner drinks of whisky and Baileys (for those who didn't drink whisky) had been served.

"It's Tobermory, I think," Thane said in answer to Brodan's question.

"We drink Macallan," Brodan replied, indignant.

"It was a gift. I thought we'd try it."

"We don't just drink Macallan," Lachlan added. "I quite like a bit of Talisker."

"Aye, Talisker is nice," Mac agreed.

"I prefer a peatier whisky," Walker offered. "Like Caol Ila."

"Nah, too smoky," Arran disagreed.

"Exactly." Walker glowered at him.

I looked at Sloane and mouthed, "Seriously?"

She hid a smile behind her glass of Baileys.

"Hey, that's an idea." Brodan stared at Lachlan like he'd been struck by lightning. "You and I should open a distillery."

Lachlan snorted. "Aye, I'll just hand over a few million pounds to do that, shall I?"

Brodan shrugged. "We can afford it."

"Arsehole," Arran teased.

His brother flashed a middle finger at him as he continued to talk to Lachlan. "Seriously, Lachlan. An Ardnoch whisky promoted by the famous Adair brothers. Folk will eat it up. And we could create a whisky that we all can agree on."

Lachlan considered it, while my heart beat a little faster for Brodan. He was genuinely excited by this idea. "Do the research, bring me the numbers and what's required, and we can talk."

"Really?" Brodan grinned, definitely excited.

His eldest brother chuckled. "Really."

"Must be nice to throw a few million away on a distillery," Arran said jokingly and raised his glass. "To pricks with too much money."

Walker clinked his glass off Arran's.

Lachlan and Brodan stared at each other, shrugged, and then raised their glasses too, making us laugh.

Thane, however, raised his and said seriously, "To men who worked hard for every penny and brought prosperity back to the place they call home."

"Aw, big brother." Arran launched himself at Thane, hugging him hard.

"Get off!" Thane shoved him away, laughing.

"Don't spill your whisky!" Regan yelled from across the room, noting the friendly tussle.

"Don't worry, it's not Macallan," Brodan called back.

"Oh, for Christ's sake, I'll find you the bloody Macallan," Thane huffed and stalked toward the kitchen.

"Thanks, big bro," Brodan called after him.

"You're awful to him. The both of you." Lachlan shook his head, smirking.

"He's just so easy." Brodan smirked.

"Be nice to your brother, Brodan Adair," I warned.

He turned to look at me, eyes glinting beneath the Christmas lights. "I tell you what, I'll be nice if you come with me."

"Where?"

Holding out his hand, he insisted, "Just come with me."

I gave Sloane a bemused look before placing my hand in Brodan's. He began leading me through the living room, and my cheeks flushed for no reason at all.

"Are you leaving, Uncle Brodan?" Eilidh yelled from her spot on the floor with Callie. They were building the Lego version of the house from the movie *Home Alone*.

"Not yet, princess." He winked at her. "I'll be back soon."

"Will you help us with this when you come back?"

"Of course," he promised.

My heart melted because I knew it wasn't an empty promise.

We left behind the noise of the main room, and Brodan pulled me down the hallway toward the front entrance. Just before the mistletoe, he opened a door and led us into an office. He shut the door quietly behind us and then took my glass from my hand and rested it on the desk with his. Pulse racing, I faced him, trying to maintain a calm expression.

"First things first. Why would you think you don't deserve me?" he asked without preamble.

Damn it.

I knew he'd be a dog with a bone about that.

There was no point hedging. If the ache of longing inside me was anything to go by, I was already losing this battle to protect my heart from him.

"I've forgiven you for the way you treated me," I said. "But I'm not sure I've forgiven myself for Arran. I thought I had. But I keep asking myself, every time he comes near me, how you can watch on and not remember that night and how it ruined us. I know you and I weren't together, but you were my best friend, and I hurt you."

He frowned deeply but stepped toward me to clasp my face in his hands. "For a start, I hurt you first. And second, when you told me what it was like for you that night, how it was just blankness until the moment I appeared, I felt nothing but sympathy for you. Because I've been there, and I know how scary that feeling is."

Surprised, I asked, "What happened?"

He moved his hands from my face to my shoulders, then smoothed them down my arms to my hands to thread his fingers through mine. "A few years ago, when I got that note from Vanessa?"

I nodded for him to continue.

"Like I said, I spiraled. It was on the heels of Fergus's psychotic break. I was drinking and partying a lot. Then one morning, I woke up and ..." He gave me a wary look. "There were multiple naked strangers in the room. Women and men. And I couldn't remember a fucking thing. But I was naked too."

My hands tightened on his. "Brodan."

"It scared the hell out of me. So I know what it feels like to black out on alcohol and not know what the fuck you're doing. Side note, I got every sexual health check under the sun done after that, so no need to worry about our night together. As for yours and Arran's night together ... I'm not angry at you and Arran. Or jealous when you hug. Arran is head over heels for Ery, and I know you don't feel that way about him. I don't see that night as something you made happen. It was a night that happened *to* you. I'm just sorry that it did. I'm sorry it happened to us all."

His compassion broke me.

Tugging on his hand, I wrenched open the door and

gestured for him to follow me into the hall. He did so, his nose wrinkled in confusion.

I stood us beneath the mistletoe and stared up into his beautiful face. "The bet is off, Brodan. I don't want to play games anymore. I just want you."

Relief flooded his expression and was quickly followed by heated determination. He yanked me against his hard body, bending to reach me.

Then his hot mouth was on mine, and it felt like coming home.

I didn't know how I patiently got through the rest of the evening.

Brodan, as promised, helped Eilidh build some of her Lego. Walker took Sloane and Callie home because Callie was growing tired. By this point, Robyn, Lachlan, Arro, and Mac had left with their wee ones too. When Eilidh's eyes drooped with tiredness, Regan told her it was time to get ready for bed. When she burst into tears, it reminded me of how young Eilidh really was. She was exhausted, but she didn't want to stop playing with Uncle Brodan. I swear I melted into a puddle of goo as Brodan cuddled the long-legged child into his arms, soothing her as he carried her upstairs past a grateful Thane, who followed him up.

Between that and our heated kiss in the hallway, I knew I was ready.

Brodan didn't know.

But he was about to.

Our drive back to the cottage after our goodbyes was silent, and I knew Brodan was probably worried about why.

I made it clear to him, however, when I said, "Park your car around the back of the cottage."

"What?" He glanced quickly at me.

"Stay with me tonight."

Brodan's grip on the wheel tightened, and he gave me an abrupt nod, like he couldn't quite speak, as the atmosphere between us sizzled. I was in a fog of lust during our walk from the car to the cottage. Once we were inside, I locked up, not bothering to switch on the lights. Instead, I kicked off my shoes and strolled toward the staircase, shrugging out of my jacket and dropping it on the floor. I moved with a casualness that belied the rapid beating of my heart. The last time we did this, Brodan had wounded my feelings beyond measure.

It was a massive leap of faith that he wouldn't again.

I heard Brodan's swift intake of breath as my Christmas jumper followed my jacket, and I ascended the stairs in nothing but my bra. My hair brushed the naked skin of my mid back, and I shivered in anticipation of feeling Brodan's fingers caress me instead.

The stairs creaked beneath his heavy footsteps as he followed me up.

With a glance over my shoulder as I walked across the hall, my stomach somersaulted at the heated intensity etched harshly across Brodan's face. He almost seemed like a stranger, and yet his expression excited the hell out of me. Goose bumps scattered down my spine, and my breasts felt suddenly heavy.

My breathing increased as I moved into the bedroom and crossed to the window to close the blinds. A soft light filled the dark room, and I turned to see Brodan had switched on one of the bedside lamps.

I felt nervous. It wasn't like traveling back to when we

were eighteen and I couldn't believe all my teenage dreams were coming true. Too much time had worn over us like sandpaper, reshaping us, changing us into something made from the same material as before, but ... different. Corners had been shaved off, and experiences had rubbed away the polish of youth and naiveté.

And yet, I still wanted this new version of Brodan as much as I'd ever wanted the boy I'd loved all those years ago. Tears swam in my eyes as I gazed across the room at him, seeing my thoughts mirrored in his eyes.

"It hurts," he whispered hoarsely. "How much time we've lost."

I nodded. "I know."

Brodan let out a shuddering breath as he crossed the room to clasp my face in his hands and pressed his forehead to mine. "I don't want to lose anymore," he said raggedly against my lips.

"I ... I can't make promises," I told him with quiet honesty. "But I want to try. I'll regret it for my whole life if I don't."

He lifted his head to stare into my eyes. "We don't have to ... tonight. If it feels like too much."

I gave him a wry smile. "It always feels like too much with you, Brodan."

The corner of his mouth tilted up. "Aye, with you too."

Then, before I could stop the words, I blurted, "What do you see in me?"

My cheeks heated with embarrassment that I'd allowed the insecure question to escape. However, I'd harbored it for months. When we were kids, I never really blamed myself for Brodan supposedly not returning my feelings. I think I'd known him so well that deep down, I'd always believed he kept a distance romantically because he was afraid to love me like that. That *I* wasn't the problem. But now ... knowing he was used to traveling the world, experiencing extraordinary things, and having endured the stupid and painful task of googling him and all his glamorous casual women, I couldn't help but feel that a petite primary school teacher who had only ever traveled out of the country once didn't exactly measure up.

Brodan's eyebrows rose at my query.

"Never mind." I laughed, embarrassed. "Stupid question. I'm awesome, of course. Why wouldn't you want me?"

He saw through my false bravado, his hands sliding down my neck and across my shoulders. "I see a woman who has endured pain since she was a child with a strength that humbles me."

I tensed.

But Brodan forged ahead, his tone growing more passionate. "I see a woman who protects those she thinks can't protect themselves, who finds genuine pleasure in molding the minds of children who would test most people's patience if they had to be around that many on a daily basis."

I chuckled because that was true.

Brodan smiled at the sound of my laughter, but he never lost his intensity as he continued, "I see a woman who has put herself before others to the detriment of her own well-being. I see a woman who is the greatest friend, the most loyal friend, who can talk about the weird and wonderful for hours, or, if you need it, can create the biggest shoulder to lean on out of the tiny one she carries." He leaned down to press a kiss to said shoulder, and I had to blink back tears at his tenderness.

When he raised his head, he whispered, "I see a good woman I don't deserve ... but then I've always been a selfish bastard, and when I want something, I rarely care if I deserve it."

"Brodan."

"Now let me show you all the ways I *want* you, my love."

Anticipation flooded my belly, and I nodded mutely.

He searched my face and bent to press the gentlest kiss to my forehead, then the corner of my right eye. "You have new freckles on your forehead and one right there on the corner of your eye," he whispered hoarsely, sounding almost pained. "It bothers me more than I can stand that I don't know when they first appeared."

"Brodan," I whispered tearfully. "Stop making me cry. It's not sexy right now."

He laughed against my lips and lightly brushed his mouth across mine. I reached into it, wanting more, but he held back. "I noticed the ones on your stomach are still there."

"What?" I murmured, feeling pulled into a daze of imprisoned lust.

"Your freckles on your stomach. When we were teenagers, sometimes your top would ride up, and I'd see those freckles and think about exploring every single one. Fuck, you have no idea how many times I had to hide a stiffy from you."

I gave a bark of laughter. "I didn't know."

He grinned. "I know. You were adorably innocent."

My smile felt almost sultry. "If you move this along a bit, you might find I'm not innocent anymore."

Brodan's expression darkened. "I want to take my time with you."

"You want to torture us, you mean?"

"Maybe a wee bit," he teased, pressing a quick kiss to my throat.

My fingers twitched at my side, desperate to reach for him. But I was also curious to see how this would play out.

"You had no idea what your smile did to me. How fucking beautiful you were. There were so many nights I wrapped my hand around my dick and fantasized about what it would be like between us if I just let myself have you."

My breath hitched.

"Did you think about me back then? Did you touch yourself thinking about me?"

I nodded.

His eyes narrowed. "Did you think about me when you were with other blokes?"

Indignation rippled through my desire. "Did you think about me when you were with other lassies?" I countered.

Brodan nodded. "I'm ashamed to say I did."

I closed my eyes. "We're quite the pair."

"Does that mean you did too?"

"Yes," I confessed. More than once, I'd closed my eyes when I was with a boy and got off imagining it was Brodan. It wasn't fair to them. It wasn't fair to either of us.

"I did it a year ago," Brodan murmured.

My eyes flew open.

"It was February 8."

I let out a gasp. "My birthday."

He nodded, his hands dropping to settle on my waist, as if he was afraid I might move away. "I … she was just some woman I met at a bar. The entire experience was empty. Once we started, I felt trapped in my own skin. I wanted to push her off, tell her to get out, but it felt like to admit that was to admit I was broken somehow," he confessed with a sheepish, unhappy smirk. "You were on my mind. I wondered where you were, who you were with, if he had splashed out on your birthday, if there were kids that made cards with 'Happy Birthday, Mum' on them. And it still fucking hurt," he whispered incredulously, "imagining it. Imagining your life without me. So I closed my eyes, and I pretended she was you."

Heart beating wildly, I reached up and caressed his cheek. Brodan bussed into my touch, closing his eyes as if in pain. "We don't have to imagine anymore. Let's stop …

279

okay? Let's just be here. Right now. We're here together now."

His eyes opened, and a fierceness lit them as he nodded. "We are. And you're still so fucking beautiful it kills me."

"Aye?" I smiled, my skin flushing with pleasure. "Show me. Show me how beautiful you think I am, Brodan Adair."

And so he did.

His hands moved up my waist, fingertips caressing across my ribs, and goose bumps prickled over my breasts. They were so heavy, desperate for his hands, his mouth.

"Brodan ..."

His palms skated slowly down my stomach, and Brodan dug his thumbs into the waistband of my jeans, expression determined and hot as our eyes stayed connected. Slowly, he unbuttoned and unzipped me, then tugged the denim down over my hips. They were my best skinny jeans and they clung tightly to me, so he had to guide them down, lowering to his haunches to do so. I felt his hot breath on my cotton underwear, and I shuddered with need. Bracing a hand on his strong shoulder, I lifted one foot after the other so he could pull off the jeans.

When he curled his large hands around my calves, looked up into my eyes, I felt a tug deep in my womb. It caused another rush of wet to dampen the material between my legs, and Brodan's gaze lowered there. His hands climbed higher and then he glided his thumbs toward my inner thighs and demanded, "Open your legs."

Another wave of arousal pulsed through me, and I moaned as I complied. Gently, he pushed beneath my underwear, and I gasped as two thick fingers slid easily inside me.

"Fuck, aye, fuck," he muttered excitedly and then groaned as he rested his forehead against my stomach. "I forgot how amazing you feel."

"I'd like to be reminded of how amazing you feel," I said a little breathlessly.

Brodan looked up at me and grinned. "Soon, my love." Then he eased his fingers from me, only to tug my underwear down my legs. I stepped out of them, my body trembling with need. Brodan surprised me by lifting my left leg over his shoulder. I gasped, grabbing onto his other shoulder for balance. He flashed me another wicked grin. "I think my Sunset needs a good licking before the main course, don't you?"

I didn't even know what noise I made, just that it was one of guttural agreement. My fingernails bit into his shoulder as I was held open to him, vulnerable and yet totally uninhibited. I wanted his mouth on me. It was imperative that it happened immediately.

"Is that a yes, my love?" He teased my clit with his thumb.

"Yes, yes, yes," I murmured, undulating toward him.

His eyes flashed with triumph and then he bent his head between my thighs and licked me from entrance to clit.

"Uhhh," I groaned, one hand sliding into his hair, my fingers curling into the soft strands as his tongue relished me. Need slammed through me, and I tried to move against his mouth. His fingers dug into my thigh, and I felt his groan in every nerve ending.

"Brodan," I gasped.

He suckled my clit, pulling on it hard, and I panted as beautiful tension built deep inside. His tongue circled my clit and then slid down in a dirty, voracious lick before pushing inside me.

"Yes," I cried, desperately thrusting against his mouth as I climbed higher and higher toward breaking apart completely.

Feeling my desperation, Brodan returned to my clit and gently pushed two fingers inside me. He fucked me slowly as he sucked on the bundle of nerves at my apex, and I was done for.

My orgasm was like a fiery explosion that filled my vision with light, the release quaking deliciously through me as I shuddered against Brodan's mouth.

He gently lowered my trembling leg, and I swayed against him, my inner muscles throbbing. Brodan stood, and I leaned into him. I was stunned, not just by the majesty of my release, but that my body still felt strung taut despite it.

I wanted more.

Brodan's grip on my waist tightened as he stared at me like a starving man. All that lust, that desire, that savage need in his expression, was for me. He'd thought of me when he was with other women. That broke my heart, but it also made me triumphantly territorial. Like he was mine.

At that moment, I didn't care if he possessed every inch of me in return.

My chest heaved with my labored, excited breaths as he brought his hands to my shoulders. His eyes followed his fingertips as they trailed with excruciating slowness across my collarbone and down toward the rise of my breasts. I wanted my bra off. I wanted his mouth on me again. My nipples peaked against my bra with anticipation.

"Stop tormenting me," I whispered plaintively.

In answer to my needy plea, Brodan gripped my hips and pulled me to him so I could feel the steel of his erection against my bare stomach.

Gently, he cupped my face in his hands and kissed me so deeply, I could taste myself. I marveled at his control. If I was setting the pace, our kiss would be hungry, wet, wicked. But Brodan's kiss was languid, sexy, and so tender I could almost cry again. My hands curled around his biceps, feeling his strength, and I didn't know what I wanted to do more: take him inside me or let him hold me while we both cried a lifetime of tears.

But I'd told him no more. Tonight we would stop looking back and just be in the moment.

I returned his kiss, channeling all those years of longing into it, and, as if he felt it, Brodan squeezed my waist, his fingers almost biting into my skin with his need. Then he seemed to regain control of himself. His breathing slowed, his tension eased. His hands moved over my body with light strokes. He learned every inch of me—my ribs, my waist, my stomach. His palms glided around to my ass to squeeze my cheeks in his hands, and that control he'd just gained snapped.

Brodan's kiss deepened, grew hungrier, and he drew me against his cock. I kissed him back with the same hunger, and our tongues caressed in deep, wet strokes. Throbbing between my legs, I grasped harder onto his biceps, pushing my hips against his erection, wanting him inside me.

I stroked my hands down his arms, learning the hard, muscular shape of him through his sweater. He was so much bigger than me. That night in the caravan, I'd been so aware of that. I loved it. I loved how delicate and feminine he made me feel. My exploration calmed him, and Brodan's kiss grew gentler. He nipped at my lower lip and then he eased away, only to stare into my eyes as he glided his hands up my back to my bra. With an ease that spoke of his experience, he unfastened it and then nudged the straps down my arms until it fell to the floor.

His gaze slowly disconnected from mine, and I shivered as his expression grew hooded. His hands tightened around my biceps while he feasted on the sight of my naked breasts. My nipples peaked under his perusal, tight, needy buds that begged for his mouth.

"Sunset," he murmured as he cupped me.

I moaned and arched into his touch. Ripples of desire undulated low in my belly as he played with my breasts, sculpting and kneading them, stroking and pinching my nipples. All the time, his attention vacillated between my face and my breasts. I thrust into his touch. "Brodan, Brodan ..."

His name had barely broken past my lips a second time when his mouth found mine. This kiss was rough, hard, desperate, and his groan filled me as he pinched both my nipples between his forefingers and thumbs. I gasped, and his growl of satisfaction made me flush with pleasure. I was beyond ready. Feeling the fabric of his sweater beneath my hands, I curled my fists into it and jerked my lips from his. I tugged on the material, wanting to see him bared. Of course, I'd seen him in the movies, but that was a stranger on film. This was Brodan. My Brodan. Hopefully. Finally?

Brodan released me, stepped back, and yanked his sweater up and off. As he threw it behind him and then worked on his boots and jeans, I gaped at him. I'd known that he was made beautifully, carved like a sculpture of male perfection through rigorous training. But I wasn't quite prepared. He seemed larger naked. His shoulders were so broad, he almost didn't seem real. Smooth, olive skin rippled over defined pecs, a six-pack, and the tapered waist of a swimmer. His thick thighs and muscular calves caused another hard flip in my lower belly, and I longed to see his ass.

I moaned when he had to peel his boxer briefs over his erection, and when freed, his cock was so hard it strained toward his abs.

He was ... beautiful. So beautiful, I was in awe.

And yet, I knew if Brodan Adair stood before me, an ordinary man with no abs or flexing muscles in his thighs and biceps ... he would still be extraordinary.

He held my gaze, affection and lust mingling in his. Every

part of my body swelled toward him as I watched him take a condom out of his wallet and roll it down his erection.

He reached for me, taking my hand as he lowered himself onto the edge of the bed. Then he guided me to straddle him, his arousal hot against my stomach. My breath stuttered at the vulnerability of being spread over him.

My fingers curled into his big shoulders as I took in Brodan's expression. Need, fierce need, battled with gentleness. I loved him for it. As soon as that word crossed my mind, I threw it from my head. I wasn't quite ready to give myself to him in *every* way.

For a second, doubt crept in.

But Brodan easily distracted me by sliding his hand along the nape of my neck, tangling in my hair to grab a handful. Then he gently tugged my head back, arched my chest, and covered my right nipple with his mouth.

I gasped as sensation slammed through me, my hips automatically undulating against him as he sucked, laved, and nipped. Tension coiled between my legs, tightening and tightening as he moved between my breasts, his hot mouth, his tongue—

"Brodan," I groaned.

Then he stopped, and I lifted my head to beg, to plead for him to keep touching me, but halted when he gripped my hips. Guiding me, he lifted me up, and I stared down at him, waiting as he took his cock in hand and put it between my legs. *Yes, yes, yes.* My excitement throbbed as I lowered myself onto him, feeling the hot tip of him against my slick opening. Electric tingles cascaded down my spine and around my belly, deep in my sex.

Brodan grasped my hip, fingers clenching into my skin, while he cupped my right breast with his other hand and squeezed. I gasped at the overwhelming, thick sensation of him as I lowered.

The coiling tension left over from my last orgasm teetered me on the edge of coming again. I cried out and clung to his shoulders as I rose and plunged back down. Brodan's grip tightened as I rode him for what only felt like seconds before my climax tore through me, my inner muscles rippling, tugging, and drawing Brodan deeper. Shuddering, my hips jerking, my abs spasming, I wrapped my arms around his neck to hold on. He rested his forehead against mine, his shoulders moving up and down with his excitement.

As the last of the tremors passed, I felt the overwhelming fullness of him inside me and knew I wasn't done. Oh my God. The man was turning me into a sex fiend.

Flushing, I lifted my head to see his reaction, and the firestorm of desire in his eyes made my inner muscles pulse around him.

Brodan grunted at the feeling and then said, voice hoarse, "Do you know how hard it was not to come with you?"

"Why didn't you?" I asked against his soft lips.

In answer, Brodan stood up with me wrapped around him, and then turned to drop us on the bed, me on my back. The motion made him drive deep inside me, and I let out a strangled cry of pleasure.

"Fuck, fuck, fuck," Brodan murmured thickly and then wrapped his hands around my wrists and pinned them to the bed at either side of my head.

His control snapped.

He thrust into me. Hard.

"Oh, God!"

Satisfaction blazed in his eyes as he moved inside me. I wanted to feel him; I wanted to grip his ass in my hands and feel it clench and release with each stroke, but he held me down.

That only excited me more.

The tension built in me again with every thick drag of him in and out. His drives came faster, harder. Then he released my wrists, but only so he could get up on his knees. Grabbing my legs, he spread me wider and tilted my hips up off the bed, his fingers biting into the back of my thighs. Then he pumped inside me even faster, harder. His hips snapped against mine as his features strained taut with desire. His gaze dragged over my body, watching my breasts shake and tremble with the force of his thrusts, and I saw his expression darken with pure lust. The sight of him above me, between me, fucking me like he couldn't get enough, was my undoing.

I shattered again. The exquisite feel of my muscles milking Brodan's cock prolonged my climax. I shuddered and shivered beneath him, gasping and panting in disbelief as the sensation rolled through me.

"Fuck, Sunset. Fuck!" Brodan's grip on my thighs was almost painful as he pulled me tighter against him and let go. I felt his cock swell inside me and contract as he climaxed, throbbing and pulsing, his long groan almost animalistic as he shuddered through the release.

His grip on me eased as he panted for breath, his gaze meeting mine in shattered awe.

I understood completely.

He gently pulled out of me, and I hissed at the sensation, feeling a slight twinge.

"You all right?" He poised above me, concern etched into his relaxed features.

"I don't know," I whispered back. "I think you've ruined sex for me with anyone else forever."

He grinned, slow, languorous, sexy as he pushed between my spread thighs and leaned over me. The damp skin of his hard stomach brushed against mine as he cupped me possessively between my legs. "Good. Because this is mine now."

I smirked against his lips. "Does that kind of talk work with other women, Brodan Adair?"

A hard glint entered his eyes. "I've never said or wanted to say it to another woman."

"Well, let me educate you," I murmured sleepily, wrung out from the most amazing orgasms of all time. "What you're petting with your hand right now belongs only to me. But since you just pleasured the life out of me, I'm willing to maybe, possibly, offer co-ownership. Sixty–forty, perhaps."

Brodan barked a laugh, his eyes crinkling at the corners. "That's good to hear because my dick just experienced a version of heaven it didn't know existed until now, and we're both feeling quite attached."

"It wasn't just me, then. That was …" I had no words.

"Fucking epic," Brodan supplied, and he kissed me hungrily. When he released me, he murmured, "I'm going to deal with this condom, then we'll sleep. You're going to need your rest because I don't plan to let you out of this bed for the next week."

I got out of bed with him to clean up, and he grinned at me in the bathroom mirror the whole time. It was surreal. There was a giddiness in me, like I was a teenager again. But I could feel the dark murmur of fear hovering in the background of my thoughts. Brodan didn't seem to share the same fears, which surprised me, considering how terrified he'd once been of commitment.

Instead, he took me by the hand, led me back to the bedroom, and helped me draw on a nightie because I didn't like sleeping naked.

We were just about to climb into bed when he said, "Shit. I forgot to give you your present."

"Oh, that does—"

But he was already hurrying out of the room and downstairs. Seconds later, I heard him ascending, and then he was there in nothing but his boxer briefs with a long velvet jewelry box in hand.

Oh my.

"Brodan …"

He wrapped his arm around my waist, cuddling me into his side as he held out the box. "Merry Christmas, Sunset."

"But …" My hand hovered over the black velvet. "I … I only got you aftershave."

Brodan shook against me with laughter. "Just open it."

With butterflies rioting in my belly, I took the box and pried it open.

Surprise, awe, then tenderness filled me.

Lying on the black velvet was a thin gold chain with a gold pendant. But not just any pendant. It was a circle, the lower half a solid gold, the upper laser cut to resemble a sun and its rays as it set on the horizon. In the center of the sun was a cluster of small diamonds. It was modern and unusual.

And so meaningful.

"It's a sunset," I whispered, gently touching the metal as my vision blurred.

"I bought it the day after I confronted your mum about my letter," Brodan confessed. "I wanted to believe that we'd be in a place I could give this to you on Christmas Day."

I smiled up at him, blinking back my tears. "I love it. It's perfect. Thank you."

He pressed a kiss to my temple. "Thank you, my love."

For a moment, I could only stare at the necklace, still discombobulated by all that happened between us in the last few weeks alone. Brodan chuckled and took the necklace from me, setting it down on my bedside table. "You can look at it in the morning. Let's get some sleep."

I nodded, dazed.

Once in bed, we spooned in the dark of the room, no sound around us except for our gentle breathing.

Brodan's arm wrapped tightly around me, his hand resting between my breasts. I covered his with mine and closed my eyes, deciding to accept the unbelievable night. To not overthink it.

To just take pleasure in sleeping with the man I'd dreamed of sleeping with for too many years to count.

30

BRODAN

I'd always considered myself attuned to Monroe. As an actor, I liked to think I was adept at reading people, sensing their moods. That I was empathetic. But with Roe, it was more. When we were children and I first became aware of how crappy her home life was, I'd watched Roe like a hawk. Ready to swoop down and rescue her the moment she needed it. Monroe rarely needed rescuing, but often she needed the comfort of knowing someone cared about her. Therefore, I watched for those moments when she needed me to be that person.

It was a habit that evolved until I was always aware of her changing moods.

Apparently, I still was.

And I was worried.

The days after Christmas were fucking magical. There was no other word for it. We'd canceled Boxing Day plans with my family because I'd turned into a horny eighteen-year-old and couldn't get enough of Roe. For two magnificent, unforgettable days, we'd learned every curve and hollow of each other's bodies. Our mouths had covered every inch. Just thinking about it made me hard.

Unfortunately, we had to return to the land of the living. I had to grab some clothes from the estate. And we needed food. Yet I was determined we walk into the village as a couple. I didn't want to hide it, even if it meant gossip among the villagers. The one thing Ardnoch could be counted upon for, however, was appreciating the positive consequences of the economic boom brought by my brother's exclusive club. In return, they respected the privacy of the celebrities who stayed there. I had faith I would be afforded the same privacy, and that they'd keep any gossip among themselves.

We ventured out, and since I couldn't seem to go five minutes without touching or kissing Roe, it was probably well known among the villagers that we were a couple by the time we got home from buying coffee and groceries. We'd also visited my family members individually, and I knew they were happy for us. Arro had texted after our visit:

Well, it's about bloody time!

This was followed by a series of dancing-women emojis. I guessed that was a good thing.

Some of my family were gearing up for Lachlan's Hogmanay party on the estate. Every year he rang in the new year with his members, and despite Vivien's birth, Robyn had insisted he not miss it. It was a tradition. Eredine disliked Hogmanay, so she and Arran had opted to babysit Eilidh and Lewis, and Arro and Mac were joining them along with Skye and Vivien. That meant Robyn, Lachlan, Regan, and Thane would attend the party.

I'd told Roe I wasn't going. I'd rather ring in the new year with her, hoping it would be a good omen for the future. But mostly, I was worried that if I took her into that world, the world of glitz and glamour and fame, it might scare her off. She was already cagey about my celebrity.

As we sat on the couch in her cottage, however, just a few days out from the party, I watched Roe warily over the top of the science fiction book I read.

I thought by now my fear would have set in. About losing her. There was an occasional flicker, but the euphoria of actually being with her pushed it out.

Now there was fear.

Fear of her withdrawing.

Changing her mind.

I'd leaned in to kiss her in the kitchen an hour ago and she turned, so I caught just the corner of her mouth. She'd given me a small smile that didn't reach her eyes.

Now, she was sitting on the other sofa when we hadn't detached ourselves from each other in days.

She was glued to the show playing quietly on the television. We'd watched a movie two nights ago, and she thought it hilarious as we flicked through a streaming app to click on all the movies I'd starred in. "Jesus, Brodan, people are bound to be sick of seeing that gorgeous face everywhere."

After I'd tickled the life out of her to get the remote back and her giggles had died down, she'd given me an admonishing look and said, "In all seriousness, no wonder you collapsed. You were working yourself to the bone."

It was true. I'd become obsessed with chasing a distraction. Because of it, I'd made some films I wasn't proud of. It was a life lesson, to be sure.

I didn't want Roe to be my next obsession. A passionate burst of flame that burned out too quickly.

I was going to slow down and not ignore moments like these. "There's something wrong," I finally said after stewing for hours.

Monroe's gaze jerked to mine. "Oh? What happened?"

Sighing, I dropped my book and leaned toward her,

elbows on my knees. "With you. There's something wrong with you."

She turned fully to look at me. "There's nothing wrong with me."

"Ever since we got back from Arro's, you've been strange. Distant."

"No, I haven't." She frowned and turned back to the TV. "I'm right here."

Frustration bubbled within me because I'd heard friends complain about their partners asking them the same question. I'd thanked fuck I didn't have to put up with that level of interrogation. Look at me now.

"Roe. Don't make me sound like a whiny girlfriend."

She cut me a glare. "Don't say sexist shit."

"How is that sexist?"

"Uh, because men ask what you're asking just as much as women do. But we're the insecure ones? Pfft."

"I'm right to ask? There is something on your mind?"

"It's not important." She gave me a tight smile. "Are you bored? Do you need a different book? Or do you want to watch something else?"

Irritated, I got off the couch and then lowered to my knees in front of her, pushing her legs wide before yanking her to me.

"Brodan," she spluttered, her hands coming to rest on my shoulders as she gaped. "What are you doing?"

"I wanted your full attention."

Her hands slid down my arms and around my back, and heat flashed through me.

Stay focused.

"Well, you certainly have it," she murmured, eyes narrowed with heat.

Fuck.

"I'm serious, Sunset." I squeezed her small waist. "What did I miss?"

Roe sighed. "Brodan, it's nothing. I'm just … being silly."

"Tell me."

She nibbled on her lower lip.

"Monroe?"

Another heavy sigh. "Fine … I'm just … Are you ashamed of me?"

"What the fuck?" It slipped out angrily.

She tensed and tried to pull away, but I held on tight.

"No, you don't get to ask that shit and run away. Explain."

Her eyes flashed. "Don't boss me around, Brodan Adair."

A different kind of heat simmered.

Stay focused.

"Tell me, Monroe."

She released me, crossing her arms over her chest, expression mulish. "Are you going to be an arsehole about it?"

Taking a deep breath, I shook my head. "No. I'm sorry. Continue."

Her expression was suspicious, but to my relief, she explained, "I don't mean in general. Obviously, you're happy for everyone here to know that we're together, but … you didn't even consider the invitation to your brother's Hogmanay party. Am I … do you … would it be embarrassing for you to attend one of those things with a primary school teacher?"

Shock held me frozen and speechless for a few seconds. It never even occurred to me she would assume that. Fuck. I tugged her closer, and her arms dropped from across her chest to rest on my shoulders again. "Sunset, no. Of course not." Deciding that too many lies had derailed us in the past, I answered honestly, "I didn't want to take you there because I'm worried being surrounded by those people, being in that world, will drive you away from me. You ... you told me you're not sure you can handle the fame."

Understanding softened Monroe's countenance, and she moved into me, wrapping her legs around my back until her chest pressed to mine. "I'm sorry I made you feel that way. I don't want you ever to feel insecure about that part of your life. If we want to make this work, I'll deal with it."

"Aye?" My doubts dissipated with relief. "You want to go to this shindig, then?"

She gave me a sad smile. "As much as I would love to see what's happened to the old castle ... I don't have a dress for that kind of thing."

If it were up to me, she'd have a million dresses, but my Roe had an independent streak a mile wide, and I didn't want to bruise her pride by telling her I'd take care of the dress. It would have to be done in a way she didn't feel bad about it. I'd figure it out.

For now, I murmured against her lips, "Well, there's nothing stopping me from showing you around the castle if you're curious about it."

She kissed me softly. "Really? Because I'd like to see it."

"We can arrange that, but first ..." I lifted her in my arms as I stood, and her squeal of fright made me laugh as I marched toward the staircase.

"Again?" she asked breathlessly, her cheeks flushed.

"You made me feel very insecure, my love," I teased. "I need some reassurance."

"And thus does your cock?" she asked wryly.

Said appendage hardened. "I love it when you talk fancy and dirty all in one sentence."

Her laughter filled the stairwell and my fast-beating heart. Too many emotions ran through my blood, raw and wild. By the time we got to the bedroom, I threw her on the bed and didn't even give her time to fully undress before I thrust inside her hot, tight body and poured every thought and every feeling into her with mine.

~

MONROE

I had some work I needed to set up for class starting back in January, so when Brodan announced he'd promised to visit Lachlan to help him with details for the Hogmanay party, I didn't question it. Instead, as much as I loved our wee bubble, I took the opportunity to work on my schedule and create homework sheets the kids could complete online. Being organized for work just put me in a better mood, and Brodan and I had plans to ring in the new year tonight. I'd rather do so with nothing else on my mind.

It was a shock, then, when Brodan showed up with two garment bags later that afternoon.

I gaped up at him from my laptop when he draped them over the couch and said, "I'll be back," before he disappeared out of the cottage and then returned a minute later with two shoeboxes.

"What on earth …?" I asked, closing my computer to stand up.

Brodan reached for a garment bag, unzipped it, and revealed a kilt and jacket.

"*Okay?*"

He grinned mischievously, and I couldn't help but smile back as he unzipped the next garment bag and revealed a stunning, dark green dress. "For you," he said. "For tonight. We're going to the party."

∼

"I can't believe I let you talk me into this," I murmured. Butterflies fluttered like crazy in my stomach as I walked into Ardnoch Castle for the first time in eighteen years. And on Brodan Adair's arm, no less. Wearing four-inch heels I hoped I wouldn't break my ankle in.

Brodan looked incredible in his kilt of Sutherland tartan in dark green, red, black, and white. He wore a dark gray jacket and waistcoat over a white shirt. Kilts were made for Scots like Brodan.

And despite not having a makeup artist or hairdresser to style my hair, I think I'd scrubbed up pretty well too. How Brodan had found me a dress and shoes on such short notice that fitted me to perfection was one of the man's many mysteries. He delighted in not telling me how he'd done it either, laughing when I became mulishly curious about it. He loved to torment me. The dress was something I might never have chosen for myself, but I had to admit, I felt pretty in it. There was an old Hollywood edge to the satin tea-length dress, with its layered, full skirt, cinched waist, and dramatically cut strapless sweetheart neckline. My boobs were pushed up impressively, and nestled just above my cleavage was the gold necklace Brodan bought me for Christmas. It was the only jewelry I wore.

To go with the old Hollywood theme, I'd given my hair some height and then pinned it into a side ponytail of soft waves. The shoes were strappy green sandals to match the dress.

I'd wanted to balk at Brodan buying me a dress, but he was so excited about taking me to the Hogmanay party, I accepted the gift. My gut reaction was to deny him his generosity because of how Steven had used his against me in our relationship. However, Brodan wasn't Steven, and I had to trust that his generosity came from a good place.

I had to trust that I knew who Brodan was.

"Wow." I gawked as we entered the main reception.

While its beautiful bones still existed, Lachlan had transformed the castle back to its glorious majesty. The parquet flooring had been restored and polished. The décor was traditional Scottish, but opulent too. The grand staircase was fitted with a new red-and-gray tartan wool runner instead of the worn one we'd tripped over as children. It led to the landing where Lachlan had replaced the three windows with floor-to-ceiling stained glass that looked like it had always been there. Beautiful Christmas garlands and fairy lights hung in strings along the galleried balconies at either end of the reception hall. I remembered us shouting to each other from across the balconies. Someone had miraculously restored the painted ceiling.

A fire burned in the huge hearth on the wall adjacent to the entrance and opposite the staircase. Tiffany lamps scattered throughout on end tables gave the space a warm glow, as did the massive Christmas tree in the corner.

There were guests everywhere. Famous faces among others I didn't recognize. Servers with trays of canapés and champagne flutes moved through the room to offer refreshment to the revelers.

"Lachlan's Hogmanay party is coveted. Members fly in from all over to be here," Brodan had told me before we left. I could see the proof before me. It was a bit of a squeeze.

"Brodan Adair, as I live and breathe." A familiar beauty with a lovely plummy British accent stopped before us.

Angeline Potter.

I tried not to gape.

But I loved her movies.

Her eyes flicked to me before moving back to Brodan.

"They told me you were living here, but I was beginning to think it was a lie. Where have you been?" She rubbed a hand over his lapel in a familiar, flirty way.

Suddenly, I didn't like her as much. My eyes narrowed on her hand, and Brodan cleared his throat and pulled me tighter against his side. "I've been around."

"Well, I'm here for a few weeks ... Duchess's Suite. Look me up." She gave him a sultry smirk.

"I won't be doing that," he said bluntly. "This is my girl-friend, Monroe."

It was the first time he'd actually said the words out loud.

For a moment, they shocked me, but I managed a small smile.

Angeline eyed me now, thoughtfully. "You do look famil-iar. Are you in Andy Bradshaw's latest movie?"

She thought I was a movie star?

Feeling mischievous, I shrugged.

"I've heard you're rather good." She took my shrug as a yes before turning back to Brodan. "If you're not free, darling, please tell me that rugged head of security has gotten over your sister."

Mac?

Brodan smirked. "Angeline, Mackennon Galbraith will never be over my sister. Or the baby girl they just had."

"Right." She pouted and then sighed heavily, looking around. "Oh, well then. Looks like I'm shagging someone I've already shagged tonight. Ta ra." With that, she sashayed away.

I snorted, and Brodan grinned down at me. "That was Angeline Potter," I whispered.

"It was."

"And she thought I was an actor."

"She did."

"She's quite funny in real life."

Brodan's lips pinched together.

"You don't like her? She seems so likable in her movies."

"She's the opposite of likable. Causes problems on set, and she fucked a friend of mine's husband while they were making a movie together. By all accounts, selfish to the core, that one. And a drama queen. Plus, it's like she bloody lives here. Lachlan jokes that she's trying to get more out of her membership than she's paying, but he might not be wrong. I once heard she—"

"Don't tell me any more." I wrinkled my nose. "You're ruining some of my favorite films."

Laughing, Brodan pulled me deeper into his side. "Come, let's find people we do like and maybe some of those canapés that keep whizzing by us."

The night was unlike anything I'd ever experienced. In fact, it might have been a wee bit too much if not for Brodan, his brothers, and their partners. Although Lachlan was forced from our sides much of the evening along with Robyn to play hostess, we had a good laugh with Thane and Regan. There was no pretension. We regaled Regan with stories of our childhood, and I realized for the first time that those stories were hurting less. It had only been a week, but already I felt like I was healing from the past.

In the background, a small orchestra entertained, but they played instrumental versions of modern pop music. Regan told me that one year the indie rock band High Voltage had played at the Hogmanay party.

As fire was a big part of Hogmanay celebrations, it didn't surprise me when Brodan led me outside with everyone else to watch the fire dancers. But I was taken aback by how spectacular the visual was of the procession of dancers down the extensive estate driveway, their flames lighting up the pitch-blackness beyond the castle. I gasped alongside everyone else as fire-breathers shot fireballs into the night sky and dancers twirled fans of fire and others spun by them in aerial cartwheels.

It was so otherworldly that I almost forgot I stood on Ardnoch Estate. It was a moment I was unlikely to forget, and after such a difficult year, it was surreal.

How quickly life can change.

For once, mine had changed for the better, and I wondered if I was really prepared to possibly walk away from this at the end of this year's school term. The thought filled me with dread, even as I knew I wasn't ready to admit that I wanted to stay with Brodan in Ardnoch.

MONROE

Once the fire dancers finished their display, we returned to find servers with more food waiting as Lachlan announced the procession of the haggis. It had been a long time since I'd taken part in such a traditional Hogmanay celebration, and I shoved my earlier morose thoughts aside to enjoy it. I felt a warm ache of pride in my chest as the bagpiper led in the haggis, the mournful tune of "Auld Lang Syne" seeming to fill the entire castle. Goose bumps prickled my exposed skin, and Brodan, somehow noticing, soothed his palms up and down my arms to warm me.

The servers descended upon us holding more champagne and delicious haggis pastry thingies drizzled in whisky sauce, and I was in food heaven. When the music suddenly stopped, we all turned to see Lachlan standing on the first landing of the main staircase. As the conversation died down, Brodan's brother raised his glass. "Thank you, honored guests," his deep voice resonated around the large hall, "for being here to celebrate Hogmanay at Ardnoch."

I raised my glass with everyone else to cheer, grinning up at Brodan, who smiled tenderly at me.

"There have been some changes here at Ardnoch this year. We welcomed Aria Howard to our staff." He gestured with his glass to a beautiful, curvy brunette who stood next to Robyn. "As our new hospitality manager, Aria has kept this place running like clockwork while I took some time with my wife and our new daughter, Vivien. To Aria!"

We raised our glasses to her, and the brunette smiled politely at everyone. This was the woman who helped Sloane get the job here. That's all the information I had so far from Sloane about her mysterious immigration. My curiosity was piqued. Who was Aria Howard? And why did she look so familiar?

"And if you might indulge me—to Robyn and Vivien. I always thought of Ardnoch as home, but as soon as I met you both"—his gaze rested on his wife, his expression blazing with such love, it made me lean back into Brodan—"I realized it was just a place until you. To my true home. To Robyn and Vivien."

"To Robyn and Vivien!" we cheered. Regan cackled delightedly at the uncomfortable smile on Robyn's face.

"She hates being the center of attention," Regan told us gleefully.

"You have a funny way of showing your love sometimes. Do you know that, wife?" Thane said dryly.

"You don't seem to mind how I show my love to you."

"Och, enough." Brodan grimaced. "No brother needs that visual."

Thane grinned smugly.

Lachlan spoke again over the growing murmurs of the crowd. "I hope as I look out upon you all that you've each found your own home, a place where you look forward to being as we enter this new year. Tonight, we let go of yesterday and embrace new beginnings." Lachlan raised his glass again, and we followed suit. "May ye for'er be happy an' yer enemies know it! *Slàinte Mhath!*"

"*Slàinte Mhath!*" we yelled.

Despite the glamour, the glitz, the famous faces, I had to admit I was enjoying myself. It didn't surprise me that Lachlan would host a Hogmanay that not only entertained his guests, but respected his Scottish heritage. And honestly, I'd felt nothing but pride to be Scottish and be a part of it, to see all these people from different places all over the world enjoy our traditions too. I'd been so nervous about coming tonight, and yet, I was having a wonderful time. I couldn't wait to tell Brodan because I knew he'd been nervous about bringing me into this area of his life.

The clock steadily eased toward midnight, and a while later, as Regan and Thane followed Lachlan and Robyn and all the guests outside for the drone display to count down to the bells, Brodan surprised me by holding me back.

I waited with rampant curiosity until only the staff remained in their traditional tailcoats and white gloves.

Once the last guest had gone, an older man in a dark green waistcoat that differentiated him from the rest of the staff approached Brodan. He gave him a small nod and said, "Mr. Adair, we have seen to your requirements."

Brodan smiled. "Thank you, Wakefield." Then he tugged on my hand. "Come on."

"Brodan, where are we going?" I asked, gasping with a bubble of giddiness fed by three glasses of champagne.

He led me past the small orchestra and upstairs.

"Brodan!" I hissed, tugging on his hand.

"It's not forbidden, Roe," he teased over his shoulder. "In fact, this is the way to my suite."

"Is that where we're going?"

"Nope."

"Brodan—"

"It's a surprise."

I tried to take in the many changes to the castle, disbelieving we were hurrying down the plush carpeted corridors of parts of the castle that had lain dark, dank, and empty when we were kids. The underskirts of my dress rustled as I rushed to keep up with him, my feet aching in the strappy sandals.

"Bro—" I cut off as he halted at the entrance to …

The castle turret.

No way.

My gaze flew to his. "What have you been up to?"

"Wait and see." He opened the door and held out a hand, pulling me in. The spiral staircase was still tight, but it was no longer dimly lit, cold, and damp, and the stone floors had been laid with carpet runner. My breathing echoed in my ears as Brodan pulled me upward and out into the turret space that had once been our place.

The place where the barriers of friendship first fell between us as he'd brought me to climax with his fingers.

Memories flooded me even as I took in the renovation. The turret had been transformed into a small library snug. Built-in bookshelves filled to the brim with books, a cozy armchair, and carpet beneath my feet. It was warm too, so Lachlan must have installed some kind of heating system and insulation. And on a side table by the armchair was what I imagined were the requirements Wakefield mentioned.

Two glasses of champagne, a champagne bottle in a bucket of ice, a vase with a few red amaryllis flowers, and a small cake covered in shiny chocolate ganache and gold leaf decoration. It looked straight out of a French patisserie. Two forks sat beside it. Soft music played from a phone nestled by the bucket.

"What have you been up to?" I asked quietly, a smile prodding my lips.

I felt Brodan's heat at my back and then shivered as he kissed my bare shoulder, whisper-soft kisses that tightened my nipples behind my strapless bra. Then he tugged on the zipper of my dress, the sound resonating around the room as he slowly lowered it, the fabric loosening around my breasts and waist.

"I wanted to bring you here," he said, his voice gruff, "to finish what I started all those years ago. To make you mine like I should have that day."

It was like a dream as I turned in his arms and let the dress drop to the floor. I stepped out of it as I unbuttoned his waistcoat. We'd explored every inch of each other's bodies, and yet the hunger for more persisted. To experience the bliss of Brodan inside me repeatedly.

I removed the strapless bra that matched my underwear, also courtesy of Brodan, but he murmured thickly for me to keep on my underwear as he stripped to his naked ass. Then he lowered me to the plush rug, stretching me out beneath him, and stared into my eyes as he braced his hands above my head.

A million emotions roiled in his striking pale gaze.

"What is it?" I asked.

He shook his head a little. "Just needed to remind myself this is real."

Loud voices counting down from ten rent the air outside before I could say anything, and I smiled as Brodan murmured the countdown along with them.

Cheers filled the air with cries welcoming in the new year.

"Happy New Year, Brodan."

"Happy New Year, my love." He kissed me soft, sweet. But I could feel him hard and hot between my legs.

I caressed his naked, strong back and whispered in anticipation, "You really need to remove my underwear if we want to take this any further."

"I intend to," he promised, trailing kisses over my breast. "But first, a little reminder ..." His hand coasted down my stomach and my muscles contracted with desire as his fingers slid beneath the fabric of the high-cut lingerie. Then his fingers were on that nub of nerves, rolling and pressing, pleasure zinging down my spine. I arched my hips into his touch. He looked up and watched me with savage determination on his face as I climbed toward climax. "That's it, Sunset. Find it."

As soon as I did, he swallowed my moans in his mouth. His fierce, yearning kiss that swept me up. I felt him brace himself over me again, pouring himself into me until we were both panting. When his mouth left mine, it was so he could kiss me all over. His tender kisses trailed a path down my neck, my chest, my breasts, to my stomach where he took his time over every freckle he seemed so fascinated by.

By the time he reached the waistband of my underwear, I was needy with want all over again. Our eyes met as his fingers curled into the fabric, and I lifted my hips to help him remove them. There was something about this act that turned Brodan on, and I reminded myself to always leave on my knickers so he could take them off. The thought made me smile, and curiosity gleamed in his eyes at the sight.

But then my underwear were off, and Brodan's mouth was on me, his tongue circling my clit, his fingers gripping tight to my thighs as he feasted. He kissed and licked and laved until I exploded with relief. I'd barely stopped shuddering through it when Brodan braced himself over me again, holding my gaze as he nudged into me.

"Protection?" I had the forethought to gasp.

Brodan smirked. "I put it on while you were coming very hard, my love."

I chuckled until it petered into a moan as he pressed inside in a slow, thick glide. He kissed me again, deep but languidly, and I wrapped him up, my thighs clasping his hips, my arms around his back, clutching him to me.

Eventually, I broke the sweetness of our kiss because I couldn't contain my moans. With every slow thrust, Brodan pushed me toward climax. Seeing and feeling my pleasure seemed to be Brodan's undoing, and I felt the strain and tension in his body as he forced himself to keep a steady, torturous pace.

"Brodan," I whispered in a plea. "Brodan."

"I'll never get enough of that," he told me hoarsely. "Hearing you say my name as you come."

His words only pushed me further toward that cliff of satisfaction. My nails dug into his shoulders and he gritted his teeth, powering harder into me even as he kept up that tormenting pace. "Come for me, Sunset. Let me feel you come."

And just like that, I did.

I cried out, throwing my head back and tightening my thighs around him, arching into his thrusts as my inner muscles spasmed around his cock.

Brodan stiffened and then let out an animalistic growl as he throbbed inside me, his hips slowing to a judder as he climaxed.

He groaned, collapsing over me, careful to keep much of his weight off me even as he buried his head against my throat. He ground his lower body into mine as the last of the shudders rippled through him.

I caressed his damp back as I stared into the stone ceiling above. The thought of ringing in every new year with Brodan like this crossed my mind, only to be chased out by fear. I didn't want to think too far ahead. To make promises to myself that he nor I could keep.

So when Brodan lifted his head, kissed me sweetly, looked deep in my eyes, and confessed thickly, "I love you so much, Monroe Sinclair," I froze.

I literally froze in his arms.

Part ecstatic, part utterly terrified.

Because I loved him too. I knew, despite everything that had happened between us, that I had never stopped loving Brodan Adair.

But I ... the people I loved tended to hurt me.

"Brodan ..."

Disappointment flared in his eyes, but to my shock, he whispered against my lips, "It's okay. I'm not a patient man, my love. But for you, I'd wait a thousand lifetimes."

Tears burned in my eyes, and I cried shakily, "You're such a romantic bastard. I hate you."

Brodan threw his head back in laughter and, because he was still inside me, I felt the sensation through my whole body. I giggled through my tears until Brodan kissed them off my cheeks. "No, you don't," he murmured with each kiss. "You love me. But I can wait until you're ready to tell me that yourself."

32

BRODAN

Over the hiss of the frying pan, I heard the cottage door open and shut.

"Ugh, that was the longest first week back at school ever," Monroe called out, and I could hear her dropping her bags, possibly kicking off her shoes. Anticipation filled me, and I turned to watch her walk through the kitchen doorway.

I'd seen my face plastered over billboards, had hundreds of screaming fans greet me at premieres … but waiting for Monroe Sinclair to come home to me was the dream I couldn't believe had come true.

She smiled a weary but happy smile. "Something smells good."

"Chicken fajitas," I told her seconds before I bent down to kiss the mouth she offered me. "Rough day?"

Roe sighed heavily, and I gestured to the glass of wine I'd already poured for her. "You are my hero." She took the glass and leaned against the counter, pushing her hair off her face. "It was like the kids were bouncing off the walls . I mean, we all knew the first day back after Christmas would be bad, it always is … but this lasted the whole bloody week. Hyper doesn't even cover it."

I nodded, my gaze dancing between her and the chicken spice mix in the frying pan. "Thane got a phone call from the school this week about Eilidh. Apparently, another girl was bullying Eilidh's wee pal about what she got, or didn't get, for Christmas. So Eilidh took it upon herself to smack her across the face. Is it wrong that I'm proud of her?"

Monroe shoved me playfully. "You better not have told her that, Brodan Adair."

"What? That I'm proud my niece stood up for her friend?"

"It's not that simple, and you know it. She can't go around smacking people in the face, no matter how much they deserve it."

I grinned. "That's a terrible rule."

She rolled her eyes, shaking her head. "Anyway, I heard about it from Eilidh's teacher. It was quite a moment. Apparently, the girl was stunned. And while we can't condone physical violence, perhaps she'll think twice about tormenting people who have less than she does."

"Aye. According to Thane, Eilidh was just as surprised by the moment as anyone. She cried, the wee darling. She knows she did wrong."

Monroe moved closer to me. "I love how you love her."

The words *Do you love how I love you?* hung on the tip of my tongue, but I forced them back. It had been two weeks since I told Monroe I loved her. I'd said it once more, and she hadn't said it back. While it stung, I understood. And I could wait.

"Dinner is ready." I took the pan off the heat and spooned the chicken into the tortillas I'd laid out.

"Do you know how amazing it is to come home after a hard week at work to a sexy man cooking dinner?" Monroe teased gleefully as she threw toppings onto her fajitas. "Where did you learn to cook?"

"I played a chef in a movie once."

"Oh, aye, I remember that one. It was a horror film, right? Kind of gross, if I remember correctly." She wrinkled her nose.

An ache panged in my chest. Over the last few months, I'd realized from the bits and pieces Roe told me that she'd probably watched every single one of my films. I never teased her about it because if things were the other way around, I would have watched every one of her films too. And it would have killed me to see her but feel so disconnected.

I cleared my throat. "Aye, it was a horror about a sous chef my character hires who starts putting human—"

"Ick, don't. Eating." She took a massive bite of fajita to make her point, and I snorted.

"Anyway," I said, following her into the living room with my dinner, "the director wanted me to take some culinary lessons, so I looked like I knew what I was doing. A top British chef trained me on how to slice and dice like a real chef, and I got him to give me some cooking tips and recipes. He said I was a natural."

"Of course you are." She sat down, her feet curled under her. "You're good at anything you put your mind to."

"Do you think so?" I asked in all seriousness.

Catching my tone, Roe swallowed her bite and asked, "What's going on?"

What was going on was that I was ready to fully commit to Ardnoch, and sitting around waiting for someone to like the screenplay I'd written would not cut it as a job. I'd been busy this week and had made two very big decisions that I knew I had to run by Monroe. I hoped that she'd be sharing in them in some capacity or another. Then there was a third issue concerning her entirely that I needed to raise. "Three things. One is that I've been working with Thane for the past few weeks on drawings for a house."

She stopped eating; her eyes widened a little.

I forged ahead, feeling more nervous than I thought I would be at this moment. "As part of our inheritance, Lachlan divided up some land in Caelmore so we'd all have a plot to build a house. My plot is close to Arran's and Arro's plots. View right over the water. The build will be in keeping with my brothers' and sister's homes. A large family home, modern design, lots of glass overlooking the water."

Roe swallowed. "That's … that's … amazing."

"You think?"

"Of course."

"I'd … I'd like you to look at the drawings. I'd like your opinion." *Because I hope like hell this will be your home as much as it is mine.*

She nodded slowly. "I'd be happy to look at them."

"I really want your opinion, Sunset."

Whatever she saw in my expression made realization dawn in hers. Her lips formed an *O*. Then the breath whooshed out of her. "Brodan … I … you know I haven't decided to stay …"

Hurt flared, but I tried not to show it. "Aye, I know. But just in case you do."

At the sudden, sad uncertainty on her face, I changed the subject. "Two, Lachlan and I looked at our holdings, and we think we've found some land that would work well for a distillery. Lachlan wants to go into business with me, and so I'm gearing up to do all the research."

Her gorgeous smile was genuine. "Brodan, that's wonderful news! I'm so excited for you. I think a whisky from you and Lachlan would be a massive hit. You have a hook already for your advertising. It'll be fantastic."

"You think so?" A flood of anticipation rushed through me at the thought of running a business I loved—and doing it at home. It would bring more jobs and boost the local economy too.

"Of course I do." She reached over and squeezed my leg. "Like I said, you can do anything you put your mind to."

That was what I was banking on.

And not for the distillery.

I was banking on my ability to fill Monroe Sinclair's life with so many bloody good times, she'd never think of leaving me.

But there was something else we needed to discuss. And this one I wasn't looking forward to. We talked more about Roe's week at school, our plans for the weekend, and once we'd finished dinner and were sitting together on the sofa, I broached the subject.

"There's that third thing I wanted to discuss. Something I need to tell you."

She turned toward me, our faces inches apart. "You sound serious. Have you decided to open a woolen mill as well as a distillery?"

At her teasing, I tickled her ribs and she squealed, trying to get away. Laughing, I pulled her into my arms. "Quit wriggling."

"Don't tickle me, then." Roe pouted, and I stole a quick kiss because her mouth was right there and that was reason enough. When I pulled back, I brushed her hair off her face, hating that she was about to lose that happy, almost dreamy expression.

"Are you ready to talk about your dad?"

She stiffened in my arms. But she didn't pull away. Instead, the shadows I hated so much crept into her gray eyes, and she answered quietly, "I do want to find him, Brodan. Maybe … maybe finding his grave … maybe I can still say goodbye. Maybe I can still forgive him. If that's what he wanted. I have to believe that's what he wanted."

Lifting my arse off the couch, I pulled out the piece of paper that had been burning a hole in my back pocket, and I held it out to her. It had the address of a cemetery in Dumfries and Galloway on it. "I found him for you."

A small gasp escaped her as she took the paper. She devoured the words on it. "What was he doing that far south?"

"I don't know."

"Brodan, how did you find him?"

"I have contacts. People who know how to find people."

Tears pooled in her eyes, but they didn't spill over as she whispered, "Thank you. Thank you so much." She threw her arms around me and mine banded around her, holding her to me, almost afraid to let go. I breathed in the scent of the citrus that lingered in her hair from her shampoo. I just … breathed *her* in, holding her there. Afraid to exhale.

A few hours later, the fire crackled in the fireplace and Roe lay naked, her back to my chest, on the couch. She drew lazy circles on my forearm as I held her, and we listened to the silence only broken by the pop of flames.

Peace unlike anything I remembered settled over me. I'd made love to the woman I loved after a night of conversation about everything and nothing. For the first time in eighteen years, I wasn't chasing this empty feeling inside. With her in my arms, I felt whole.

"I never imagined I could ever be this happy," I confessed.

Monroe turned her head, her hair tickling my chest as she looked up at me. "Are you scared, Brodan?"

The fear tightened like a fist around my throat, and I could only nod.

"Me too," she admitted.

Then she moved in my arms, turning to straddle me. Cupping my nape in her hands, she whispered, "I want to hold on, though. Will you hold on with me?"

In answer, I wrapped my arms around and pulled her close, burying my face in the crook of her neck. I'd hold on for fucking forever now. That's not what terrified me. What terrified me was what happened if she slipped from my hold or was yanked away from me by forces stronger than my grip?

Fuck.

I took a calming breath, reminding myself that it was that kind of thinking that cost us eighteen years together.

We had to take one day at a time.

One day at a time.

And maybe, I'd eventually settle into the feeling of being genuinely happy for the first time in my life.

33
MONROE

Guilt and shame kicked my arse all the way down the street as I walked to meet Sloane at a café in the neighboring village of Golspie. Although we'd texted, we hadn't seen each other since the holidays, and we wanted to catch up without the nosy ears and eyes of Ardnoch watching. Plus, Flora's was always so busy on Saturdays, it made it hard to get a table.

Brodan was in research mode for the day, and Sloane had the afternoon off. This proved to be a rarity between Callie, the housekeeping job at the castle, and the side gig of baking and selling cakes. Today, however, Callie was spending the afternoon again with Lewis. Thane and Regan were taking the kids for lunch and shopping in Inverness.

Which meant Sloane was free.

And I was glad, because I desperately needed someone to talk to.

This morning, hours after I'd asked Brodan to hold on to me and promised him the same in return, I'd opened my personal email to find I'd been selected for an interview for a teaching job in the Lowlands. Near Edinburgh.

A frightened part of me wanted to go to the interview. But in doing so, wouldn't it make me just as bad as Brodan when we were kids? I'd be running from him like he'd run from me.

The difference was, I never treated Brodan poorly when we were teens. When he returned to Ardnoch, he'd shown me a side of him that I didn't like. I knew now he didn't like that side of himself either, but I'd be going on pure faith that he'd never treat me like that again. Or that he wouldn't one day give in to his fear and leave me behind.

Everything was wonderful now between us, but the rest of the world hadn't intruded yet. No one knew we were dating, but as soon as that hit the news, my face would be plastered all over the internet. My anonymity—a precious thing I did not take for granted—would be lost. It didn't matter if Brodan had retired from acting. He was Hollywood royalty now. His name was on a star on the Hollywood Walk of Fame. I thought I'd figured this all out, but the interview invitation confused me all over again.

Mind whirring, heart thumping, and stomach roiling, I felt a headache coming on as I pushed into the quiet café down a village side street. A few other people were in for a cup of tea, but I spotted Sloane at a table in the corner, away from prying ears.

She stood up to hug me, and I gave her a tight squeeze back. "How are you?"

"A little tired," Sloane answered, and I noted the dark circles under her eyes.

"You're working too hard."

Shrugging, she sighed. "I have to. I can't stay on the estate forever. It would be nice to give Callie a real home."

Concern filled me because if I couldn't afford a place by myself in Ardnoch on a teacher's salary, how was Sloane supposed to with the money she made? As if she read my thoughts, she said, "I'm hoping if I build up enough business with my baking, between that and housekeeping, I'll have enough for rent."

"And in the meantime, you'll work yourself into the ground?"

"What can I get you, ladies?" asked the server, a woman around my age.

We ordered and once she was gone, I lectured like a big sister. "You'll be no use to Callie if you exhaust yourself to the point you make yourself sick."

Sloane gave me a weary smile. "I know. I just … I want to make it work for us here. I don't want us to be scrimping and saving all the time."

"You will make it work … but you have to take care of yourself too."

"Okay. I promise I will try."

"Good. Then I can stop lecturing you."

"It's nice you care enough to want to."

We shared a warm look and then I launched right into it. "I need advice."

"From me?" Sloane pressed a hand to her chest. "From this disorganized mess you see before you?"

Chuckling, I nodded. "I could really use a sounding board."

"Okay. Then tell me all the things, and I will try to be helpful."

"First, I need to give you a bit more background on me and Brodan." I told her our story and explained as much as I could about our friendship and love for each other as teens, without going into too much detail. I told her how it ended and what he was like when he came back into my life. Then I explained about the interview and how I didn't know if I should go for it. "Brodan's like a different man to how he was when he first came back. He seems committed to Ardnoch, to me. He's confided things I know he hasn't told anyone else. And he's told me he loves me."

Sloane's eyes brightened. "Really? He said, 'I love you.'"

"Twice now. And I have not said it back."

"Why haven't you?"

"I'm afraid," I admitted. "I'm afraid that another person I love will disappoint me. Will hurt me. He has the power to break me, and it's scary."

"Do you love him?" Sloane asked, tone serious.

Emotion almost choked me as I nodded.

"Thirty-two years is an awfully long time to love someone, Monroe. That won't just go away because *you* decide to go away. It will follow you, and I'm afraid you'll regret not taking the risk. I ... if it were me, I would stay." She reached over and squeezed my fisted hand. "Plus, you're my closest friend here, and I selfishly don't want to lose you."

I covered her hand with mine. "Thank you."

"Does that mean you'll stay?"

I thought of where I was mentally and emotionally when I applied for the job down south. Then I considered what life in Ardnoch would be like if I took Brodan out of the equation. If he did decide life in the Highlands was too small for him. What would I be left with?

Friends.

Friends I hadn't had before.

Sloane and Arran and Arro. My colleagues at school. Flora. Belle.

They were all part of my life now.

Ardnoch wasn't home without Brodan, but it was something like that, even with him gone. I just had to trust that I wouldn't need to worry about that. That Brodan meant it when he said he loved me. That planning the house and taking my opinion into account in the design was because he was adamant I'd be living in it with him.

I want to, I admitted, heart aching.

I wanted to come home to Brodan every evening and lie in his arms on the couch, watching crap television and moaning about my day.

I wanted to make love to him in the dark hours of the night and fall asleep beside him, feeling cherished and needed.

I wanted what I'd had for the last few weeks, and I wanted it to last forever.

"Something tells me you just made a decision," Sloane guessed, her gaze searching.

"I think I did." Smiling at her through bright tears, I shook my head. "I swear to God, that man is turning me into mush." Exhaling, I waved a hand. "Okay, less of that now. Let's talk about you. I don't want to pry and you can tell me to mind my own business and I promise I won't be offended … but why the Highlands?"

If Sloane had looked exhausted before, she suddenly seemed completely drained as she nodded solemnly. "Okay. What I'm about to tell you has to stay between us."

I tensed but replied, "I know how to keep a secret, Sloane. I grew up in a village that made it difficult, so trust me, I'm a vault."

She nodded, the muscle in her jaw flexing. And then she began to tell a tale that shocked and dismayed me.

By the end, I felt nothing but relief that she was here and safe. Both her and Callie.

I vowed, now that I'd decided to stay in Ardnoch for good, that I would do whatever it took to make sure Sloane and her daughter flourished here. To make sure they stayed protected.

∾

My pulse raced like mad as I let myself into the cottage later that afternoon. I was doing it.

Even though I was still terrified, I was doing it.

I was going to tell Brodan that I was in love with him, too, and that I was staying in Ardnoch for good.

"You would not believe what it takes to launch a distillery," Brodan announced as I shut the door behind me. He had the fire blazing in the grate, and it warmed my cold cheeks. Shrugging out of my coat, I felt myself deflate from being hyped up to tell him I loved him, only to be halted by his greeting.

He stood from the computer and gestured to it. "Never mind the millions of pounds it'll take, there are things to consider I never even realized. For a start, the land we thought might work for the distillery will need investigating because we'll need a consistent water supply from it all year round. A distillery on one of the islands has suspended production a few times because of droughts on the island. Land with a consistent water supply is a must." He gestured emphatically, eyes a little wide with excitement or fear, or both, maybe.

"And there's a five-year waiting list for the copper stills we'll need. I mean, we could probably shop elsewhere, but these are the best companies in the world, and we'll want the best. And waiting for the best costs time and money. Then we'll need to finesse the whisky itself, get it how we want it, which will also take time, and then it needs a minimum of three years to mature. We might as well build the main distillery while we create the actual whisky off-site some-where smaller. We'll have to get around this copper stills thing because we can't wait *eight* years to get it off the ground." He rubbed his forehead, suddenly looking exhausted.

All thoughts of telling him I loved him were put on hold

as I rounded the couch to rub a soothing palm down his arm. "Hey, you know you don't have to go ahead with this if you don't want to. But ... you have the money and the palate, Brodan. And you're learning patience very quickly, handsome."

Brodan's expression softened and he cuddled me into his side. "I just ... I'm a bit overwhelmed by the facts."

"This whole venture would require time and money, and it's out of your comfort zone ... but you've done it before. A few things this year have pushed you out of your comfort zone. Look how those turned out."

At my teasing, he smirked. "Aye, they turned out quite nicely, didn't they?"

Thinking this was my moment, the perfect moment, I opened my mouth to say it. To tell him. But the words got stuck, and before I could drag them out, Brodan pulled me down beside him on the couch. "Now the other thing we'd need to decide is if we'd open the distillery to the public. I want your opinion on a few things. Here, look ..."

Just like that, my moment was gone.

Or I'd choked on it.

Pushing my frustration aside, I forced myself to engage in the conversation.

34

MONROE

I noticed nothing out of the ordinary that morning when I got my coffee from Flora's, but I was distracted because I hadn't told Brodan I loved him yet. For the past few days, I'd allowed myself to be waylaid by other things, and it was pure nonsense on my part. I loved him. I loved Brodan. There was no denying it, so what was the point in not telling him? Ugh, I had to get it together.

Tonight, I promised myself. I would tell him tonight come hell or high water.

Having made that decision just in time for the kids coming in that morning, I was more cognizant of my surroundings, and I noted that, not only did colleagues I passed in the hall look at me strangely, but parents beyond the waiting children were grouped together, whispering and staring.

I thought maybe I was being paranoid … but nope.

They were definitely a lot of parents eyeballing me as I welcomed the kids inside the building at the sound of the bell. Once the kids were settled, I shrugged off the strange feeling until a teaching assistant from P4 came into my class to ask a question on behalf of her teacher. She stared hard at me, eyes a wee bit round and dazed.

What on earth?

Finally, when I walked into the staff room at break and all talking ceased upon my arrival, my indignation rose. I strode toward Ellen. "Right, what's going on?" I asked her.

She raised an eyebrow at my tone. "What are you talking about?"

"Everybody staring at me and whispering. Have I done something?"

Ellen looked at me like I'd lost my mind. "Monroe, I really have no idea what you're talking about."

She genuinely didn't seem to.

Someone cleared their throat behind me, and I turned to see Summer Smith, the young P2 teacher, holding out her phone. She gave me a sheepish smile. "I think this might be why."

Frowning, I took her phone, and as soon as I read the screen, my stomach plummeted. It was an article on a national tabloid's website with the headline, "Star Finds Love in the Highlands," along with a great big bloody photograph of Brodan kissing me passionately on Castle Street, near the cottage. Smaller images followed of us walking down the street arm in arm. I looked tiny next to him. It was almost funny. In one of them, I was laughing at something he'd said, looking straight ahead while he gazed down at me with such tenderness, my breath caught. Anyone looking at that photo would know he loved me.

It took me a moment to drag my eyes from the photograph to the article. I sped-read the story, and dread filled me as they named a familiar social media influencer as their source for the original story. I clicked on the link, and her profile opened.

Harriet Bloody Blume.

I'd met her last summer, and she'd tried to get me to spill details about the Adairs.

Seeing the picture of Brodan and me on her grid, I clicked it and opened a video in which she sat with books in her background. Uncaring that everyone in the staff room could hear, I listened as she spewed lies.

Panic built up from my gut until my heart raced way too hard. Sweat slickened my palm as I listened to the vicious wee cow tell her five million followers, and thus the world, that I'd talked to her exclusively. And someone—say, Brodan —might believe her because she had details about our relationship. She knew we were friends since school. She knew I'd loved him and that he'd left. She knew I felt abandoned by him. And now she knew we were dating and living together in the cottage on Castle Street. That I spent Christmas and New Year's with his family. That we were serious.

How did she know all these things?

"She's lying," I whispered, feeling a comforting hand on my shoulder. "I didn't tell her any of this. She's lying."

But Brodan ... What if he didn't believe me? What if he thought Harriet was telling the truth? He'd jumped to conclusions before. He'd hated me before.

Oh my God.

He'd hate me for this.

Nausea rose inside me, and I just managed to give Summer her phone back before I dashed from the room and across the hall into the bathroom. I fell before the nearest toilet and threw up all my fear and humiliation.

BRODAN

Arran had the Gloaming looking like a million dollars. I walked downstairs from inspecting the vacant rooms he'd redone and wandered through the restaurant to the bar. My brother was behind it, cleaning glasses, and there were only a few patrons in at this time of the day. A fire crackled in the large hearth at the back, giving the dark, historic room life and warmth.

"I'm proud of you," I said as I slid onto a stool at the bar. "The place looks like a boutique, not an inn."

Arran grinned. "Aye, well, it seems to have worked because we're fully booked May through October."

"That's amazing, Arr. Seriously."

"Thanks, Bro. You want anything?"

"Aye, give us an Irn-Bru. Then I'll need to go in a bit. I'm heading into Inverness to finalize drawings with Thane for the house."

Arran considered this. "So ... how does your agent feel now about your retirement?"

"In denial." I shrugged. "I've spoken to my publicist, though, and we're getting ready to announce it."

"And you're happy?"

Looking my brother straight in the eye, I answered honestly, "For years, I thought I loved acting. I got a high from it. But I'd confused loving the escape for love of the actual job. Deciding to retire ... being home with you lot, being with Monroe ... it's like this massive weight I was carrying has lifted from my shoulders. I feel free, Arran."

Arran relaxed with relief. "I couldn't be happier to hear that. I'm glad you're home."

"I'm glad you are."

He chuckled. "Aye, did you ever think you and I would return home to become one-woman blokes?"

"Never," I admitted. "It scares the shit out of me. But it's worth it."

My phone dinged in my pocket, and I pulled it out to see a text from my publicist, Annie.

We need to talk.

Beneath her text was a link. I clicked it, and a video of Harriet Blume opened. I pushed the volume up, and I felt my brother stop what he was doing as we listened to the social media influencer.

Fuck.

My anger built as images of Monroe and me on Castle Street filled the screen. Private fucking moments.

Not that I wasn't used to the tabloids sharing private moments … but this was different. This was Monroe.

Arran had rounded the bar to watch the video, and he sucked in a breath. "No, Bro, this is that wee snake who was hanging around last summer. I came across her harassing Monroe, and Roe was definitely keeping her mouth shut even then, and that was before you and she had reconciled. There's no way she gave this viper any of this information."

A different fury filled me as I turned to my brother, who staunchly defended Roe … like I'd believe a stranger over the woman I loved. "I fucking know that." I glared at him. "Do you think I'd trust a celebrity vlogger over Roe?"

My brother held up his hands defensively. "Of course not. Sorry."

"But someone told that brat about us." I quickly googled my name and, sure enough, article after article popped up about me and Monroe. I pushed off the stool. "This is every-where. And the vlogger knows things that only the people here would know. Someone talked. So much for this village keeping our privacy, eh?"

"Where are you going?" Arran hurried after me as I marched toward the door.

"To Roe. It's everywhere, Arran. She probably knows and is freaking out at school."

I tried to drive as calmly as possible to the primary school, while I called Thane to explain the bloody mess. He was as angry on my behalf, and he promised we'd get to the bottom of it. Whoever talked, we'd find them.

When I got to the school, however, the receptionist told me Roe had already left early because she was sick.

What the hell?

I tried calling her as I drove back toward Castle Street, but her phone was going straight to voicemail. My worry and fury mingled. I was desperate to get to her.

Seeing her car parked in her spot made me feel better as I drove the Range Rover in beside it. I threw myself out of the car and jogged around the building and into the cottage.

Roe was on the sofa facing the door, her face chalk white as I barged inside. She shot up from her seat and raised trembling hands. "Brodan, I promise it wasn't me. She's lying. I know she knows things about us she shouldn't, but it wasn't me. She's lying."

At the begging, pleading tone, at the fear and panic in her glazed eyes ... my heart crashed in my chest.

It scared her I believed Harriet Blume.

What the fuck?

For a moment, I wanted to be angry, but gazing at the woman I loved in distress, I took a few calming breaths and thought about why she'd think that.

And decided ... why *wouldn't* she think that? After the way I'd treated her in the past.

I could see it clear as day in front of me.

The damage I'd done. It hadn't just magically disappeared because I told her I loved her.

I strode across the room, and her eyes widened before I

pulled her into my arms and kissed the top of her head, holding her so bloody tight. "My love, I know. I know," I assured her.

Her trembling body melted and she sobbed against me.

Fuck!

"I know, I know," I kept whispering. "I know you'd never do that. Come on, Sunset. It's all right. You're killing me here." My voice cracked as emotion thickened my throat.

Her hands clutched at my jacket, pulling on it hard as she tried to soothe her cries. "I'm sorry," she managed through tears. "I'm sorry for thinking … for thinking you wouldn't believe me."

I rested my cheek on top of her head. "I'm sorry for giving you reason to doubt me."

She shifted as if to pull back, so I lifted my head. She tilted her chin. "I won't again. I … I love you, Brodan. Since I was twelve years old, I have been in love with you."

Relief and joy cut through my darker emotions, and I kissed her. I kissed her as if that one kiss might keep her with me forever. "I love you too," I whispered against her now swollen lips.

"I know who told her."

That made me jerk back from her. "Who?"

Anger lit her eyes, but there was also the shadow of fear there. That just made me want to kill someone. Turning, she reached for a piece of card on the coffee table and handed it to me. "This was posted through the letter box. No stamp. It was hand delivered."

I took the card.

Handwritten across it were the words:

Enjoy the fame, bitch. That's what you get for sending thugs to my door.

Understanding dawned. Steven Shaw.

"I'm going to destroy the bastard," I growled slowly.

"Brodan, no." Monroe yanked the card out of my hand, expression mulish. "I told him things when we were together. Before I realized he was a prick. I told him I knew you, that we grew up together, that I loved you. I didn't tell him everything, but I told him enough. At the time, I honestly didn't think he believed me. But when you sent him that message after the Christmas card—"

"He realized it was all true." My eyes flew to the window. "He must have been watching us, Roe. He took those photos."

"And sold the story to Harriet."

Furious, I glowered at her. "And you want me to just sit by and let him get away with it?"

She gestured with the card. "Look what antagonizing him did. He's a sociopath, Brodan. Giving him attention is what he feeds off. We just need to ignore him."

"Ignore him? Everyone and their uncle knows about us, Roe."

"Wouldn't it have come out, eventually?"

"Aye, of course. But in a way I could somewhat control."

"It's done." She dropped the card on the table and pressed her hands to my chest. "I don't want to give him or her any more of our time." Roe's expression softened with amazement. "We love each other, Brodan. It took us over two decades to get here. I don't want anything to ruin that."

For her, I tried to let my anger go. I enclosed her in my arms again. "All right."

She sighed with relief and burrowed her head against my chest.

Then I remembered the receptionist at her school. "The school said you went home because you were sick?"

Roe pulled back, expression sheepish. "I found out in the staff room about the articles and the video ... I got so panicked, I threw up."

"Fuck." My rage returned.

"Brodan. Please. I'm okay."

I clasped her face in my hands. "We trust each other now, right? Going forward … nothing but love and trust."

She nodded, happiness cutting through the shadows in her eyes. "Nothing but love and trust."

3 5

MONROE

teven and Harriet Blume outing Brodan and me meant I
finally got a taste of what Brodan's life was like. When
he called to speak to his publicist, Annie, he put her on
speaker and introduced us. Annie was a bit surprised to hear
I was Brodan's girlfriend, but she moved past it with blunt
professionalism. She insisted that if Brodan wanted to take
back some control from the tabloids, then he should post to
his social media. It was apparently harder to get readers to
follow the clickbait if celebrities were already posting their
personal lives to socials.

So that night, we went to the Gloaming, and Arran
snapped a few candid photos of Bro and me cuddled in the
pub booth. Brodan posted one of them to his socials with the
caption, "It's good to be home with my love."

He told me his comment section went wild, but he wasn't
looking at them. Brodan closed the app as soon as he posted,
and I was never more thankful that I didn't have social media
accounts.

The real problem, Annie had told us, was that once
Brodan announced his retirement from acting, we had to

prepare for the speculation that I was the reason. Some of that speculation would turn negative, and fans might blame me. The thought didn't fill me with as much dread as I'd anticipated. In fact, it reminded me I rarely cared what strangers thought of me. All I cared about in the end was Brodan.

We were inundated with requests from chat shows and morning television for live interviews that Brodan had his people shut down immediately. And before we could even get to dealing with the upcoming announcement of Brodan's retirement, we had to endure the paparazzi that descended on Ardnoch. Walker took leave from his position on the estate to be Brodan's full-time bodyguard, and a security guard from the estate, who was ex-Special Forces, agreed to be *my* temporary bodyguard. His name was Jock, and he was professional but a lot warmer than Walker. It was scary leaving the cottage in the mornings to a crowd of paps, pushing their cameras in my face as Jock shoved them back. When one of them grabbed at my arm hard enough to leave bruises, Brodan had enough. We packed up some things and moved into his suite in the castle where they couldn't get to us.

He and Lachlan were pretty certain it wouldn't take long for the tabloids to grow bored and leave. The village *did* protect the celebrities who stayed at Ardnoch Castle, and they were getting nowhere with our neighbors. They were also unable to get into the castle or follow me into the school because Anita had asked for a police presence. I'd felt awful creating such a stir, but I had the feeling Anita found it exciting, so I let my guilt go.

After a week of being hounded, however, a politician in London got caught on video snorting cocaine while a half-naked woman, who wasn't his wife, draped herself over him. Brodan and I were old news, and while it was nice to be catered to in the castle, I was glad to return to our cottage. To not have to be tailed by Jock and Walker wherever we went.

Yet having my love life plastered all over the internet, all the speculation and gossip, and hounding by the media wasn't even the worst moment during it all.

A few nights ago, while we were still staying in the castle, Brodan was showering and I was on the bed, creating online worksheets for the kids. He'd left his phone beside me and, while he'd silenced all social media notifications, he'd kept his ringer and text notifications on. His phone buzzed a few times, and every time I'd instinctually glance at the screen.

The third time it buzzed, I noted the name Lotte, and the first line of the text was visible on the notification screen.

Hey, sexy. So is the redhead why you didn't take me up on ...

Heart thumping in my chest, I desperately wanted to know what Brodan hadn't taken her up on. Who was she? I racked my brain and then suddenly, it hit me.

Holy shit.

Lotte Fischer. Gorgeous German American actor who starred in a romantic thriller with Brodan a few years ago.

What was she doing texting Brodan?

The urge to read the rest of the text was real, but if Brodan invaded my privacy in that way, I'd be so disappointed that he didn't trust me. Still, I'd sat nauseated on the bed, unable to concentrate until he came out of the shower. He was rubbing his hair dry with a towel as he stepped into the main bedroom, wearing nothing but boxer briefs and looking like something out of a Calvin Klein ad. I didn't want to be jealous of his previous relationships, but what the hell was Lotte Fischer doing texting him?

Whatever he saw in my expression made him pause. "What's wrong?"

"Your phone buzzed a few times." I couldn't help my sullen tone.

"Okay?"

"I didn't read your texts, but I can see part of them when they come up on the screen."

Brodan tensed. "What is it?"

"Lotte thinks you're sexy and wants to know if the redhead is the reason you didn't take her up on ..." I shrugged. "That's all I saw on the screen, so who knows what you didn't take her up on."

He dropped the towel as a muscle ticked in his jaw. Brodan rounded the bed to sit at my feet. He held my gaze for a second before he reached for his phone and unlocked the screen. His eyes moved over it and then back to me. "She wants to know why I didn't take her up on her invitation to join her in London on New Year's."

Hurt I wasn't sure I was allowed to feel made me draw my knees in. "So a woman asked you to spend New Year's with her, and you didn't tell me?"

Brodan studied me warily. "I didn't think it mattered, since I had no intention of taking her up on it."

"Is it Lotte Fischer?" I nodded at his phone.

"It is."

"She was your ...?"

"Fuck buddy," he said bluntly. "Whenever she's single and we're in the same place, she calls me up."

"You had a few of those, then?"

"Aye. I never hid that from you."

"But you're still texting with her. With the others? Have they been in contact recently?" Blood whooshed in my ears as I waited impatiently for him to respond.

Brodan sighed heavily. "A few have reached out, and I told them I wasn't available anymore."

SAMANTHA YOUNG

"But you still text with them? They're still on your phone?"

He glanced at his phone and uttered a slight huff. "Well ... they're still my friends."

"Either they're your fuck buddies or your friends, Brodan, but they can't be both."

"Of course they can."

"Maybe before you were in a serious relationship."

He narrowed his eyes. "You want to dictate who I can be friends with?"

That he couldn't see how hurtful this was made me want to scream in his face. Instead, I shoved my laptop aside and pushed off the bed with a scoff of bitter laughter. Shoving my feet into my boots, I skewered him with a dark look. "I'd like to see your reaction if my fuck buddies were still texting me."

"Roe ..." He stood up.

I took hold of the door handle. "I'm going for a walk because if I stay, I might throw something at you. But think on this, Brodan, while I'm gone ... what do you think it says to me you need to keep in contact with your fuck buddies? If you can't guess, let me tell you." Tears burned my eyes, and I hated him for it. "It tells me that deep down, you think you'll need them again, and you don't want to burn those bridges."

"Monroe—"

I slammed out of the room before he could respond because I wasn't kidding when I said I might throw something at him.

As I hurried down the corridor, Angeline Potter, of all people, appeared around the corner, heading toward her suite.

"Monroe!" Brodan shouted behind me, and I glanced back to catch him practically falling out of the room as he pulled up his jeans and zipped them.

Ugh. I couldn't even get space to run away from an argument.

"Trouble in paradise?" Angeline asked snidely as I passed.

"Oh, fuck off, Potter," I snarled.

"Uh!" She squeaked in outrage behind me.

"Monroe!"

I turned the corner, almost running now as I tried to make my escape without Brodan seeing which way I'd gone. I fled toward the turret, the only place in the whole damn castle that ever seemed to be free of other humans.

But I'd barely made it into the circular room when I heard the door below me open and shut and footsteps thunder upward. Brodan appeared at the top, not even out of breath, bare of foot and chest.

"You chased after me in front of Angeline Potter half-naked, so now our spat will be all over the estate," I snapped without preamble.

Brodan's eyes gleamed as he prowled toward me. "I'm not the one who told her to fuck off."

"You heard that?"

"No, she screeched it at me as I ran past her. Well done, by the way."

I placed a hand in front of me to halt him.

He walked right into my palm. I felt his heartbeat thudding underneath the smooth, hot skin and dropped my hand as if he'd burned me. "Don't run away from me in the middle of an argument. I can't stand it," he growled.

"Don't be an arsehole, then."

Brodan pulled his phone out of the back pocket of his jeans, tapped the screen, and held it up. Lotte's name glared at me. Then he tapped the screen next to her name and deleted the contact.

I sucked in a breath as he scrolled through and deleted five other women's names from it.

SAMANTHA YOUNG

"That's all of them. I need you to believe that."

Adrenaline still rushed through me from my jealousy and hurt, but now relief loosened my shoulders.

"Do you believe me?"

Studying his panicked expression, I felt remorse. "I believe you."

Brodan nodded, panic turning quickly to irritation, as he threw the phone on the side table with a hard clatter. "You're right. If you were in contact with men you'd had a sexual relationship with, it would bother me. I never want you thinking I've got one foot out the door in this. I'm in this with you, Monroe. You know how hard it was for me to get to this point, but I'm here ... and you can run here or run all the way to fucking Timbuktu ... and I will follow you. I will never give up on you without a fight."

I nodded, feeling silly now for my outburst. "I ran to the one place you knew I'd run, Brodan. Hardly speaks of any real intention to run away from you, does it?"

The corner of his mouth tugged up. "I noticed that."

"I try to be rational about it, but it hurts to think of you with all those glamorous women. But I know you never loved any of them. I do know that. I'm sorry too."

"Don't be." He grinned, pulling me into his arms. "Things were getting a bit monotonous around here."

Feeling something hard prod into me, I let out a huff of disbelief. "Are you turned on by this fight?"

Brodan smiled shamelessly. "So hard right now, I want to bend you over that chair and fuck you senseless."

My breath caught as tingles exploded to life between my legs. "Then why don't you?"

At my challenge, heat flared in Brodan's eyes and, seconds later, I found myself bent over a chair with my dress pushed up. Cool air caressed my skin as he ripped down my underwear until it hit my ankles and then I heard his zipper. A crinkle of foil. My chest heaved against the chair as I glanced over my shoulder at him.

Wicked, stark need stared back at me.

Then I felt the thick, hot push of him inside.

His thrusts were fast and furious, his grip bruising on my hips.

But it was what I needed. What he needed.

Our passion couldn't be replicated. I knew he'd never had this with anyone else. This overwhelming need to be a part of the other. To claim something that no one else had of us.

I was his, and he was mine.

My jealousy abated as we climaxed together and he stayed buried inside me, pressing kisses to the back of my neck and murmuring his love for me over and over again.

～

Once the paparazzi left Ardnoch and I was assured of my place in Brodan's heart, I could breathe again.

Sort of.

There was the small matter of me hiding my morning sickness from Brodan.

The morning after our heated encounter in the turret, I was sick again … and realized that my period was late. Since we'd been using protection (because birth control made me ill, so I couldn't take it), it hadn't occurred to me that the sickness was anything but nerves. Until I missed my period.

It turned out it might not have been panic that made me throw up at school. The paparazzi were gone. Life was returning to some semblance of normality, and I was still sick every morning. Thankfully, unlike some women I knew, my nausea only hit in the morning.

There had been no opportunity to buy a pregnancy test without someone at my side, but now that Jock had returned to Ardnoch Estate, I was going to drive to a pharmacy a few villages away and buy one.

I didn't want to think about how Brodan might feel about me falling pregnant so soon. Or at all. I didn't think it would happen so easily, considering my age, but there I was ... possibly pregnant. A huge part of me was giddy with excitement and gratitude. However, I also didn't want to ruin what was building between us. So I wouldn't think about it until I knew for certain. First a pregnancy test and then a trip to the doctor.

The kids had left for the day, and I was just crossing the emptying car park to my car when someone called out to me.

I turned, yanked from my worries, to find Michelle Kingsley standing at the driver's-side door of her car. Her son, whom I taught, was already in the back of the Ford, not paying attention. "Ms. Kingsley?"

She smiled, but a gleam in her eyes made me wary. "I just wanted to say I'm sorry about all the nasty things people are saying about you online."

I stiffened. "I wouldn't know about that." And I wouldn't, because I'd promised Brodan I wouldn't google our names.

"Oh, people are vicious," Michelle said, taking great delight in telling me. "I mean, just because you're not a glamour model doesn't mean you can't be appealing to someone like Brodan. Attraction sometimes isn't apparent to the rest of us."

Bitch.

"I don't believe them when they say a small-town primary school teacher can't keep Brodan Adair entertained for long. It's not like he'll get bored and run off with a jet-setting beauty who fits his lifestyle better, is it? You're not worried that he'll leave you. Again? Are you?" She couldn't hide her smirk.

Shaking my head, I felt nothing but pity for her. "You

never understood Brodan. Or what was between us. You didn't when we were kids, and you don't now. And that you find pleasure in trying to upset me just makes me feel sorry for you, Michelle."

Her expression slackened with surprise and disbelief.

"Have a good evening." I got in my car and wasted not another thought on her. Or anyone else who allowed their jealousy to control their words and actions.

Shaking off the unpleasant encounter, sure it might not be the last, I drove through Golspie and onto Brora to pop into the pharmacy there. My phone rang, connecting to my car, and Brodan's name came up on the screen. I hit the answer button on my steering wheel. "Hello, handsome," I answered, smiling just at the thought of him.

God, I made myself sick with how loved up we were.

"Hello, my love," he answered in that deep voice that made me tingle all over. "Are you on your way home?"

Home.

My grin deepened. "Not yet. What are you making for dinner?"

"I was actually thinking we could eat at the Gloaming tonight, now that the paps are gone."

"Aye, that'll work."

"I'm just heading home from a meeting in Inverness with Thane about the house. I can't wait to share the new drawings with you."

Excitement bubbled inside me. "Me too."

"So, where are you now? Will you beat me home?"

"Um …" I didn't want to lie totally, so noting the package on my seat I'd collected from the post office during my lunch break, I replied, "I'm driving to Brora. The gift I got you for your birthday that didn't show up in time was delivered to Brora's post office instead of ours." It was a half lie. The truth was that I had ordered a gift for Brodan's birthday (January

3) before Christmas, and it had taken weeks to arrive. I'd had his first script turned into a book, leather-bound and every-thing. There had been some interest from a director, but nothing solid had come of it yet. But I still thought his writing it was momentous and should be celebrated.

"So, you're on your way to Brora?"

"Yep."

"Okay, I will probably be home first, then. See you soon, Sunset."

"See you soon, handsome."

I will not feel guilty, I told myself as I hung up. There was no point telling Brodan my suspicions until I knew for certain.

Once I parked in Brora, I shoved my hair under my knit wool hat, feeling paranoid after the last week. I didn't want anyone to recognize me and leak it to the internet that I'd bought a pregnancy test. Bloody Nora, I should have called Sloane and asked her to buy it for me.

Well, I was here now.

The pharmacy had a few people in it, but I kept my head low, found a couple of tests, and brought them to the counter. Thankfully, the young man at the till was so bored he didn't even look at me as he rang me up. I left the store breathing easy that I hadn't been seen and got back into the car.

It was growing dark as I drove back down the A9 toward home. The traffic had been fairly busy on the way here, but it had thinned out, and my headlights were the only ones on a stretch of road. There was a field on my left and the sea beyond that and a low stone wall set before woodlands on my right.

Headlights suddenly appeared on the opposite side of the road. I thought nothing of it.

Until the lights swerved onto my side.

My heart leapt in my throat as the vehicle raced straight toward me.

"What on—" I cried, instinct making me yank my wheel to the right to avoid a head-on collision. My body jolted, head slamming backward as the airbag burst from the steering wheel. A bang exploded in my ears, followed by a crunching sound and a loud hiss. Dazed, shaking with adrenaline, pain radiating down my neck, I tried to make sense of what had happened.

Before I could, my door was yanked open, and I felt the cold press of metal to my temple. Disbelief filled me as I glanced up and saw a masked figure peering into the car. The metal at my temple belonged to the muzzle of the gun in their hand.

Terror cut through my discombobulation.

"Get out of the car," a male voice demanded. Was that voice familiar?

What the fuck?

"Now!" he barked.

Trembling, I unclipped my belt and pushed the airbag out of my way. My upper body groaned with pain from the crash, and as I staggered out of the car, I saw the front of it had crumpled when it hit the stone wall.

Headlights beamed in the distance, and I felt a surge of relief …

Until pain shot across the back of my head and everything went black.

36

BRODAN

Monroe should have been home by now.

A feeling of dread came over me not long ago, and I'd called Monroe to check on her. No answer. I paced the cottage and tried phoning her again.

She hadn't answered her phone in thirty minutes.

It wasn't like her.

And she should be home by now.

I didn't want to succumb to my paranoia and fear. Even though it had only been thirty minutes, I could not forget that my brother woke up to his first wife dead in his bed from an aneurysm, that Mum died in childbirth and our aunt Imogen followed her not too long later. That Robyn was almost taken out by Lucy, that Regan was hunted in the night by a bloke who'd become obsessed with her. That my sister was almost killed by an ex, and Eredine by her sister's ex.

I didn't want to believe we Adair men were cursed, but, fuck—it was hard not to when our women had been put through the wringer over the years.

Dread in the pit of my stomach would not abate.

My first thought was to phone Arran, but to tell him

what? To look like a paranoid fool because my girlfriend wasn't answering?

Glancing at my phone, I saw the time had crept up to forty minutes. "Fuck it," I murmured and tried calling her again.

After two rings, I heard the click of the phone picking up, and my stomach stopped somersaulting. "Sunset?"

"I have your girlfriend," an unfamiliar male voice answered, and icy fear froze me to the spot.

It took me a second to bite out, "Who the fuck is this?"

"I have your girlfriend," he repeated. "And if you want her to remain alive, you'll come alone. I'll know if you don't come alone, and I will kill her."

Rage unlike anything I'd ever felt flooded my veins. "If you lay one hand on Monroe, I will end you. Do you hear me? I will fucking end you."

"Let's not waste time with empty threats. If you want your girlfriend to be alive next time you see her, you'll come alone. I'm going to hang up and text you directions to a location. Be there in twenty minutes, or she dies."

The fucker hung up before I could say anything else, and I stared blankly at my phone in shock. What was happening? Was this for ransom? Was it a crazy fan?

Then something occurred to me.

Shaw.

Steven Shaw.

The phone buzzed in my hand as my fury simmered to near exploding. The text from Monroe's phone was directions to a cabin in Claymore Woods, a national scenic area inland from Caelmore, and while there would be some foot traffic there during the summer months, it was mostly isolated during the winter.

Hurrying upstairs, I fell to my knees at the bed and reached under it for the locked safe box I'd placed there when I'd started living with Roe. Inside was the Glock I had a license for. I'd trained to use weapons years ago for one of my first action roles. I grabbed its holster, stood and attached it to the back of my waistband. With the gun fitted safely into the holster, I pulled my jacket on over it to hide it.

Rushing downstairs, I grabbed my keys and phone and raced to my Range Rover.

I was about two minutes from the turnoff for where I was instructed to get out and walk into the woods. I hit the screen in the middle of my dash and tapped on recent calls. Finding Walker, I pressed his name. My hands shook with adrenaline.

He answered on two rings. "Can I call you back? We're in the middle of—"

"Walk, someone has Roe."

He was quiet for a second and then ordered, "Talk to me."

I relayed what had happened and where I was.

"Don't you move a muscle," he commanded. "Stay in that fucking car, Brodan, until I can get a team to the location."

Pulling to a stop, I switched off the engine and grabbed my phone. "I'm forwarding the text to you now. But I'm going in, Walk. He has Monroe, and I can't just sit here."

"Brodan, I swear to—"

"Just get here as fast as you can." I hung up, put my phone on silent, and hopped out of the SUV. The small car park before the entrance to the woods was empty. There was no one in sight. Blood rushing in my ears, I struggled to hear over the whooshing as I stepped toward the path that would take me into the woods.

I'd maybe made it six or seven steps when I heard the crunch of bracken and whirled.

Too late.

A handgun pointed in my face. A man I didn't recognize held it, his expression filled with fury.

It was his rage and me not knowing him that made me certain this was Steven Shaw.

"Turn around and keep walking," he demanded. "Or I'll blow that pretty head off."

"Where's Monroe?" I asked, cool, calm.

His lip curled. "Safe. For now. Walk or die."

"Shaw?" I asked.

He narrowed his eyes. "Walk."

Aye.

Definitely Shaw.

And as soon as I got the opportunity, I would kill him for this.

37

MONROE

A strange sound filtered into my consciousness and then the smell. It was pungent. Like fish. The noise continued pushing me toward the surface, and I groaned.

"Looks like your bitch is waking up in time for the show," a voice said nearby.

Fear shuddered through me, and I didn't know why. Uneasy, I forced open my eyes like I would if I'd been having a bad dream. My blurry vision cleared, and I became cognizant of the freezing cold, the damp. The smell of wet wood filtered through the fishy odor, and I realized why as the tiny cabin came into focus. On the walls before me hung fishing tackle.

A fishing cabin.

What?

A throbbing pain shot through my head, and I reached to touch it, hissing at the lump I found.

It all came flooding back.

The car.

The masked man.

I flew upward, head spinning, nausea rising, and a cry of

terror caught in my throat at the sight of Brodan tied to a chair, his face bruised and bloody. My fear was mirrored in his eyes as he stared back at me in mute horror.

My gaze flew to the man standing over him.

A man I didn't recognize.

"Who are you?" I choked out. "What do you want?"

"You don't know him?" Brodan's voice sounded hoarse. "This isn't Shaw?"

I shook my head as Brodan's eyes flew to the stranger. He was tall with dark hair and blue eyes and looked to be around our age. He might even have been considered good-looking if he hadn't beaten the shit out of Brodan and wasn't brandishing a handgun.

Noting the ropes wrapped tightly around each of Brodan's ankles, that his hands were restrained behind the chair, I knew I was our only hope. I needed to get that handgun if we had any chance of escaping alive. Any thought of why we were here, what the fuck was going on, was pushed to the back of my mind as it raced to find a solution.

The stranger sneered at Brodan. "I don't know who Shaw is, but he's not the reason I'm going to kill you and make your girlfriend watch."

I stifled my whimper as Brodan glared at him. "If you're going to kill me, I think I deserve to know who you are first. Because I've never seen you before in my life."

"No, you haven't." He pulled a photograph out of his back pocket and held it up to Brodan's face. Whoever was on it made Brodan's face go slack with shock. "Aye, you remember her, though, eh?"

"Vanessa," he whispered.

Vanessa? His ex-girlfriend from uni Vanessa? The one who killed herself?

"About a year ago, I found drafts of letters she'd written

before she killed herself. Five letters to the people she believed had ruined her. You were one of them."

Brodan stared stonily at the photo. "I'm not responsible for Vanessa's demons."

The stranger punched Brodan so hard, I screamed. He raised the handgun to me. "Shut the fuck up, bitch."

I bared my teeth, wanting to kill him.

Brodan shook his head as blood trickled down his eyebrow.

Brodan.

"I tried to pick up the pieces," the stranger said, his voice cracking with emotion. "Because I loved her so much. I tried to make her want to stay, but what her dad did to her … it broke her in ways I couldn't fix. And I barely knew half of it. I read the rest in her letter to him. And what he did to her … Well, I made him pay for it two nights ago."

"What?" Brodan asked, seeming as confused as I was.

"I killed him. First, I tortured him, and then I killed him."

Renewed terror gripped me, but I fought through it, searching the tiny fishing cabin, looking for a weapon, as the man continued to talk. "They'll find his body soon enough, but not before I'm done. You're shit out of luck because I don't care what happens to me after I deal with every single one of you. And you're next for abandoning her when she needed you. I didn't know how the hell I'd get someone like you alone, but then you decided to play house back at home with the redhead. It was all over the papers. And I knew it was time to make my move. You were the first man she ever loved." I heard the hatred in his voice as my eyes snagged on an ice pick near a bucket of tackle. "You're the reason she couldn't fully trust me. But now, I'm going to show her I would do anything for her."

"You've lost your fucking mind," Brodan observed calmly.

"Huh … you know … now that I have you here … now that I can see how scared you are for her …"

My eyes flew back to them to find the stranger smirking at me.

"I might make you watch while I kill her first."

A tortured roar erupted from Brodan, and I watched as he used his impressive strength to throw himself and the chair at the stranger.

I didn't wait around.

Through my dizziness and nausea, I shoved myself up and lunged across the small space for the ice pick. Turning, I saw the stranger push Brodan off him. He shoved the chair onto its back, causing Brodan to cry out as his hands smashed against the floor.

The man was so consumed with Brodan, he wasn't paying attention to me.

And something primal came over me.

I rushed him with a cry of fury, and he straightened in shock at the sight. He'd dropped the handgun in the tussle. He had nothing to protect himself.

Adrenaline filled me with a strength I could never have imagined as I plunged the ice pick into his chest.

His face slackened with shock, and he stumbled. My attention moved to the handgun he'd dropped, and I rushed to grab it before he could remember its existence.

I pointed the gun at him as he fell to his knees and pulled out the ice pick. Blood poured from the wound, too fast, too much. He turned deathly pale before he collapsed onto his back.

Eyes open but vacant.

Nausea rose, but a sound from Brodan reminded me there was no time to think about the fact that I'd probably just killed a man. I pulled Brodan's chair up with gritted teeth and then dropped behind it to untie his bruised hands.

"Sunset," he said gruffly, his anguish so noticeable, it was like a scream through the croaky quiet of his nickname for me. "Sunset."

The cabin door blasted open, swinging so hard against the inside wall it cracked off its hinge. I cried out, raising the handgun at whoever was coming inside.

My sob burst free at the sight of an armed Walker Ironside.

"Sunset," Brodan whispered, and I rounded the chair to clasp his face in my hands.

Sorrow and relief mingled in his gaze.

"Sunset, I'm so sorry ..." His voice broke on the last syllable.

I shook my head. No. This wasn't his fault.

"Fuck." Walker bit out gruffly as he strode inside, followed by two other armed men. One of them was Mac, I realized. "Are you two all right?"

"Roe might have a concussion," Brodan replied quietly.

I huffed. "He needs an ambulance."

"You both do," Mac said, gaze furious. "There's already one on the way. We need to get you back to the car park."

"Who is this?" Walker lowered himself to his haunches and checked the stranger's pulse. "Dead."

I remembered the feel of the ice pick plunging through his chest and felt my nausea rise. "I ... I ..."

"It was self-defense," Brodan offered. "I did it in self-defense."

My eyes flew to his. "Brodan, no—"

"With your hands tied behind your back?" Walker asked dryly. "Don't worry. Monroe won't be charged for self-defense." He pushed open the stranger's jacket and patted his inside pockets. Finding something, he pulled out a wallet and flipped it open. "Ian Moffat." He looked at us. "You know him?"

Brodan shook his head as one of the other men freed his hands and legs. "From what he was saying, he dated Vanessa Woodridge. He found her letters to me and others on her computer. He admitted to killing her father."

Walker nodded and stood up. "The police are on their way. We can tell them all this, but first, let's get you to the hospital."

I didn't want to leave Brodan's side. So I didn't. We held on to each other as Mac, Walker, and the others guided us through the woods to the car park.

"What time is it?" I asked over our footsteps crunching through the undergrowth.

Walk answered.

Huh.

"Two hours," I whispered.

"Sunset?" Brodan squeezed my hand.

"It's been less than two hours." Though those moments in the cabin had felt like an eternity.

And I knew when I closed my eyes tonight, I'd see Ian Moffat's face slacken into death.

"I've got you," Brodan promised as if he could hear my thoughts. "I'm not letting go, Sunset. I'm never letting go."

38
MONROE

We were on our way to the hospital in the ambulance when I remembered the pregnancy test in my car.

Renewed terror I couldn't speak of held me tense as we rode to Inverness. The paramedics reckoned I had a concussion.

I could only hope that was the worst of my injuries.

Brodan was beaten and bruised, a possible concussion too, and a cracked rib or two where Moffat had disabled him. While I'd been out, Moffat had led Brodan into the cabin and knocked him unconscious with the butt of his gun. Brodan had been out just long enough for the bastard to tie him to the chair. As soon as Brodan regained consciousness, Ian Moffat had started hitting him, which I assumed was the noise that woke me up.

I felt sick every time I thought about it.

While I was horrified and stunned and still not quite able to process that I'd killed a man, I wouldn't feel guilty about it. He'd admitted to murdering another man, and I knew he'd intended to kill us.

There was a real possibility he'd killed more than just

Vanessa's father, and I wasn't ashamed to admit that if it was true, I'd be glad I stuck that ice pick in him.

They separated us at the hospital, despite Brodan's protests, and Mac had insisted on being allowed to wait outside my exam room. As soon as the doctor appeared, I cried as I told him I suspected I was pregnant and was afraid physical trauma might have hurt the baby.

Everything moved faster at that news as the doctor and nurses rushed to run tests.

Tears I couldn't stop rolled down my cheeks.

For years, I'd wanted Brodan, and I'd wanted to be the mother of his child.

For a few beautiful days, it seemed like all that might be possible.

But life had already proven that it didn't know how to play fair with me.

BRODAN

Monroe was paler than normal, the freckles on her forehead seeming brighter under the hospital lights. Her eyelashes fluttered, and I wondered what she was dreaming about.

I shifted in the chair by her bed, my ribs protesting at the movement, but I refused to get up and go back to my own bed. The nurse had stopped insisting a while ago.

I couldn't leave Monroe. The doctors had advised we both stay overnight because of our concussions, and that was fine. As long as I got to be with her.

Those moments in the cabin, when I'd first entered and

saw her unconscious, when I'd come to only to find myself bound and unable to save her …

Fuck, I'd never felt more powerless.

She'd saved me.

Again.

Walker, ever the superdetective, had run a check on Ian Moffat even before the police could give us more information. Moffat was from Vanessa's hometown, and it appeared he might have known her his whole life. There was a rental agreement with both their names on it, so they'd lived together, and Walker somehow got his hands on police reports for Vanessa's death. Moffat had been the one to find her. According to his medical records, Ian Moffat was being treated with therapy and antipsychotics for hallucinations and paranoia triggered by Vanessa's suicide.

A small part of me sympathized with him. But only a small part, considering he'd threatened to murder the love of my life.

Reaching for Monroe's hand, I clasped it between both of mine and bent my head to kiss the inside of her wrist. Feeling her pulse there, I tried to relax. But I got this weird feeling from her doctor. Like they weren't telling me something. It was making me uneasy as fuck.

Staring at her—damaged by my past in more ways than one—should have made me want to get up and walk away. Leave her again. Protect myself from a kind of yawning pain that would break me if something happened to her.

But I couldn't anymore.

I didn't want to.

I'd tasted what life with Monroe was like. What our love was like.

It was worth the inevitable indescribable grief I'd feel if she left this world before me.

I wouldn't run. Even if she deserved better than me.

After all, I'd always been a selfish bastard when it came to Monroe Sinclair.

She was mine.

Forever.

As I was hers.

Even if forever couldn't last.

Emotion thickened my throat, and I pressed another kiss to her hand.

Her fingers twitched, drawing my gaze to her face. Those perfect gray eyes were open and looking right into me. "What's wrong?" she whispered.

"Your doctor is hiding something from me," I blurted out.

Monroe searched my face as she curled her fingers around my hand. "I'm pregnant, Brodan."

Her words took a second to penetrate.

Then relief, unlike anything I could remember, flooded me. I let out a huff of disbelief, and it turned into quiet laughter.

Roe's eyes widened. "Not exactly the reaction I expected."

"You're not dying … you're pregnant?"

Her hand flexed in mine. "You thought I was dying?"

"I thought something was really wrong, aye." I stood, ignoring the pain in my ribs to lean over and press a quick but desperate kiss to her lips. "But you're pregnant."

"You're okay with that?" she whispered.

I grinned, bracing my hands on either side of her head. "I am more than okay with that. Of course, we should get married first."

"Brodan, I'm not marrying you because I'm pregnant," she snapped.

Relieved to see her fire, I shrugged. "Nah, we're getting married because you're the love of my fucking life, and I don't want to waste anymore time."

359

Laughter lit her eyes. "So, you're telling me we're getting married? You're not asking?"

"The question was implicit."

"Was it?"

My mind raced, the fear of fatherhood overshadowed by the anticipation of it. "I wonder if the house will be ready in time for the baby? How far along are you?"

Monroe shifted into a sitting position, forcing me back a bit. "You're seriously okay that I'm pregnant? Brodan, we've been dating less than two months."

"But we've been in love since we were kids. Technically, I've been yours since I was five years old, so that's thirty-three years. I'd say that's a perfectly adequate length of time to be in love before having a baby."

A slow smile lit up her beautiful face. "Well, when you put it like that …"

Matching her smile, I leaned in to kiss her, a slow, sweet kiss that grew with my euphoria. It was a bit manic to go from such terror to such happiness in less than twenty-four hours, but that was life, I supposed.

Monroe broke the kiss, her fingers gentle on my face as she warned, "I'm thirty-eight in a few weeks, Brodan. This is a high-risk pregnancy."

A wee bit of reality leaked in, but I wouldn't let fear rule me anymore. "Then we'll take each day as it comes. Whatever happens, I won't leave your side. Ever again."

Roe leaned her forehead against mine, her warm breath puffing against my lips. "I love you so much, Brodan Adair."

"I love you too, soon to be Monroe Adair."

She smiled at that but said, "Your official proposal better be an upgrade from a command in a hospital room, Mr. Adair."

"Oh, I'll think of something good." I kissed her again, sliding my hands down her waist to feel her solid warmth, to reassure myself she was here and well. My hand slid down over her stomach as we kissed, and I marveled at the idea of our baby growing in there.

"Mr. Adair, I must insist you go back to your room," a sharp voice cut through the moment.

I glanced over my shoulder to find the nurse, and Walker behind her, standing guard. I could have sworn I saw a smirk on that usually stoic expression. "Walker."

He moved into the doorway. "Aye?"

"I want you to be the first to know that Roe and I are having a baby."

This time, I definitely saw a curl to the corner of his mouth as he nodded at me. "Glad for you both."

"Yes, yes, congratulations. However, I really—"

"Must insist I return to my room," I cut off the nurse. "Not a chance in hell."

"Brodan," Monroe said quietly. "I'll be okay."

I looked back at her. "They'll have to physically remove me."

She raised an eyebrow but said nothing else.

The nurse huffed. "Fine. But please do not pester my patient with your amorous notions."

Monroe snorted, and I grinned down at her. "Am I pestering you with my amorous notions?"

Her shoulders shook with laughter. "How do you think I got pregnant?"

Love, tenderness, amusement filled me, and gratitude that we could laugh after the night we'd had. "I didn't realize I was *pestering* you?"

"Oh, I definitely feel pestered," she teased.

"So that's what the screaming is? I thought that was you coming really hard."

"Brodan!" She smacked me across the arm, and I chuckled

like a kid as the nurse, affronted, fled the room. "You're awful."

"It got rid of her, didn't it? Now, prepare yourself because I intend to pester you with my amorous notions."

Monroe's giggles soothed my ravaged emotions as I kissed the laughter off her lips, ignoring the flare of pain in my ribs. I didn't pester her, though. Instead, she shifted over on the bed and I slid in beside her, holding her while we slept and vowing to myself that on the days we couldn't hold back the dark, I'd be there to make her laugh through it. I'd be there to make her life easier, not harder. I'd be there to soften the harshness of bad days and to make sure the good days outweighed the bad.

I'd just ... be there.

EPILOGUE

BRODAN

THREE MONTHS LATER

"I'm not sure we should be here," Monroe whispered, like we were breaking into someone else's home.

I shot a grin over my shoulder as I led her to the door, hand tight around hers. "We own it, Sunset. We're allowed to be here."

"But it's not ready yet."

"I need to show you something." Unlocking the front door to our home that was but a two-minute walk to Arran's and Arro's homes and less than a ten-minute walk to Lachlan's and Thane's, I guided Monroe into what would eventually be our finished front entrance of the main house. Like Thane, we had a secondary building, but while his was a guest annex, ours was a large secure garage with an apartment above it. The garage was to protect my Black Shadow and the small collection of cars I'd had shipped from storage.

The Black Shadow made Monroe a bit uneasy, but as soon as she was no longer pregnant, I was determined to get her on the back of it. She was an adventurer at heart, always jumping into whatever us boys were doing when we were kids, so I more than suspected she'd love it. Besides, there was no way I was ridding myself of a vehicle that I felt was partly credited for bringing Monroe and me together. I'd told her about my bet with Walker, and she'd laughed her arse off at Walker's mischief that had forced me to spend time with her. I think he endeared himself to her even more that day.

As for the main house, we'd opted for something more open than Thane's and Lachlan's, with an impressive staircase greeting us in the middle of a massive space. To our left would be our finished kitchen and, to the right, our living room. A wall of windows ran from one end to the other, giving us awesome views over the North Sea.

"What the …" Monroe gaped at what I had Arro do for me just minutes before our arrival.

In what would be our living room, a picnic blanket was laid out with pastries and petit fours Sloane had baked especially for the occasion, two glasses of non-alcoholic sparkling wine, and a bottle in a bucket. And along the edges of the room were candles upon lit candles. The flames flickered and glowed, dancing in the reflection of the windows.

"Come on." I led her inside and helped her out of her light spring coat. I draped it carefully over one of the stacked boxes that contained pieces of our kitchen. Then I shrugged out of mine, my eyes going to Monroe's small, rounded belly as she turned to gaze at the candles.

"What is all this?"

She was four months pregnant, and other than morning sickness that dissipated after her first trimester, Monroe was doing well. Which was a good thing because who knew your fiancée being pregnant could make her hornier than a teenager? Roe's libido was in overdrive at the moment, and she was extremely sensitive. We were taking advantage of it now since Arro and Robyn had warned Roe that she probably "wouldn't want to touch me with a barge pole by the middle of the third trimester."

The candles cast a glow over Roe's hair, making it dance like the sunset. We didn't know if we were having a boy or a girl yet, but I was hoping for a girl with hair like her mother's. And a heart like Roe's. I'd love a boy, too, of course. Whatever the universe saw fit, I would be grateful. I was just bloody in awe and amazed that I was standing in a house that belonged to me and Monroe Sinclair, that she was pregnant with my child and wanted to spend the rest of her life with me.

Speaking of … "Come here." I took her hand and led her over to the layers of picnic blankets. "Stay there." I lowered myself down to one knee and her eyes rounded as I raised the black velvet ring box before her, snapping it open to reveal the ring that had taken me weeks to pick from the selections jewelers had sent me. I watched Roe's face like a hawk for her reaction.

To my utter relief, her jaw dropped, and she lifted her hands as if to touch it, but then stopped, delight and disbelief dancing in her eyes. "Brodan." Her gaze flew to mine. "It's perfect."

I hadn't wanted to get her a ring that was too modern or too old-fashioned. Finally, I'd found one that had a vintage edge that I immediately could see on Roe's finger. The jeweler told me it had a vertical marquise center, which I think was just a posh word for oval. Smaller marquise diamond petals on either side, then two single horizontal marquise diamonds on a knife-edge, rose-gold band.

"I'm sorry it took me so long to make good on my promise to propose properly ... but I wanted to find the perfect ring."

Her eyes brightened with emotion. "You certainly did that."

I grinned, relieved, and she reached out to clasp my face in her palms. I leaned into her touch, feeling so much, too much. More than I could ever deserve to feel. "I have loved you, Monroe Sinclair, since I was a boy. I've loved you as my best friend, I've loved you as a teenage boy's fantasy"—I laughed as she rolled her eyes—"I've loved you as a scared young man. I've loved you even when I didn't realize I loved you."

She nodded in tender understanding.

"I have loved you most of my life, and I know with a certainty that awes and terrifies me in equal measure ... that I will love you until my last breath. Maybe even then."

Tears spilled down her cheeks, and she lowered to her knees beside me.

"And I promise I will love our child with the same fierce-ness. That I will do everything in my power to make our family happy. To spend the rest of our lives loving you the way you've always deserved to be loved." At her choked sob, I felt my emotion rise, and I released the ring from the box and took hold of Roe's left hand. "Will you spare me the agony of life without you, Monroe Sinclair, and do me the honor of becoming my wife?"

She laughed through her tears and nodded frantically. "Yes, I'll marry you, Brodan."

Even though I'd been pretty certain of her answer, I laughed with pure joy and slipped the ring on her finger. It winked in the candlelight, and she shook her head, marveling at it. "It's so beautiful."

"You're so beautiful." I cradled her face in my palms and drew her in for a deep kiss. She melted into me, winding her arms around my neck, and I felt her baby bump rest against my stomach. I kissed her like there was no tomorrow until she broke the kiss, panting for breath. Resting her forehead to mine, she whispered against my lips, "I have loved you every minute, every second of my life too. There has been no one else. Only you."

I closed my eyes, feeling the magical pleasure pain of those words. So much time lost. So much time to make up for. But we'd do it.

"I can't wait to make you my wife." I settled onto the blanket, pulling her over my lap. "For us to begin our lives together."

"We already have," Monroe assured me, taking a hand to rest it on her belly. "And we deserve this, handsome. After everything we've been through to get here."

She wasn't just speaking of the eighteen years we'd spent apart, but of the night Ian Moffat attacked us. It had taken weeks for Monroe to find sleep easily, and I knew guilt rode her. But my constant assurances that she'd not only protected us but the life of our unborn child eventually seemed to sink in, and she was on the path to forgiving herself.

No charges were brought against Monroe as it was cut-and-dry self-defense. Moreover, they found Vanessa's father's body, which confirmed everything we'd told the police. Moffat had murdered the man horrifically, and while I wished no one ever had to meet such an end, I couldn't feel too sorry for Mr. Woodridge. He'd traumatized a bunch of college students, and I feared, from what Ian told us, that he'd done much worse to Vanessa over the years.

It was a tragedy I would never forget. However, it was a tragedy I was determined to move on from for the sake of my family.

We'd decided to move on together. And that included from Monroe's parents too. We'd driven south to Dumfries and Galloway, where we not only found Monroe's father's grave, but the woman he'd spent the rest of his life with. Her name was Isabelle, and she'd paid for Roe's dad's funeral. She'd also told Roe that he'd tried to get in touch with her while he was dying of cancer. That he wanted to apologize for his abuse and abandonment. It wasn't everything, but I knew it gave Monroe some peace to know her father was sorry. And while we stood at his grave, I held her while she cried and offered him a forgiveness I'm not sure many other people would.

As for Monroe's mother, she was recovering from her hip replacement and we'd spotted her out in the village with her cane. She ignored us, and Monroe knew from Belle that Mrs. Sinclair was aware of Roe's pregnancy. She didn't reach out. But Roe had already decided she didn't want our child around someone as toxic as her mother. Their relationship was over, and while it was heartbreaking to see mother and daughter brought to such a place, I couldn't help but feel relieved she was out of our lives. I blamed her for the eighteen years we'd spent apart as much as I blamed myself. But mostly, I blamed her for not loving her daughter the way she deserved to be loved.

So that was done.

Roe had a new family now, and we were determined to fill her life with so much love, she'd forget she'd ever been alone.

"Want cake?" I asked, reaching for the tray of petit fours.

"Sloane?" Roe literally rubbed her palms together in

excitement, her engagement ring sparkling. Lust hit me hard, and I felt myself thicken beneath her arse.

Roe side-eyed me. "I thought I was the only one turned on by cake right now."

"It's not the cake," I answered gruffly, holding the tray to her. "It's that ring on your finger."

Understanding dawned, and she grinned as she picked up a cake and commented, "You are such a caveman," before popping it into her mouth.

I watched her eat, having to agree. My possessiveness over this woman was something I curbed and controlled on a daily basis. I never wanted to treat her like I owned her, but I couldn't deny that she felt so intrinsically a part of me, I definitely saw her as mine. And I was hers.

She raised an eyebrow, feeling me grow harder. Wicked mischief gleamed in her eyes. "Do you need me?"

"Always."

Biting her bottom lip with excitement, she turned in my lap until she was straddling me. "I'm already ready," she murmured hotly against my lips.

Heat flushed through me with anticipation as I gripped her waist. "After this one, we're knocking you up again."

She laughed against my lips as she unzipped my jeans. "Let's just see how we get on with this one."

I grabbed her hand, the one with the ring, and brought it to my mouth to kiss her wrist. "I want to marry you this week."

Monroe froze. "I ... I thought we were going to wait until after the baby. Plan a proper wedding."

"I don't want to wait. Do you?"

She shook her head, a different excitement on her expression. "I don't need a big fancy wedding, Brodan. That's not me." Her eyes widened with an idea. "Let's get married, just you, me, and Lachlan to officiate ... in the turret."

A rightness moved through me at the plan. "I love it."

Monroe beamed, wrapping her arms around my neck to pull me close. "So we're getting married this week?"

"This week," I promised.

"Okay, now that's sorted, let's get it on in our new home."

I grinned. "Get it on? You're so romantic."

"I know." She laughed against my lips and then kissed me. Deep. Sexy. Needful. Then she pulled back, suddenly serious as she promised in a husky whisper, "Only you, Brodan."

"Only you," I vowed in return.

THE END… ALMOST…
READ ON FOR A SPECIAL SECOND EPILOGUE

EPILOGUE II

A YEAR OR SO LATER...

LACHLAN

Robyn had shoved the bedcovers off in her sleep, and I stared broodingly at her long, bare legs. Her sleep shorts had ridden high, and I could see the curve of her perfect arse, while her tee had hiked up, revealing her stomach. Impatience rode me as I stood over the bed with the phone to my ear.

"You're sure it's normal?" Brodan asked, his voice raspy with lack of sleep.

Grasping on to my patience and sympathy when all I wanted to do was hang up and make love to my wife before our child wakened, I nodded and replied quietly, "At six months, Vivien screamed and cried whenever Robyn left the room. It's just separation anxiety." He'd called me at five in the morning because Monroe was unable to leave their six-month-old son without him wailing. He wouldn't sleep unless she was there, and this was a new development.

"Right." Brodan still sounded troubled.

"Look, if it's bothering you that much, call your health visitor to ask her for some advice."

"Nah, nah, I'm sure you're right."

I thought of what I'd done with Vivien's cot during that time. "Why don't you bring Lennox's cot right up to Monroe's side of the bed? That way he can see her, and they can both get some sleep."

They'd named their son after me. Lennox was my middle name. I'd not only been privileged to marry them in the castle turret that I'd forgotten had been their place as children, but they'd honored me by naming my nephew after me.

Which was why I was being as patient as I was right now.

Brodan sucked in a breath. "Aye, that's what I'll do. Thanks, Lachlan. Sorry I woke you."

"Don't be. You can call me anytime ..." I smirked as my eyes lingered longingly on my wife's magnificent legs. "Just not anytime in the next hour, all right?"

My brother chuckled. "I hear you." Then he groaned, "Fuck, I miss my wife."

Understanding, I assured him, "The first few months are the hardest. Trust me, you find the energy and time for each other again."

"I'm clinging to that reminder," he joked. "Anyway, I'll let you go. Talk soon."

We hung up and I placed my phone on silent before settling it on the bedside table. The baby monitor beside it barely crackled, informing me my wee angel was still asleep in the next room.

Which was great news for Mum and Dad.

Anticipation and heat thrummed through me as I stared down at this woman who had become everything to me. If I'd thought I loved her before we had Vivien, I was shocked to discover how much more I could adore Robyn Adair after she gave me our daughter. I had friends whose marriages fell apart once they had kids … but ours had only strengthened. Robyn was so calm and collected in the face of the exhaustion and stress of being parents to a newborn. Her patience awed me. We'd cared for each other during the transition from two to three, and it hadn't pushed us apart at all. Vivien had bound us so tightly together, we were two halves of a whole.

Needing Robyn, I whipped off my pajamas and pushed the duvet cover aside. She shifted in her sleep, lashes fluttering with dreams. I didn't consider leaving her to sleep. My wife had woken me in the middle of the night last weekend to slake her lust. I grinned at the memory and curled my fingers into her shorts and knickers.

She grumbled as I pulled them down her legs, but her hips shifted instinctually. My cock grew hard as I nudged her legs apart and took in the sight of her.

Robyn awoke with an aroused gasp a few seconds later with my head between her thighs and my mouth on her.

"Lachlan!" she cried and then slapped her hand over her mouth to be quiet.

I lapped at her, licking and sucking her clit. Robyn's fingers tangled in my hair, tight, holding me to her as she urged her hips against me, riding me.

My grip on her thighs tightened as I devoured my wife.

It didn't take long.

She came, teeth clenched against the cry of release that wanted to tear from her throat. I missed being loud. Listening to Robyn's excitement got me off. But our three-year wedding anniversary was coming up very soon, and Arro and Mac had agreed to babysit Vivien for the weekend. I was surprising Robyn with three nights in Paris, and I was going to make my wife scream the roof off our hotel with as many orgasms as we could fit into our stay. I was a bit anxious about leaving Vivien for the first time, but she'd be in safe hands.

And I believed it was good for me and Robyn to have those moments together.

My wife glided her hands over my arms and chest, drawing me to her for a kiss as she still trembled from her release. I took her mouth hungrily as I gripped her by the thigh and opened her. I pushed into her wet heat and growled into the kiss.

Robyn lifted her legs, wrapping them around my hips as I braced myself over her and thrust. Our lips parted on her gasp, and I held her gaze as I slowly fucked her.

"Take off your T-shirt," I demanded, stilling inside her.

She scrambled to haul it off, her naked breasts trembling with the movement. Her tight nipples taunted me, and I bent my head to suck one into my mouth before she'd even thrown her tee away.

"Lachlan," she moaned, fingers biting into my back as she undulated in perfect rhythm against me. "Keep going."

I moved inside her again, lifting my head to watch her flushed reaction.

"Honey, harder!"

"Shh," I hushed even as I increased the power behind my drives into her.

"Oh, God, yes …" She smoothed her hands down my back to grab my arse. "Harder."

At the feverish need in her eyes, I got up on my knees, forcing her to unwrap her legs, and gripped the back of her thighs, tilting her hips up. Robyn lost her purchase on me, arms falling to her sides, as she could do nothing but enjoy being fucked as hard as she needed. Her breasts shook with my every thrust, and Robyn's mouth was wide with her escaping moans, her eyes narrow with lust, her cheeks flushed.

So goddamn beautiful.

So very mine.

"Lachlan!"

I forgot to tell her to be quiet.

I forgot everything but making her come.

"That's it, get there, Braveheart," I urged harshly as I felt her wet heat tighten around my cock. She was heaven. "Come around me. Let me feel you."

"Harder!"

Her thighs would bruise from my grip, but my wife liked all kinds of sex and obviously this morning, she was in the mood for rough. It took every ounce of willpower to drag my throbbing cock out of her, but I did. "Get on your knees, hands on the headboard," I ordered.

Excitement danced in Robyn's eyes as she took no time at all following direction. Cupping her perfect arse in my hands, I nudged her knees wide with mine and then I drove back into her. Her cry rent the air. Wrapping one hand in her hair to hold her to me while I gripped her hip with the other, I thrust into her with such force the bed creaked with each snap of my hips.

She pushed back into me. "Yes!"

"Is this what you need?" I asked harshly, desperately.

"Yes. Lachlan!"

I lost myself in her, roughly taking what she wanted to give.

"I'm gonna come," she whimpered.

Cognizance returned to me at that moment, and I angled her head back to cover her mouth with mine as her husky shout of release was swallowed by my kiss. At the hard, pulsing tug around me, I came seconds later, groaning into Robyn as I released savagely inside her.

She melted against the headboard as I pressed into her, my face buried in the crook of her neck as my cock still throbbed inside her and her inner muscles contracted around me.

"Well, that was pretty effing amazing," Robyn said breathlessly with a smile in her voice.

Grinning, I lifted my head to answer when the sound of Vivien's crying suddenly blasted through the baby monitor.

"Shit." I pulled out of my wife, and she turned to stare at me with a mix of hazy lust and guilt.

"Did we wake her?" Robyn asked.

"I don't know, Braveheart. I'll go see to her."

"I can do it."

I smirked and pressed a kiss to her nose. "I doubt you'll be able to walk straight right now."

"Cocky bastard," she teased, rolling her eyes.

As much as I would have loved to pull Robyn into my arms and just hold her for a bit, I hastened. Hurrying into the bathroom, I quickly cleaned up and then drew on my pajamas. Vivien's cries still filled our suite.

"I'm coming, angel," I whispered to myself as I rushed from the bathroom.

Robyn laid on the bed, naked, relaxed, and so inviting it physically hurt. She smiled lovingly at me as I passed, and I winked at her before disappearing from the room.

Vivien's nursery was just down the hall. Like us, she had a magnificent view of the North Sea.

That view was nothing compared to my wee girl as she stood in her cot, face scrunched, cheeks red and tears streaming. My chest caved at the sight as it always did. No one prepared me for that. To feel Vivien's tears like a score across my heart, no matter what had produced them.

"Aw, wee angel, Daddy's here," I told her, feeling guilty that we might have woken her.

She reached her chubby arms out to me, and it was then I noted how easily she could have crawled out of her cot. It was maybe time to move her to a bed, but the thought filled me with a weird sense of panic. Time was moving too quickly. "Isn't it, angel?" I lifted her warm body into my arms, and her cries instantly quieted to hiccups and sniffles. I pressed kisses to her face and coaxed a smile from her.

"Dada," she said with exhausted, relieved weariness before leaning her head on my shoulder.

I overflowed with love, unable to contain its magnitude as I wandered over to Vivien's large window to show her the morning sun spilling across the water.

"It's a beautiful morning, Viv," I whispered as she stared sleepily out the window. "See the sun sparkling on the water? Like diamonds."

"Cookie," she replied.

I grinned. While she wasn't yet ready to string entire sentences together, Vivien had learned a fair few words. However, after being treated to a bit of Sloane Harrow's cookies, *cookie* was Viv's new favorite word. Robyn was not pleased as she was determined Vivien would be sweet-free until at least two years old on the guidance from our health advisor. Regan, the cookie giver, to my amusement, got a guilty look on her face every time Viv said *cookie*. "How about some banana instead?"

Vivien lifted her head to blink at me, her tear tracks still staining her cheeks. "Nana?"

"Aye, banana."

She made a face and sighed wearily again as she rested her head on my shoulder. I took that as a reluctant yes.

Pressing another kiss to her head and breathing in her scent, I tightened my hold. A few years ago, if anyone had told me I'd be married and a father, I'd have laughed at the absurdity of it.

Yet, here I was. Wedding band on my left ring finger. Daughter in my arms. Watching the sun rise over Caelmore.

In a few hours, I'd head onto the estate to see to business. I'd then drive to the small distillery I owned with Brodan to check on the building of the main distillery, as well as the progress of our whisky production. It was a slow process, but one I knew would be worth it. From there, I'd call Robyn to see where she'd taken Vivien on her travels for the day, camera in hand, and I'd drive to find them. Be with them. I was on call if anyone needed me. Perhaps I'd settle back into a more normal routine as Vivien grew. But for now, I didn't want to miss a thing.

Footsteps sounded behind us, and Robyn, dressed in her robe, hair still a wild mess from our spectacular sex, drew up beside us.

"Mummy." Vivien lifted an arm to her without raising her head from my shoulder and Robyn grinned, leaning into kiss Viv all over. Giggles erupted from our daughter, and she smiled sleepily as Robyn lifted her head.

Our eyes met, and she smiled at me.

Fear tickled the back of my mind. Its shadow never left me, the terrifying thought of one day losing her, losing Viv. But I fought it back each day. I chose gratitude. Because very few people in this world were given the chance to love like I loved.

I wouldn't waste that gift by worrying about tomorrow.

My wife slid her arm around my waist, leaning into my side, our daughter between us.

"Beautiful morning," she whispered, staring out at the water with us.

"Aye," I answered, voice gruff with emotion. "It is that."

THANE

For my wife, I'd do anything.

Even hover outside our shared office, eavesdropping on her like a spying creep.

Why would I do something that raised a red flag in any relationship?

Because for the last few weeks, I'd noted Regan's preoccupation. While she came easily into my arms anytime I reached for her, I could sense her mind was elsewhere. This made me extremely uneasy because Regan was one of the most open people I'd ever met. And there would always be that tiny voice in the back of my head questioning why a gorgeous young woman would want to stay in the Scottish Highlands to be wife to a man thirteen years her senior and stepmum to his kids.

I'd gotten very good at silencing that voice. Regan made it easy. She showed us every day that she was more than content with our life together.

This sudden distance I felt from her bothered me to where it was all I could think about. Was she sick? Was she growing discontent? Had I forgotten something important or said the wrong thing? What the fuck was going on? I was not a man who enjoyed this unfamiliar feeling of insecurity. When I asked her to tell me what was wrong, she gave me a smile that didn't reach her eyes, kissed me, and told me she was tired.

Construction had commenced on her soon-to-be preschool just as she was finishing her business degree while also dealing with all the agencies she needed to register herself and the business with. It was a plausible excuse. But I knew she was lying.

And that worried the fuck out of me too.

My concern morphed and changed three days ago when I was putting out the rubbish and the bag broke. I was outside, muttering curse words under my breath, trying to shove everything back in and grimacing at the unknown substance deposited on my hands, when I spotted an object that had fallen out with the waste.

A pregnancy test.

For a moment, I could only stare at it.

Then, shaking out of my shock, I picked it up. Moving into the bright outdoor light, I squinted at the words printed on the white stick.

Pregnant = two lines.

Not pregnant = one line.

Two red lines stared up at me.

Suddenly Regan's distance made sense.

Sort of.

A mix of elation and fear and anticipation filled me. I'd felt those emotions twice before. They were definitely more heightened with Lewis because I was a first-time dad. I felt more assured with Eilidh. Now I felt more of the excitement than the fear.

A child with Regan.

Ours.

But why would this preoccupy her? Why would she keep it from me?

I waited over the next few days for her to tell me the news. But nothing. In fact, Regan seemed to grow even more distant. When I woke in the morning, she was already up and about and keeping herself so busy, as if to avoid talking to me. I couldn't work it out.

Did she not want a child with me?

That made little sense. She'd told me before we ever got engaged that as much as she loved Eilidh and Lewis, she would like another child.

We'd not spoken of it since, though.

The fear that Regan didn't want a child with me was

probably irrational, but I couldn't ignore it. It made me act like a fool.

That's how I found myself eavesdropping on my wife's phone call to her sister instead of manning up and telling her I knew she was pregnant.

"I can't really talk here." I heard Regan say softly. I strained to hear better. "No, Thane's home. The kids are out with Arran and Ery ... I did go ... I didn't call you last night because I couldn't get away from Thane."

I frowned at that. Get away from me?

"He knows something's wrong," she whispered. "I feel so bad for keeping this from him ... Yeah, the doc confirmed it yesterday ... I know ... Robbie, I know ... I'm not making this up in my head and turning it into an unnecessary drama," she snapped. There was silence on her end, then a quiet, "I know you didn't mean it like that, but when Vivien and Skye were born, Thane said, and I quote, 'The thought of going through that again makes me tired in my very bones.'"

With the heavy suddenness of an anvil dropping, understanding slammed into me.

"That's a pretty emphatic thing to say."

Dammit, I did say that.

I closed my eyes and squeezed the bridge of my nose. What a stupid fucking thing to say to her.

"What if ... Robbie, we're so happy ... what if this screws it up?" More silence and then my chest caved at the sound of her sniffle. "I want this baby so badly ... I know ... I don't know why I'm freaking out so much ... Really? You think it's hormones?"

Right.

My wife was afraid to tell me she was pregnant because of a stupid unthinking comment I'd made months ago.

Something needed to be done about that.

Walking quietly away from the office, I hurried upstairs

and made my way to the end of the hallway. Grabbing the pole hook, I latched it to the attic door and pulled, revealing the collapsing stairs. Using the hook, I pulled the stairs down, stabilized them, and ventured up. The attic space was massive, and we had furniture and all kinds of things up here in storage, including the huge collection of Christmas decorations Regan had amassed over the last few years.

Striding toward the back, I moved a few boxes out of the way to reveal Eilidh's cot. We had a couple of travel cots stored next to them we used for Vivien and Skye whenever they visited, but Eilidh's old cot was a classic white wooden frame. It came with a green canopy that fastened to the ceiling above it. We'd need a new mattress, but for my purposes, I had what I required. Spying a box of Eilidh's old toys and books, I grinned.

Perfect.

Hoping Regan would continue avoiding me for a while, I unscrewed parts of the cot so I could get it down the stairs without making too much noise. It took me just over half an hour and thankfully, my wife didn't come up to see what I was doing.

Once I was done, I wandered downstairs, hot from my exertions and bloody eager to have this strangeness over between us.

I strode into the office, and she turned from her computer. Noting the dark circles under her eyes, I frowned. Once everything was out in the open, we'd have words about her being afraid to tell me the truth. "Come with me. I need to show you something."

She smirked. "A please might get my ass off this chair."

"Please come with me." I held out my hand.

Curiosity sparked in her gaze and she got up, placing her hand in mine. I squeezed hers tight, staring into her gorgeous hazel eyes for a few seconds. Didn't she know by now I'd do anything for her?

"Thane?"

"Come." I tugged on her hand and led her into the kitchen/living room and upstairs.

"Is this an afternoon booty call, because I ... I have something to tell you first."

I glanced over my shoulder and saw her nervous expression. Oh, she was ready now, was she? "Sex with your husband is never a booty call," I corrected. "And no, this is not an afternoon delight. Yet."

She snorted, and I was relieved to hear the sound.

"Then what are we doing ..." Regan's words trailed off into a gasp as we entered our bedroom.

Turning, I studied her as she gaped at the makeshift nursery I'd created.

Eilidh's old cot sat by the window. I'd put a temporary plastic hook on the ceiling and hung the canopy so it draped down the middle and over the sides of the cot. I filled the cot with Eilidh's old toys and books and placed the armchair and side table we already had in the room by the baby's bed.

Regan's eyes flew to mine, her perfect lips parted in stupefaction. Her expression asked *How*?

"A pregnancy test fell out of the rubbish bag a few days ago," I explained. "And I just overheard your conversation with Robyn." Pulling her into me, she stumbled, her arms resting on my chest. "Never, ever, be afraid to tell me anything."

Hearing the censure in my tone, she stiffened. "You can hardly blame me. After what you said about Vivien and Skye."

I sighed. "A stupid remark I am deeply regretful of now. But how could you let that stand in your way of telling me you were pregnant?"

"Because!" She pushed at my chest, but I wouldn't let her

go. Tears glistened in her eyes. "I don't want to change what we have. I want a baby really badly, but I don't want to force you into this. I don't want Eilidh and Lewis to feel like I don't love them because I want a baby." She cried sore, hard sobs that were completely uncharacteristic of her.

Pregnancy hormones.

Smiling tenderly, I hauled her close and let her cry against me as I smoothed my hand over her hair. "Aw, *mo leannan*, I could never feel forced into having a child with you. I'm over the moon that you're pregnant."

Her head snapped back, tears smearing her makeup. "Really?"

"Of course." I clasped her face in my hands. "Regan, when will you realize I am happy as long as you're happy? As long as the kids are happy. Speaking of, there is no way Eilidh and Lewis will feel abandoned. We won't let them. Eilidh will be ecstatic that she's no longer the youngest." Fuck. We were going to have a child. "We're having a baby." I grinned at her in realization.

Regan laughed through her tears. "We're having a baby."

I kissed her slow and languid, pouring everything I felt into it. Regan clung to me, pushing into the kiss, turning it fierce, hungry. Then she maneuvered me back to the bed.

"Afternoon delight time," she whispered breathlessly against my mouth as she fumbled for my zipper.

Laughing against her lips, I let myself be pushed back onto the bed. I clasped her hand as she shoved inside my jeans. "*Mo leannan*," I groaned. "As much as I hate to put a stop to this, we need to talk. I need to know what the doctor said."

"I'm eight weeks pregnant," she said hurriedly, and pushed her free hand inside my boxers instead. "I have my first screening test and blood work next week, scan and another screening a few weeks after that. Otherwise, it's all good. I'm young, I'm healthy, Doc has no concerns, so now I would like to make love to my husband to celebrate the fact that we're having a baby and you're happy about it. That okay with you?"

I fucking growled as she tightened her hold on my cock, the blood rushing from my brain.

"I'll take that as a yes," she said smugly before kissing the life out of me.

A while later, after we'd celebrated our pregnancy news twice, I held Regan in my arms as we laid in bed and stared at the cot.

"You told Robyn first," I said, a wee bit put out.

"I'm sorry." Regan lifted her head off my chest, her hair tickling my skin. "I ... I don't know why I got so freaked out. I guess it's everything. Changing our life, especially just as I'm about to open the preschool. It's a lot. I worried that we'd grown so comfortable that you would be disappointed. That the kids would be disappointed. It was silly. I'm sorry."

"It wasn't silly. I understand. But never be afraid to tell me anything, *mo leannan*. Anything."

"I know. I won't."

"And I promise to push harder to find out what's going on in that head of yours so I don't have to resort to eavesdropping on your conversations like a creep."

"Yeah, that wasn't cool."

"I'm sorry."

"I'm sorry too." She pressed a soft kiss to my lips, her fingers tickling across my beard, before she settled back against me. "I wonder if we'll have a boy or a girl."

The thought made me smile. "I hope he or she gets your dimples."

"I hope they get your accent."

Shaking with laughter at that, I replied, "It's likely. Children develop their accent from their peers, not their parents."

"I knew that." She smiled. "I'm just rambling nonsense. Is it possible to have baby brain this early in the pregnancy? I mean, my hormones are all over the place, obviously."

I glanced at the clock. "The kids will be home soon."

"I know. But let's just lie here as long as we can."

In answer, I pulled her closer, and we fell into companionable silence. Trailing my fingers over her shoulder, I imagined the future. I imagined her growing belly, and then our child. I imagined Eilidh acting like a wee mother over the baby and Lewis's watchfulness, his quiet protectiveness, just as he was with his sister.

It filled me up.

This woman, our children, this life … it filled every part of me until there was no emptiness to be found.

"Happy here?" I asked Regan, as I often did.

She smoothed her left hand over my stomach, her fingertips tickling me, her engagement ring and wedding band glinting in the afternoon light. And she gave me the words I loved to hear. "I'm happy wherever I am, as long as I'm there with you."

ARROCHAR

An hour commute to work never used to bother me. It was part of the business of being a forest engineer. But the drive to the forest near Loch Garve in Strathpeffer meant I was an hour there and an hour back. Two hours of my day on top of my working hours I wasn't spending with my husband and daughter.

Thankfully, the days of logistical planning were over.

Everything was almost implemented, and harvesting would begin soon. My next job was a bit closer to home. Still, I missed Mackennon and Skye in a way I had never imagined before I became a mum.

After little discussion, Mackennon had insisted I return to work after maternity leave and he take a hiatus from his job as head of security at Ardnoch to be a full-time dad. He'd saved a lot of money during his career that would allow us to manage financially. It was a relief because my job was a bit trickier to find my way back to if I took more time off.

As it was, Marcello, my project manager, had left the industry to teach. Marcello and I had gotten along so well. It was disappointing then to return from maternity leave to a new project manager, Scott, who subtly undermined me at every turn. I pushed through; I stood my ground, and I did my job. I just wished Scott would make my life a bit easier. It was hard enough being away from Skye, knowing she and Mackennon were off on their adventures for the day without me.

When she was in a grumbly mood, Skye wanted her dad. Always. Part of me couldn't blame her because when I was in a grumbly mood, Mackennon's arms were the best place ever. Yet it hurt so much when she lifted her little arms and cried for Daddy instead of Mummy.

It was a dry morning, the timber harvest was underway, and I was standing by in case adjustments were required for our temporary bridge we'd built to get the harvester over a small stream. Scott was up front, watching everyone like a hawk.

Then, suddenly, I saw a familiar Range Rover pull in next to my Defender in our makeshift car park. My heart jumped at the sight of Mackennon behind the wheel. He hopped out, flashing me a smile before he opened the back passenger door. I hurried over, grinning from ear to ear.

"What are you doing here?"

"Mummy!" Skye cried from inside her car seat as Mackennon hurried to unbuckle her.

"Hullo, my sweet, gorgeous baby girl," I cooed back, heart melting at the sight of her big smile.

"Mummy, Mummy, Mummy!"

I heard Mackennon chuckle. "Give me a second, sweet pea."

He lifted her out of the seat and into his arms as he straightened beside the car. She reached for me, and the worries I'd been harboring about leaving her so much lifted for a second as I took her and covered her face in kisses. Her giggles filled me with so much emotion, I laughed to release it. Then I raised my face for Mackennon's lips as he bent to take a much longer kiss than I'd anticipated. I sighed into him, and he brushed his thumb over my mouth as we parted.

"What are you doing here?" I turned to Skye. "Eh, Skye Pie? You've come a long way to see Mummy."

"Aye," she agreed, and I chuckled. "Mummy away."

My smile fell a little. "Mummy's here, Skye Pie."

"We just thought we'd come see you. I hope that's okay." Mackennon caressed my cheek. "You seemed a bit down this morning."

I leaned into my husband in gratitude. "It's lovely to see you."

"Arrochar!"

I tensed at the sound of Scott's voice, and Mackennon's eyes narrowed at my reaction. There might have been a slight chance I hadn't told him about Scott being a shitty project manager, mostly because my husband was overprotective and I didn't want him worrying.

Turning with Skye in my arms chattering to me in baby talk that made little sense yet, I watched warily as Scott marched toward us. His eyes drifted over my husband and daughter, and he let out an exasperated sigh as he drew to a stop. "What the hell is this?"

Mackennon grunted behind me, which signaled he was not amused by Scott's tone.

"If you could watch your language in front of my daughter, that would be great," I told Scott tonelessly.

"Your daughter?"

"Skye. And this is my husband, Mackennon. Mackennon, this is my project manager, Scott."

Stepping forward, Mac held out his hand. "Nice to meet you."

Scott had to tilt his head back a little to meet Mackennon's gaze. He reluctantly shook his hand. He then dropped it and curled his lip at me. "Last time I checked, it wasn't lunch break."

"You might want to watch your tone when you're talking to my wife," Mac warned quietly.

Oh, shit.

"Excuse me?"

"You heard me. That's twice you've addressed her aggressively."

"Mackennon."

My husband cut me an annoyed look, but I shook my head, then turned to Scott. "They just popped by. They're not staying."

"Mummy away?" Skye rested her hand on my cheek, and I had to fight back emotion.

"I need you here and focused today," Scott said, softening his tone a little.

"I am here."

"My fault," Mackennon offered, still glowering at Scott. "We just dropped by. We'll get out of your hair."

"Yes, do. A construction site is no place for a baby." Scott turned on his heel and marched away.

"Well, he's a plucking flick," Mackennon muttered, making me laugh.

He'd started substituting curse words for silly words around Skye, and it was hilarious coming out of his mouth. Gathering he meant *fucking prick*, I murmured my agreement and kissed Skye's cheek.

"But he's right. Sorry, I shouldn't have dropped by without notice. I just …" Mackennon stepped into me. "I'm worried about you."

"I love you." I leaned into him. "It's just that I miss you guys, that's all. Scott isn't exactly Prince Charming, and I'm … I just miss you. I'll be okay, though, eh, Skye Pie? You'll see Mummy when I get home tonight and we'll read *Zog*?" I referred to her favorite book.

"Aye," she said before chewing on the ear of her favorite teddy bear.

"Come on, sweet pea." Mackennon reached for her, and Skye, suddenly realizing what was happening, began to cry. It started as a soft whimper as she cried, "No, no, no!" repeatedly and then she was full-on screaming.

Tears filled my eyes as Mackennon took her, and I saw the worry and regret in his.

"I'm sorry, darlin'." I heard him over her mournful sobs. "I shouldn't have brought her here."

"It was a nice thought," I promised him, even as I strained to hold back my own tears. I smoothed a hand over my daughter's back as she buried her face in Mackennon's throat. "Mummy will be home soon, Skye Pie." My words caught.

I waited, biting my lip to hold back more emotion as Mac put our still-crying daughter into the car seat and closed the door. He strode over to me, clasped my face in his hands, and pressed a hard kiss to my mouth. When he pulled back, those dark eyes stared intensely into mine. "Whatever will make you happy is what we'll do, but never feel guilty for wanting your career. As for that prick over there, I want to know if he gives you any hassle."

I smirked sadly at him. "I have to fight my own battles, Mackennon."

"Okay. But remember, I'm always here when you need me to fight them with you."

"I know. I love you."

"I love you too. Skye will be fine. I'll take her to see the horses outside Caelmore, and that will cheer her up. You'll be home before she knows it."

Covering his hands with mine, I whispered, "I feel like I'm missing everything."

"You're not," he promised. "You're showing our daughter what it means to balance being a loving, caring mother and strong, capable, successful woman. Because that's what you want for her, right?"

My husband always made me feel better. "Thank you."

He gave me another quick kiss. "See you at home, darlin'."

While Mackennon had taken the edge off my guilt and sadness, as I watched him reverse and drive away with Skye, I could feel the panicked melancholy push in at my edges.

"Arrochar!"

Scott's voice sent indignation rushing through me.

If I was going to sacrifice time with my daughter for this job, then it would not be under these circumstances. Marching toward my project manager, I only stopped once there were inches between us, and I said calmly but sternly, "If you ever speak to me in that tone again, I will file a complaint against you. If you ever undermine my decisions again, I will file a complaint against you. Every time you step out of line with me, Scott, I am going to be there with HR on your arse, making your life miserable. Because I will not let an arrogant misogynist ruin a job that I love, a job I happen to be bloody excellent at. Are we clear?"

Scott blinked at me, stunned. Then he sneered, "If anyone should put in a complaint, it should be me. Your husband and daughter here? On a construction site. Really?"

Enough.

"Try me," I hissed in his face. "Try pushing me, Scott. Because I'm done taking your shit, and I've faced bigger and badder in this job, believe me, and I came out winning. In fact, let's just put this to rest. The next project that comes up, I will make sure you and I are not on it together. Until then, we have to deal with each other. I can be professional. Can you?" I walked away, striding toward two of my fellers to discuss progress.

I left Scott gaping like a goldfish behind me.

The next morning, I woke up to the relief of knowing it was a Saturday. What I didn't wake up to was my husband's warm, hard body wrapped around mine. Grumbling under my breath, I threw off the covers and got up, thinking Skye must have woken him. I hit the remote on our blinds and they rose, letting the dull morning light spill into the room.

The clouds hung low over the North Sea beyond our windows, and I cursed the imminent rain because I'd planned to take Skye to the petting zoo at John O'Groats today. It was a bit of a journey, but she was great in the car.

Padding down the hall in my slippers, I peeked into her bedroom and found it empty. As I drew closer to the stairs, I heard Skye's giggles and Mackennon's deep murmur. What I hadn't expected when I descended into our open-plan living and kitchen area was to discover sheets draped over furniture, creating lots of tents.

Mackennon and Skye were nowhere in sight.

Laughter bubbled on my lips. "And what's all this?"

"Is that Mum?" Mackennon's voice sounded from beneath a sheet between the armchair and sofa.

"Mummy!" Skye squealed. "Mummy, hide!"

Grinning, I followed her voice and got down on my hands and knees. Sure enough, inside the makeshift tent, Skye hobbled along on wobbly legs back and forth to collect toys she'd scattered everywhere. Mackennon laid on his back as Skye rested her toys along his torso, one by one.

"What is going on in here?"

Skye turned with a squeal and beamed at me, her arms flapping excitedly. "Mummy!" She hurried toward me and I crawled quickly in her direction because she wasn't entirely stable on her feet yet. I caught her, turning to fall on my back so I could lift her in the air above me.

Her delighted giggles spilled over me as I rested her on my tummy and tickled her gorgeous wee belly. After our laughter died down, she said, "Mummy, see!" and proceeded to show me how she was displaying her toys on her very patient father.

I crawled over to Mackennon and kissed him. "Good morning."

He grinned. "Morning."

"What is all this, then?"

"I was trying to keep her entertained so you could sleep in," he explained.

I kissed him again, longer, until Skye cried, "Mummy, no!"

As I pulled back, Mackennon grumbled, "She's a wee rock blocker."

Chuckling, I sat up. "She is that. Has she had breakfast?"

"Wouldn't eat anything," he said, placing one of her toys back on his chest after it fell off.

"Daddy, no." Skye took the teddy bear and placed it a few inches left of where he had.

"That was me told then."

Laughter trembled on my lips. "I'm going to make us all some breakfast. We'll eat it in here, I think. Do you want to eat your breakfast in the tent, Skye Pie?"

"Aye."

I shook my head with a grin. "What about you, Daddy?"

Mackennon rested his hands behind his head, his biceps flexing in a way I felt between my legs. "Whatever you're having, darlin'."

"Scrambled eggs on toast?"

"Sounds good."

A while later, I returned with a snack plate for Skye with the dry cereal she liked, a wee drop of scrambled egg, some cut-up banana and strawberries, and a veggie smoothie Mac had devised that she actually enjoyed. Skye reluctantly allowed Mackennon to sit up, and he did so, hunched over beneath the tent. And even though he couldn't be the most comfortable, he ate his breakfast and coffee like that, while I ate mine between feeding Skye.

That day, we did go to the petting zoo after all. When a goat frightened her, Skye burst into tears and reached for me, wanting her mummy. It reminded me that children went through phases and just because I wasn't with her every second of the day didn't mean she didn't need me or didn't feel my love.

I knew my working mum's guilt would never fully dissipate, but I held on to Mackennon's words of wisdom and vowed to fully enjoy the time I had with my daughter.

At around seven that night, after a long day out, Skye drifted off to sleep. We'd had a rough first nine months with her, both of us shattered every day from lack of sleep, but around the ten-month mark, she started to sleep regularly, which was more than I could say for her cousin and half-niece, Vivien, who still wasn't sleeping wonderfully.

I came downstairs from putting Skye to bed after reading *Room on the Broom* to her, feeling much, much lighter than I had the day before.

Mackennon was sprawled on the couch, watching an action flick on low volume, and he lifted his arm for me. I settled in beside him, cuddled into his side, tangling my legs with his. His fingers drifted through my hair as he commented, "You seem in a better mood today."

"I am." I kissed his chest. "I had words with Scott yesterday, and I think he got the message. Then I spent a brilliant day with my husband and daughter, and she drifted off to sleep, no problem. It's been a good day."

"Words with Scott?"

I sighed and told Mackennon what I'd been dealing with.

"Why didn't you say anything?" he asked gruffly.

"Like I said yesterday, I wanted to deal with it without you worrying about me."

"But I knew something was up and was worried, anyway."

"I'm sorry. I just … I thought maybe I was being sensitive because I miss Skye, but after you said that to him about his attitude, I realized I really wasn't. So I let him have it."

"Good. I'm glad."

"Anyway, what are we watching?"

In answer, Mackennon abruptly switched off the TV and threw the remote to the other end of the couch.

"What—oof!" I found myself flat on my back as he slid out to brace himself above me. Grinning, I spread my legs so he could fit better between them. "Oh, I see."

He grinned as he caressed the skin beneath my shirt. "I feel like watching you, darlin'," Mackennon replied, voice thick with desire, "as you come around me."

Heat flushed over me as I tingled between my legs in response. "That sounds like an excellent plan."

His chuckle died against my lips as he kissed me with a passion and hunger I hoped never died between us. I said as much to him as we made love quietly on our living room sofa. Afterward, I thanked him for staying home to watch Skye. I thanked him for supporting me through everything, and I thanked him for loving me.

"You never have to thank me for these things," Mackennon replied, his hand coasting down my stomach, signaling he was ready to make me come again. "It's my fucking honor, Arro. My honor to love you."

"And mine to love you," I whispered against his mouth, undulating into his touch as his thumb found my clit. "Thank you for a beautiful life."

"It's only going to get better, darlin'," he vowed before he captured my moans on his lips.

~

ARRAN

"Nervous?" Brodan asked at my side.

Though my pulse raced like the clappers, it was more to do with anticipation than nervousness. "Eager to get it done."

My brother snorted. "You make it sound like a bad thing."

I cut him a dirty look. "You know what I mean, Mr. I Couldn't Wait Five Seconds to Marry My Wife."

"Aye, my marrying Roe so soon certainly made *you* look bad." He smirked. "Took you long enough to get here."

I rolled my eyes at him before staring straight ahead, waiting for her. It was true Ery and I hadn't rushed into matrimony like the rest of my siblings, but we wanted to wait until the ordeal with her sister's murderer, Ezra Jefferson, was over. Months had passed since the evil brute killed himself. Months since Eredine could finally, truly breathe. And only a few months since I'd proposed to her.

Now here we were.

My family stood on the private beach at Ardnoch, facing Brodan, the officiate, and me. It was a warm late spring day, and thankfully the breeze was minimal. The Adairs and Galbraiths were dressed in their best, even Skye and Vivien, who were already growing restless. Lewis tugged at the collar of his shirt while Eilidh kept smoothing down her dress, looking way too tall and grown up for a nine-year-old for my liking.

I caught Arro's eye and shared a smile with my sister as she leaned into her husband, who cradled their daughter in his arms. Ery and I talked about kids and decided when we were ready, we'd like to try adoption. She was a big advocate for "found family," and I wanted to give her whatever would make her happy. Our child would be our child, blood or not.

The thought of our future and all it held made me rub my hands together impatiently. "Do you think there's something wrong? She's taking forever."

"Lachlan probably made her cry with some mushy speech and she's fixing her makeup," Brodan joked.

"I hope that's all it is."

Suddenly, the music changed. The violinists we'd hired played an instrumental version of "Infinity" by Jaymes Young, the song we'd chosen for Ery to "walk down the aisle." I glimpsed Lachlan's head through the dune grass seconds before they both appeared, and I swear my fucking breath caught.

"Wow. She's stunning," I murmured in awe.

"She is that," Brodan agreed, clapping a hand on my shoulder and giving it a squeeze.

Eredine had her arm threaded through Lachlan's as he led

her onto the beach, her bare feet peeking beneath the white silk dress that molded to her exquisite body. Her light brown skin glowed against the white of the wedding dress, and her hair hung loose in its natural curls.

She was perfect.

Classy and sexy and the kindest soul I'd ever encountered.

And she wanted to be mine.

I sucked in a breath, still surprised that was true.

Our eyes met and held as my eldest brother walked her toward me. Instead of a father, Eredine had chosen Lachlan because, even though they weren't related (thank fuck for that), she thought of Lachlan like a big brother. He'd protected her long before I ever came on the scene. I'd be grateful to him forever for that.

We'd chosen to marry with just our family present. Thane, Regan, and the kids (including the one in Regan's belly), Lachlan, Robyn, and Vivien, Arro, Mac, and Skye, Brodan (as my best man), and Monroe, who held my nephew Lennox in her arms.

Our family.

The best bloody family anyone could ever hope for.

That was all Eredine and I needed here today.

Lachlan kissed Ery's cheek and released her. I took her hand, drawing her before me and in front of our officiate.

"You look stunning," I told her quietly.

"So do you," Ery said with a loving smile.

"You ready?"

"I am. Are you?"

"I've been ready since I met you," I promised.

"Adairs and Galbraiths," our officiate announced over the softly lapping waves at our backs, "we're gathered here today to witness the joining of this man, Arran Adair, and this woman, Eredine Willows, in loving matrimony ..."

BRODAN

As Monroe watched Eredine and Arran dance, Lachlan and Robyn swaying next to them and Thane twirling a laughing Eilidh around the dance floor, I noted my wife's worried frown.

Arran and Lachlan had shut down the Gloaming for our private party for Ery and Arran's reception. However, half an hour ago, the nannies we'd hired had arrived to take Lennox, Skye, and Vivien. These were men and women hired by celebrities, and security guards accompanied them from our estate. The children couldn't be in safer hands, and yet I knew Monroe couldn't enjoy herself.

Our wee boy was almost seven months old, and this was the first time we'd left him with someone who wasn't family.

"He'll be fine," I whispered in Monroe's ear.

She jerked in surprise and then turned to me with wide, guilty eyes. At the sight, I sighed inwardly. Maybe we'd be better off leaving the reception early. But then she surprised me. "I'm sorry. I want to be here." Roe clasped my face in her hands. "It's just a bit of separation anxiety."

"I know. If you want, we can go."

"No." She shook her head and held out a hand to me. "We're going to enjoy your brother's wedding."

Grinning, I let my wife lead me onto the dance floor, then I drew her deep against my body and watched her eyes flare. Anticipation filled me as I moved my pelvis against hers. Sex had been a thing of the past for what felt like forever, but we were finding our rhythm again. Still, we didn't have time for much more than quick and quiet. I was eager to make love to my wife properly.

I knew by her expression that her mind was in the same filthy gutter as mine.

"You know, I think my brother would understand if we disappeared upstairs for a while. I might have gotten us a room."

Monroe's eyes widened, her cheeks flushing with the telltale sign of arousal. "Really?"

"Really, Sunset."

"Well, what the bloody hell are we waiting for?"

Throwing my head back in laughter, I cuddled her close. "What happened to separation anxiety?"

Roe scowled. "Teasing me about that is one way not to get laid, Brodan Adair."

Straining not to smile, I nodded. "Good point."

"Well?"

"What?"

"Uh … room … upstairs … now."

She didn't have to tell me twice. Taking her hand, I tugged her across the dance floor, meeting Arran's knowing gaze, and ignoring the equally knowing gazes of my brothers and sisters.

"They all know," Monroe whispered a little breathlessly as we left the pub and hurried upstairs.

"And they all completely understand," I replied over my shoulder.

By the time we reached our room, Monroe was giggling at my side, making me chuckle. As soon as I unlocked the door, she shoved me inside impatiently.

She still wore her dress, and I'd only dropped trews and undies when she jumped me.

"We're supposed to be taking our time," I panted, holding her hips tight as I sat on the edge of the bed while she rode me.

"We'll take our time after this," Roe huffed against my lips. "I need you now."

"Fuck," I groaned as her tight heat stroked me.

We came like sex-starved teens, and as I held her in my arms, I smiled as I felt Monroe shake with laughter. "That was fast." She chuckled, pulling back to look at me.

I reached for a soft, slow kiss and then murmured, "It was exceptional. But I'm calling the shots for round two. First order of business is to get you very, very naked, Mrs. Adair."

Monroe beamed, as she always did when I called her Mrs. Adair. I'd achieved many a thing in my life, but nothing filled me with more pride than my son's very existence or my wife taking pleasure in sharing my name.

As if she read my mind, her face fell. "Do you think Lennox is okay?"

I nodded reassuringly. "I wouldn't let anyone near him I didn't trust."

Hearing the hard truth in my words, Roe relaxed.

When the world found out that not only was I retiring but settling down at home with my pregnant wife, we were unprepared for the media storm. The paparazzi hit Ardnoch like never before, and it was so bad, we had to move back into Ardnoch Castle temporarily. The entire family was given protective detail, and it seemed to go on for weeks, even though it probably only lasted a fortnight. My fans showed a mix of support and love and blame and viciousness toward Monroe. I stayed off social media, no longer required to keep up in the way I had as a working actor.

By the time it was announced I was producing the film I'd written after a renowned director picked it up, the attitudes of the masses softened a bit. They were excited I was still working in film in some capacity. The movie, about childhood friends who fall in love with each other at different times and drift apart only to find each other again eventually, would go into production next month. I'd be away from home for the first time since returning. Thankfully, I wouldn't be needed on set for the entire shoot, so my trips down there would just be a few days at a time.

As for the distillery, it was coming along. Lachlan and I had finally decided on our whisky, and it was now maturing. The distiller would open to the public once our first bottles were ready to be sold.

Life in Ardnoch had grown quiet again. Monroe, Lennox, and I had a fairly normal life, considering. True, if we ventured farther afield, photos of us ended up on the internet somewhere. Once we started planning holidays abroad, I'd hire security to accompany us. We might be safe at home, but that didn't mean I was comfortable traveling with my wife and son without protection.

"Ery and Arran seem so happy," Monroe observed as she stared into my eyes.

My grip on her tightened. "If they're half as happy as we are, they can count themselves lucky."

She studied me thoughtfully. "You're still happy, then?"

"So fucking happy it's terrifying," I promised her.

Roe gave me an understanding smile. "Me too."

"I'll be even happier if you get naked right now."

My wife barked a laugh before she eased herself off me. Her gaze turned sultry. "Would you like a striptease, Mr. Adair?"

Leaning back on my hands, uncaring of my half-nakedness, I felt a renewed rush of blood flood my cock. "I would like that very much, Mrs. Adair."

A bang on the hotel door made us both jump in fright. "Brodan, you're missing your brother's reception!" Thane's voice was filled with laughter and more than a small hint of whisky.

"Fuck off! I'm making love to my wife!" I shouted back.

"You can make love to your wife anytime!"

"If you don't get away from that door, I will end you, you sadistic bastard!"

Thane's deep, booming laughter filtered through the walls, and then I heard Regan's voice. "Thane Adair, get away from that door!"

"Aw, I'm just having fun, *mo leannan*."

"Yeah, well, you just see how you like it when you haven't had sex in months after the baby's born, and someone interrupts our opportunity."

"What do you mean *months?*" We heard his outraged question just as their voices trailed off.

I looked at Monroe and found her chuckling hysterically to herself as she tried to strip off her clothes.

Seeing her there, mirth in her eyes, amusement flushing her cheeks as she struggled to undress through her giggles, it wasn't quite what I'd imagined when she'd offered a striptease.

But fuck, the sight of her was perfect, anyway.

I wouldn't want her or the life with our son that we'd fought hard to win to be anything other than what it was.

It was about family.

And we were an imperfect but bloody great family, we Adairs.

"Come here, wife. Let me help you with that dress."

THE END

COMING SOON

Beyond the Thistles (The Highlands Series #1)

It's been a long time since Walker Ironside left behind Scotland and the memories that haunt him. Yet after years of traveling the world as a bodyguard, Walker misses his homeland enough to return. To a village in the Scottish Highlands that plays host to an exclusive members-only club, Ardnoch Estate. If not happy, Walker is content working with the elite security at the club and maintaining his bachelor lifestyle. What he doesn't need is distraction in the form of the enticing but too-young newcomer, single mother Sloane Harrow.

Sloane never imagined she'd get pregnant at sixteen. Or that a decade later she'd escape from California with her daughter, Callie, to start over in the Scottish Highlands. Hidden and safe from Callie's dangerous father, Sloane is satisfied with their new lives. Her daughter is happy. Sloane has a stable job, a quaint cottage, a passion for baking that might just be turning into a business, and a huge crush on brooding security guard Walker Ironside. Unfortunately, the grumpy Scot seems immune to Sloane's charm, but she can't help but try to seduce him with cupcakes and baked treats whenever the opportunity arises.

However, when someone arrives in Ardnoch intent on destroying Sloane's life, Walker is the first to step forward to protect her and Callie. Even if it means giving into temptation and awakening his own demons. Because in doing so, Walker faces failing not only to shield Sloane from her past, but to safeguard her against his own.

Out May 2nd 2023 in ebook & paperback
Audiobook coming Summer 2023
Amazon US
Amazon UK

Barnes & Noble
Apple US
Apple UK
Kobo US
Kobo UK

Made in United States
Orlando, FL
16 July 2023

35161278R00250